D0057957

THE BEST SHORT STORIES

THE BEST SHORT STORIES

Rudyard Kipling

WORDSWORTH CLASSICS

This edition published 1997 by
Wordsworth Editions Limited
Cumberland House, Crib Street
Ware, Hertfordshire SG12 9ET

ISBN 1 85326 179 3

© Wordsworth Editions Limited 1997

Wordsworth® is a registered trade mark of
Wordsworth Editions Ltd

All rights reserved. This publication may not be
reproduced, stored in a retrieval system, or
transmitted, in any form or by any means, electronic,
mechanical, photocopying, recording or otherwise,
without the prior permission of the publishers.

Typeset by Antony Gray
Printed and bound in Great Britain by
Mackays of Chatham plc, Chatham, Kent

INTRODUCTION

Rudyard Kipling has always been a controversial literary figure. Enormously successful during his own lifetime, at one stage he achieved virtually the status of a national hero. Yet even then he had his critics, and was accused by some of crudeness and brutality. Though sales of his books never faltered, his reputation declined after he returned to England from the Boer War, and in recent times the jingoistic note and strident championing of British imperialism that mark his work have made him unfashionable. However, Kipling was the first British writer ever to win the Nobel Prize for Literature, and if some of his attitudes now seem questionable, his work has an undeniable power. He remains a cherished children's author, an esteemed and widely quoted poet, and a very fine storyteller of a particular era.

Kipling's tales for children are perhaps his best-loved, yet all his stories have admirable features. This representative selection comprises thirteen tales taken from four of his many published volumes, *The Day's Work* of 1889, *Life's Handicap* of 1891, *Many Inventions* of 1893 and *Traffics and Discoveries* of 1904. Subjects and locations vary widely, reflecting the much travelled author's own experience, and the vast range of his interests.

Like his poetry, many of Kipling's earliest stories celebrate the daily lives of ordinary British soldiers, far from home, employed in the business of maintaining an empire. This subject matter, which broke new ground, proved immensely popular. Kipling was dubbed 'the soldier's friend' for his insight into the feelings of the rankers. 'The Courting of Dinah Shadd' and 'On Greenhow Hill' feature Mulvaney, Ortheris and Learoyd, the principals of Kipling's earlier collection, *Soldiers Three*. Discriminated chiefly by marked differences of dialect, the three characters are vehicles for anecdotes full of variety and humour that reflect an admiration for action and power.

Badalia, heroine of 'The Record of Badalia Herodsfoot' (a stark account of survival in the slums of London in the 1890s), is, like Ortheris and indeed many of Kipling's characters, an exemplar of a self-imposed code of conduct that derives from Kipling's sense of British sportsmanship, decency and public-school honour. Allegorical or symbolic tales, such as 'The Ship that Found Herself', which conveys Kipling's passion for machinery and technology, 'Below the Mill Dam' and 'The Maltese Cat' (an expression of the extraordinary feeling for animals that culminates in *The Jungle Books* and *Just So Stories*), illustrate in various ways the strong respect for social order and the sense of responsibility to all parts of a community that Kipling's discipline demands. Other tales such as 'The Finest Story in the World', 'Wireless' and 'They' (a very personal story that Kipling wrote after the death of his young daughter) display his fascination with fantasy, the supernatural, previous incarnation and after-life. Oriental wisdom, superstitions and philosophy colour much of his work, and Kipling's geographical reference points spread from England to the far-flung corners of India, Africa, New Zealand, Indonesia and beyond.

Kipling's training as a journalist furnished him with a keen eye for the dramatic moment, just as his upbringing gave him a sense of order and a respect for rules. These qualities are evident in the fine construction and skilful handling of narrative that characterise his short stories, and they are coupled to great effect with vigour, a powerful sense of place and a clear focus on moral conflict. Kipling has had countless worthy champions, among them Winston Churchill whose high praise seems irrefutable: 'no one has ever written like Kipling before, and his work has been successfully imitated by none. He was unique and irreplaceable'.

FURTHER READING

Lord Birkenhead, *Rudyard Kipling*
R. L. Green (ed.), *Kipling: The Critical Heritage*, 1971
Angus Wilson, *The Strange Ride of Rudyard Kipling*, 1977

CONTENTS

The Courting of Dinah Shadd

What did the colonel's lady think?
  Nobody never knew.
Somebody asked the sergeant's wife
  An' she told 'em true.
When you git to a man in the case
  They're like a row o' pins,
For the colonel's lady an' Judy O'Grady
  Are sisters under their skins.
                              Barrack-Room Ballads

ALL DAY I had followed at the heels of a pursuing army engaged on one of the finest battles that ever camp of exercise beheld. Thirty thousand troops had, by the wisdom of the Government of India, been turned loose over a few thousand square miles of country to practise in peace what they would never attempt in war. Consequently cavalry charged unshaken infantry at the trot. Infantry captured artillery by frontal attacks delivered in line of quarter columns, and mounted infantry skirmished up to the wheels of an armoured train which carried nothing more deadly than a twenty-five pounder Armstrong, two Nordenfeldts, and a few score volunteers all cased in three-eighths-inch boiler-plate. Yet it was a very lifelike camp. Operations did not cease at sundown; nobody knew the country and nobody spared man or horse. There was unending cavalry scouting and almost unending forced work over broken ground. The Army of the South had finally pierced the centre of the Army of the North, and was pouring through the gap hot-foot to capture a city of strategic importance. Its front extended fanwise, the sticks being represented by regiments strung out along the line of route backwards to the divisional transport columns and all the lumber that trails behind an army on the move. On its right the broken left of the Army of the North was flying in mass, chased by the Southern horse and hammered by the Southern guns till these had been pushed far beyond the limits of their last support. Then the flying sat down to rest, while the elated commandant of the pursuing force telegraphed that he held all in check and observation.

Unluckily he did not observe that three miles to his right flank a flying column of Northern horse with a detachment of Gurkhas and British troops had been pushed round as fast as the failing light allowed, to cut across the entire rear of the Southern Army – to break, as it were, all the ribs of the fan where they converged by striking at the transport, reserve ammunition, and artillery supplies. Their instructions were to go in, avoiding the few scouts who might not have been drawn off by the pursuit, and create sufficient excitement to impress the Southern Army with the wisdom of guarding their own flank and rear before they captured cities. It was a pretty manoeuvre, neatly carried out.

Speaking for the second division of the Southern Army, our first intimation of the attack was at twilight, when the artillery were labouring in deep sand, most of the escort were trying to help them out, and the main body of the infantry had gone on. A Noah's Ark of elephants, camels, and the mixed menagerie of an Indian transport-train bubbled and squealed behind the guns, when there appeared from nowhere in particular British infantry to the extent of three companies, who sprang to the heads of the gun-horses and brought all to a standstill amid oaths and cheers.

'How's that, umpire?' said the major commanding the attack, and with one voice the drivers and limber gunners answered 'Hout!' while the colonel of artillery sputtered.

'All your scouts are charging our main body,' said the major. 'Your flanks are unprotected for two miles. I think we've broken the back of this division. And listen – there go the Gurkhas!'

A weak fire broke from the rear-guard more than a mile away, and was answered by cheerful howlings. The Gurkhas, who should have swung clear of the second division, had stepped on its tail in the dark, but drawing off hastened to reach the next line of attack, which lay almost parallel to us five or six miles away.

Our column swayed and surged irresolutely – three batteries, the divisional ammunition reserve, the baggage, and a section of the hospital and bearer corps. The commandant ruefully promised to report himself 'cut up' to the nearest umpire and, commending his cavalry and all other cavalry to the special care of Eblis, toiled on to resume touch with the rest of the division.

'We'll bivouac here tonight,' said the major. 'I have a notion that the Gurkhas will get caught. They may want us to re-form on. Stand easy till the transport gets away.'

A hand caught my beast's bridle and led him out of the choking dust; a larger hand deftly canted me out of the saddle; and two of the hugest hands in the world received me sliding. Pleasant is the lot of the special correspondent who falls into such hands as those of Privates Mulvaney, Ortheris, and Learoyd.

'An' that's all right,' said the Irishman calmly. 'We thought we'd find you somewheres here by. Is there anything av yours in the transport? Orth'ris'll fetch ut out.'

Ortheris did 'fetch ut out', from under the trunk of an elephant, in the shape of a servant and an animal both laden with medical comforts. The little man's eyes sparkled.

'If the brutil an' licentious soldiery av these parts gets sight av the thruck,' said Mulvaney, making practised investigation, 'they'll loot ev'rything. They're bein' fed on iron-filin's an' dog-biscuit these days, but glory's no compensation for a bellyache. Praise be, we're here to protect you, sorr. Beer, sausage, bread (soft an' that's a cur'osity), soup in a tin, whisky by the smell av ut, an' fowls! Mother av Moses, but ye take the field like a confectioner! 'Tis scand'lus.'

' 'Ere's a orficer,' said Ortheris significantly. 'When the sergent's done lushin' the privit may clean the pot.'

I bundled several things into Mulvaney's haversack before the major's hand fell on my shoulder and he said tenderly, 'Requisitioned for the Queen's service. Wolseley was quite wrong about special correspondents: they are the soldier's best friends. Come and take pot luck with us tonight.'

And so it happened amid laughter and shoutings that my well-considered commissariat melted away to reappear later at the mess table, which was a waterproof sheet spread on the ground. The flying column had taken three days' rations with it, and there be few things nastier than Government rations – especially when Government is experimenting with German toys. Erbswurst, tinned beef of surpassing tinniness, compressed vegetables, and meat-biscuits may be nourishing, but what Thomas Atkins needs is bulk in his inside. The major, assisted by his brother officers, purchased goats for the camp, and so made the experiment of no effect. Long before the fatigue-party sent to collect brushwood had returned, the men were settled down by their valises, kettles and pots had appeared from the surrounding country, and were dangling over fires as the kid and the compressed vegetable bubbled together; there rose a cheerful clinking of mess-tins; outrageous demands for 'a little more stuffin' with that there liver-wing'; and gust on gust of chaff as pointed as a bayonet and as delicate as a gun-butt.

'The boys are in a good temper,' said the major. 'They'll be singing presently. Well, a night like this is enough to keep them happy.'

Over our heads burned the wonderful Indian stars, which are not all pricked in on one plane, but, preserving an orderly perspective, draw the eye through the velvet darkness of the void up to the barred doors of heaven itself. The earth was a grey shadow more unreal than the sky. We could hear her breathing lightly in the pauses between the howling of the jackals, the movement of the wind in the tamarisks, and the fitful mutter of musketry fire leagues away to the left. A native woman from some unseen hut began to sing, the mail-train thundered past on its way to Delhi, and a roosting crow cawed drowsily. Then there was a belt-loosening silence about the fires, and the even breathing of the crowded earth took up the story.

The men, full fed, turned to tobacco and song – their officers with them. The subaltern is happy who can win the approval of the musical critics in his regiment, and is honoured among the more intricate step-dancers. By him, as by him who plays cricket cleverly, Thomas Atkins will stand in time of need, when he will let a better officer go on alone. The ruined tombs of forgotten Mussulman saints heard *The ballad of Agra Town*, *The Buffalo Battery*, *Marching to Kabul*, *The Long, Long Indian Day*, *The Place where the Punkah-coolie Died*, and that crashing chorus which announces,

> Youth's daring spirit, manhood's fire,
>   Firm hand and eagle eye,
> Must he acquire, who would aspire
>   To see the grey boar die.

Today, of all those jovial thieves who appropriated my commissariat and lay and laughed round that waterproof sheet, not one remains. They went to camps that were not of exercise and to battles without umpires. Burma, the Sudan, and the frontier – fever and fight – took them in their time.

I drifted across to the men's fires in search of Mulvaney, whom I found strategically greasing his feet by the blaze. There is nothing particularly lovely in the sight of a private thus engaged after a long day's march, but when you reflect on the exact proportion of the 'might, majesty, dominion, and power' of the British Empire which stands on those feet you take an interest in the proceedings.

'There's a blister, bad luck to ut, on the heel,' said Mulvaney. 'I can't touch ut. Prick ut out, little man.'

Ortheris took out his housewife, eased the trouble with a needle, stabbed Mulvaney in the calf with the same weapon, and was swiftly kicked into the fire.

'I've bruk the best av my toes over you, ye grinnin' child av disruption,' said Mulvaney, sitting cross-legged and nursing his feet; then seeing me, 'Oh, ut's you, sorr! Be welkim, an' take that maraudin' scutt's place. Jock, hold him down on the cindhers for a bit.'

But Ortheris escaped and went elsewhere, as I took possession of the hollow he had scraped for himself and lined with his greatcoat. Learoyd on the other side of the fire grinned affably and in a minute fell fast asleep.

'There's the height av politeness for you,' said Mulvaney, lighting his pipe with a flaming branch. 'But Jock's eaten half a box av your sardines at wan gulp, an' I think the tin too. What's the best wid you, sorr, an' how did you happen to be on the losin' side this day whin we captured you?'

'The Army of the South is winning all along the line,' I said.

'Then that line's the hangman's rope, savin' your presence. You'll learn tomorrow how we rethreated to dhraw thim on before we made thim trouble, an' that's what a woman does. By the same tokin, we'll be attacked before the dawnin' an' ut would be betther not to slip your boots. How do I know that? By the light av pure reason. Here are three companies av us ever so far inside av the enemy's flank an' a crowd av roarin', tarin', squealin' cavalry gone on just to turn out the whole hornet's nest av them. Av course the enemy will pursue, by brigades like as not, an' thin we'll have to run for ut. Mark my words. I am av the opinion av Polonius whin he said, "Don't fight wid ivry scutt for the pure joy av fightin', but if you do, knock the nose av him first an' frequint." We ought to ha' gone on an' helped the Gurkhas.'

'But what do you know about Polonius?' I demanded. This was a new side of Mulvaney's character.

'All that Shakespeare iver wrote an' a dale more that the gallery shouted,' said the man of war, carefully lacing his boots. 'Did I not tell you av Silver's theatre in Dublin whin I was younger than I am now an' a patron av the drama? Ould Silver wud never pay actor-man or woman their just dues, an' by consequince his comp'nies was collapsible at the last minut. Thin the bhoys wud clamour to take a part, an' oft as not ould Silver made them pay for the fun. Faith, I've seen Hamlut played wid a new black eye an' the queen as full as a cornucopia. I remimber wanst Hogin that 'listed in the Black Tyrone an' was shot in South Africa, he sejuced ould Silver into givin' him Hamlut's part instid av me that had a fine fancy for rhetoric in those days. Av course I wint into the gallery an' began to fill the pit wid other people's hats, an' I passed the time av day to Hogin walkin' through Denmark like a hamstrung mule wid a pall on his back. "Hamlut," sez I, "there's a hole in your heel. Pull up your shtockin's, Hamlut," sez I.

"Hamlut, Hamlut, for the love av decincy dhrop that skull an' pull up
your shtockin's." The whole house begun to tell him that. He stopped
his soliloquishms mid-between. "My shtockin's may be comin' down
or they may not," sez he, screwin' his eye into the gallery, for well he
knew who I was. "But afther this performince is over me an' the
Ghost'll trample the tripes out av you, Terence, wid your ass's bray!"
An' that's how I come to know about Hamlut. Eyah! Those days, those
days! Did you iver have onendin' devilmint an' nothin' to pay for it in
your life, sorr?'

'Never, without having to pay,' I said.

'That's thrue! 'Tis mane whin you considher on ut; but ut's the same
wid horse or fut. A headache if you dhrink, an' a bellyache if you eat too
much, an' a heartache to kape all down. Faith, the beast only gets the
colic, an' he's the lucky man.'

He dropped his head and stared into the fire, fingering his moustache the while. From the far side of the bivouac the voice of Corbet-
Nolan, senior subaltern of B company, uplifted itself in an ancient and
much appreciated song of sentiment, the men moaning melodiously
behind him.

> 'The north wind blew coldly, she drooped from that hour,
> My own little Kathleen, my sweet little Kathleen,
> Kathleen, my Kathleen, Kathleen O'Moore!'

With forty-five O's in the last word: even at that distance you might
have cut the soft South Irish accent with a shovel.

'For all we take we must pay, but the price is cruel high,' murmured
Mulvaney when the chorus had ceased.

'What's the trouble?' I said gently, for I knew that he was a man of an
inextinguishable sorrow.

'Hear now,' said he. 'Ye know what I am now. *I* know what I mint to
be at the beginnin' av my service. I've tould you time an' again, an'
what I have not Dinah Shadd has. An' what am I? Oh, Mary Mother av
Hiven, an ould dhrunken, untrustable baste av a privit that has seen the
reg'ment change out from colonel to drummer-boy, not wanst or
twice, but scores av times! Ay, scores! An' me not so near gettin'
promotion as in the first! An' me livin' on an' kapin' clear av clink, not
by my own good conduck, but the kindness av some orf'cer-bhoy
young enough to be son to me! Do I not know ut? Can I not tell whin
I'm passed over at p'rade, tho' I'm rockin' full av liquor an' ready to fall
all in wan piece, such as even a suckin' child might see, bekaze, "Oh, 'tis
only ould Mulvaney!" An' whin I'm let off in ord'ly-room through
some thrick of the tongue an' a ready answer an' the ould man's mercy,

is ut smilin' I feel whin I fall away an' go back to Dinah Shadd, thryin' to carry ut all off as a joke? Not I! 'Tis hell to me, dumb hell through ut all; an' next time whin the fit comes I will be as bad again. Good cause the reg'ment has to know me for the best soldier in ut. Better cause have I to know mesilf for the worst man. I'm only fit to tache the new drafts what I'll niver learn myself; an' I am sure, as tho' I heard ut, that the minut wan av these pink-eyed recruities gets away from my "Mind ye now" an' "Listen to this, Jim, bhoy" – sure I am that the sergint houlds me up to him for a warnin'. So I tache, as they say at musketry instruction, by direct and ricochet fire. Lord be good to me, for I have stud some throuble!'

'Lie down and go to sleep,' said I, not being able to comfort or advise. 'You're the best man in the regiment, and, next to Ortheris, the biggest fool. Lie down and wait till we're attacked. What force will they turn out? Guns, think you?'

'Try that wid your lorrds an' ladies, twistin' an turnin' the talk, tho' you mint ut well. Ye cud say nothin' to help me, an' yet ye niver knew what cause I had to be what I am.'

'Begin at the beginning and go on to the end,' I said royally. 'But rake up the fire a bit first.'

I passed Ortheris's bayonet for a poker.

'That shows how little we know what we do,' said Mulvaney, putting it aside. 'Fire takes all the heart out av the steel, an' the next time, may be, that our little man is fighting for his life his bradawl'll break, an' so you'll ha' killed him, manin' no more than to kape yourself warm. 'Tis a recruity's thrick that. Pass the clanin'-rod, sorr.'

I snuggled down abashed; and after an interval the voice of Mulvaney began.

'Did I iver tell you how Dinah Shadd came to be wife av mine?'

I dissembled a burning anxiety that I had felt for some months – ever since Dinah Shadd, the strong, the patient, and the infinitely tender, had of her own good love and free will washed a shirt for me, moving in a barren land where washing was not.

'I can't remember,' I said casually. 'Was it before or after you made love to Annie Bragin, and got no satisfaction?'

The story of Annie Bragin is written in another place. It is one of the many less respectable episodes in Mulvaney's chequered career.

'Before – before – long before, was that business av Annie Bragin an' the corp'ril's ghost. Niver woman was the worse for me whin I had married Dinah. There's a time for all things, an' I know how to kape all things in place – barrin' the dhrink, that kapes me in my place wid no hope av comin' to be aught else.'

'Begin at the beginning,' I insisted. 'Mrs Mulvaney told me that you married her when you were quartered in Krab Bokhar barracks.'

'An' the same is a cesspit,' said Mulvaney piously. 'She spoke thrue, did Dinah. 'Twas this way. Talkin' av that, have ye iver fallen in love, sorr?'

I preserved the silence of the damned. Mulvaney continued –

'Thin I will assume that ye have not. *I* did. In the days av my youth, as I have more than wanst tould you, I was a man that filled the eye an' delighted the sowl av women. Niver man was hated as I have bin. Niver man was loved as I – no, not within half a day's march av ut! For the first five years av my service, whin I was what I wud give my sowl to be now, I tuk whatever was within my reach an' digested ut – an' that's more than most men can say. Dhrink I tuk, an' ut did me no harm. By the Hollow av Hiven, I cud play wid four women at wanst, an' kape them from findin' out anythin' about the other three, an' smile like a full-blown marigold through ut all. Dick Coulhan, av the battery we'll have down on us tonight, could drive his team no better than I mine, an' I hild the worser cattle! An' so I lived, an' so I was happy till afther that business wid Annie Bragin – she that turned me off as cool as a meat-safe, an' taught me where I stud in the mind av an honest woman. 'Twas no sweet dose to swallow.

'Afther that I sickened awhile an' tuk thought to my reg'mental work; conceiting mesilf I wud study an' be a sargint, an' a major-gineral twinty minutes afther that. But on top av my ambitiousness there was an empty place in my sowl, an' me own opinion av mesilf cud not fill ut. Sez I to mesilf, "Terence, you're a great man an' the best set-up in the reg'mint. Go on an' get promotion." Sez mesilf to me, "What for?" Sez I to mesilf, "For the glory av ut!" Sez mesilf to me, "Will that fill these two strong arrums av yours, Terence?" – "Go to the devil," sez I to mesilf. "Go to the married lines," sez mesilf to me. " 'Tis the same thing," sez I to mesilf. "Av you're the same man, ut is," said mesilf to me; an' wid that I considhered on ut a long while. Did you iver feel that way, sorr?'

I snored gently, knowing that if Mulvaney were uninterrupted he would go on. The clamour from the bivouac fires beat up to the stars, as the rival singers of the companies were pitted against each other.

'So I felt that way an' a bad time ut was. Wanst, bein' a fool, I wint into the married lines more for the sake av spakin' to our ould colour-sergint Shadd than for any thruck wid womenfolk. I was a corp'ril then – rejuced afthcrwards, but a corp'ril then. I've got a photograft av mesilf to prove ut. "You'll take a cup av tay wid us?" sez Shadd. "I will that," I sez, "tho' tay is not my divarsion."

' " 'Twud be better for you if ut were," sez ould Mother Shadd, an' she had ought to know, for Shadd, in the ind av his service, dhrank bungfull each night.

'Wid that I tuk off my gloves – there was pipeclay in thim, so that they stud alone – an' pulled up my chair, lookin' round at the china ornaments an' bits av things in the Shadds' quarters. They were things that belonged to a man, an' no camp-kit, here today an' dishipated next. "You're comfortable in this place, sergint," sez I. " 'Tis the wife that did ut, boy," sez he, pointin' the stem av his pipe to ould Mother Shadd, an' she smacked the top av his bald head apon the compliment. "That manes you want money," sez she.

'An' thin – an' thin whin the kettle was to be filled, Dinah came in – my Dinah – her sleeves rowled up to the elbow an' her hair in a winkin' glory over her forehead, the big blue eyes beneath twinklin' like stars on a frosty night, an' the tread av her two feet lighter than waste-paper from the colonel's basket in ord'ly-room whin ut's emptied. Bein' but a shlip av a girl she went pink at seein' me, an' I twisted me moustache an' looked at a picture forninst the wall. Niver show a woman that ye care the snap av a finger for her, an' begad she'll come bleatin' to your boot-heels!'

'I suppose that's why you followed Annie Bragin till everybody in the married quarters laughed at you,' said I, remembering that unhallowed wooing and casting off the disguise of drowsiness.

'I'm layin' down the gin'ral theory av the attack,' said Mulvaney, driving his boot into the dying fire. 'If you read the *Soldier's Pocket Book*, which niver any soldier reads, you'll see that there are exceptions. Whin Dinah was out av the door (an' 'twas as tho' the sunlight had shut too) – "Mother av Hiven, sergint," sez I, "but is that your daughter?" – "I've believed that way these eighteen years," sez ould Shadd, his eyes twinklin', "but Mrs Shadd has her own opinion, like iv'ry woman." – " 'Tis wid yours this time, for a mericle," sez Mother Shadd. "Thin why in the name av fortune did I niver see her before?" sez I. "Bekaze you've been thrapesin' round wid the married women these three years past. She was a bit av a child till last year, an' she shot up wid the spring," sez ould Mother Shadd. "I'll thrapese no more," sez I. "D'you mane that?" sez ould Mother Shadd, lookin' at me sideways like a hen looks at a hawk whin the chickens are runnin' free. "Try me, an' tell," sez I. Wid that I pulled on my gloves, dhrank off the tay, an' went out av the house as stiff as at gin'ral p'rade, for well I knew that Dinah Shadd's eyes were in the small av my back out av the scullery window. Faith! that was the only time I mourned I was not a cav'l'ry man for the pride av the spurs to jingle.'

'I wint out to think, an' I did a powerful lot av thinkin', but ut all came round to that shlip av a girl in the dotted blue dhress, wid the blue eyes an' the sparkil in them. Thin I kept off canteen, an' I kept to the married quarthers, or near by, on the chanst av meetin' Dinah. Did I meet her? Oh, my time past, did I not; wid a lump in my throat as big as my valise an' my heart goin' like a farrier's forge on a Saturday morning? 'Twas "Good-day to ye, Miss Dinah," an "Good-day t'you, corp'ril," for a week or two, and divil a bit further could I get bekaze av the respect I had to that girl that I cud ha' broken betune finger an' thumb.'

Here I giggled as I recalled the gigantic figure of Dinah Shadd when she handed me my shirt.

'Ye may laugh,' grunted Mulvaney. 'But I'm speakin' the trut', an' 'tis you that are in fault. Dinah was a girl that wud ha' taken the imperiousness out av the Duchess av Clonmel in those days. Flower hand, foot av shod air, an' the eyes av the livin' mornin' she had that is my wife today – ould Dinah, and niver aught else than Dinah Shadd to me.

' 'Twas after three weeks standin' off an' on, an' niver makin' headway excipt through the eyes, that a little drummer-boy grinned in me face whin I had admonished him wid the buckle av my belt for riotin' all over the place. "An' I'm not the only wan that doesn't kape to barricks," sez he. I tuk him by the scruff av his neck – my heart was hung on a hair-thrigger those days, you will onderstand – an' "Out wid ut," sez I, "or I'll lave no bone av you unbreakable." – "Speak to Dempsey," sez he howlin'. "Dempsey which?" sez I, "ye unwashed limb av Satan." – "Av the Bobtailed Dhragoons," sez he. "He's seen her home from her aunt's house in the civil lines four times this fortnight." – "Child!" sez I, dhroppin' him, "your tongue's stronger than your body. Go to your quarters. I'm sorry I dhressed you down."

'At that I went four ways to wanst huntin' Dempsey. I was mad to think that wid all my airs among women I shud ha' been chated by a basin-faced fool av a cav'lryman not fit to trust on a trunk. Presintly I found him in our lines – the Bobtails was quartered next us – an' a tallowy, topheavy son av a she-mule he was wid his big brass spurs an' his plastrons on his epigastrons an' all. But he niver flinched a hair.

' "A word wid you, Dempsey," sez I. "You've walked wid Dinah Shadd four times this fortnight gone.'

' "What's that to you?" sez he. "I'll walk forty times more, an' forty on top av that, ye shovel-futted clod-breakin' infantry lance-corp'ril."

'Before I cud gyard he had his gloved fist home on my cheek an' down I went full-sprawl. "Will that content you?" sez he, blowin' on his knuckles for all the world like a Scots Greys orf'cer. "Content!" sez I. "For your own sake, man, take off your spurs, peel your jackut, an' onglove. 'Tis the beginnin' av the overture; stand up!"

'He stud all he know, but he niver peeled his jacket, an' his shoulders had no fair play. I was fightin' for Dinah Shadd an' that cut on my cheek. What hope had he forninst me? "Stand up," sez I, time an' again whin he was beginnin' to quarter the ground an' gyard high an' go large. "This isn't ridin' school," I sez. "O man, stand up an' let me get in at ye." But whin I saw he wud be runnin' about, I grup his shtock in my left an' his waist-belt in my right an' swung him clear to my right front, head undher, he hammerin' my nose till the wind was knocked out av him on the bare ground. "Stand up," sez I, "or I'll kick your head into your chest!" and I wud ha' done ut too, so ragin' mad I was.

' "My collar-bone's bruk," sez he. "Help me back to lines. I'll walk wid her no more." So I helped him back.'

'And was his collar-bone broken?' I asked, for I fancied that only Learoyd could neatly accomplish that terrible throw.

'He pitched on his left shoulder-point. Ut was. Next day the news was in both barricks, an' whin I met Dinah Shadd wid a cheek on me like all the reg'mintal tailor's samples there was no "Good-mornin', corp'ril," or aught else. "An' what have I done, Miss Shadd," sez I, very bould, plantin' mesilf forninst her, "that ye should not pass the time of day?"

' "Ye've half-killed rough-rider Dempsey," sez she, her dear blue eyes fillin' up.

' "May be," sez I. "Was he a friend av yours that saw ye home four times in the fortnight?"

' "Yes," sez she, but her mouth was down at the corners. "An' – an' what's that to you?" she sez.

' "Ask Dempsey," sez I, purtendin' to go away.

' "Did you fight for me then, ye silly man?" she sez, tho' she knew ut all along.

' "Who else?" sez I, an' I tuk wan pace to the front.

' "I wasn't worth ut," sez she, fingerin' in her apron.

' "That's for me to say," sez I. "Shall I say ut?"

' "Yes," sez she in a saint's whisper, an' at that I explained mesilf; and she tould me what ivry man that is a man, an' many that is a woman, hears wanst in his life.

' "But what made ye cry at startin', Dinah, darlin'?" sez I.

' "Your – your bloody cheek," sez she, duckin' her little head down on my sash (I was on duty for the day) an' whimperin' like a sorrowful angil.

'Now a man cud take that two ways. I tuk ut as pleased me best an' my first kiss wid ut. Mother av Innocence! but I kissed her on the tip av the nose an' undher the eye; an' a girl that lets a kiss come tumbleways like that has never been kissed before. Take note av that, sorr. Thin we wint hand in hand to ould Mother Shadd like two little childher, an' she said 'twas no bad thing, an' ould Shadd nodded behind his pipe, an' Dinah ran away to her own room. That day I throd on rollin' clouds. All earth was too small to hould me. Begad, I cud ha' hiked the sun out av the sky for a live coal to my pipe, so magnificent I was. But I tuk recruities at squad-drill instid, an' began wid general battalion advance whin I shud ha' been balance-steppin' them. Eyah! that day! that day!'

A very long pause. 'Well?' said I.

' 'Twas all wrong,' said Mulvaney, with an enormous sigh. 'An' I know that ev'ry bit av ut was my own foolishness. That night I tuk maybe the half av three pints – not enough to turn the hair of a man in his natural senses. But I was more than half drunk wid pure joy, an' that canteen beer was so much whisky to me. I can't tell how it came about, but *bekaze* I had no thought for anywan except Dinah, *bekaze* I hadn't slipped her little white arms from my neck five minuts, *bekaze* the breath of her kiss was not gone from my mouth, I must go through the married lines on my way to quarters, an' I must stay talkin' to a red-headed Mullingar heifer av a girl, Judy Sheehy, that was daughter to Mother Sheehy, the wife of Nick Sheehy, the canteen-sergint – the Black Curse av Shielygh be on the whole brood that are above groun' this day!

' "An' what are ye houldin' your head that high for, corp'ril?" sez Judy. "Come in an' thry a cup av tay," she sez, standin' in the doorway. Bein' an ontrustable fool, an' thinkin' av anything but tay, I wint.

' "Mother's at canteen," sez Judy, smoothin' the hair av hers that was like red snakes, an' lookin' at me corner-ways out av her green cats' eyes. "Ye will not mind, corp'ril?"

' "I can endure," sez I; ould Mother Sheehy bein' no divarsion av mine, nor her daughter too. Judy fetched the tea things an' put thim on the table, leanin' over me very close to get thim square. I dhrew back, thinkin' av Dinah.

' "Is ut afraid you are av a girl alone?" sez Judy.

' "No," sez I. "Why should I be?"

' "That rests wid the girl," sez Judy, dhrawin' her chair next to mine.

' "Thin there let ut rest," sez I; an' thinkin' I'd been a trifle onpolite, I sez, "The tay's not quite sweet enough for my taste. Put your little finger in the cup, Judy. 'Twill make ut necthar."

' "What's necthar?" sez she.

' "Somethin' very sweet," sez I; an' for the sinful life av me I cud not help lookin' at her out av the corner av my eye, as I was used to look at a woman.

' "Go on wid ye, corp'ril," sez she. "You're a flirrt."

' "On me sowl I'm not," sez I.

' "Then you're a cruel handsome man, an' that's worse," sez she, heaving big sighs an' lookin' crossways.

' "You know your own mind," sez I.

' " 'Twud be better for me if I did not," she sez.

' "There's a dale to be said on both sides av that," sez I, unthinkin'.

' "Say your own part av ut, then, Terence, darlin'," sez she, "for begad I'm thinkin' I've said too much or too little for an honest girl," an' wid that she put her arms round my neck an' kissed me.

' "There's no more to be said afther that," sez I, kissin' her back again – Oh the mane scutt that I was, my head ringin' wid Dinah Shadd! How does ut come about, sorr, that when a man has put the comether on wan woman, he's sure bound to put it on another? 'Tis the same thing at musketry. Wan day ivry shot goes wide or into the bank, an' the next, lay high lay low, sight or snap, ye can't get off the bull's-eye for ten shots runnin'.'

'That only happens to a man who has had a good deal of experience. He does it without thinking,' I replied.

'Thankin' you for the complimint, sorr, ut may be so. But I'm doubtful whether you mint ut for a complimint. Hear now; I sat there wid Judy on my knee tellin' me all manner av nonsinse an' only sayin' "yes" an' "no" when I'd much better ha' kept tongue betune teeth. An' that was not an hour afther I had left Dinah! What I was thinkin' av I cannot say. Presintly, quiet as a cat, ould Mother Sheehy came in velvet-dhrunk. She had her daughter's red hair, but 'twas bald in patches, an' I cud see in her wicked ould face, clear as lightnin', what Judy wud be twenty years to come. I was for jumpin' up, but Judy niver moved.

' "Terence has promust, mother," sez she, an' the could sweat bruk out all over me. Ould Mother Sheehy sat down of a heap an' began playin' wid the cups. "Thin you're a well-matched pair," she sez very thick. "For he's the biggest rogue that iver spoiled the Queen's shoe-leather," an' –

' "I'm off, Judy," sez I. "Ye should not talk nonsinse to your mother. Get her to bed, girl."

' "Nonsinse!" sez the ould woman, prickin' up her ears like a cat an' grippin' the table edge. " 'Twill be the most nonsinsical nonsinse for you, ye grinnin' badger, if nonsinse 'tis. Git clear, you. I'm goin' to bed."

'I ran out into the dhark, my head in a stew an' my heart sick, but I had sinse enough to see that I'd brought ut all on mysilf. "It's this to pass the time av day to a panjandhrum av hellcats," sez I. "What I've said, an' what I've not said do not matther. Judy an' her dam will hould me for a promust man, an' Dinah will give me the go, an' I desarve ut. I will go an' get dhrunk," sez I, "an' forget about ut, for 'tis plain I'm not a marrin' man."

'On my way to canteen I ran against Lascelles, colour-sergeant that was av E Comp'ny, a hard, hard man, wid a torment av a wife. "You've the head av a drowned man on your shoulders," sez he, "an' you're goin' where you'll get a worse wan. Come back," sez he. "Let me go," sez I. "I've thrown my luck over the wall wid my own hand!" – "Then that's not the way to get ut back again," sez he. "Have out wid your throuble, ye fool-bhoy." An' I tould him how the matther was.

'He sucked in his lower lip. "You've been thrapped," sez he. "Ju Sheehy wud be the betther for a man's name to hers as soon as can. An' ye thought ye'd put the comether on her – that's the natural vanity of the baste. Terence, you're a big born fool, but you're not bad enough to marry into that comp'ny. If you said anythin', an' for all your protestations I'm sure ye did – or did not, which is worse – eat ut all – lie like the father of all lies, but come out av ut free av Judy. Do I not know what ut is to marry a woman that was the very spit an' image av Judy whin she was young? I'm gettin' old an' I've larnt patience, but you, Terence, you'd raise hand on Judy an' kill her in a year. Never mind if Dinah gives you the go, you've desarved ut; never mind if the whole reg'mint laughs you all day. Get shut av Judy an' her mother. They can't dhrag you to church, but if they do, they'll dhrag you to hell. Go back to your quarters and lie down," sez he. Thin over his shoulder, "You *must* ha' done with thim."

'Next day I wint to see Dinah, but there was no tucker in me as I walked. I knew the throuble wud come soon enough widout any handlin' av mine, an' I dreaded ut sore.

'I heard Judy callin' me, but I hild straight on to the Shadds' quarthers, an' Dinah wud ha' kissed me but I put her back.

' "Whin all's said, darlin'," sez I, "you can give ut me if ye will, tho' I misdoubt 'twill be so easy to come by then."

'I had scarce begun to put the explanation into shape before Judy an' her mother came to the door. I think there was a verandah, but I'm forgettin'.

' "Will ye not step in?" sez Dinah, pretty and polite, though the Shadds had no dealin's with the Sheehys. Old Mother Shadd looked up quick, an' she was the fust to see the throuble; for Dinah was her daughter.

' "I'm pressed for time today," sez Judy as bould as brass, "an' I've only come for Terence – my promust man. 'Tis strange to find him here the day afther the day."

'Dinah looked at me as though I had hit her, an' I answered straight.

' "There was some nonsinse last night at the Sheehys' quarthers, an' Judy's carryin' on the joke, darlin'," sez I.

' "At the Sheehys' quarthers?" sez Dinah very slow, an' Judy cut in wid: "He was there from nine till ten, Dinah Shadd, an' the betther half av that time I was sittin' on his knee, Dinah Shadd. Ye may look and ye may look an' ye may look me up an' down, but ye won't look away that Terence is my promust man. Terence, darlin', 'tis time for us to be comin' home."

'Dinah Shadd niver said word to Judy. "Ye left me at half-past eight," she sez to me, "an' I niver thought that ye'd leave me for Judy – promises or no promises. Go back wid her, you that have to be fetched by a girl! I'm done with you," sez she, and she ran into her own room, her mother followin'. So I was alone wid those two women and at liberty to spake my sentiments.

' "Judy Sheehy," sez I, "if you made a fool av me betune the lights you shall not do ut in the day. I niver promised you words or lines."

' "You lie," sez ould Mother Sheehy, "an' may ut choke you where you stand!" She was far gone in dhrink.

' "An' tho' ut choked me where I stud I'd not change," sez I. "Go home, Judy. I take shame for a decent girl like you dhraggin' your mother out bare-headed on this errand. Hear now, and have ut for an answer. I gave my word to Dinah Shadd yesterday, an', more blame to me, I was wid you last night talkin' nonsinse but nothin' more. You've chosen to thry to hould me on ut. I will not be held thereby for anythin' in the world. Is that enough?"

'Judy wint pink all over. "An' I wish you joy av the perjury," sez she, duckin' a curtsey. "You've lost a woman that would ha' wore her hand to the bone for your pleasure; an' 'deed, Terence, ye were not thrapped . . . " Lascelles must ha' spoken plain to her. "I am such as Dinah is – 'deed I am! Ye've lost a fool av a girl that'll niver look at you again, an' ye've lost what ye niver had – your common honesty. If you manage your men as you manage your love-makin', small wondher they call you the worst corp'ril in the comp'ny. Come away, mother," sez she.

'But divil a fut would the ould woman budge! "D'you hould by that?" sez she, peerin' up under her thick grey eyebrows.

' "Ay, an' wud," sez I, "tho' Dinah gave me the go twenty times. I'll have no thruck with you or yours," sez I. "Take your child away, ye shameless woman."

' "An' am I shameless?" sez she, bringin' her hands up above her head. "Thin what are you, ye lyin', schamin', weak-kneed, dhirty-souled son av a sutler? Am *I* shameless? Who put the open shame on me an' my child that we shud go beggin' through the lines in the broad daylight for the broken word of a man? Double portion of my shame be on you, Terence Mulvaney, that think yourself so strong! By Mary and the saints, by blood and water an' by ivry sorrow that came into the world since the beginnin', the black blight fall on you and yours, so that you may niver be free from pain for another when ut's not your own! May your heart bleed in your breast drop by drop wid all your friends laughin' at the bleedin'! Strong you think yourself? May your strength be a curse to you to dhrive you into the divil's hands against your own will! Clear-eyed you are? May your eyes see clear evry step av the dark path you take till the hot cindhers av hell put thim out! May the ragin' dry thirst in my own ould bones go to you that you shall niver pass bottle full nor glass empty. God preserve the light av your onderstandin' to you, my jewel av à bhoy, that ye may niver forget what you mint to be an' do, whin you're wallowin' in the muck! May ye see the betther and follow the worse as long as there's breath in your body; an' may ye die quick in a strange land, watchin' your death before ut takes you, an' onable to stir hand or foot!"

'I heard a scufflin' in the room behind, and thin Dinah Shadd's hand dhropped into mine like a rose-leaf into a muddy road.

' "The half av that I'll take," sez she, "an' more too if I can. Go home, ye silly talkin' woman – go home an' confess."

' "Come away! Come away!" sez Judy, pullin' her mother by the shawl. " 'Twas none av Terence's fault. For the love av Mary stop the talkin'!"

' "An' you!" said ould Mother Sheehy, spinnin' round forninst Dinah. "Will ye take the half av that man's load? Stand off from him, Dinah Shadd, before he takes you down too – you that look to be a quarthermaster-sergeant's wife in five years. You look too high, child. You shall *wash* for the quarthermaster-sergeant, whin he plases to give you the job out av charity; but a privit's wife you shall be to the end, an' evry sorrow of a privit's wife you shall know and niver a joy but wan, that shall go from you like the running tide from a rock. The pain av bearin' you shall know but niver the pleasure av giving the breast; an' you shall put away a man-child into the common ground wid niver a priest to say a prayer over him, an' on that man-child ye shall think ivry day av your life. Think long, Dinah Shadd, for you'll niver have another tho' you pray till your knees are bleedin'. The mothers av childer shall mock you behind your back when you're wringing over the wash-tub. You shall know what ut is to help a dhrunken husband home an' see him go to the gyard-room. Will that plase you, Dinah Shadd, that won't be seen talkin' to my daughter? You shall talk to worse than Judy before all's over. The sergints' wives shall look down on you contemptuous, daughter av a sergint, an' you shall cover ut all up wid a smiling face whin your heart's burstin'. Stand off av him, Dinah Shadd, for I've put the Black Curse of Shielygh upon him an' his own mouth shall make ut good."

'She pitched forward on her head an' began foamin' at the mouth. Dinah Shadd ran out wid water, an' Judy dhragged the ould woman into the verandah till she sat up.

' "I'm old an' forlore," she sez, thremblin' an' cryin', "and 'tis like I say a dale more than I mane."

' "When you're able to walk – go," says ould Mother Shadd. "This house has no place for the likes av you that have cursed my daughter."

' "Eyah!" said the ould woman. "Hard words break no bones, an' Dinah Shadd 'll kape the love av her husband till my bones are green corn. Judy darlin', I misremember what I came here for. Can you lend us the bottom av a taycup av tay, Mrs Shadd?"

'But Judy dhragged her off cryin' as tho' her heart wud break. An' Dinah Shadd an' I, in ten minutes we had forgot ut all.'

'Then why do you remember it now?' said I.

'Is ut like I'd forget? Ivry word that wicked ould woman spoke fell thrue in my life afthrwards, an' I cud ha' stud ut all – stud ut all – excipt when my little Shadd was born. That was on the line av march three months afther the regiment was taken with cholera. We were betune Umballa an' Kalka thin, an' I was on picket. Whin I came off duty the women showed me the child, an' ut turned on uts side an' died as I looked. We buried him by the road, an' Father Victor was a day's march behind wid the heavy baggage, so the comp'ny captain read a prayer. An' since then I've been a childless man, an' all else that ould Mother Sheehy put upon me an' Dinah Shadd. What do you think, sorr?'

I thought a good deal, but it seemed better then to reach out for Mulvaney's hand. The demonstration nearly cost me the use of three fingers. Whatever he knows of his weaknesses, Mulvaney is entirely ignorant of his strength.

'But what do you think?' he repeated, as I was straightening out the crushed fingers.

My reply was drowned in yells and outcries from the next fire, where ten men were shouting for 'Orth'ris', 'Privit Orth'ris', 'Mistah

Or – ther – ris!' 'Deah boy', 'Cap'n Orth'ris', 'Field-marshal Orth'ris', 'Stanley, you pen'north o' pop come 'ere to your own comp'ny!' And the cockney, who had been delighting another audience with recondite and Rabelaisian yarns, was shot down among his admirers by the major force.

'You've crumpled my dress-shirt 'orrid,' said he, 'an' I shan't sing no more to this 'ere bloomin' drawin'-room.'

Learoyd, roused by the confusion, uncoiled himself, crept behind Ortheris, and slung him aloft on his shoulders.

'Sing, ye bloomin' hummin' bird!' said he, and Ortheris, beating time on Learoyd's skull, delivered himself, in the raucous voice of the Ratcliffe Highway, of this song –

> 'My girl she give me the go onst,
>   When I was a London lad,
> An' I went on the drink for a fortnight,
>   An' then I went to the bad.
> The Queen she give me a shillin'
>   To fight for 'er over the seas;
> But Guv'ment built me a fever-trap,
>   An' Injia give me disease.
>
> *Chorus*
> Ho! don't you 'eed what a girl says,
>   An' don't you go for the beer;
> But I was an ass when I was at grass,
>   An' that is why I'm here.
>
> I fired a shot at a Afghan,
>   The beggar 'e fired again,
> An' I lay on my bed with a 'ole in my 'ed,
>   An' missed the next campaign!
> I up with my gun at a Burman
>   Who carried a bloomin' *dah*,
> But the cartridge stuck and the bay'nit bruk,
>   An' all I got was the scar.
>
> *Chorus*
> Ho! don't you aim at a Afghan,
>   When you stand on the skyline clear
> An' don't you go for a Burman
>   If none o' your friends is near.

I served my time for a corp'ral,
An' wetted my stripes with pop,
For I went on the bend with a intimate friend,
An' finished the night in the "shop".
I served my time for a sergeant;
The colonel 'e sez, "No!
The most you'll see is a full CB."*
An' . . . very next night 'twas so.

Chorus
Ho! don't you go for a corp'ral
Unless your 'ed is clear;
But I was an ass when I was at grass,
An' that is why I'm 'ere.

I've tasted the luck o' the army
In barrack an' camp an' clink,
An' I lost my tip through the bloomin' trip
Along o' the women an' drink.
I'm down at the heel o' my service,
An' when I am laid on the shelf,
My very wust friend from beginning to end
By the blood of a mouse was myself!

Chorus
Ho! don't you 'eed what a girl says,
An' don't you go for the beer;
But I was an ass when I was at grass
An' that is why I'm 'ere.'

'Ay, listen to our little man now, singin' an' shoutin' as tho' trouble had niver touched him. D' you remember when he went mad with the home-sickness?' said Mulvaney, recalling a never-to-be-forgotten season when Ortheris waded through the deep waters of affliction and behaved abominably. 'But he's talkin' bitter truth, though. Eyah!

My very worst frind from beginnin' to ind
By the blood av a mouse was mesilf!'

When I woke I saw Mulvaney, the night-dew gemming his moustache, leaning on his rifle at picket, lonely as Prometheus on his rock, with I know not what vultures tearing his liver.

* confined to barracks

On Greenhow Hill

To Love's low voice she lent a careless ear;
Her hand within his rosy fingers lay,
A chilling weight. She would not turn or hear;
But with averted face went on her way.
But when pale Death, all featureless and grim,
Lifted his bony hand, and beckoning
Held out his cypress-wreath, she followed him,
And Love was left forlorn and wondering,
That she who for his bidding would not stay,
At Death's first whisper rose and went away.

Rivals

'*Ohé, Ahmed Din! Shafiz Ullah ahoo!* Bandur Khan, where are you? Come out of the tents, as I have done, and fight against the English. Don't kill your own kin! Come out to me!'

The deserter from a native corps was crawling round the outskirts of the camp, firing at intervals, and shouting invitations to his old comrades. Misled by the rain and the darkness, he came to the English wing of the camp, and with his yelping and rifle-practice disturbed the men. They had been making roads all day, and were tired.

Ortheris was sleeping at Learoyd's feet. 'Wot's all that?' he said thickly. Learoyd snored, and a Snider bullet ripped its way through the tent wall. The men swore. 'It's that bloomin' deserter from the Aurangabadis,' said Ortheris. 'Git up, someone, an' tell 'im 'e's come to the wrong shop.'

'Go to sleep, little man,' said Mulvaney, who was steaming nearest the door. 'I can't arise an' expaytiate with him. 'Tis rainin' entrenchin' tools outside.'

' 'Tain't because you bloomin' can't. It's 'cause you bloomin' won't, ye long, limp, lousy, lazy beggar, you. 'Ark to 'im 'owlin'!'

'Wot's the good of argifying? Put a bullet into the swine!' 'E's keepin' us awake!' said another voice.

A subaltern shouted angrily, and a dripping sentry whined from the darkness –

' 'Tain't no good, sir. I can't see 'im. 'E's 'idin' somewhere down 'ill.'

THE BEST SHORT STORIES

Ortheris tumbled out of his blanket. 'Shall I try to get 'im, sir?' said he.

'No,' was the answer. 'Lie down. I won't have the whole camp shooting all round the clock. Tell him to go and pot his friends.'

Ortheris considered for a moment. Then, putting his head under the tent wall, he called, as a 'bus conductor calls in a block, ' 'Igher up, there! 'Igher up!'

The men laughed, and the laughter was carried downwind to the deserter, who, hearing that he had made a mistake, went off to worry his own regiment half a mile away. He was received with shots; the Aurangabadis were very angry with him for disgracing their colours.

'An' that's all right,' said Ortheris, withdrawing his head as he heard the hiccough of the Sniders in the distance. 'S'elp me Gawd, tho', that man's not fit to live – messin' with my beauty sleep this way.'

'Go out and shoot him in the morning, then,' said the subaltern incautiously. 'Silence in the tents now. Get your rest, men.'

Ortheris lay down with a happy little sigh, and in two minutes there was no sound except the rain on the canvas and the all-embracing and elemental snoring of Learoyd.

The camp lay on a bare ridge of the Himalayas, and for a week had been waiting for a flying column to make connection. The nightly rounds of the deserter and his friends had become a nuisance.

In the morning the men dried themselves in hot sunshine and cleaned their grimy accoutrements. The native regiment was to take its turn of road-making that day while the Old Regiment loafed.

'I'm goin' to lay for a shot at that man,' said Ortheris, when he had finished washing out his rifle. ' 'E comes up the watercourse every evenin' about five o'clock. If we go and lie out on the north 'ill a bit this afternoon we'll get 'im.'

'You're a bloodthirsty little mosquito,' said Mulvaney, blowing blue clouds into the air. 'But I suppose I will have to come wid you. Fwhere's Jock?'

'Gone out with the Mixed Pickles, 'cause 'e thinks 'isself a bloomin' marksman,' said Ortheris with scorn.

The 'Mixed Pickles' were a detachment of picked shots, generally employed in clearing spurs of hills when the enemy were too impertinent. This taught the young officers how to handle men, and did not do the enemy much harm. Mulvaney and Ortheris strolled out of camp, and passed the Aurangabadis going to their road-making.

'You've got to sweat today,' said Ortheris genially. 'We're going to get your man. You didn't knock 'im out last night by any chance, any of you?'

'No. The pig went away mocking us. I had one shot at him,' said a private. 'He's my cousin, and *I* ought to have cleared our dishonour. But good luck to you.'

They went cautiously to the north hill, Ortheris leading, because, as he explained, 'this is a long-range show, an' I've got to do it.' His was an almost passionate devotion to his rifle, whom, by barrack-room report, he was supposed to kiss every night before turning in. Charges and scuffles he held in contempt, and, when they were inevitable, slipped between Mulvaney and Learoyd, bidding them to fight for his skin as well as their own. They never failed him. He trotted along, questing like a hound on a broken trail, through the wood of the north hill. At last he was satisfied, and threw himself down on the soft pine-needled slope that commanded a clear view of the watercourse and a brown, bare hillside beyond it. The trees made a scented darkness in which an army corps could have hidden from the sun-glare without.

' 'Ere's the tail o' the wood,' said Ortheris. ' 'E's got to come up the watercourse, 'cause it gives 'im cover. We'll lay 'ere. 'Tain't not 'arf so bloomin' dusty neither.'

He buried his nose in a clump of scentless white violets. No one had come to tell the flowers that the season of their strength was long past, and they had bloomed merrily in the twilight of the pines.

'This is something like,' he said luxuriously. 'Wot a 'evinly clear drop for a bullet acrost. How much d'you make it, Mulvaney?'

'Seven hunder. Maybe a trifle less, bekaze the air's so thin.'

Wop! wop! wop! went a volley of musketry on the rear face of the north hill.

'Curse them Mixed Pickles firin' at nothin'! They'll scare 'arf the country.'

'Thry a sightin' shot in the middle of the row,' said Mulvaney, the man of many wiles. 'There's a red rock yonder he'll be sure to pass. Quick!'

Ortheris ran his sight up to six hundred yards and fired. The bullet threw up a feather of dust by a clump of gentians at the base of the rock.

'Good enough!' said Ortheris, snapping the scale down. 'You snick your sights to mine or a little lower. You're always firin' high. But remember, first shot to me. O Lordy! but it's a lovely afternoon.'

The noise of the firing grew louder, and there was a tramping of men in the wood. The two lay very quiet, for they knew that the British soldier is desperately prone to fire at anything that moves or calls. Then Learoyd appeared, his tunic ripped across the breast by a bullet, looking ashamed of himself. He flung down on the pine needles, breathing in snorts.

'One o' them damned gardeners o' th' Pickles,' said he, fingering the rent. 'Firin' to th' right flank, when he knowed I was there. If I knew who he was I'd 'a' rippen the hide offan him. Look at ma tunic!'

'That's the spishil trustability av a marksman. Train him to hit a fly wid a stiddy rest at seven hunder, an' he loose on anythin' he sees or hears up to th' mile. You're well out av that fancy-firin' gang, Jock. Stay here.'

'Bin firin' at the bloomin' wind in the bloomin' treetops,' said Ortheris with a chuckle. 'I'll show you some firin' later on.'

They wallowed in the pine-needles, and the sun warmed them where they lay. The Mixed Pickles ceased firing, and returned to camp, and left the wood to a few scared apes. The watercourse lifted up its voice in the silence, and talked foolishly to the rocks. Now and again the dull thump of a blasting charge three miles away told that the Aurangabadis were in difficulties with their road-making. The men smiled as they listened and lay still, soaking in the warm leisure. Presently Learoyd, between the whiffs of his pipe –

'Seems queer – about 'im yonder – desertin' at all.'

' 'E'll be a bloomin' side queerer when I've done with 'im,' said Ortheris. They were talking in whispers, for the stillness of the wood and the desire of slaughter lay heavy upon them.

'I make no doubt he had his reasons for desertin'; but, my faith! I make less doubt ivry man has good reason for killin' him,' said Mulvaney.

'Happen there was a lass tewed up wi' it. Men do more than more for th' sake of a lass.'

'They make most av us 'list. They've no manner av right to make us desert.'

'Ah; they make us 'list, or their fathers do,' said Learoyd softly, his helmet over his eyes.

Ortheris's brows contracted savagely. He was watching the valley. 'If it's a girl I'll shoot the beggar twice over, an' second time for bein' a fool. You're blasted sentimental all of a sudden. Thinkin' o' your last near shave?'

'Nay, lad; ah was but thinkin' o' what has happened.'

'An' fwhat has happened, ye lumberin' child av calamity, that you're lowing like a cow-calf at the back av the pasture, an' suggestin' invidious excuses for the man Stanley's goin' to kill. Ye'll have to wait another hour yet, little man. Spit it out, Jock, an' bellow melojus to the moon. It takes an earthquake or a bullet graze to fetch aught out av you. Discourse, Don Juan! The a-moors av Lotharius Learoyd!

Stanley, kape a rowlin' rig'mental eye on the valley.'

'It's along o' yon hill there,' said Learoyd, watching the bare sub-Himalayan spur that reminded him of his Yorkshire moors. He was speaking more to himself than his fellows. 'Ay,' said he, 'Rumbolds Moor stands up ower Skipton town, an' Greenhow Hill stands up ower Pately Brig. I reckon you've never heeard tell o' Greenhow Hill, but yon bit o' bare stuff if there was nobbut a white road windin' is like ut; strangely like. Moors an' moors an' moors, wi' never a tree for shelter, an' grey houses wi' flagstone rooves, and pewits cryin', an' a windhover goin' to and fro just like these kites. And cold! A wind that cuts you like a knife. You could tell Greenhow Hill folk by the red-apple colour o' their cheeks an' nose tips, and their blue eyes, driven into pin-points by the wind. Miners mostly, burrowin' for lead i' th' hillsides, followin' the trail of th' ore vein same as a field-rat. It was the roughest minin' I ever seen. Yo'd come on a bit o' creakin' wood windlass like a well-head, an' you was let down i' th' bight of a rope, fendin' yoursen off the side wi' one hand, carryin' a candle stuck in a lump o' clay with t'other, an' clickin' hold of a rope with t'other hand.'

'An' that's three of them,' said Mulvaney. 'Must be a good climate in those parts.'

Learoyd took no heed.

'An' then yo' came to a level, where you crept on your hands and knees through a mile o' windin' drift, an' you come out into a cave-place as big as Leeds Townhall, with a engine pumpin' water from workin's 'at went deeper still. It's a queer country, let alone minin', for the hill is full of those natural caves, an' the rivers an' the becks drops into what they call pot-holes, an' come out again miles away.'

'Wot was you doin' there?' said Ortheris.

'I was a young chap then, an' mostly went wi' 'osses, leadin' coal and lead ore; but at th' time I'm tellin' on I was drivin' the wagon-team i' th' big sumph. I didn't belong to that countryside by rights. I went there because of a little difference at home, an' at fust I took up wi' a rough lot. One night we'd been drinkin', an' I must ha' hed more than I could stand, or happen th' ale was none so good. Though i' them days, By for God, I never seed bad ale.' He flung his arms over his head, and gripped a vast handful of white violets. 'Nah,' said he, 'I never seed the ale I could not drink, the bacca I could not smoke, nor the lass I could not kiss. Well, we mun have a race home, the lot on us. I lost all th' others, an' when I was climbin' ower one of them walls built o' loose stones, I comes down into the ditch, stones and all, an' broke my arm. Not as I knawed much about it, for I fell on th' back of my head, an' was knocked stupid like. An' when I come to mysen it were mornin', an' I were lyin' on the settle i' Jesse Roantree's house-place, an' 'Liza Roantree was settin' sewin'. I ached all ovver, and my mouth were like a lime-kiln. She gave me a drink out of a china mug wi' gold letters – "A Present from Leeds" – as I looked at many and many a time at after. "Yo're to lie still while Dr Warbottom comes, because your arm's broken, and father has sent a lad to fetch him. He found yo' when he was goin' to work, an' carried you here on his back," sez she. "Oa!" sez I, an' I shet my eyes, for I felt ashamed o' mysen. "Father's gone to his work these three hours, an' he said he'd tell 'em to get somebody to drive the tram." The clock ticked, an' a bee comed in the house, an' they rung i' my head like mill-wheels. An' she give me another drink an' settled the pillow. "Eh, but yo're young to be getten drunk an' such like, but yo' won't do it again, will yo'?" – "Noa," sez I, "I wouldn't if she'd not but stop they mill-wheels clatterin'." '

'Faith, it's a good thing to be nursed by a woman when you're sick!' said Mulvaney. 'Dir' cheap at the price av twenty broken heads.'

Ortheris turned to frown across the valley. He had not been nursed by many women in his life.

'An' then Dr Warbottom comes ridin' up, an' Jesse Roantree along with 'im. He was a high-larned doctor, but he talked wi' poor folk same as theirsens. "What's ta bin agaate on naa?" he sings out. "Brekkin' tha thick head?" An' he felt me all ovver. "That's none broken. Tha' nobbut knocked a bit sillier than ordinary, an' that's daaft eneaf." An' soa he went on, callin' me all the names he could think on, but settin' my arm, wi' Jesse's help, as careful as could be. "Yo' mun let the big óaf bide here a bit, Jesse," he says, when he hed strapped me up an' given me a dose o' physic, "an' you an' 'Liza will tend him, though he's scarcelins worth the trouble. An' tha'll lose tha work," sez he, "an' tha'll be upon th' Sick Club for a couple o' months an' more. Doesn't tha think tha's a fool?" '

'But whin was a young man, high or low, the other av a fool, I'd like to know?' said Mulvaney. 'Sure, folly's the only safe way to wisdom, for I've thried it.'

'Wisdom!' grinned Ortheris, scanning his comrades with uplifted chin. 'You're bloomin' Solomons, you two, ain't you?'

Learoyd went calmly on, with a steady eye like an ox chewin the cud.

'And that was how I comed to know 'Liza Roantree. There's some tunes as she used to sing – aw, she were always singin' – that fetches Greenhow Hill before my eyes as fair as yon brow across there. And she would learn me to sing bass, an' I was to go to th' chapel wi' 'em, where Jesse and she led the singin', th' old man playin' the fiddle. He was a strange chap, old Jesse, fair mad wi' music, an' he made me promise to learn the big fiddle when my arm was better. It belonged to him, and it stood up in a big case alongside o' th' eight-day clock, but Willie Satterthwaite, as played it in the chapel, had getten deaf as a doorpost, and it vexed Jesse, as he had to rap him ower his head wi' th' fiddlestick to make him give ower sawin' at th' right time.

'But there was a black drop in it all, an' it was a man in a black coat that brought it. When th' Primitive Methodist preacher came to Greenhow, he would always stop wi' Jesse Roantree, an' he laid hold of me from th' beginning. It seemed I wor a soul to be saved, and he meaned to do it. At th' same time I jealoused 'at he were keen o' savin' 'Liza Roantree's soul as well, and I could ha' killed him many a time. An' this went on till one day I broke out, an' borrowed th' brass for a drink from 'Liza. After fower days I come back, wi' my tail between my legs, just to see 'Liza again. But Jesse were at home an' th' preacher – th' Reverend Amos Barraclough. 'Liza said naught, but a bit o' red come into her face as were white of a regular thing. Says Jesse, tryin' his best to be civil, "Nay, lad, it's like this. You've getten to choose which way it's goin' to be. I'll ha' nobody across ma doorstep as goes a-drinkin', an' borrows my lass's money to spend i' their drink. Ho'd tha tongue, 'Liza," sez he, when she wanted to put in a word 'at I were welcome to th' brass, and she were none afraid that I wouldn't pay it back. Then the Reverend cuts in, seein' as Jesse were losin' his temper, an' they fair beat me among them. But it were 'Liza, as looked an' said naught, as did more than either o' their tongues, an' soa I concluded to get converted.'

'Fwhat!' shouted Mulvaney. Then, checking himself, he said softly, 'Let be! Let be! Sure the Blessed Virgin is the mother of all religion an' most women; an' there's a dale av piety in a girl if the men would only let ut stay there. I'd ha' been converted myself under the circumstances.'

'Nay, but,' pursued Learoyd with a blush, 'I meaned it.'

Ortheris laughed as loudly as he dared, having regard to his business at the time.

'Ay, Ortheris, you may laugh, but you didn't know yon preacher Barraclough – a little white-faced chap, wi' a voice as 'ud wile a bird off an a bush, and a way o' layin' hold of folks as made them think they'd never had a live man for a friend before. You never saw him, an' – an' – you never seed 'Liza Roantree – never seed 'Liza Roantree . . . Happen it was as much 'Liza as th' preacher and her father, but anyways they all meaned it, an' I was fair shamed o' mysen, an' so I become what they called a changed character. And when I think on, it's hard to believe as yon chap going to prayer-meetin's, chapel, and class-meetin's were me. But I never had naught to say for mysen, though there was a deal o' shoutin', and old Sammy Strother, as were almost clemmed to death and doubled up with the rheumatics, would sing out, "Joyful! Joyful!" and 'at it were better to go up to heaven in a coal-basket than down to hell i' a coach an' six. And he would put his poor old claw on my shoulder, sayin', "Doesn't tha feel it, tha great lump? Doesn't tha feel it?" An' sometimes I thought I did, and then again I thought I didn't, an' how was that?'

'The iverlastin' nature av mankind,' said Mulvaney. 'An', furthermore, I misdoubt you were built for the Primitive Methodians. They're a new corps anyways. I hold by the Ould Church, for she's the mother of them all – ay, an' the father, too. I like her bekaze she's most remarkable regimental in her fittings. I may die in Honolulu, Nova Zambra, or Cape Cayenne, but wherever I die, me bein' fwhat I am, an' a priest handy, I go under the same orders an' the same words an' the same unction as tho' the Pope himself come down from the roof av St Peter's to see me off. There's neither high nor low, nor broad nor deep, nor betwixt nor between wid her, an' that's what I like. But mark you, she's no manner av Church for a wake man, bekaze she takes the body and the soul av him, unless he has his proper work to do. I remember when my father died that was three months comin' to his grave; begad he'd ha' sold the shebeen above our heads for ten minutes' quittance of purgathory. An' he did all he could. That's why I say ut takes a strong man to deal with the Ould Church, an' for that reason you'll find so many women go there. An' that sames a conundrum.'

'Wot's the use o' worrittin' 'bout these things?' said Ortheris. 'You're bound to find all out quicker nor you want to, any'ow.' He jerked the cartridge out of the breech-block into the palm of his hand. ' 'Ere's my chaplain,' he said, and made the venomous black-headed bullet bow like a marionette. ' 'E's goin' to teach a man all about which is which, an' wot's true, after all, before sundown. But wot 'appened after that, Jock?'

'There was one thing they boggled at, and almost shut th' gate i' my face for, and that were my dog Blast, th' only one saved out o' a litter o' pups as was blowed up when a keg o' minin' powder loosed off in th' store-keeper's hut. They liked his name no better than his business, which were fightin' every dog he comed across; a rare good dog, wi' spots o' black and pink on his face, one ear gone, and lame o' one side wi' being driven in a basket through an iron roof, a matter of half a mile.

'They said I mun give him up 'cause he were worldly and low; and would I let mysen be shut out of heaven for the sake on a dog? "Nay," says I, "if th' door isn't wide enough for th' pair on us, we'll stop outside, for we'll none be parted." And th' preacher spoke up for Blast, as had a likin' for him from th' first – I reckon that was why I come to like th' preacher – and wouldn't hear o' changin' his name to Bless, as some o' them wanted. So th' pair on us became reg'lar chapel-members. But it's hard for a young chap o' my build to cut traces from the world, th' flesh, an' the devil all uv a heap. Yet I stuck to it for a long time, while th' lads as used to stand about th' town-end an' lean ower th' bridge, spittin' into th' beck o' a Sunday, would call after me, "Sitha, Learoyd, when's ta bean to preach, 'cause we're comin' to hear tha." – "Ho'd tha jaw. He hasn't getten th' white choaker on ta morn," another lad would say, and I had to double my fists hard i' th' bottom of my Sunday coat, and say to mysen, "If 'twere Monday and I warn't a member o' the Primitive Methodists, I'd leather all th' lot of yond'." That was th' hardest of all – to know that I could fight and I mustn't fight.'

Sympathetic grunts from Mulvaney.

'So what wi' singin', practisin', and class-meetin's, and th' big fiddle, as he made me take between my knees, I spent a deal o' time i' Jesse Roantree's house-place. But often as I was there, th' preacher fared to me to go oftener, and both th' old man an' th' young woman were pleased to have him. He lived i' Pately Brig, as were a goodish step off, but he come. He come all the same. I liked him as well or better as any man I'd ever seen i' one way, and yet I hated him wi' all my heart i' t'other, and we watched each other like cat and mouse, but civil as you please, for I was on my best behaviour, and he was that fair and open that I was bound to be fair with him. Rare good company he was, if I hadn't wanted to wring his cliver little neck half of the time. Often and often when he was goin' from Jesse's I'd set him a bit on the road.'

'See 'im 'ome, you mean?' said Ortheris.

'Ay. It's a way we have i' Yorkshire o' seein' friends off. Yon was a friend as I didn't want to come back, and he didn't want me to come back neither, and so we'd walk together towards Pately, and then he'd set me back again, and there we'd be wal two o'clock i' the mornin' settin' each other to an' fro like a blasted pair o' pendulums twixt hill and valley, long after th' light had gone out i' 'Liza's window, as both on us had been looking at, pretending to watch the moon.'

'Ah!' broke in Mulvaney, 'ye'd no chanst against the maraudin' psalm-singer. They'll take the airs an' the graces instid av the man nine times out av ten, an' they only find the blunder later – the wimmen.'

'That's just where yo're wrong,' said Learoyd, reddening under the freckled tan of his cheeks. 'I was th' first wi 'Liza, an' yo'd think that were enough. But th' parson were a steady-gaited sort o' chap, and Jesse were strong o' his side, and all th' women i' the congregation dinned it to 'Liza 'at she were fair fond to take up wi' a wastrel ne'er-do-weel like me, as was scarcelins respectable an' a fighting dog at his heels. It was all very well for her to be doing me good and saving my soul, but she must mind as she didn't do herself harm. They talk o' rich folk bein' stuck up an' genteel, but for cast-iron pride o' respectability there's naught like poor chapel folk. It's as cold as th' wind o' Greenhow Hill – ay, and colder, for 'twill never change. And now I come to think on it, one at strangest things I know is 'at they couldn't abide th' thought o' soldiering. There's a vast o' fightin' i' th' Bible, and there's a deal of Methodists i' th' army; but to hear chapel folk talk yo'd think that soldierin' were next door, an' t'other side, to hangin'. I' their meetin's all their talk is o' fightin'. When Sammy Strother were stuck for summat to say in his prayers, he'd sing out, "Th' sword o' th' Lord and o' Gideon." They were allus at it about puttin' on th' whole armour o' righteousness, an' fightin' the good fight o' faith. And then, atop o' 't all, they held a prayer-meetin' ower a young chap as wanted to 'list, and nearly deafened him, till he picked up his hat and fair ran away. And they'd tell tales in th' Sunday-school o' bad lads as had been thumped and brayed for bird-nesting o' Sundays and playin' truant o' weekdays, and how they took to wrestlin', dog-fightin', rabbit-runnin', and drinkin', till at last, as if 'twere a hepitaph on a gravestone, they damned him across th' moors wi', "an' then he went and 'listed for a soldier," an' they'd all fetch a deep breath, and throw up their eyes like a hen drinkin'.'

'Fwhy is ut?' said Mulvaney, bringing down his hand on his thigh with a crack. 'In the name av God, fwhy is ut? I've seen ut, tu. They cheat an' they swindle an' they lie an' they slander, an' fifty things fifty times worse; but the last an' the worst by their reckonin' is to serve the Widdy* honest. It's like the talk av childer – seein' things all round.'

'Plucky lot of fightin' good fights of whatsername they'd do if we didn't see they had a quiet place to fight in. And such fightin' as theirs is! Cats on the tiles. T'other callin' to which to come on. I'd give a month's pay to get some o' them broad-backed beggars in London sweatin' through a day's road-makin' an' a night's rain. They'd carry on a deal afterwards – same as we're supposed to carry on. I've bin turned out of a measly 'arf-license pub down Lambeth way, full o' greasy kebmen, 'fore now,' said Ortheris with an oath.

'Maybe you were dhrunk,' said Mulvaney soothingly.

'Worse nor that. The Forders were drunk. *I* was wearin' the Queen's uniform.'

* Queeen Victoria

'I'd no particular thought to be a soldier i' them days,' said Learoyd, still keeping his eye on the bare hill opposite, 'but this sort o' talk put it i' my head. They was so good, th' chapel folk, that they tumbled ower t'other side. But I stuck to it for 'Liza's sake, specially as she was learning me to sing the bass part in a horotorio as Jesse were gettin' up. She sung like a throstle hersen, and we had practisin's night after night for a matter of three months.'

'I know what a horotorio is,' said Ortheris pertly. 'It's a sort of chaplain's sing-song – words all out of the Bible, and hullabaloojah choruses.'

'Most Greenhow Hill folks played some instrument or t'other, an' they all sung so you might have heard them miles away, and they were so pleased wi' the noise they made they didn't fair to want anybody to listen. The preacher sung high seconds when he wasn't playin' the flute, an' they set me, as hadn't got far with big fiddle, against Willie Satterthwaite, to jog his elbow when he had to get a' gate playin'. Old Jesse was happy if ever a man was, for he were th' conductor an' th' first fiddle an' th' leadin' singer, beatin' time wi' his fiddle-stick, till at times he'd rap with it on the table, and cry out, "Now, you mun all stop; it's my turn." And he'd face round to his front, fair sweating wi' pride, to sing th' tenor solos. But he were grandest i' th' choruses, waggin' his head, flinging his arms round like a windmill, and singin' hisself black in the face. A rare singer were Jesse.

'Yo' see, I was not o' much account wi' 'em all exceptin' to 'Liza Roantree, and I had a deal o' time settin' quiet at meetings and horotorio practises to hearken their talk, and if it were strange to me at beginnin', it got stranger still at after, when I was shut on it, and could study what it meaned.

'Just after th' horotorios came off, 'Liza, as had allus been weakly like, was took very bad. I walked Dr Warbottom's horse up and down a deal of times while he were inside, where they wouldn't let me go, though I fair ached to see her.

' "She'll be better i' noo, lad – better i' noo," he used to say. "Tha mun ha' patience." Then they said if I was quiet I might go in, and th' Reverend Amos Barraclough used to read to her lyin' propped up among th' pillows. Then she began to mend a bit, and they let me carry her on to th' settle, and when it got warm again she went about same as afore. Th' preacher and me and Blast was a deal together i' them days, and i' one way we was rare good comrades. But I could ha' stretched him time and again with a good will. I mind one day he said he would like to go down into th' bowels o' th' earth, and see how th' Lord had builded th' framework o' th' everlastin' hills. He were one of them chaps as had a gift o' sayin' things. They rolled off the tip of his clever tongue, same as Mulvaney here, as would ha' made a rare good preacher if he had nobbut given his mind to it. I lent him a suit o' miner's kit as almost buried th' little man, and his white face down i' th' coat-collar and hat-flap looked like the face of a boggart, and he cowered down i' th' bottom o' the wagon. I was drivin' a tram as led up a bit of an incline up to th' cave where the engine was pumpin', and where th' ore was brought up and put into th' wagons as went down o' themselves, me puttin' th' brake on and th' horses a-trottin' after. Long as it was daylight we were good friends, but when we got fair into th' dark, and could nobbut see th' day shinin' at the hole like a lamp at a street-end, I feeled downright wicked. Ma religion dropped all away from me when I looked back at him as were always comin' between me and 'Liza. The talk was 'at they were to be wed when she got better, an' I couldn't get her to say yes or nay to it. He began to sing a hymn in his thin voice, and I came out wi' a chorus that was all cussin' an' swearin' at my horses, an' I began to know how I hated him. He were such a little chap, too. I could drop him wi' one hand down Garstang's Copper-hole – a place where th' beck slithered ower th' edge on a rock, and fell wi' a bit of a whisper into a pit as no rope i' Greenhow could plump.'

Again Learoyd rooted up the innocent violets. 'Ay, he should see th' bowels o' th' earth an' never naught else. I could take him a mile or two along th' drift, and leave him wi' his candle doused to cry hallelujah, wi' none to hear him and say amen. I was to lead him down th' ladder-way to th' drift where Jesse Roantree was workin', and why shouldn't he slip on th' ladder, wi' my feet on his fingers till they loosed grip, and I put him down wi' my heel? If I went fust down th' ladder I could click hold on him and chuck him over my head, so as he should go squshin' down the shaft, breakin' his bones at ev'ry timberin' as Bill Appleton did when he was fresh, and hadn't a bone left when he wrought to th' bottom. Niver a blasted leg to walk from Pately. Niver an arm to put round 'Liza Roantree's waist. Niver no more – niver no more.'

The thick lips curled back over the yellow teeth, and that flushed face was not pretty to look upon. Mulvaney nodded sympathy, and Ortheris, moved by his comrade's passion, brought up the rifle to his shoulder, and searched the hillside for his quarry, muttering ribaldry about a sparrow, a spout, and a thunderstorm. The voice of the watercourse supplied the necessary small talk till Learoyd picked up his story.

'But it's none so easy to kill a man like yon. When I'd given up my horses to th' lad as took my place and I was showin' th' preacher th' workin's, shoutin' into his ear across th' clang o' th' pumpin' engines, I saw he were afraid o' naught; and when the lamplight showed his black eyes, I could feel as he was masterin' me again. I were no better nor Blast chained up short and growlin' i' the depths of him while a strange dog went safe past.

' "Th'art a coward and a fool," I said to mysen; an' I wrestled i' my mind again' him till, when we come to Garstang's Copper-hole, I laid hold o' the preacher and lifted him up over my head and held him into the darkest on it. "Now, lad," I says, "it's to be one or t'other on us – thee or me – for 'Liza Roantree. Why, isn't thee afraid for thysen?" I says, for he were still i' my arms as a sack. "Nay; I'm but afraid for thee, my poor lad, as knows naught," says he. I set him down on th' edge, an' th' beck run stiller, an' there was no more buzzin' in my head like when th' bee come through th' window o' Jesse's house. "What dost tha mean?" says I.

' "I've often thought as thou ought to know," says he, "but 'twas hard to tell thee. 'Liza Roantree's for neither on us, nor for nobody o' this earth. Dr Warbottom says – and he knows her, and her mother before her – that she is in a decline, and she cannot live six months longer. He's known it for many a day. Steady, John! Steady!" says he. And that weak little man pulled me further back and set me again' him, and talked it all over quiet and still, me turnin' a bunch o' candles in my hand, and counting them ower and ower again as I listened. A deal on it were th' regular preachin' talk, but there were a vast lot as made me begin to think as he were more of a man than I'd ever given him credit for, till I were cut as deep for him as I were for mysen.

'Six candles we had, and we crawled and climbed all that day while they lasted, and I said to mysen, " 'Liza Roantree hasn't six months to live." And when we came into th' daylight again we were like dead men to look at, an' Blast come behind us without so much as waggin' his tail. When I saw 'Liza again she looked at me a minute and says, "Who's telled tha? For I see tha knows." And she tried to smile as she kissed me, and I fair broke down.

'Yo'see, I was a young chap i' them days, and had seen naught o' life, let alone death, as is allus a-waitin'. She told me as Dr Warbottom said as Greenhow air was too keen, and they were goin' to Bradford, to Jesse's brother David, as worked i' a mill, and I mun hold up like a man and a Christian, and she'd pray for me. Well, and they went away, and the preacher that same back end o' th' year were appointed to another circuit, as they call it, and I were left alone on Greenhow Hill.

'I tried, and I tried hard, to stick to th' chapel, but 'tweren't th' same thing at after. I hadn't 'Liza's voice to follow i' th' singin', nor her eyes a'shinin' acrost their heads. And i' th' class-meetings they said as I mun have some experiences to tell, and I hadn't a word to say for mysen.

'Blast and me moped a good deal, and happen we didn't behave ourselves over well, for they dropped us and wondered however they'd come to take us up. I can't tell how we got through th' time, while i' th' winter I gave up my job and went to Bradford. Old Jesse were at th' door o' th' house, in a long street o' little houses. He'd been sendin' th' children 'way as were clatterin' their clogs in th' causeway, for she were asleep.

' "Is it thee?" he says, "but you're not to see her. I'll none have her wakened for a nowt like thee. She's goin' fast, and she mun go in peace. Thou'lt never be good for naught i' th' world, and as long as thou lives thou'll never play the big fiddle. Get away, lad, get away!" So he shut the door softly i' my face.

'Nobody never made Jesse my master, but it seemed to me he was about right, and I went away into the town and knocked up against a recruiting sergeant. The old tales o' th' chapel folk came buzzin' into my head. I was to get away, and this were th' regular road for the likes o' me. I 'listed there and then, took th' Widow's shillin', and had a bunch o' ribbons pinned i' my hat.

'But next day I found my way to David Roantree's door, and Jesse came to open it. Says he, "Thou's come back again wi' th' devil's colours flyin' – thy true colours, as I always told thee."

'But I begged and prayed of him to let me see her nobbut to say goodbye, till a woman calls down th' stairway, "She says John Learoyd's to come up." Th' old man shifts aside in a flash, and lays his hand on my arm, quite gentle like. "But thou'lt be quiet, John," says he, "for she's rare and weak. Thou was allus a good lad."

'Her eyes were all alive wi' light, and her hair was thick on the pillow round her, but her cheeks were thin – thin to frighten a man that's strong. "Nay, father, yo mayn't say th' devil's colours. Them ribbons is pretty." An' she held out her hands for th' hat, an' she put all straight as a woman will wi' ribbons. "Nay, but what they're pretty," she says. "Eh, but I'd ha' liked to see thee i' thy red coat, John, for thou was allus my own lad – my very own lad, and none else."

'She lifted up her arms, and they come round my neck i' a gentle grip, and they slacked away, and she seemed fainting. "Now yo' mun get away, lad," says Jesse, and I picked up my hat and I came downstairs.

'Th' recruiting sergeant were waitin' for me at th' corner public-house. "Yo've seen your sweetheart?" says he. "Yes, I've seen her," says I. "Well, we'll have a quart now, and you'll do your best to forget her," says he, bein' one o' them smart, bustlin' chaps. "Ay, sergeant," says I. "Forget her." And I've been forgettin' her ever since.'

He threw away the wilted clump of white violets as he spoke. Ortheris suddenly rose to his knees, his rifle at his shoulder, and peered across the valley in the clear afternoon light. His chin cuddled the stock, and there was a twitching of the muscles of the right cheek as he sighted; Private Stanley Ortheris was engaged on his business. A speck of white crawled up the watercourse.

'See that beggar? . . . Got 'im.'

Seven hundred yards away, and a full two hundred down the hillside, the deserter of the Aurangabadis pitched forward, rolled down a red rock, and lay very still, with his face in a clump of blue gentians, while a big raven flapped out of the pine wood to make investigation.

'That's a clean shot, little man,' said Mulvaney.

Learoyd thoughtfully watched the smoke clear away. 'Happen there was a lass tewed up wi' him, too,' said he.

Ortheris did not reply. He was staring across the valley, with the smile of the artist who looks on the completed work.

At the End of the Passage

The sky is lead and our faces are red,
   And the gates of Hell are opened and riven,
   And the winds of Hell are loosened and driven,
And the dust flies up in the face of Heaven,
   And the clouds come down in a fiery sheet,
Heavy to raise and hard to be borne.
   And the soul of man is turned from his meat,
Turned from the trifles for which he has striven,
   Sick in his body, and heavy hearted,
   And his soul flies up like the dust in the sheet,
   Breaks from his flesh and is gone and departed,
As the blasts they blow on the cholera-horn.

                                Himalayan

FOUR MEN, each entitled to 'life, liberty, and the pursuit of happiness', sat at a table playing whist. The thermometer marked – for them – one hundred and one degrees of heat. The room was darkened till it was only just possible to distinguish the pips of the cards and the very white faces of the players. A tattered, rotten punkah of whitewashed calico was puddling the hot air and whining dolefully at each stroke. Outside lay gloom of a November day in London. There was neither sky, sun, nor horizon – nothing but a brown purple haze of heat. It was as though the earth were dying of apoplexy.

From time to time clouds of tawny dust rose from the ground without wind or warning, flung themselves tablecloth-wise among the tops of the parched trees, and came down again. Then a whirling dust-devil would scutter across the plain for a couple of miles, break, and fall outward, though there was nothing to check its flight save a long low line of piled railway-sleepers white with the dust, a cluster of huts made of mud, condemned rails, and canvas, and the one squat four-roomed bungalow that belonged to the assistant engineer in charge of a section of the Gaudhari State line then under construction.

The four, stripped to the thinnest of sleeping-suits, played whist crossly, with wranglings as to leads and returns. It was not the best kind of whist, but they had taken some trouble to arrive at it. Mottram of the

Indian Survey had ridden thirty and railed one hundred miles from his
lonely post in the desert since the night before; Lowndes of the Civil
Service, on special duty in the political department, had come as far to
escape for an instant the miserable intrigues of an impoverished native
State whose king alternately fawned and blustered for more money
from the pitiful revenues contributed by hard-wrung peasants and
despairing camel-breeders; Spurstow, the doctor of the line, had left a
cholera-stricken camp of coolies to look after itself for forty-eight
hours while he associated with white men once more. Hummil, the
assistant engineer, was the host. He stood fast and received his friends
thus every Sunday if they could come in. When one of them failed to
appear, he would send a telegram to his last address, in order that he
might know whether the defaulter were dead or alive. There are very
many places in the East where it is not good or kind to let your
acquaintances drop out of sight even for one short week.

The players were not conscious of any special regard for each other.
They squabbled whenever they met; but they ardently desired to meet,
as men without water desire to drink. They were lonely folk who
understood the dread meaning of loneliness. They were all under
thirty years of age – which is too soon for any man to possess that
knowledge.

'Pilsener?' said Spurstow, after the second rubber, mopping his
forehead.

'Beer's out, I'm sorry to say, and there's hardly enough soda-water
for tonight,' said Hummil.

'What filthy bad management!' Spurstow snarled.

'Can't help it. I've written and wired; but the trains don't come
through regularly yet. Last week the ice ran out – as Lowndes knows.'

'Glad I didn't come. I could ha' sent you some if I had known,
though. Phew! it's too hot to go on playing bumblepuppy.' This with a
savage scowl at Lowndes, who only laughed. He was a hardened
offender.

Mottram rose from the table and looked out of a chink in the
shutters.

'What a sweet day!' said he.

The company yawned all together and betook themselves to an
aimless investigation of all Hummil's possessions – guns, tattered
novels, saddlery, spurs, and the like. They had fingered them a score of
times before, but there was really nothing else to do.

'Got anything fresh?' said Lowndes.

'Last week's *Gazette of India*, and a cutting from a home paper. My
father sent it out. It's rather amusing.'

THE BEST SHORT STORIES

'One of those vestrymen that call 'emselves MPs again, is it?' said Spurstow, who read his newspapers when he could get them.

'Yes. Listen to this. It's to your address, Lowndes. The man was making a speech to his constituents, and he piled it on. Here's a sample, "And I assert unhesitatingly that the Civil Service in India is the preserve – the pet preserve – of the aristocracy of England. What does the democracy – what do the masses – get from that country, which we have step by step fraudulently annexed? I answer, nothing whatever. It is farmed with a single eye to their own interests by the scions of the aristocracy. They take good care to maintain their lavish scale of incomes, to avoid or stifle any enquiries into the nature and conduct of their administration, while they themselves force the unhappy peasant to pay with the sweat of his brow for all the luxuries in which they are lapped." ' Hummil waved the cutting above his head. ' 'Ear! 'ear!' said his audience.

Then Lowndes, meditatively, 'I'd give – I'd give three months' pay to have that gentleman spend one month with me and see how the free and independent native prince works things. Old Timbersides' – this was his flippant title for an honoured and decorated feudatory prince – 'has been wearing my life out this week past for money. By Jove, his latest performance was to send me one of his women as a bribe!'

'Good for you! Did you accept it?' said Mottram.

'No. I rather wish I had, now. She was a pretty little person, and she yarned away to me about the horrible destitution among the king's womenfolk. The darlings haven't had any new clothes for nearly a month, and the old man wants to buy a new drag from Calcutta – solid silver railings and silver lamps, and trifles of that kind. I've tried to make him understand that he has played the deuce with the revenues for the last twenty years and must go slow. He can't see it.'

'But he has the ancestral treasure-vaults to draw on. There must be three millions at least in jewels and coin under his palace,' said Hummil.

'Catch a native king disturbing the family treasure! The priests forbid it except as the last resort. Old Timbersides has added something like a quarter of a million to the deposit in his reign.'

'Where the mischief does it all come from?' said Mottram.

'The country. The state of the people is enough to make you sick. I've known the tax-men wait by a milch-camel till the foal was born and then hurry off the mother for arrears. And what can I do? I can't get the court clerks to give me any accounts; I can't raise anything more than a fat smile from the commander-in-chief when I find out the troops are three months in arrears; and old Timbersides begins to weep when I speak to him. He has taken to the King's Peg heavily – liqueur brandy for whisky, and Heidsieck for soda-water.'

'That's what the Rao of Jubela took to. Even a native can't last long at that,' said Spurstow. 'He'll go out.'

'And a good thing, too. Then I suppose we'll have a council of regency, and a tutor for the young prince, and hand him back his kingdom with ten years' accumulations.'

'Whereupon that young prince, having been taught all the vices of the English, will play ducks and drakes with the money and undo ten years' work in eighteen months. I've seen that business before,' said Spurstow. 'I should tackle the king with a light hand if I were you, Lowndes. They'll hate you quite enough under any circumstances.'

'That's all very well. The man who looks on can talk about the light hand; but you can't clean a pig-stye with a pen dipped in rose-water. I know my risks; but nothing has happened yet. My servant's an old Pathan, and he cooks for me. They are hardly likely to bribe him, and I don't accept food from my true friends, as they call themselves. Oh, but it's weary work! I'd sooner be with you, Spurstow. There's shooting near your camp.'

'Would you? I don't think it. About fifteen deaths a day don't incite a man to shoot anything but himself. And the worst of it is that the poor devils look at you as though you ought to save them. Lord knows, I've tried everything. My last attempt was empirical, but it pulled an old man through. He was brought to me apparently past hope, and I gave him gin and Worcester sauce with cayenne. It cured him; but I don't recommend it.'

'How do the cases run generally?' said Hummil.

'Very simply indeed. Chlorodyne, opium pill, chlorodyne, collapse, nitre, bricks to the feet, and then – the burning-ghaut. The last seems to be the only thing that stops the trouble. It's black cholera, you know. Poor devils! But, I will say, little Bunsee Lal, my apothecary, works like a demon. I've recommended him for promotion if he comes through it all alive.'

'And what are your chances, old man?' said Mottram.

'Don't know; don't care much; but I've sent the letter in. What are you doing with yourself generally?'

'Sitting under a table in the tent and spitting on the sextant to keep it cool,' said the man of the survey. 'Washing my eyes to avoid ophthalmia, which I shall certainly get, and trying to make a sub-surveyor understand that an error of five degrees in an angle isn't quite so small as it looks. I'm altogether alone, y' know, and shall be till the end of the hot weather.'

'Hummil's the lucky man,' said Lowndes, flinging himself into a long chair. 'He has an actual roof – torn as to the ceiling-cloth, but still a roof – over his head. He sees one train daily. He can get beer and soda-water and ice 'em when God is good. He has books, pictures' – they were torn from the *Graphic* – 'and the society of the excellent sub-contractor Jevins, besides the pleasure of receiving us weekly.'

Hummil smiled grimly. 'Yes, I'm the lucky man, I suppose. Jevins is luckier.'

'How? Not – '

'Yes. Went out. Last Monday.'

'By his own hand?' said Spurstow quickly, hinting the suspicion that was in everybody's mind. There was no cholera near Hummil's section. Even fever gives a man at least a week's grace, and sudden death generally implied self-slaughter.

'I judge no man this weather,' said Hummil. 'He had a touch of the sun, I fancy; for last week, after you fellows had left, he came into the verandah and told me that he was going home to see his wife, in Market Street, Liverpool, that evening.

'I got the apothecary in to look at him, and we tried to make him lie down. After an hour or two he rubbed his eyes and said he believed he had had a fit – hoped he hadn't said anything rude. Jevins had a great idea of bettering himself socially. He was very like Chucks in his language.'

'Well?'

'Then he went to his own bungalow and began cleaning a rifle. He told the servant that he was going to shoot buck in the morning. Naturally he fumbled with the trigger, and shot himself through the head – accidentally. The apothecary sent in a report to my chief, and Jevins is buried somewhere out there. I'd have wired to you, Spurstow, if you could have done anything.'

'You're a queer chap,' said Mottram. 'If you'd killed the man yourself you couldn't have been more quiet about the business.'

'Good Lord! what does it matter?' said Hummil calmly. 'I've got to do a lot of his overseeing work in addition to my own. I'm the only person that suffers. Jevins is out of it – by pure accident, of course, but out of it. The apothecary was going to write a long screed on suicide. Trust a babu to drivel when he gets the chance.'

'Why didn't you let it go in as suicide?' said Lowndes.

'No direct proof. A man hasn't many privileges in this country, but he might at least be allowed to mishandle his own rifle. Besides, someday I may need a man to smother up an accident to myself. Live and let live. Die and let die.'

'You take a pill,' said Spurstow, who had been watching Hummil's white face narrowly. 'Take a pill, and don't be an ass. That sort of talk is skittles. Anyhow, suicide is shirking your work. If I were Job ten times over, I should be so interested in what was going to happen next that I'd stay on and watch.'

'Ah! I've lost that curiosity,' said Hummil.

'Liver out of order?' said Lowndes feelingly.

'No. Can't sleep. That's worse.'

'By Jove, it is!' said Mottram. 'I'm that way every now and then, and the fit has to wear itself out. What do you take for it?'

'Nothing. What's the use? I haven't had ten minutes' sleep since Friday morning.'

'Poor chap! Spurstow, you ought to attend to this,' said Mottram. 'Now you mention it, your eyes are rather gummy and swollen.'

Spurstow, still watching Hummil, laughed lightly. 'I'll patch him up, later on. Is it too hot, do you think, to go for a ride?'

'Where to?' said Lowndes wearily. 'We shall have to go away at eight, and there'll be riding enough for us then. I hate a horse when I have to use him as a necessity. Oh, heavens! what is there to do?'

'Begin whist again, at chick points [a 'chick' is supposed to be eight shillings] and a gold mohur on the rub,' said Spurstow promptly.

'Poker. A month's pay all round for the pool – no limit – and fifty-rupee raises. Somebody would be broken before we got up,' said Lowndes.

'Can't say that it would give me any pleasure to break any man in this company,' said Mottram. 'There isn't enough excitement in it, and it's foolish.' He crossed over to the worn and battered little camp-piano – wreckage of a married household that had once held the bungalow – and opened the case.

'It's used up long ago,' said Hummil. 'The servants have picked it to pieces.'

The piano was indeed hopelessly out of order, but Mottram managed to bring the rebellious notes into a sort of agreement, and there rose from the ragged keyboard something that might once have been the ghost of a popular music-hall song. The men in the long chairs turned with evident interest as Mottram banged the more lustily.

'That's good!' said Lowndes. 'By Jove! the last time I heard that song was in '79, or thereabouts, just before I came out.'

'Ah!' said Spurstow with pride, 'I was home in '80.' And he mentioned a song of the streets popular at that date.

Mottram executed it roughly. Lowndes criticised and volunteered emendations. Mottram dashed into another ditty, not of the music-hall character, and made as if to rise.

'Sit down,' said Hummil. 'I didn't know that you had any music in your composition. Go on playing until you can't think of anything more. I'll have that piano tuned up before you come again. Play something festive.'

Very simple indeed were the tunes to which Mottram's art and the limitations of the piano could give effect, but the men listened with pleasure, and in the pauses talked all together of what they had seen or heard when they were last at home. A dense dust-storm sprung up outside, and swept roaring over the house, enveloping it in the choking darkness of midnight, but Mottram continued unheeding, and the crazy tinkle reached the ears of the listeners above the flapping of the tattered ceiling-cloth.

In the silence after the storm he glided from the more directly personal songs of Scotland, half humming them as he played, into the Evening Hymn.

'Sunday,' said he, nodding his head.

'Go on. Don't apologise for it,' said Spurstow.

Hummil laughed long and riotously. 'Play it, by all means. You're full of surprises today. I didn't know you had such a gift of finished sarcasm. How does that thing go?'

Mottram took up the tune.

'Too slow by half. You miss the note of gratitude,' said Hummil. 'It ought to go to the "Grasshopper's Polka" – this way.' And he chanted, *prestissimo* –

> 'Glory to thee, my God, this night,
> For all the blessings of the light.

That shows we really feel our blessings. How does it go on? –

> If in the night I sleepless lie,
> My soul with sacred thoughts supply;
> May no ill dreams disturb my rest –

Quicker, Mottram! –

> Or powers of darkness me molest!'

'Bah! what an old hypocrite you are!'

'Don't be an ass,' said Lowndes. 'You are at full liberty to make fun of anything else you like, but leave that hymn alone. It's associated in my mind with the most sacred recollections – '

'Summer evenings in the country – stained-glass window – light going out, and you and she jamming your heads together over one hymn-book,' said Mottram.

'Yes, and a fat old cockchafer hitting you in the eye when you walked home. Smell of hay, and a moon as big as a bandbox sitting on the top of a haycock; bats – roses – milk and midges,' said Lowndes.

'Also mothers. I can just recollect my mother singing me to sleep with that when I was a little chap,' said Spurstow.

The darkness had fallen on the room. They could hear Hummil squirming in his chair.

'Consequently,' said he testily, 'you sing it when you are seven fathom deep in Hell! It's an insult to the intelligence of the Deity to pretend we're anything but tortured rebels.'

'Take *two* pills,' said Spurstow, 'that's tortured liver.'

'The usually placid Hummil is in a vile bad temper. I'm sorry for his coolies tomorrow,' said Lowndes, as the servants brought in the lights and prepared the table for dinner.

As they were settling into their places about the miserable goat-chops, and the smoked tapioca pudding, Spurstow took occasion to whisper to Mottram, 'Well done, David!'

'Look after Saul, then,' was the reply.

'What are you two whispering about?' said Hummil suspiciously.

'Only saying that you are a damned poor host. This fowl can't be cut,' returned Spurstow with a sweet smile. 'Call this a dinner?'

'I can't help it. You don't expect a banquet, do you?'

Throughout that meal Hummil contrived laboriously to insult directly and pointedly all his guests in succession, and at each insult Spurstow kicked the aggrieved persons under the table; but he dared not exchange a glance of intelligence with either of them. Hummil's face was white and pinched, while his eyes were unnaturally large. No man dreamed for a moment of resenting his savage personalities, but as soon as the meal was over they made haste to get away.

'Don't go. You're just getting amusing, you fellows. I hope I haven't said anything that annoyed you. You're such touchy devils.' Then, changing the note into one of almost abject entreaty, Hummil added, 'I say, you surely aren't going?'

'In the language of the blessed Jorrocks, where I dines I sleeps,' said Spurstow. 'I want to have a look at your coolies tomorrow, if you don't mind. You can give me a place to lie down in, I suppose?'

The others pleaded the urgency of their several duties next day, and, saddling up, departed together, Hummil begging them to come next

Sunday. As they jogged off, Lowndes unbosomed himself to Mottram –

' . . . And I never felt so like kicking a man at his own table in my life. He said I cheated at whist, and reminded me I was in debt! Told you you were as good as a liar to your face! You aren't half indignant enough over it.'

'Not I,' said Mottram. 'Poor devil! Did you ever know old Hummy behave like that before or within a hundred miles of it?'

'That's no excuse. Spurstow was hacking my shin all the time, so I kept a hand on myself. Else I should have – '

'No, you wouldn't. You'd have done as Hummy did about Jevins; judge no man this weather. By Jove! the buckle of my bridle is hot in my hand! Trot out a bit, and 'ware rat-holes.'

Ten minutes' trotting jerked out of Lowndes one very sage remark when he pulled up, sweating from every pore –

'Good thing Spurstow's with him tonight.'

'Ye–es. Good man, Spurstow. Our roads turn here. See you again next Sunday, if the sun doesn't bowl me over.'

'S'pose so, unless old Timbersides' finance minister manages to dress some of my food. Good-night, and – God bless you!'

'What's wrong now?'

'Oh, nothing.' Lowndes gathered up his whip, and, as he flicked Mottram's mare on the flank, added, 'You're not a bad little chap – that's all.' And the mare bolted half a mile across the sand, on the word.

In the assistant engineer's bungalow Spurstow and Hummil smoked the pipe of silence together, each narrowly watching the other. The capacity of a bachelor's establishment is as elastic as its arrangements are simple. A servant cleared away the dining-room table, brought in a couple of rude native bedsteads made of tape strung on a light wood frame, flung a square of cool Calcutta matting over each, set them side by side, pinned two towels to the punkah so that their fringes should just sweep clear of the sleeper's nose and mouth, and announced that the couches were ready.

The men flung themselves down, ordering the punkah-coolies by all the powers of Hell to pull. Every door and window was shut, for the outside air was that of an oven. The atmosphere within was only 104°, as the thermometer bore witness, and heavy with the foul smell of badly-trimmed kerosene lamps; and this stench, combined with that of native tobacco, baked brick, and dried earth, sends the heart of many a strong man down to his boots, for it is the smell of the Great Indian Empire when she turns herself for six months into a house of torment. Spurstow packed his pillows craftily so that he reclined rather than lay, his head at a safe elevation above his feet. It is not good to sleep on a low pillow in the hot weather if you happen to be of thick-necked build, for you may pass with lively snores and gugglings from natural sleep into the deep slumber of heat-apoplexy.

'Pack your pillows,' said the doctor sharply, as he saw Hummil preparing to lie down at full length.

The night-light was trimmed; the shadow of the punkah wavered across the room, and the '*flick*' of the punkah-towel and the soft whine of the rope through the wall-hole followed it. Then the punkah flagged, almost ceased. The sweat poured from Spurstow's brow. Should he go out and harangue the coolie? It started forward again with a savage jerk, and a pin came out of the towels. When this was replaced, a tomtom in the coolie-lines began to beat with the steady throb of a swollen artery inside some brain-fevered skull. Spurstow turned on his side and swore gently. There was no movement on Hummil's part. The man had composed himself as rigidly as a corpse, his hands clinched at his sides. The respiration was too hurried for any suspicion of sleep. Spurstow looked at the set face. The jaws were clinched, and there was a pucker round the quivering eyelids.

'He's holding himself as tightly as ever he can,' thought Spurstow. 'What in the world is the matter with him? – Hummil!'

'Yes,' in a thick constrained voice.

'Can't you get to sleep?'

'No.'

'Head hot? Throat feeling bulgy? or how?'

'Neither, thanks. I don't sleep much, you know.'

'Feel pretty bad?'

'Pretty bad, thanks. There is a tomtom outside, isn't there? I thought it was my head at first . . . Oh, Spurstow, for pity's sake give me something that will put me asleep – sound asleep – if it's only for six hours!' He sprang up, trembling from head to foot. 'I haven't been able to sleep naturally for days, and I can't stand it! – I can't stand it!'

'Poor old chap!'

'That's no use. Give me something to make me sleep. I tell you I'm nearly mad. I don't know what I say half my time. For three weeks I've had to think and spell out every word that has come through my lips before I dared say it. Isn't that enough to drive a man mad? I can't see things correctly now, and I've lost my sense of touch. My skin aches – my skin aches! Make me sleep. Oh, Spurstow, for the love of God make me sleep sound. It isn't enough merely to let me dream. Let me sleep!'

'All right, old man, all right. Go slow; you aren't half as bad as you think.'

The flood-gates of reserve once broken, Hummil was clinging to him like a frightened child. 'You're pinching my arm to pieces.'

'I'll break your neck if you don't do something for me. No, I didn't mean that. Don't be angry, old fellow.' He wiped the sweat off himself as he fought to regain composure. 'I'm a bit restless and off my oats, and perhaps you could recommend some sort of sleeping mixture – bromide of potassium.'

'Bromide of skittles! Why didn't you tell me this before? Let go of my arm, and I'll see if there's anything in my cigarette-case to suit your complaint.' Spurstow hunted among his day-clothes, turned up the lamp, opened a little silver cigarette-case, and advanced on the expectant Hummil with the daintiest of fairy squirts.

'The last appeal of civilisation,' said he, 'and a thing I hate to use. Hold out your arm. Well, your sleeplessness hasn't ruined your muscle; and what a thick hide it is! Might as well inject a buffalo subcutaneously. Now in a few minutes the morphia will begin working. Lie down and wait.'

A smile of unalloyed and idiotic delight began to creep over Hummil's face. 'I think,' he whispered, 'I think I'm going off now. Gad! it's positively heavenly! Spurstow, you must give me that case to keep; you – ' The voice ceased as the head fell back.

'Not for a good deal,' said Spurstow to the unconscious form. 'And now, my friend, sleeplessness of your kind being very apt to relax the moral fibre in little matters of life and death, I'll just take the liberty of spiking your guns.'

He padded into Hummil's saddle-room in his bare feet and uncased a twelve-bore rifle, an express, and a revolver. Of the first he unscrewed the nipples and hid them in the bottom of a saddlery-case; of the second he abstracted the lever, kicking it behind a big wardrobe. The third he merely opened, and knocked the doll-head bolt of the grip up with the heel of a riding-boot.

'That's settled,' he said, as he shook the sweat off his hands. 'These little precautions will at least give you time to turn. You have too much sympathy with gun-room accidents.'

And as he rose from his knees, the thick muffled voice of Hummil cried in the doorway, 'You fool!'

Such tones they use who speak in the lucid intervals of delirium to their friends a little before they die.

Spurstow started, dropping the pistol. Hummil stood in the doorway, rocking with helpless laughter.

'That was awf'ly good of you, I'm sure,' he said, very slowly, feeling for his words. 'I don't intend to go out by my own hand at present. I say, Spurstow, that stuff won't work. What shall I do? What shall I do?'

And panic terror stood in his eyes.

'Lie down and give it a chance. Lie down at once.'

'I daren't. It will only take me half-way again, and I shan't be able to get away this time. Do you know it was all I could do to come out just now? Generally I am as quick as lightning; but you had clogged my feet. I was nearly caught.'

'Oh yes, I understand. Go and lie down.'

'No, it isn't delirium; but it was an awfully mean trick to play on me. Do you know I might have died?'

As a sponge rubs a slate clean, so some power unknown to Spurstow had wiped out of Hummil's face all that stamped it for the face of a man, and he stood at the doorway in the expression of his lost innocence. He had slept back into terrified childhood.

'Is he going to die on the spot?' thought Spurstow. Then, aloud, 'All right, my son. Come back to bed, and tell me all about it. You couldn't sleep; but what was all the rest of the nonsense?'

'A place – a place down there,' said Hummil, with simple sincerity. The drug was acting on him by waves, and he was flung from the fear of a strong man to the fright of a child as his nerves gathered sense or were dulled.

'Good God! I've been afraid of it for months past, Spurstow. It has made every night hell to me; and yet I'm not conscious of having done anything wrong.'

'Be still, and I'll give you another dose. We'll stop your nightmares, you unutterable idiot!'

'Yes, but you must give me so much that I can't get away. You must make me quite sleepy – not just a little sleepy. It's so hard to run then.'

'I know it; I know it. I've felt it myself. The symptoms are exactly as you describe.'

'Oh, don't laugh at me, confound you! Before this awful sleeplessness came to me I've tried to rest on my elbow and put a spur in the bed to sting me when I fell back. Look!'

'By Jove! the man has been rowelled like a horse! Ridden by the nightmare with a vengeance! And we all thought him sensible enough. Heaven send us understanding! You like to talk, don't you?'

'Yes, sometimes. Not when I'm frightened. *Then* I want to run. Don't you?'

'Always. Before I give you your second dose try to tell me exactly what your trouble is.'

Hummil spoke in broken whispers for nearly ten minutes, whilst Spurstow looked into the pupils of his eyes and passed his hand before them once or twice.

At the end of the narrative the silver cigarette-case was produced, and the last words that Hummil said as he fell back for the second time were, 'Put me quite to sleep; for if I'm caught I die – I die!'

'Yes, yes; we all do that sooner or later – thank Heaven who has set a term to our miseries,' said Spurstow, settling the cushions under the head. 'It occurs to me that unless I drink something I shall go out before my time. I've stopped sweating, and – I wear a seventeen-inch collar.' He brewed himself scalding hot tea, which is an excellent remedy against heat-apoplexy if you take three or four cups of it in time. Then he watched the sleeper.

'A blind face that cries and can't wipe its eyes, a blind face that chases him down corridors! H'm! Decidedly, Hummil ought to go on leave as soon as possible; and, sane or otherwise, he undoubtedly did rowel himself most cruelly. Well, Heaven send us understanding!'

At midday Hummil rose, with an evil taste in his mouth, but an unclouded eye and a joyful heart.

'I was pretty bad last night, wasn't I?' said he.

'I have seen healthier men. You must have had a touch of the sun. Look here: if I write you a swingeing medical certificate, will you apply for leave on the spot?'

'No.'

'Why not? You want it.'

'Yes, but I can hold on till the weather's a little cooler.'

'Why should you, if you can get relieved on the spot?'

'Burkett is the only man who could be sent; and he's a born fool.'

'Oh, never mind about the line. You aren't so important as all that. Wire for leave, if necessary.'

Hummil looked very uncomfortable.

'I can hold on till the Rains,' he said evasively.

'You can't. Wire to headquarters for Burkett.'

'I won't. If you want to know why, particularly, Burkett is married, and his wife's just had a kid, and she's up at Simla, in the cool, and Burkett has a very nice billet that takes him into Simla from Saturday to Monday. That little woman isn't at all well. If Burkett was transferred she'd try to follow him. If she left the baby behind she'd fret herself to death. If she came – and Burkett's one of those selfish little beasts who are always talking about a wife's place being with her husband – she'd die. It's murder to bring a woman here just now. Burkett hasn't the physique of a rat. If he came here he'd go out; and I know she hasn't any money, and I'm pretty sure she'd go out too. I'm salted in a sort of way, and I'm not married. Wait till the Rains, and then Burkett can get thin down here. It'll do him heaps of good.'

'Do you mean to say that you intend to face – what you have faced, till the Rains break?'

'Oh, it won't be so bad, now you've shown me a way out of it. I can always wire to you. Besides, now I've once got into the way of sleeping, it'll be all right. Anyhow, I shan't put in for leave. That's the long and the short of it.'

'My great Scott! I thought all that sort of thing was dead and done with.'

'Bosh! You'd do the same yourself. I feel a new man, thanks to that cigarette-case. You're going over to camp now, aren't you?'

'Yes; but I'll try to look you up every other day, if I can.'

'I'm not bad enough for that. I don't want you to bother. Give the coolies gin and ketchup.'

'Then you feel all right?'

'Fit to fight for my life, but not to stand out in the sun talking to you. Go along, old man, and bless you!'

Hummil turned on his heel to face the echoing desolation of his bungalow, and the first thing he saw standing in the verandah was the figure of himself. He had met a similar apparition once before, when he was suffering from overwork and the strain of the hot weather.

'This is bad – already,' he said, rubbing his eyes. 'If the thing slides away from me all in one piece, like a ghost, I shall know it is only my eyes and stomach that are out or order. If it walks – my head is going.'

He approached the figure, which naturally kept at an unvarying distance from him, as is the use of all spectres that are born of overwork. It slid through the house and dissolved into swimming specks within the eyeball as soon as it reached the burning light of the garden. Hummil went about his business till even. When he came in to dinner he found himself sitting at the table. The vision rose and walked out hastily. Except that it cast no shadow it was in all respects real.

No living man knows what that week held for Hummil. An increase of the epidemic kept Spurstow in camp among the coolies, and all he could do was to telegraph to Mottram, bidding him go to the bungalow and sleep there. But Mottram was forty miles away from the nearest telegraph, and knew nothing of anything save the needs of the survey till he met, early on Sunday morning, Lowndes and Spurstow heading towards Hummil's for the weekly gathering.

'Hope the poor chap's in a better temper,' said the former, swinging himself off his horse at the door. 'I suppose he isn't up yet.'

'I'll just have a look at him,' said the doctor. 'If he's asleep there's no need to wake him.'

And an instant later, by the tone of Spurstow's voice calling upon them to enter, the men knew what had happened. There was no need to wake him.

The punkah was still being pulled over the bed, but Hummil had departed this life at least three hours.

The body lay on its back, hands clinched by the side, as Spurstow had seen it lying seven nights previously. In the staring eyes was written terror beyond the expression of any pen.

Mottram, who had entered behind Lowndes, bent over the dead and touched the forehead lightly with his lips. 'Oh, you lucky, lucky devil!' he whispered.

But Lowndes had seen the eyes, and withdrew shuddering to the other side of the room.

'Poor chap! poor old chap! And the last time I met him I was angry. Spurstow, we should have watched him. Has he – ?'

Deftly Spurstow continued his investigations, ending by a search round the room.

'No, he hasn't,' he snapped. 'There's no trace of anything. Call the servants.'

They came, eight or ten of them, whispering and peering over each other's shoulders.

'When did your Sahib go to bed?' said Spurstow.

'At eleven or ten, we think,' said Hummil's personal servant.

'He was well then? But how should you know?'

'He was not ill, as far as our comprehension extended. But he had slept very little for three nights. This I know, because I saw him walking much, and specially in the heart of the night.'

As Spurstow was arranging the sheet, a big straight-necked hunting-spur tumbled on the ground. The doctor groaned. The personal servant peeped at the body.

'What do you think, Chuma?' said Spurstow, catching the look on the dark face.

'Heaven-born, in my poor opinion, this that was my master has descended into the Dark Places, and there has been caught because he was not able to escape with sufficient speed. We have the spur for evidence that he fought with Fear. Thus have I seen men of my race do with thorns when a spell was laid upon them to overtake them in their sleeping hours and they dared not sleep.'

'Chuma, you're a mud-head. Go out and prepare seals to be set on the Sahib's property.'

'God has made the Heaven-born. God has made me. Who are we, to enquire into the dispensations of God? I will bid the other servants hold aloof while you are reckoning the tale of the Sahib's property.

They are all thieves, and would steal.'

'As far as I can make out, he died from – oh, anything; stoppage of the heart's action, heat-apoplexy, or some other visitation,' said Spurstow to his companions. 'We must make an inventory of his effects, and so on.'

'He was scared to death,' insisted Lowndes. 'Look at those eyes! For pity's sake don't let him be buried with them open!'

'Whatever it was, he's clear of all the trouble now,' said Mottram softly.

Spurstow was peering into the open eyes.

'Come here,' said he. 'Can you see anything there?'

'I can't face it!' whimpered Lowndes. 'Cover up the face! Is there any fear on earth that can turn a man into that likeness? It's ghastly. Oh, Spurstow, cover it up!'

'No fear – on earth,' said Spurstow. Mottram leaned over his shoulder and looked intently.

'I see nothing except some grey blurs in the pupil. There can be nothing there, you know.'

'Even so. Well, let's think. It'll take half a day to knock up any sort of coffin; and he must have died at midnight. Lowndes, old man, go out and tell the coolies to break ground next to Jevins's grave. Mottram, go round the house with Chuma and see that the seals are put on things. Send a couple of men to me here, and I'll arrange.'

The strong-armed servants when they returned to their own kind told a strange story of the doctor Sahib vainly trying to call their master back to life by magic arts – to wit, the holding of a little green box that clicked to each of the dead man's eyes, and of a bewildered muttering on the part of the doctor Sahib, who took the little green box away with him.

The resonant hammering of a coffin-lid is no pleasant thing to hear, but those who have experience maintain that much more terrible is the soft swish of the bed-linen, the reeving and unreeving of the bed-tapes, when he who has fallen by the roadside is apparelled for burial, sinking gradually as the tapes are tied over, till the swaddled shape touches the floor and there is no protest against the indignity of hasty disposal.

At the last moment Lowndes was seized with scruples of conscience. 'Ought you to read the service – from beginning to end?' said he to Spurstow.

'I intend to. You're my senior as a civilian. You can take it if you like.'

'I didn't mean that for a moment. I only thought if we could get a chaplain from somewhere – I'm willing to ride anywhere – and give poor Hummil a better chance. That's all.'

'Bosh!' said Spurstow, as he framed his lips to the tremendous words that stand at the head of the burial service.

After breakfast they smoked a pipe in silence to the memory of the dead. Then Spurstow said absently –

' 'Tisn't in medical science.'

'What?'

'Things in a dead man's eye.'

'For goodness' sake leave that horror alone!' said Lowndes. 'I've seen a native die of pure fright when a tiger chivied him. I know what killed Hummil.'

'The deuce you do! I'm going to try to see.' And the doctor retreated into the bathroom with a Kodak camera. After a few minutes there was the sound of something being hammered to pieces, and he emerged, very white indeed.

'Have you got a picture?' said Mottram. 'What does the thing look like?'

'It was impossible, of course. You needn't look, Mottram. I've torn up the films. There was nothing there. It was impossible.'

'That,' said Lowndes, very distinctly, watching the shaking hand striving to relight the pipe, 'is a damned lie.'

Mottram laughed uneasily. 'Spurstow's right,' he said. 'We're all in such a state now that we'd believe anything. For pity's sake let's try to be rational.'

There was no further speech for a long time. The hot wind whistled without, and the dry trees sobbed. Presently the daily train, winking brass, burnished steel, and spouting steam, pulled up panting in the intense glare. 'We'd better go on on that,' said Spurstow. 'Go back to work. I've written my certificate. We can't do any more good here, and work'll keep our wits together. Come on.'

No one moved. It is not pleasant to face railway journeys at midday in June. Spurstow gathered up his hat and whip, and, turning in the doorway, said –

'There may be Heaven – there must be Hell.
Meantime, there is our life here. We-ell?'

Neither Mottram nor Lowndes had any answer to the question.

The Limitations of Pambé Serang

IF YOU CONSIDER the circumstances of the case, it was the only thing that he could do. But Pambé Serang has been hanged by the neck till he is dead, and Nurkeed is dead also.

Three years ago, when the Elsass-Lothringen steamer *Saarbruck* was coaling at Aden and the weather was very hot indeed, Nurkeed, the big fat Zanzibar stoker who fed the second right furnace thirty feet down in the hold, got leave to go ashore. He departed a 'Seedee boy', as they call the stokers; he returned the full-blooded Sultan of Zanzibar – His Highness Sayyid Burgash, with a bottle in each hand. Then he sat on the fore-hatch grating, eating salt fish and onions, and singing the songs of a far country. The food belonged to Pambé, the Serang or head man of the lascar sailors. He had just cooked it for himself, turned to borrow some salt, and when he came back Nurkeed's dirty black fingers were spading into the rice.

A serang is a person of importance, far above a stoker, though the stoker draws better pay. He sets the chorus of 'Hya! Hulla! Hee-ah! Heh!' when the captain's gig is pulled up to the davits; he heaves the lead too; and sometimes, when all the ship is lazy, he puts on his whitest muslin and a big red sash, and plays with the passengers' children on the quarter-deck. Then the passengers give him money, and he saves it all up for an orgy at Bombay or Calcutta, or Pulu Penang.

'Ho! you fat black barrel, you're eating my food!' said Pambé, in the other lingua franca that begins where the Levant tongue stops, and runs from Port Said eastward till east is west, and the sealing-brigs of the Kurile Islands gossip with the strayed Hakodate junks.

'Son of Eblis, monkey-face, dried shark's liver, pig-man, I am the Sultan Sayyid Burgash, and the commander of all this ship. Take away your garbage,' and Nurkeed thrust the empty pewter rice-plate into Pambé's hand.

Pambé beat it into a basin over Nurkeed's woolly head. Nurkeed drew his sheath-knife and stabbed Pambé in the leg. Pambé drew *his* sheath-knife; but Nurkeed dropped down into the darkness of the hold and spat through the grating at Pambé, who was staining the clean fore-deck with his blood.

Only the white moon saw these things; for the officers were looking after the coaling, and the passengers were tossing in their close cabins. 'All right,' said Pambé – and went forward to tie up his leg – 'we will settle the account later on.'

He was a Malay born in India: married once in Burma, where his wife had a cigar-shop on the Shwe-Dagon road; once in Singapore, to a Chinese girl; and once in Madras, to a Mahomedan woman who sold fowls. The English sailor cannot, owing to postal and telegraph facilities, marry as profusely as he used to do; but native sailors can, being uninfluenced by the barbarous inventions of the Western savage. Pambé was a good husband when he happened to remember the existence of a wife; but he was also a very good Malay; and it is not wise to offend a Malay, because he does not forget anything. Moreover, in Pambé's case blood had been drawn and food spoiled.

Next morning Nurkeed rose with a blank mind. He was no longer Sultan of Zanzibar, but a very hot stoker. So he went on deck and opened his jacket to the morning breeze, till a sheath-knife came like a flying-fish and stuck into the woodwork of the cook's galley half an inch from his right armpit. He ran down below before his time, trying to remember what he could have said to the owner of the weapon. At noon, when all the ship's lascars were feeding, Nurkeed advanced into their midst, and, being a placid man with a large regard for his own skin, he opened negotiations, saying, 'Men of the ship, last night I was drunk, and this morning I know that I behaved unseemly to someone or another of you. Who was that man, that I may meet him face to face and say that I was drunk?'

Pambé measured the distance to Nurkeed's naked breast. If he sprang at him he might be tripped up, and a blind blow at the chest sometimes only means a gash on the breast-bone. Ribs are difficult to thrust between unless the subject be asleep. So he said nothing; nor did the other lascars. Their faces immediately dropped all expression, as is the custom of the Oriental when there is killing on the carpet or any chance of trouble. Nurkeed looked long at the white eyeballs. He was only an African, and could not read characters. A big sigh – almost a groan – broke from him, and he went back to the furnaces. The lascars took up the conversation where he had interrupted it. They talked of the best methods of cooking rice.

Nurkeed suffered considerably from lack of fresh air during the run to Bombay. He only came on deck to breathe when all the world was about; and even then a heavy block once dropped from a derrick within a foot of his head, and an apparently firm-lashed grating on which he set his foot began to turn over with the intention of dropping him on the cased cargo fifteen feet below; and one insupportable night the sheath-knife dropped from the fo'c's'le, and this time it drew blood. So Nurkeed made complaint; and, when the *Saarbruck* reached Bombay, fled and buried himself among eight hundred thousand people, and did not sign articles till the ship had been a month gone from the port. Pambé waited too; but his Bombay wife grew clamorous, and he was forced to sign in the *Spicheren* to Hongkong, because he realised that all play and no work gives Jack a ragged shirt. In the foggy China seas he thought a great deal of Nurkeed, and, when Elsass-Lothringen steamers lay in port with the *Spicheren*, enquired after him and found he had gone to England via the Cape, on the *Gravelotte*. Pambé came to England on the *Worth*. The *Spicheren* met her by the Nore Light. Nurkeed was going out with the *Spicheren* to the Calicut coast.

'Want to find a friend, my trap-mouthed coal-scuttle?' said a gentleman in the mercantile service. 'Nothing easier. Wait at the Nyanza Docks till he comes. Everyone comes to the Nyanza Docks. Wait, you poor heathen.' The gentleman spoke truth. There are three great doors in the world where, if you stand long enough, you shall meet anyone you wish. The head of the Suez Canal is one, but there Death comes also; Charing Cross Station is the second – for inland work; and the Nyanza Docks is the third. At each of these places are men and women looking eternally for those who will surely come. So Pambé waited at the docks. Time was no object to him; and the wives could wait, as he did from day to day, week to week, and month to month, by the Blue Diamond funnels, the Red Dot smoke-stacks, the Yellow Streaks, and the nameless dingy gypsies of the sea that loaded and unloaded, jostled, whistled, and roared in the everlasting fog. When money failed, a kind gentleman told Pambé to become a Christian; and Pambé became one with great speed, getting his religious teachings between ship and ship's arrival, and six or seven shillings a week for distributing tracts to mariners. What the faith was Pambé did not in the least care; but he knew if he said 'Native Ki-lis-ti-an, Sar' to men with long black coats he might get a few coppers; and the tracts were vendible at a little public-house that sold shag by the 'dottel', which is even smaller weight than the 'half-screw', which is less than the half-ounce, and a most profitable retail trade.

But after eight months Pambé fell sick with pneumonia, contracted from long standing still in slush; and much against his will he was forced to lie down in his two-and-sixpenny room raging against Fate.

The kind gentleman sat by his bedside, and grieved to find that Pambé talked in strange tongues, instead of listening to good books, and almost seemed to become a benighted heathen again – till one day

he was roused from semi-stupor by a voice in the street by the dock-head. 'My friend – he,' whispered Pambé. 'Call now – call Nurkeed. Quick! God has sent him!'

'He wanted one of his own race,' said the kind gentleman; and, going out, he called 'Nurkeed!' at the top of his voice. An excessively coloured man in a rasping white shirt and brand-new slops, a shining hat, and a breast-pin, turned round. Many voyages had taught Nurkeed how to spend his money and made him a citizen of the world.

'Hi! Yes!' said he, when the situation was explained. 'Command him – black nigger – when I was in the *Saarbruck*. Ole Pambé, good ole Pambé. Damn lascar. Show him up, Sar,' and he followed into the room. One glance told the stoker what the kind gentleman had overlooked. Pambé was desperately poor. Nurkeed drove his hands deep into his pockets, then advanced with clenched fists on the sick, shouting, 'Hya, Pambé. Hya! Hee-ah! Hulla! Heh! Takilo! Takilo! Make fast aft, Pambé. You know, Pambé. You know me. Dekho, jee! Look! Damn big fat lazy lascar!'

Pambé beckoned with his left hand. His right was under his pillow. Nurkeed removed his gorgeous hat and stooped over Pambé till he could catch a faint whisper. 'How beautiful!' said the kind gentleman. 'How these Orientals love like children!'

'Spit him out,' said Nurkeed, leaning over Pambé yet more closely.

'Touching the matter of that fish and onions – ' said Pambé – and sent the knife home under the edge of the rib-bone upwards and forwards.

There was a thick sick cough, and the body of the African slid slowly from the bed, his clutching hands letting fall a shower of silver pieces that ran across the room.

'Now I can die!' said Pambé.

But he did not die. He was nursed back to life with all the skill that money could buy, for the Law wanted him; and in the end he grew sufficiently healthy to be hanged in due and proper form.

Pambé did not care particularly; but it was a sad blow to the kind gentleman.

The Disturber of Traffic

From the wheel and the drift of Things
    Deliver us, good Lord;
And we will meet the wrath of kings,
    The faggot, and the sword.

Lay not Thy toil before our eyes,
    Nor vex us with Thy wars,
Lest we should feel the straining skies
    O'ertrod by trampling stars.

A veil 'twixt us and Thee, dread Lord,
    A veil 'twixt us and Thee:
Lest we should hear too clear, too clear,
    And unto madness see!

MIRIAM COHEN

THE BROTHERS OF THE TRINITY order that none unconnected with their service shall be found in or on one of their Lights during the hours of darkness; but their servants can be made to think otherwise. If you are fair-spoken and take an interest in their duties, they will allow you to sit with them through the long night and help to scare the ships into mid-channel.

Of the English south-coast Lights, that of St Cecilia-under-the-Cliff is the most powerful, for it guards a very foggy coast. When the sea-mist veils all, St Cecilia turns a hooded head to the sea and sings a song of two words once every minute. From the land that song resembles the bellowing of a brazen bull; but off-shore they understand, and the steamers grunt gratefully in answer.

Fenwick, who was on duty one night, lent me a pair of black glass spectacles, without which no man can look at the Light unblinded, and busied himself in last touches to the lenses before twilight fell. The width of the English Channel beneath us lay as smooth and as many-coloured as the inside of an oyster shell. A little Sunderland cargo-boat had made her signal to Lloyd's Agency, half a mile up the coast, and was lumbering down to the sunset, her wake lying white behind her. One star came out over the cliffs, the waters turned to lead colour, and

St Cecilia's Light shot out across the sea in eight long pencils that wheeled slowly from right to left, melted into one beam of solid light laid down directly in front of the tower, dissolved again into eight, and passed away. The light-frame of the thousand lenses circled on its rollers, and the compressed-air engine that drove it hummed like a bluebottle under a glass. The hand of the indicator on the wall pulsed from mark to mark. Eight pulse-beats timed one half-revolution of the Light; neither more nor less.

Fenwick checked the first few revolutions carefully; he opened the engine's feed-pipe a trifle, looked at the racing governor, and again at the indicator, and said: 'She'll do for the next few hours. We've just sent our regular engine to London, and this spare one's not by any manner so accurate.'

'And what would happen if the compressed air gave out?' I asked.

'We'd have to turn the flash by hand, keeping an eye on the indicator. There's a regular crank for that. But it hasn't happened yet. We'll need all our compressed air tonight.'

'Why?' said I. I had been watching him for not more than a minute.

'Look,' he answered, and I saw that the dead sea-mist had risen out of the lifeless sea and wrapped us while my back had been turned. The pencils of the Light marched staggeringly across tilted floors of white cloud. From the balcony round the light-room the white walls of the lighthouse ran down into swirling, smoking space. The noise of the tide coming in very lazily over the rocks was choked down to a thick drawl.

'That's the way our sea-fogs come,' said Fenwick, with an air of ownership. 'Hark, now, to that little fool calling out 'fore he's hurt.'

Something in the mist was bleating like an indignant calf; it might have been half a mile or half a hundred miles away.

'Does he suppose we've gone to bed?' continued Fenwick. 'You'll hear us talk to him in a minute. He knows puffickly where he is, and he's carrying on to be told like if he was insured.'

'Who is "he"?'

'That Sunderland boat, o' course. Ah!'

I could hear a steam-engine hiss down below in the mist where the dynamos that fed the Light were clacking together. Then there came a roar that split the fog and shook the lighthouse.

'GIT-*toot*!' blared the fog-horn of St Cecilia. The bleating ceased.

'Little fool!' Fenwick repeated. Then, listening: 'Blest if that aren't another of them! Well, well, they always say that a fog do draw the ships of the sea together. They'll be calling all night, and so'll the siren. We're expecting some tea-ships up-Channel . . . If you put my coat on that chair, you'll feel more so-fash, sir.'

It is no pleasant thing to thrust your company upon a man for the night. I looked at Fenwick, and Fenwick looked at me; each gauging the other's capacities for boring and being bored. Fenwick was an old, clean-shaven, grey-haired man who had followed the sea for thirty years, and knew nothing of the land except the lighthouse in which he served. He fenced cautiously to find out the little that I knew and talked down to my level, till it came out that I had met a captain in the merchant service who had once commanded a ship in which Fenwick's son had served; and further, that I had seen some places that Fenwick had touched at. He began with a dissertation on pilotage in the Hugli. I had been privileged to know a Hugli pilot intimately. Fenwick had only seen the imposing and masterful breed from a ship's chains, and his intercourse had been cut down to 'Quarter less five', and remarks of a strictly business-like nature. Hereupon he ceased to talk down to me, and became so amazingly technical that I was forced to beg him to explain every other sentence. This set him fully at his ease; and then we spoke as men together, each too interested to think of anything except the subject in hand. And that subject was wrecks, and voyages, and old-time trading, and ships cast away in desolate seas, steamers we both had known, their merits and demerits, lading, Lloyd's, and, above all, Lights. The talk always came back to Lights: Lights of the Channel; Lights on forgotten islands, and men forgotten on them; Light-ships – two months' duty and one month's leave – tossing on kinked cables in ever troubled tideways; and Lights that men had seen where never lighthouse was marked on the charts.

Omitting all those stories, and omitting also the wonderful ways by which he arrived at them, I tell here, from Fenwick's mouth, one that was not the least amazing. It was delivered in pieces between the roller-skate rattle of the revolving lenses, the bellowing of the fog-horn below, the answering calls from the sea, and the sharp tap of reckless night-birds that flung themselves at the glasses. It concerned a man called Dowse, once an intimate friend of Fenwick, now a waterman at Portsmouth, believing that the guilt of blood is on his head, and finding no rest either at Portsmouth or Gosport Hard.

' . . . And if anybody was to come to you and say, "I know the Java currents," don't you listen to him; for those currents is never yet known to mortal man. Sometimes they're here, sometimes they're there, but they never runs less than five knots an hour through and among those islands of the Eastern Archipelagus. There's reverse currents in the Gulf of Boni – and that's up north in Celebes – that no man can explain; and through all those Java passages from the Bali Narrows, Dutch Gut, and Ombay, which I take it is the safest, they chop and they change, and they banks the tides fust on one shore and then on another, till your ship's tore in two. I've come through the Bali Narrows, stern first, in the heart o' the south-east monsoon, with a sou'-sou'-west wind blowing atop of the northerly flood, and our skipper said he wouldn't do it again, not for all Jamrach's. You've heard o' Jamrach's, sir?'

'Yes; and was Dowse stationed in the Bali Narrows?' I said.

'No; he was not at Bali, but much more east o' them passages, and that's Flores Strait, at the east end o' Flores. It's all on the way south to Australia when you're running through that Eastern Archipelagus. Sometimes you go through Bali Narrows if you're full-powered, and sometimes through Flores Strait, so as to stand south at once, and fetch round Timor, keeping well clear o' the Sahul Bank. Elseways, if you aren't full-powered, why it stands to reason you go round by the Ombay Passage, keeping careful to the north side. You understand that, sir?'

I was not full-powered, and judged it safer to keep to the north side – of Silence.

'And on Flores Strait, in the fairway between Adonare Island and the mainland, they put Dowse in charge of a screw-pile Light called the Wurlee Light. It's less than a mile across the head of Flores Strait. Then it opens out to ten or twelve mile for Solor Strait, and then it narrows again to a three-mile gut, with a toplin' flamin' volcano by it. That's old Loby Toby by Loby Toby Strait, and if you keep his Light and the Wurlee Light in a line you won't take much harm, not on the darkest night. That's what Dowse told me, and I can well believe him, knowing these seas myself; but you must ever be mindful of the currents. And there they put Dowse, since he was the only man that that Dutch Government which owns Flores could find that would go to Wurlee and tend a fixed Light. Mostly they uses Dutch and Italians; Englishmen being said to drink when alone. I never could rightly find out what made Dowse accept of that position, but accept he did, and used to sit for to watch the tigers come out of the forests to hunt for crabs and such like round about the lighthouse at low tide. The water was always warm in those parts, as I know well, and uncommon sticky, and it ran with the tides as thick and smooth as hogwash in a trough. There was another man along with Dowse in the Light, but he wasn't rightly a man. He was a Kling. No, nor yet a Kling he wasn't, but his skin was in little flakes and cracks all over, from living so much in the salt water as was his usual custom. His hands was all webby-foot, too.

He was called, I remember Dowse saying now, an Orange-Lord, on account of his habits. You've heard of an Orange-Lord, sir?'

'Orang-Laut?' I suggested.

'That's the name,' said Fenwick, smacking his knee. 'An Orang-Laut, of course, and his name was Challong; what they call a sea-gypsy. Dowse told me that that man, long hair and all, would go swimming up and down the straits just for something to do; running down on one tide and back again with the other, swimming side-stroke, and the tides going tremenjus strong. Elseways he'd be skipping about the beach along with the tigers at low tide, for he was most part a beast; or he'd sit in a little boat praying to old Loby Toby of an evening when the volcano was spitting red at the south end of the strait. Dowse told me that he wasn't a companionable man, like you and me might have been to Dowse.

'Now I can never rightly come at what it was that began to ail Dowse after he had been there a year or something less. He was saving of all his pay and tending to his Light, and now and again he'd have a fight with Challong and tip him off the Light into the sea. Then, he told me, his head began to feel streaky from looking at the tide so long. He said there was long streaks of white running inside it; like wall-paper that hadn't been properly pasted up, he said. The streaks, they would run with the tides, north and south, twice a day, accordin' to them currents, and he'd lie down on the planking – it was a screw-pile Light – with his eye to a crack and watch the water streaking through the piles just so quiet as hogwash. He said the only comfort he got was at slack water. Then the streaks in his head went round and round like a sampan in a tide-rip; but that was heaven, he said, to the other kind of streaks – the straight ones that looked like arrows on a wind-chart, but much more regular, and that was the trouble of it. No more he couldn't ever keep his eyes off the tides that ran up and down so strong, but as soon as ever he looked at the high hills standing all along Flores Strait for rest and comfort his eyes would be pulled down like to the nesty streaky water; and when they once got there he couldn't pull them away again till the tide changed. He told me all this himself, speaking just as though he was talking of somebody else.'

'Where did you meet him?' I asked.

'In Portsmouth harbour, a-cleaning the brasses of a Ryde boat, but I'd known him off and on through following the sea for many years. Yes, he spoke about himself very curious, and all as if he was in the next room laying there dead. Those streaks, they preyed upon his intellecks, he said; and he made up his mind, every time that the Dutch gunboat that attends to the Lights in those parts come along, that he'd ask to be took off. But as soon as she did come something went click in his throat, and he was so took up with watching her masts, because they ran longways, in the contrary direction to his streaks, that he could never say a word until she was gone away and her masts was under sea again. Then, he said, he'd cry by the hour; and Challong swum round and round the Light, laughin' at him and splashin' water with his webby-foot hands. At last he took it into his pore sick head that the ships, and particularly the steamers that came by – there wasn't many of them – made the streaks, instead of the tides as was natural. He used to sit, he told me, cursing every boat that come along – sometimes a junk, sometimes a Dutch brig, and now and again a steamer rounding Flores Head and poking about in the mouth of the strait. Or there'd come a boat from Australia running north past old Loby Toby hunting for a fair current, but never throwing out any papers that Challong might pick up for Dowse to read. Generally speaking, the steamers kept more westerly, but now and again they came looking for Timor and the west coast of Australia. Dowse used to shout to them to go round by the Ombay Passage, and not to come streaking past him, making the water all streaky, but it wasn't likely they'd hear. He says to himself after a month, "I'll give them one more chance," he says. "If the next boat don't attend to my just representations," – he says he remembers using those very words to Challong – "I'll stop the fairway."

'The next boat was a Two-streak cargo-boat very anxious to make her northing. She waddled through under old Loby Toby at the south end of the strait, and she passed within a quarter of a mile of the Wurlee Light at the north end, in seventeen fathom o' water, the tide against her. Dowse took the trouble to come out with Challong in a little prow that they had – all bamboos and leakage – and he lay in the fairway waving a palm branch, and, so he told me, wondering why and what for he was making this fool of himself. Up come the Two-streak boat, and Dowse shouts: "Don't you come this way again, making my head all streaky! Go round by Ombay, and leave me alone." Someone looks over the port bulwarks and shies a banana at Dowse, and that's all. Dowse sits down in the bottom of the boat and cries fit to break his heart. Then he says, "Challong, what am I a-crying for?" and they fetches up by the Wurlee Light on the half-flood.

' "Challong," he says, "there's too much traffic here, and that's why the water's so streaky as it is. It's the junks and the brigs and the steamers that do it," he says; and all the time he was speaking he was thinking, "Lord, Lord, what a crazy fool I am!" Challong said nothing, because he couldn't speak a word of English except say "damn", and he said that where you or me would say "yes". Dowse lay down on the planking of the Light with his eye to the crack, and he saw the muddy water streaking below, and he never said a word till slack water, because the streaks kept him tongue-tied at such times. At slack water he says, "Challong, we must buoy this fairway for wrecks," and he holds up his hands several times, showing that dozens of wrecks had come about in the fairway; and Challong says, "Damn."

'That very afternoon he and Challong rows to Wurlee, the village in the woods that the Light was named after, and buys canes – stacks and stacks of canes, and coir rope thick and fine, all sorts – and they sets to work making square floats by lashing of the canes together. Dowse said he took longer over those floats than might have been needed, because he rejoiced in the corners, they being square, and the streaks in his head all running longways. He lashed the canes together, criss-cross and thwartways – any way but longways – and they made up twelve-foot-square floats, like rafts. Then he stepped a twelve-foot bamboo or a bundle of canes in the centre, and to the head of that he lashed a big six-foot W letter, all made of canes, and painted the float dark green and the W white, as a wreck-buoy should be painted. Between them two they makes a round dozen of these new kind of wreck-buoys, and it was a two months' job. There was no big traffic, owing to it being on the turn of the monsoon, but what there was Dowse cursed at, and the streaks in his head, they ran with the tides, as usual.

'Day after day, so soon as a buoy was ready, Challong would take it out, with a big rock that half sunk the prow and a bamboo grapnel, and drop it dead in the fairway. He did this day or night, and Dowse could see him of a clear night, when the sea brimed, climbing about the buoys with the sea-fire dripping off him. They was all put into place, twelve of them, in seventeen-fathom water; not in a straight line, on account of a well-known shoal there, but slantways, and two, one behind the other, mostly in the centre of the fairway. You must keep the centre of those Java currents, for currents at the side is different, and in narrow water, before you can turn a spoke, you get your nose took round and rubbed upon the rocks and the woods. Dowse knew that just as well as any skipper. Likeways he knew that no skipper daren't run through uncharted wrecks in a six-knot current. He told me he used to lie outside the Light watching his buoys ducking and dipping so friendly with the tide; and the motion was comforting to him on account of its being different from the run of the streaks in his head.

'Three weeks after he'd done his business up comes a steamer through Loby Toby Straits, thinking she'd run into Flores Sea before night. He saw her slow down; then she backed. Then one man and another come up on the bridge, and he could see there was a regular pow-wow, and the flood was driving her right on to Dowse's wreck-buoys. After that she spun round and went back south, and Dowse nearly killed himself with laughing. But a few weeks after that a couple of junks came shouldering through from the north, arm in arm, like junks go. It takes a good deal to make a Chinaman understand danger. They junks set well in the current, and went down the fairway, right among the buoys, ten knots an hour, blowing horns and banging tin pots all the time. That made Dowse very angry; he having taken so much trouble to stop the fairway. No boats run Flores Straits by night, but it seemed to Dowse that if junks 'd do that in the day, the Lord knew but what a steamer might trip over his buoys at night; and he sent Challong to run a coir rope between three of the buoys in the middle of the fairway, and he fixed naked lights of coir steeped in oil to that rope. The tides was the only things that moved in those seas, for the airs was dead still till they began to blow, and *then* they would blow your hair off. Challong tended those lights every night after the junks had been so impident – four lights in about a quarter of a mile hung up in iron skillets on the rope; and when they was alight – and coir burns well, very like a lamp wick – the fairway seemed more madder than anything else in the world. First there was the Wurlee Light, then these four queer lights, that couldn't be riding-lights, almost flush with the water, and behind them, twenty mile off, but the biggest light of all, there was the red top of old Loby Toby volcano. Dowse told me that he used to go out in the prow and look at his handiwork, and it made him scared, being like no lights that ever was fixed.

'By and by some more steamers came along, snorting and snifting at the buoys, but never going through, and Dowse says to himself: "Thank goodness I've taught them not to come streaking through my water. Ombay Passage is good enough for them and the like of them." But he didn't remember how quick that sort of news spreads among the shipping. Every steamer that fetched up by those buoys told another steamer and all the port officers concerned in those seas that there was something wrong with Flores Straits that hadn't been charted yet. It was block-buoyed for wrecks in the fairway, they said, and no sort of passage to use. Well, the Dutch, of course they didn't know anything about it. They thought our Admiralty Survey had been there, and they thought it very queer but neighbourly. You understand us English are always looking up marks and lighting seaways all the world over, never asking with your leave or by your leave, seeing that the sea concerns us more than anyone else. So the news went to and back from Flores to Bali, and

Bali to Probolingo, where the railway is that runs to Batavia. All through the Java seas everybody got the word to keep clear o' Flores Straits, and Dowse, he was left alone except for such steamers and small craft as didn't know. They'd come up and look at the straits like a bull over a gate, but those nodding wreck-buoys scared them away. By and by the Admiralty Survey ship – the *Britomarte* I think she was – lay in Macassar Roads off Fort Rotterdam, alongside of the *Amboina*, a dirty little Dutch gunboat that used to clean there; and the Dutch captain says to our captain, "What's wrong with Flores Straits?" he says.

' "Blowed if I know," says our captain, who'd just come up from the Angelica Shoal.

' "Then why did you go and buoy it?" says the Dutchman.

' "Blowed if I have," says our captain. "That's your lookout."

' "Buoyed it is," says the Dutch captain, "according to what they tell me; and a whole fleet of wreck-buoys, too."

' "Gummy!" says our captain. "It's a dorg's life at sea, anyway. I must have a look at this. You come along after me as soon as you can," and down he skimmed that very night, round the heel of Celebes, three days' steam to Flores Head, and he met a Two-streak liner, very angry, backing out of the head of the strait; and the merchant captain gave our Survey ship something of his mind for leaving wrecks uncharted in those narrow waters and wasting his company's coal.

' "It's no fault o' mine," says our captain.

' "I don't care whose fault it is," says the merchant captain, who had come aboard to speak to him just at dusk. "The fairway's choked with wreck enough to knock a hole through a dock-gate. I saw their big ugly masts sticking up just under my forefoot. Lord ha' mercy on us!" he says, spinning round. "The place is like Regent Street of a hot summer night."

'And so it was. They two looked at Flores Straits, and they saw lights one after the other stringing across the fairway. Dowse, he had seen the steamers hanging there before dark, and he said to Challong: "We'll give 'em something to remember. Get all the skillets and iron pots you can and hang them up alongside o' the regular four lights. We must teach 'em to go round by the Ombay Passage, or they'll be streaking up our water again!" Challong took a header off the lighthouse, got aboard the little leaking prow, with his coir soaked in oil and all the skillets he could muster, and he began to show his lights, four regulation ones and half a dozen new lights hung on that rope which was a little above the water. Then he went to all the spare buoys with all his spare coir, and hung a skillet-flare on every pole that he could get at – about seven poles. So you see, taking one with another, there was the Wurlee Light, four lights on the rope between the three centre fairway wreck-buoys that was hung out as a usual custom, six or eight extry ones that Challong had hung up on the same rope, and seven dancing flares that belonged to seven wreck-buoys – eighteen or twenty lights in all crowded into a mile of seventeen-fathom water, where no tide 'd ever let a wreck rest for three weeks, let alone ten or twelve wrecks, as the flares showed.

'The Admiralty captain, he saw the lights come out one after another, same as the merchant-skipper did who was standing at his side, and he said –

' "There's been an international catastrophe here or elseways," and then he whistled. "I'm going to stand on and off all night till the Dutchman comes," he says.

' "I'm off," says the merchant skipper. "My owners don't wish for me to watch illuminations. That strait's choked with wreck, and I shouldn't wonder if a typhoon hadn't driven half the junks o' China there." With that he went away; but the Survey ship, she stayed all night at the head o' Flores Strait, and the men admired of the lights till the lights was burning out, and then they admired more than ever.

'A little bit before morning the Dutch gunboat come flustering up, and the two ships stood together watching the lights burn out and out, till there was nothing left 'cept Flores Straits, all green and wet, and a dozen wreck-buoys, and Wurlee Light.

'Dowse had slept very quiet that night, and got rid of his streaks by means of thinking of the angry steamers outside. Challong was busy, and didn't come back to his bunk till late. In the grey early morning Dowse looked out to sea, being, as he said, in torment, and saw all the navies of the world riding outside Flores Strait fairway in a half-moon, seven miles from wing to wing, most wonderful to behold. Those were the words he used to me time and again in telling the tale.

'Then, he says, he heard a gun fired with a most tremenjus explosion, and all them great navies crumbled to little pieces of clouds, and there was only two ships remaining, and a man-o'-war's boat rowing to the Light, with the oars going sideways instead o' longways as the morning tides, ebb or flow, would continually run.

' "What the devil's wrong with this strait?" says a man in the boat as soon as they was in hailing distance. "Has the whole English Navy sunk here, or what?"

' "There's nothing wrong," says Dowse, sitting on the platform outside the Light, and keeping one eye very watchful on the streakiness of the tide, which he always hated, 'specially in the mornings. "You leave me alone and I'll leave you alone. Go round by the Ombay Passage, and don't cut up my water. You're making it streaky." All the time he was saying that he kept on thinking to himself, "Now that's foolishness – now that's nothing but foolishness", and all the time he was holding tight to the edge of the platform in case the streakiness of the tide should carry him away.

'Somebody answers from the boat, very soft and quiet, "We're going round by Ombay in a minute, if you'll just come and speak to our captain and give him his bearings."

'Dowse, he felt very highly flattered, and he slipped into the boat, not paying any attention to Challong. But Challong swum along to the ship after the boat. When Dowse was in the boat, he found, so he says, he couldn't speak to the sailors 'cept to call them "white mice with chains about their neck", and Lord knows he hadn't seen or thought o' white mice since he was a little bit of a boy with them in his hankerchief. So he kept himself quiet, and so they come to the Survey ship; and the man in the boat hails the quarterdeck with something that Dowse could not rightly understand, but there was one word he spelt out again and again – m-a-d, mad – and he heard someone behind him saying of it backwards. So he had two words – m-a-d, mad, d-a-m, damn; and he put they two words together as he come on the quarter-deck, and he says to the captain very slowly, "I be damned if I am mad," but all the time his eye was held like by the coils of rope on the belaying pins, and he followed those ropes up and up with his eye till he was quite lost and comfortable among the rigging, which ran criss-cross, and slopeways, and up and down, and any way but straight along under his feet north and south. The deck-seams, they ran *that* way, and Dowse daresn't look at them. They was the same as the streaks of the water under the planking of the lighthouse.

'Then he heard the captain talking to him very kind, and for the life of him he couldn't tell why; and what he wanted to tell the captain was that Flores Strait was too streaky, like bacon, and the steamers only made it worse; but all he could do was to keep his eye very careful on the rigging and sing –

> I saw a ship a-sailing,
> A-sailing on the sea;
> And oh, it was all lading
> With pretty things for me!

Then he remembered that was foolishness, and he started off to say about the Ombay Passage, but all he said was: "The captain was a duck – meaning no offence to you, sir – but there was something on his back that I've forgotten.

And when the ship began to move
The captain says, 'Quack-quack!' "

'He notices the captain turns very red and angry, and he says to himself, "My foolish tongue's run away with me again. I'll go forward," and he went forward, and catched the reflection of himself in the binnacle brasses; and he saw that he was standing there and talking mother-naked in front of all them sailors, and he ran into the fo'c's'le howling most grievous. He must ha' gone naked for weeks on the Light, and Challong o' course never noticed it. Challong was swimmin' round and round the ship, sayin' "damn" for to please the men and to be took aboard, because he didn't know any better.

'Dowse didn't tell what happened after this, but seemingly our Survey ship lowered two boats and went over to Dowse's buoys. They took one sounding, and then finding it was all correct they cut the buoys that Dowse and Challong had made, and let the tide carry 'em out through the Loby Toby end of the strait; and the Dutch gunboat, she sent two men ashore to take care o' the Wurlee Light, and the *Britomarte*, she went away with Dowse, leaving Challong to try to follow them, a-calling "damn – damn" all among the wake of the screw, and half heaving himself out of water and joining his webby-foot hands together. He dropped astern in five minutes, and I suppose he went back to the Wurlee Light. You can't drown an Orange-Lord, not even in Flores Strait on flood-tide.

'Dowse come across me when he came to England with the Survey ship, after being more than six months in her, and cured of his streaks by working hard and not looking over the side nore than he could help. He told me what I've told you, sir, and he was very much ashamed of himself; but the trouble on his mind was to know whether he hadn't sent something or other to the bottom with his buoyings and his lightings and such like. He put it to me many times, and each time more and more sure he was that something had happened in the straits because of him. I think that distructed him, because I found him up at Fratton one day, in a red jersey, a-praying before the Salvation Army, which had produced him in their papers as a Reformed Pirate. They knew from his mouth that he had committed evil on the deep waters – that was what he told them – and piracy, which no one does now except Chineses, was all they knew of. I says to him: "Dowse, don't be a fool. Take off that jersey and come along with me." He says: "Fenwick, I'm a-saving of my soul; for I do believe that I have killed more men in Flores Strait than Trafalgar." I says: "A man that thought he'd seen all the navies of the earth standing round in a ring to watch his foolish false wreck-buoys" (those was my very words I used) "ain't fit to have a soul, and if he did he couldn't kill a louse with it. John Dowse, you was mad then, but you are a damn sight madder now. Take off that there jersey!"

'He took it off and come along with me, but he never got rid o' that suspicion that he'd sunk some ships a-cause of his foolishnesses at Flores Straits; and now he's a wherryman from Portsmouth to Gosport, where the tides run crossways and you can't row straight for ten strokes together . . . So late as all this! Look!'

Fenwick left his chair, passed to the Light, touched something that clicked, and the glare ceased with a suddenness that was pain. Day had come, and the Channel needed St Cecilia no longer. The sea-fog rolled back from the cliffs in trailed wreaths and dragged patches, as the sun rose and made the dead sea alive and splendid. The stillness of the morning held us both silent as we stepped on the balcony. A lark went up from the cliffs behind St Cecilia, and we smelt a smell of cows in the lighthouse pastures below.

Then we were both at liberty to thank the Lord for another day of clean and wholesome life.

'The Finest Story in the World'

Or ever the knightly years were gone
    With the old world to the grave,
I was a king in Babylon
    And you were a Christian slave.
                                        W. E. HENLEY

HIS NAME WAS CHARLIE MEARS; he was the only son of his mother who was a widow, and he lived in the north of London, coming into the City every day to work in a bank. He was twenty years old and was full of aspirations. I met him in a public billiard-saloon where the marker called him by his first name, and he called the marker 'Bullseye'. Charlie explained, a little nervously, that he had only come to the place to look on, and since looking on at games of skill is not a cheap amusement for the young, I suggested that Charlie should go back to his mother.

That was our first step towards better acquaintance. He would call on me sometimes in the evenings instead of running about London with his fellow-clerks; and before long, speaking of himself as a young man must, he told me of his aspirations, which were all literary. He desired to make himself an undying name chiefly through verse, though he was not above sending stories of love and death to the penny-in-the-slot journals. It was my fate to sit still while Charlie read me poems of many hundred lines, and bulky fragments of plays that would surely shake the world. My reward was his unreserved confidence, and the self-revelations and troubles of a young man are almost as holy as those of a maiden. Charlie had never fallen in love, but was anxious to do so on the first opportunity; he believed in all things good and all things honourable, but at the same time, was curiously careful to let me see that he knew his way about the world as befitted a bank-clerk on twenty-five shillings a week. He rhymed 'dove' with 'love' and 'moon' with 'June', and devoutly believed that they had never so been rhymed before. The long lame gaps in his plays he filled up with hasty words of apology and description, and swept on, seeing all that he intended to do so clearly that he esteemed it already done, and turned to me for applause.

I fancy that his mother did not encourage his aspirations; and I know that his writing-table at home was the edge of his washstand. This he told me almost at the outset of our acquaintance – when he was ravaging my bookshelves, and a little before I was implored to speak the truth as to his chances of 'writing something really great, you know'. Maybe I encouraged him too much for, one night, he called on me, his eyes flaming with excitement, and said breathlessly:

'Do you mind – can you let me stay here and write all this evening? I won't interrupt you, I won't really. There's no place for me to write in at my mother's.'

'What's the trouble?' I said, knowing well what that trouble was.

'I've a notion in my head that would make the most splendid story that was ever written. Do let me write it out here. It's *such* a notion!'

There was no resisting the appeal. I set him a table; he hardly thanked me, but plunged into his work at once. For half an hour the pen scratched without stopping. Then Charlie sighed and tugged his hair. The scratching grew slower, there were more erasures, and at last ceased. The finest story in the world would not come forth.

'It looks such awful rot now,' he said mournfully. 'And yet it seemed so good when I was thinking about it. What's wrong?'

I could not dishearten him by saying the truth. So I answered: 'Perhaps you don't feel in the mood for writing.'

'Yes I do – except when I look at this stuff. Ugh!'

'Read me what you've done,' I said.

He read, and it was wondrous bad, and he paused at all the specially turgid sentences, expecting a little approval; for he was proud of those sentences, as I knew he would be.

'It needs compression,' I suggested cautiously.

'I hate cutting my things down. I don't think you could alter a word here without spoiling the sense. It reads better aloud than when I was writing it.'

'Charlie, you're suffering from an alarming disease afflicting a numerous class. Put the thing by, and tackle it again in a week.'

'I want to do it at once. What do you think of it?'

'How can I judge from a half-written tale? Tell me the story as it lies in your head.'

Charlie told, and in the telling there was everything that his ignorance had so carefully prevented from escaping into the written word. I looked at him, wondering whether it were possible that he did not know the originality, the power of the notion that had come in his way? It was distinctly a Notion among notions. Men had been puffed up with pride by ideas not a tithe as excellent and practicable. But

Charlie babbled on serenely, interrupting the current of pure fancy with samples of horrible sentences that he purposed to use. I heard him out to the end. It would be folly to allow his thought to remain in his own inept hands, when I could do so much with it. Not all that could be done indeed; but, oh so much!

'What do you think?' he said at last. 'I fancy I shall call it "The Story of a Ship".'

'I think the idea's pretty good; but you won't be able to handle it for ever so long. Now I – '

'Would it be of any use to you? Would you care to take it? I should be proud,' said Charlie promptly.

There are few things sweeter in this world than the guileless, hot-headed, intemperate, open admiration of a junior. Even a woman in her blindest devotion does not fall into the gait of the man she adores, tilt her bonnet to the angle at which he wears his hat, or interlard her speech with his pet oaths. And Charlie did all these things. Still it was necessary to salve my conscience before I possessed myself of Charlie's thoughts.

'Let's make a bargain. I'll give you a fiver for the notion,' I said.

Charlie became a bank-clerk at once.

'Oh, that's impossible. Between two pals, you know, if I may call you so, and speaking as a man of the world, I couldn't. Take the notion if it's any use to you. I've heaps more.'

He had – none knew this better than I – but they were the notions of other men.

'Look at it as a matter of business – between men of the world,' I returned. 'Five pounds will buy you any number of poetry books. Business is business, and you may be sure I shouldn't give that price unless – '

'Oh, if you put it *that* way,' said Charlie, visibly moved by the thought of the books. The bargain was clinched with an agreement that he should at unstated intervals come to me with all the notions that he possessed, should have a table of his own to write at, and unquestioned right to inflict upon me all his poems and fragments of poems. Then I said, 'Now tell me how you came by this idea.'

'It came by itself.' Charlie's eyes opened a little.

'Yes, but you told me a great deal about the hero that you must have read before somewhere.'

'I haven't any time for reading, except when you let me sit here, and on Sundays I'm on my bicycle or down the river all day. There's nothing wrong about the hero, is there?'

'Tell me again and I shall understand clearly. You say that your hero went pirating. How did he live?'

'He was on the lower deck of this ship-thing that I was telling you about.'

'What sort of ship?'

'It was the kind rowed with oars, and the sea spurts through the oar-holes, and the men row sitting up to their knees in water. Then there's a bench running down between the two lines of oars, and an overseer with a whip walks up and down the bench to make the men work.'

'How do you know that?'

'It's in the tale. There's a rope running overhead, looped to the upper-deck, for the overseer to catch hold of when the ship rolls. When the overseer misses the rope once and falls among the rowers, remember the hero laughs at him and gets licked for it. He's chained to his oar of course – the hero.'

'How is he chained?'

'With an iron band round his waist fixed to the bench he sits on, and a sort of handcuff on his left wrist chaining him to the oar. He's on the lower deck where the worst men are sent, and the only light comes from the hatchways and through the oar-holes. Can't you imagine the sunlight just squeezing through between the handle and the hole and wobbling about as the ship moves?'

'I can, but I can't imagine your imagining it.'

'How could it be any other way? Now you listen to me. The long oars on the upper deck are managed by four men to each bench, the lower ones by three, and the lowest of all by two. Remember it's quite dark on the lowest deck and all the men there go mad. When a man dies at his oar on that deck he isn't thrown overboard, but cut up in his chains and stuffed through the oar-hole in little pieces.'

'Why?' I demanded amazed, not so much at the information as the tone of command in which it was flung out.

'To save trouble and to frighten the others. It needs two overseers to drag a man's body up to the top deck; and if the men at the lower deck oars were left alone, of course they'd stop rowing and try to pull up the benches by all standing up together in their chains.'

'You've a most provident imagination. Where have you been reading about galleys and galley-slaves?'

'Nowhere that I remember. I row a little when I get the chance. But, perhaps, if you say so, I may have read something.'

He went away shortly afterwards to deal with booksellers, and I wondered how a bank-clerk aged twenty could put into my hands with a profligate abundance of detail, all given with absolute assurance, the story of extravagant and bloodthirsty adventure, riot, piracy, and death in unnamed seas. He had led his hero a desperate dance through revolt against the overseers, to command of a ship of his own, and at last to the establishment of a kingdom on an island 'somewhere in the sea, you know'; and, delighted with my paltry five pounds, had gone out to buy the notions of other men, that these might teach him how to write. I had the consolation of knowing that this notion was mine by right of purchase, and I thought that I could make something of it.

When next he came to me he was drunk – royally drunk on many poets for the first time revealed to him. His pupils were dilated, his words tumbled over each other, and he wrapped himself in quotations – as a beggar would enfold himself in the purple of emperors. Most of all was he drunk with Longfellow.

'Isn't it splendid? Isn't it superb?' he cried, after hasty greetings. 'Listen to this –

> "Wouldst thou" – so the helmsman answered,
>   "Know the secret of the sea?
> Only those who brave its dangers
>   Comprehend its mystery."

By gum!

>   "Only those who brave its dangers
>   Comprehend its mystery," '

he repeated twenty times, walking up and down the room and forgetting me. 'But *I* can understand it too,' he said to himself. 'I don't know how to thank you for that fiver. And this; listen –

>   "I remember the black wharves and the slips
>   And the sea-tides tossing free;
>   And the Spanish sailors with bearded lips,
>   And the beauty and mystery of the ships,
>   And the magic of the sea."

I haven't braved any dangers, but I feel as if I knew all about it.'

'You certainly seem to have a grip of the sea. Have you ever seen it?'

'When I was a little chap I went to Brighton once; we used to live in Coventry, though, before we came to London. I never saw it,

>   "When descends on the Atlantic
>   The gigantic
>   Storm-wind of the Equinox." '

He shook me by the shoulder to make me understand the passion that was shaking himself.

'When that storm comes,' he continued, 'I think that all the oars in the ship that I was talking about get broken, and the rowers have their chests smashed in by the oar-heads bucking. By the way, have you done anything with that notion of mine yet?'

'No. I was waiting to hear more of it from you. Tell me how in the world you're so certain about the fittings of the ship. You know nothing of ships.'

'I don't know. It's as real as anything to me until I try to write it down. I was thinking about it only last night in bed, after you had lent me *Treasure Island*; and I made up a whole lot of new things to go into the story.'

'What sort of things?'

'About the food the men ate; rotten figs and black beans and wine in a skin bag, passed from bench to bench.'

'Was the ship built so long ago as *that*?'

'As what? I don't know whether it was long ago or not. It's only a notion, but sometimes it seems just as real as if it was true. Do I bother you with talking about it?'

'Not in the least. Did you make up anything else?'

'Yes, but it's nonsense.' Charlie flushed a little.

'Never mind; let's hear about it.'

'Well, I was thinking over the story, and after a while I got out of bed and wrote down on a piece of paper the sort of stuff the men might be supposed to scratch on their oars with the edges of their handcuffs. It seemed to make the thing more life-like. It *is* so real to me, y'know.'

'Have you the paper on you?'

'Ye–es, but what's the use of showing it? It's only a lot of scratches. All the same, we might have 'em reproduced in the book on the front page.'

'I'll attend to those details. Show me what your men wrote.'

He pulled out of his pocket a sheet of notepaper, with a single line of scratches upon it, and I put this carefully away.

'What is it supposed to mean in English?' I said.

'Oh, I don't know. I mean it to mean, "I'm beastly tired." It's great nonsense,' he repeated, 'but all those men in the ship seem as real as real people to me. Do do something to the notion soon; I should like to see it written and printed.'

'But all you've told me would make a long book.'

'Make it then. You've only to sit down and write it out.'

'Give me a little time. Have you any more notions?'

'Not just now. I'm reading all the books I've bought. They're splendid.'

When he had left I looked at the sheet of notepaper with the inscription upon it. Then I took my head tenderly between both hands, to make certain that it was not coming off or turning round. Then ... but there seemed to be no interval between quitting my rooms and finding myself arguing with a policeman outside a door marked *Private* in a corridor of the British Museum. All I demanded, as politely as possible, was 'the Greek antiquity man'. The policeman knew nothing except the rules of the Museum, and it became necessary to forage through all the houses and offices inside the gates. An elderly gentleman called away from his lunch put an end to my search by holding the notepaper between finger and thumb and sniffing at it scornfully.

'What does this mean? H'mm,' said he. 'So far as I can ascertain it is an attempt to write extremely corrupt Greek on the part' – here he glared at me with intention – 'of an extremely illiterate – ah – person.' He read slowly from the paper, *'Pollock, Erckmann, Tauchnitz, Henniker'* – four names familiar to me.

'Can you tell me what the corruption is supposed to mean – the gist of the thing?' I asked.

'I have been – many times – overcome with weariness in this particular employment. That is the meaning.' He returned me the paper, and I fled without a word of thanks, explanation, or apology.

I might have been excused for forgetting much. To me of all men had been given the chance to write the most marvellous tale in the world, nothing less than the story of a Greek galley-slave, as told by himself. Small wonder that his dreaming had seemed real to Charlie. The Fates that are so careful to shut the doors of each successive life behind us had, in this case, been neglectful, and Charlie was looking, though that he did not know, where never man had been permitted to look with full knowledge since Time began. Above all, he was absolutely ignorant of the knowledge sold to me for five pounds; and he would retain that ignorance, for bank-clerks do not understand metempsychosis, and a sound commercial education does not include Greek. He would supply me – here I capered among the dumb gods of Egypt and laughed in their battered faces – with material to make my tale sure – so sure that the world would hail it as an impudent and vamped fiction. And I – I alone would know that it was absolutely and literally true. I – I alone held this jewel to my hand for the cutting and polishing! Therefore I danced again among the gods of the Egyptian court till a policeman saw me and took steps in my direction.

It remained now only to encourage Charlie to talk, and here there was no difficulty. But I had forgotten those accursed books of poetry. He came to me time after time, as useless as a surcharged phonograph –

drunk on Byron, Shelley, or Keats. Knowing now what the boy had been in his past lives, and desperately anxious not to lose one word of his babble, I could not hide from him my respect and interest. He misconstrued both into respect for the present soul of Charlie Mears, to whom life was as new as it was to Adam, and interest in his readings; and stretched my patience to breaking point by reciting poetry – not his own now, but that of others. I wished every English poet blotted out of the memory of mankind. I blasphemed the mightiest names of song because they had drawn Charlie from the path of direct narrative, and would, later, spur him to imitate them; but I choked down my impatience until the first flood of enthusiasm should have spent itself and the boy returned to his dreams.

'What's the use of my telling you what *I* think, when these chaps wrote things for the angels to read?' he growled, one evening. 'Why don't you write something like theirs?'

'I don't think you're treating me quite fairly,' I said, speaking under strong restraint.

'I've given you the story,' he said shortly, re-plunging into 'Lara'.

'But I want the details.'

'The things I make up about that damned ship that you call a galley? They're quite easy. You can just make 'em up for yourself. Turn up the gas a little, I want to go on reading.'

I could have broken the gas globe over his head for his amazing stupidity. I could indeed make up things for myself did I only know what Charlie did not know that he knew. But since the doors were shut behind me I could only wait his youthful pleasure and strive to keep him in good temper. One minute's want of guard might spoil a priceless revelation: now and again he would toss his books aside – he kept them in my rooms, for his mother would have been shocked at the waste of good money had she seen them – and launched into his sea-dreams. Again I cursed all the poets of England. The plastic mind of the bank-clerk had been overlaid, coloured, and distorted by that which he had read, and the result as delivered was a confused tangle of other voices most like the mutter and hum through a City telephone in the busiest part of the day.

He talked of the galley – his own galley had he but known it – with illustrations borrowed from the 'Bride of Abydos'. He pointed the experiences of his hero with quotations from 'The Corsair', and threw in deep and desperate moral reflections from 'Cain' and 'Manfred', expecting me to use them all. Only when the talk turned on Longfellow were the jarring cross-currents dumb, and I knew that Charlie was speaking the truth as he remembered it.

'What do you think of this?' I said one evening, as soon as I understood the medium in which his memory worked best, and, before he could expostulate, read him nearly the whole of 'The Saga of King Olaf'.

He listened open-mouthed, flushed, his hands drumming on the back of the sofa where he lay, till I came to the Song of Einar Tamberskelver and the verse –

> 'Einar then, the arrow taking
>   From the loosened string,
> Answered, "That was Norway breaking
>   'Neath thy hand, O King." '

He gasped with pure delight of sound.

'That's better than Byron, a little?' I ventured.

'Better! Why it's *true*! How could he have known?'

I went back and repeated –

> ' "What was that?" said Olaf, standing
>   On the quarter-deck,
> "Something heard I like the stranding
>   Of a shattered wreck." '

'How could he have known how the ships crash and the oars rip out and go z-zzp all along the line? Why only the other night . . . But go back, please, and read "The Skerry of Shrieks" again.'

'No, I'm tired. Let's talk. What happened the other night?'

'I had an awful dream about that galley of ours. I dreamed I was drowned in a fight. You see we ran alongside another ship in harbour. The water was dead still except where our oars whipped it up. You know where I always sit in the galley?' He spoke haltingly at first, under a fine English fear of being laughed at.

'No. That's news to me,' I answered meekly, my heart beginning to beat.

'On the fourth oar from the bow on the right side on the upper deck. There were four of us at that oar, all chained. I remember watching the water and trying to get my handcuffs off before the row began. Then we closed up on the other ship, and all their fighting men jumped over our bulwarks, and my bench broke and I was pinned down with the three other fellows on top of me, and the big oar jammed across our backs.'

'Well?' Charlie's eyes were alive and alight. He was looking at the wall behind my chair.

'I don't know how we fought. The men were trampling all over my back, and I lay low. Then our rowers on the left side – tied to their oars, you know – began to yell and back water. I could hear the water sizzle, and we spun round like a cockchafer, and I knew, lying where I was, that there was a galley coming up bow-on to ram us on the left side. I could just lift up my head and see her sail over the bulwarks. We wanted to meet her bow to bow, but it was too late. We could only turn a little bit because the galley on our right had hooked herself on to us and stopped our moving. Then, by gum! there was a crash! Our left oars began to break as the other galley, the moving one y'know, stuck her nose into them. Then the lower-deck oars shot up through the deck planking, butt first, and one of them jumped clear up into the air and came down again close at my head.'

'How was that managed?'

'The moving galley's bow was plunking them back through their own oar-holes, and I could hear no end of a shindy in the decks below. Then her nose caught us nearly in the middle, and we tilted sideways, and the fellows in the right-hand galley unhitched their hooks and ropes, and threw things on to our upper deck – arrows, and hot pitch or something that stung – and we went up and up and up on the left side, and the right side dipped, and I twisted my head round and saw the water stand still as it topped the right bulwarks, and then it curled over and crashed down on the whole lot of us on the right side, and I felt it hit my back, and I woke.'

'One minute, Charlie. When the sea topped the bulwarks, what did it look like?' I had my reasons for asking. A man of my acquaintance had once gone down with a leaking ship in a still sea, and had seen the water-level pause for an instant ere it fell on the deck.

'It looked just like a banjo-string drawn tight, and it seemed to stay there for years,' said Charlie.

Exactly! The other man had said: 'It looked like a silver wire laid down along the bulwarks, and I thought it was never going to break.' He had paid everything except the bare life for this little valueless piece of knowledge, and I had travelled ten thousand weary miles to meet him and take his knowledge at second hand. But Charlie, the bank-clerk on twenty-five shillings a week, who had never been out of sight of a made road, knew it all. It was no consolation to me that once in his lives he had been forced to die for his gains. I also must have died scores of times, but behind me, because I could have used my knowledge, the doors were shut.

'And then?' I said, trying to put away the devil of envy.

'The funny thing was, though, in all the row I didn't feel a bit astonished or frightened. It seemed as if I'd been in a good many fights, because I told my next man so when the row began. But that cad of an overseer on my deck wouldn't unloose our chains and give us a chance. He always said that we'd all be set free after a battle, but we never were; we never were.' Charlie shook his head mournfully.

'What a scoundrel!'

'I should say he was. He never gave us enough to eat, and sometimes we were so thirsty that we used to drink salt-water. I can taste that salt-water still.'

'Now tell me something about the harbour where the fight was fought.'

'I didn't dream about that. I know it was a harbour, though, because we were tied up to a ring on a white wall and all the face of the stone under water was covered with wood to prevent our ram getting chipped when the tide made us rock.'

'That's curious. Our hero commanded the galley, didn't he?'

'Didn't he just! He stood by the bows and shouted like a good 'un. He was the man who killed the overseer.'

'But you were all drowned together, Charlie, weren't you?'

'I can't make that fit quite,' he said, with a puzzled look. 'The galley must have gone down with all hands, and yet I fancy that the hero went on living afterwards. Perhaps he climbed into the attacking ship. I wouldn't see that, of course. I was dead, you know.'

He shivered slightly and protested that he could remember no more.

I did not press him further, but to satisfy myself that he lay in ignorance of the workings of his own mind, deliberately introduced him to Mortimer Collins's *Transmigration*, and gave him a sketch of the plot before he opened the pages.

'What rot it all is!' he said frankly, at the end of an hour. 'I don't understand his nonsense about the Red Planet Mars and the King, and the rest of it. Chuck me the Longfellow again.'

I handed him the book and wrote out as much as I could remember of his description of the sea-fight, appealing to him from time to time for confirmation of fact or detail. He would answer without raising his eyes from the book, as assuredly as though all his knowledge lay before him on the printed page. I spoke under the normal key of my voice that the current might not be broken, and I knew that he was not aware of what he was saying, for his thoughts were out on the sea with Longfellow.

'Charlie,' I asked, 'when the rowers on the galleys mutinied how did they kill their overseers?'

'Tore up the benches and brained 'em. That happened when a heavy sea was running. An overseer on the lower deck slipped from the centre plank and fell among the rowers. They choked him to death against the

side of the ship with their chained hands quite quietly, and it was too
dark for the other overseer to see what had happened. When he asked,
he was pulled down too and choked, and the lower deck fought their
way up deck by deck, with the pieces of the broken benches banging
behind 'em. How they howled!'

'And what happened after that?'

'I don't know. The hero went away – red hair and red beard and all.
That was after he had captured our galley, I think.'

The sound of my voice irritated him, and he motioned slightly with
his left hand as a man does when interruption jars.

'You never told me he was red-headed before, or that he captured
your galley,' I said, after a discreet interval.

Charlie did not raise his eyes.

'He was as red as a red bear,' said he abstractedly. 'He came from the
north; they said so in the galley when he looked for rowers – not slaves,
but free men. Afterwards – years and years afterwards – news came
from another ship, or else he came back – '

His lips moved in silence. He was rapturously retasting some poem
before him.

'Where had he been, then?' I was almost whispering that the
sentence might come gently to whichever section of Charlie's brain
was working on my behalf.

'To the Beaches – the Long and Wonderful Beaches!' was the reply
after a minute of silence.

'To Furdurstrandi?' I asked, tingling from head to foot.

'Yes, to Furdurstrandi,' he pronounced the word in a new fashion.
'And I too saw – ' The voice failed.

'Do you know what you have said?' I shouted incautiously.

He lifted his eyes, fully roused now. 'No!' he snapped. 'I wish you'd
let a chap go on reading. Hark to this –

> But Othere, the old sea captain,
> He neither paused nor stirred
> Till the king listened, and then
> Once more took up his pen
> And wrote down every word.
>
> And to the King of the Saxons
> In witness of the truth
> Raising his noble head,
> He stretched his brown hand and said,
> "Behold this walrus tooth."

By Jove, what chaps those must have been, to go sailing all over the shop never knowing where they'd fetch the land! Hah!'

'Charlie,' I pleaded, 'if you'll only be sensible for a minute or two I'll make our hero in our tale every inch as good as Othere.'

'Umph! Longfellow wrote that poem. I don't care about writing things any more. I want to read.' He was thoroughly out of tune now, and raging over my own ill-luck, I left him.

Conceive yourself at the door of the world's treasure-house guarded by a child – an idle, irresponsible child playing knuckle-bones – on whose favour depends the gift of the key, and you will imagine one-half my torment. Till that evening Charlie had spoken nothing that might not lie within the experiences of a Greek galley-slave. But now, or there was no virtue in books, he had talked of some desperate adventure of the Vikings, of Thorfin Karlsefne's sailing to Wineland, which is America, in the ninth or tenth century. The battle in the harbour he had seen; and his own death he had described. But this was a much more startling plunge into the past. Was it possible that he had skipped half a dozen lives, and was then dimly remembering some episode of a thousand years later? It was a maddening jumble, and the worst of it was that Charlie Mears in his normal condition was the last person in the world to clear it up. I could only wait and watch, but I went to bed that night full of the wildest imaginings. There was nothing that was not possible if Charlie's detestable memory only held good.

I might rewrite the Saga of Thorfin Karlsefne as it had never been written before, might tell the story of the first discovery of America, myself the discoverer. But I was entirely at Charlie's mercy, and so long as there was a three-and-sixpenny Bohn volume within his reach Charlie would not tell. I dared not curse him openly; I hardly dared jog his memory, for I was dealing with the experiences of a thousand years ago, told through the mouth of a boy of today; and a boy of today is affected by every change of tone and gust of opinion, so that he must lie even when he most desires to speak the truth.

I saw no more of Charlie for nearly a week. When next I met him it was in Gracechurch Street with a bill-book chained to his waist. Business took him over London Bridge, and I accompanied him. He was very full of the importance of that book and magnified it. As we passed over the Thames we paused to look at a steamer unloading great slabs of white and brown marble. A barge drifted under the steamer's stern and a lonely ship's cow in that barge bellowed. Charlie's face changed from the face of the bank-clerk to that of an unknown and – though he would not have believed this – a much shrewder man. He flung out his arm across the parapet of the bridge and laughing very loudly, said –

'When they heard *our* bulls bellow the Skroelings ran away!'

I waited only for an instant, but the barge and the cow had disappeared under the bows of the steamer before I answered.

'Charlie, what do you suppose are Skroelings?'

'Never heard of 'em before. They sound like a new kind of seagull. What a chap you are for asking questions!' he replied. 'I have to go to the cashier of the Omnibus Company yonder. Will you wait for me and we can lunch somewhere together? I've a notion for a poem.'

'No, thanks. I'm off. You're sure you know nothing about Skroelings?'

'Not unless he's been entered for the Liverpool Handicap.' He nodded and disappeared in the crowd.

Now it is written in the Saga of Eric the Red or that of Thorfin Karlsefne, that nine hundred years ago when Karlsefne's galleys came to Leif's booths, which Leif had erected in the unknown land called Markland, which may or may not have been Rhode Island, the Skroelings – and the Lord He knows who these may or may not have been – came to trade with the Vikings, and ran away because they were frightened at the bellowing of the cattle which Thorfin had brought with him in the ships. But what in the world could a Greek slave know of that affair? I wandered up and down among the streets trying to unravel the mystery and the more I considered it the more baffling it grew. One thing only seemed certain, and that certainty took away my breath for the moment. If I came to full knowledge of anything at all, it would not be one life of the soul in Charlie Mears's body, but half a dozen – half a dozen several and separate existences spent on blue water in the morning of the world!

Then I reviewed the situation.

Obviously if I used my knowledge I should stand alone and unapproachable until all men were as wise as myself. That would be something, but, manlike, I was ungrateful. It seemed bitterly unfair that Charlie's memory should fail me when I needed it most. Great Powers Above – I looked up at them through the fog-smoke – did the Lords of Life and Death know what this meant to me? Nothing less than eternal fame of the best kind, that comes from One, and is shared by one alone. I would be content – remembering Clive, I stood astounded at my own moderation – with the mere right to tell one story, to work out one little contribution to the light literature of the day. If Charlie were permitted full recollection for one hour – for sixty short minutes – of existences that had extended over a thousand years, I would forgo all profit and honour from all that I should make of his speech. I would take no share in the commotion that would follow throughout the particular corner of the earth that calls itself 'the world'. The thing should be put forth anonymously. Nay, I would make other men believe that they had written it. They would hire bull-hided self-advertising Englishmen to bellow it abroad. Preachers would found a fresh conduct of life upon it, swearing that it was new and that they had lifted the fear of death from all mankind. Every Orientalist in Europe would patronise it discursively with Sanskrit and Pali texts. Terrible women would invent unclean variants of the men's belief for the elevation of their sisters. Churches and religions would war over it. Between the hailing and restarting of an omnibus I foresaw the scuffles that would arise among half a dozen denominations all professing 'the doctrine of the True Metempsychosis as applied to the world and the New Era'; and saw, too, the respectable English newspapers shying, like frightened kine, over the beautiful simplicity of the tale. The mind leaped forward a hundred – two hundred – a thousand years. I saw with sorrow that men would mutilate and garble the story; that rival creeds would turn it upside down till, at last, the western world which clings to the dread of death more closely than the hope of life, would set it aside as an interesting superstition and stampede after some faith so long forgotten that it seemed altogether new. Upon this I changed the terms of the bargain that I would make with the Lords of Life and Death. Only let me know, let me write, the story with sure knowledge that I wrote the truth, and I would burn the manuscript as a solemn sacrifice. Five minutes after the last line was written I would destroy it all. But I must be allowed to write it with absolute certainty.

There was no answer. The flaming colours of an Aquarium poster caught my eye, and I wondered whether it would be wise or prudent to lure Charlie into the hands of the professional mesmerist then, and whether, if he were under his power, he would speak of his past lives. If he did, and if people believed him . . . but Charlie would be frightened and flustered, or made conceited by the interviews. In either case he would begin to lie through fear or vanity. He was safest in my own hands.

'They are very funny fools, your English,' said a voice at my elbow, and turning round I recognised a casual acquaintance, a young Bengali law student, called Grish Chunder, whose father had sent him to England to become civilised. The old man was a retired native official, and on an income of five pounds a month contrived to allow his son two hundred pounds a year, and the run of his teeth in a city where he could pretend to be the cadet of a royal house, and tell stories of the brutal Indian bureaucrats who ground the faces of the poor.

Grish Chunder was a young, fat, full-bodied Bengali, dressed with scrupulous care in frock coat, tall hat, light trousers, and tan gloves. But I had known him in the days when the brutal Indian Government paid for his university education, and he contributed cheap sedition to the *Sachi Durpan*, and intrigued with the wives of his fourteen-year-old schoolmates.

'That is very funny and very foolish,' he said, nodding at the poster. 'I am going down to the Northbrook Club. Will you come too?'

I walked with him for some time. 'You are not well,' he said. 'What is there on your mind? You do not talk.'

'Grish Chunder, you've been too well educated to believe in a God, haven't you?'

'Oah, yes, *here*! But when I go home I must conciliate popular superstition, and make ceremonies of purification, and my women will anoint idols.'

'And hang up *tulsi* and feast the *purohit*, and take you back into caste again, and make a good *khuttri* of you again, you advanced Freethinker. And you'll eat *desi* food, and like it all, from the smell in the courtyard to the mustard oil over you.'

'I shall very much like it,' said Grish Chunder unguardedly. 'Once a Hindu – always a Hindu. But I like to know what the English think they know.'

'I'll tell you something that one Englishman knows. It's an old tale to you.'

I began to tell the story of Charlie in English but Grish Chunder put a question in the vernacular, and the history went forward naturally in the tongue best suited for its telling. After all, it could never have been told in English. Grish Chunder heard me, nodding from time to time, and then came up to my rooms, where I finished the tale.

'*Beshak*,' he said philosophically. '*Lekin darwaza band hai*. (Without doubt; but the door is shut.) I have heard of this remembering of previous existences among my people. It is of course an old tale with us, but, to happen to an Englishman – a cow-fed *Mlechh* – an outcast. By Jove, that is *most* peculiar!'

'Outcast yourself, Grish Chunder! You eat cow-beef every day. Let's think the thing over. The boy remembers his incarnations.'

'Does he know that?' said Grish Chunder quietly, swinging his legs as he sat on my table. He was speaking in his English now.

'He does not know anything. Would I speak to you if he did? Go on!'

'There is no going on at all. If you tell that to your friends they will say you are mad and put it in the papers. Suppose, now, you prosecute for libel.'

'Let's leave that out of the question entirely. Is there any chance of his being made to speak?'

'There is a chance. Oah, yess! But *if* he spoke it would mean that all this world would end now – *instanto* – fall down on your head. These things are not allowed, you know. As I said, the door is shut.'

'Not a ghost of a chance?'

'How can there be? You are a Christi-án, and it is forbidden to eat, in your books, of the Tree of Life, or else you would never die. How shall you all fear death if you all know what your friend does not know that he knows? I am afraid to be kicked, but I am not afraid to die, because I know what I know. You are not afraid to be kicked, but you are afraid to die. If you were not, by God! you English would be all over the shop in an hour, upsetting the balances of power, and making commotions. It would not be good. But no fear. He will remember a little and a little less, and he will call it dreams. Then he will forget altogether. When I passed my First Arts Examination in Calcutta that was all in the cram-book on Wordsworth. "Trailing clouds of glory", you know.'

'This seems to be an exception to the rule.'

'There are no exceptions to rules. Some are not so hard-looking as others, but they are all the same when you touch. If this friend of yours said so-and-so and so-and-so, indicating that he remembered all his lost lives, or one piece of a lost life, he would not be in the bank another hour. He would be what you call sacked because he was mad, and they would send him to an asylum for lunatics. You can see that, my friend.'

'Of course I can, but I wasn't thinking of him. His name need never appear in the story.'

'Ah! I see. That story will never be written. You can try.'

'I am going to.'

'For your own credit and for the sake of money, *of* course?'

'No. For the sake of writing the story. On my honour that will be all.'

'Even then there is no chance. You cannot play with the gods. It is a very pretty story now. As they say, Let it go on that – I mean at that. Be quick; he will not last long.'

'How do you mean?'

'What I say. He has never, so far, thought about a woman.'

'Hasn't he, though!' I remembered some of Charlie's confidences.

'I mean no woman has thought about him. When that comes; *bus – hogya* – all up! I know. There are millions of women here. Housemaids, for instance. They kiss you behind doors.'

I winced at the thought of my story being ruined by a housemaid. And yet nothing was more probable.

Grish Chunder grinned.

'Yes – also pretty girls – cousins of his house, and perhaps *not* of his house. One kiss that he gives back again and remembers will cure all this nonsense, or else – '

'Or else what? Remember he does not know that he knows.'

'I know that. Or else, if nothing happens he will become immersed in the trade and the financial speculation like the rest. It must be so. You can see that it must be so. But the woman will come first, *I* think.'

There was a rap at the door, and Charlie charged in impetuously. He had been released from office, and by the look in his eyes I could see that he had come over for a long talk; most probably with poems in his pockets. Charlie's poems were very wearying, but sometimes they led him to speak about the galley.

Grish Chunder looked at him keenly for a minute.

'I beg your pardon,' Charlie said uneasily; 'I didn't know you had anyone with you.'

'I am going,' said Grish Chunder.

He drew me into the lobby as he departed.

'That is your man,' he said quickly. 'I tell you he will never speak all you wish. That is rot – bosh. But he would be most good to make to see things. Suppose now we pretend that it was only play' – I had never seen Grish Chunder so excited – 'and pour the ink-pool into his hand. Eh, what do you think? I tell you that he could see *anything* that a man could see. Let me get the ink and the camphor. He is a seer and he will tell us very many things.'

'He may be all you say, but I'm not going to trust him to your gods and devils.'

'It will not hurt him. He will only feel a little stupid and dull when he wakes up. You have seen boys look into the ink-pool before.'

'That is the reason why I am not going to see it any more. You'd better go, Grish Chunder.'

He went, insisting far down the staircase that it was throwing away my only chance of looking into the future.

This left me unmoved, for I was concerned for the past, and no peering of hypnotised boys into mirrors and ink-pools would help me to that. But I recognised Grish Chunder's point of view and sympathised with it.

'What a big black brute that was!' said Charlie, when I returned to him. 'Well, look here, I've just done a poem; did it instead of playing dominoes after lunch. May I read it?'

'Let me read it to myself.'

'Then you miss the proper expression. Besides, you always make my things sound as if the rhymes were all wrong.'

'Read it aloud, then. You're like the rest of 'em.'

Charlie mouthed me his poem, and it was not much worse than the average of his verses. He had been reading his books faithfully, but he was not pleased when I told him that I preferred my Longfellow undiluted with Charlie.

Then we began to go through the MS line by line, Charlie parrying every objection and correction with:

'Yes, that may be better, but you don't catch what I'm driving at.'

Charlie was, in one way at least, very like one kind of poet.

There was a pencil scrawl at the back of the paper, and 'What's that?' I said.

'Oh, that's not poetry at all. It's some rot I wrote last night before I went to bed, and it was too much bother to hunt for rhymes; so I made it a sort of blank verse instead.'

Here is Charlie's 'blank verse':

> We pulled for you when the wind was against us and the sails were low.
>
> *Will you never let us go?*
>
> We ate bread and onions when you took towns, or ran aboard quickly when you were beaten back by the foe,
> The captains walked up and down the deck in fair weather singing songs, but we were below.
> We fainted with our chins on the oars and you did not see that we were idle for we still swung to and fro.
>
> *Will you never let us go?*
>
> The salt made the oar-handles like shark-skin; our knees were cut to the bone with salt cracks; our hair was stuck to our foreheads; and our lips were cut to our gums, and you whipped us because we could not row.
>
> *Will you never let us go?*
>
> But in a little time we shall run out of the portholes as the water runs along the oar-blade, and though you tell the others to row after us you will never catch us till you catch the oar-thresh and tie up the winds in the belly of the sail. Aho!
>
> *Will you never let us go?*

'H'm. What's oar-thresh, Charlie?'

'The water washed up by the oars. That's the sort of song they might sing in the galley y' know. Aren't you ever going to finish that story and give me some of the profits?'

'It depends on yourself. If you had only told me more about your hero in the first instance it might have been finished by now. You're so hazy in your notions.'

'I only want to give you the general notion of it – the knocking about from place to place and the fighting and all that. Can't you fill in the rest yourself? Make the hero save a girl on a pirate-galley and marry her or do something.'

'You're a really helpful collaborator. I suppose the hero went through some few adventures before he married.'

'Well then, make him a very artful card – a low sort of man – a sort of political man who went about making treaties and breaking them – a black-haired chap who hid behind the mast when the fighting began.'

'But you said the other day that he was red-haired.'

'I couldn't have. Make him black-haired of course. You've no imagination.'

Seeing that I had just discovered the entire principles upon which the half-memory falsely called imagination is based, I felt entitled to laugh, but forbore for the sake of the tale.

'You're right. *You're* the man with imagination. A black-haired chap in a decked ship,' I said.

'No, an open ship – like a big boat.'

This was maddening.

'Your ship has been built and designed, closed and decked in; you said so yourself,' I protested.

'No, no, not that ship. That was open or half-decked because – By Jove, you're right. You made me think of the hero as a red-haired chap. Of course if he were red, the ship would be an open one with painted sails.'

Surely, I thought, he would remember now that he had served in two galleys at least – in a three-decked Greek one under the black-haired 'political man', and again in a Viking's open sea-serpent under the man 'red as a red bear' who went to Markland. The devil prompted me to speak.

'Why, "of course", Charlie?' said I.

'I don't know. Are you making fun of me?'

The current was broken for the time being. I took up a note-book and pretended to make many entries in it.

'It's a pleasure to work with an imaginative chap like yourself,' I said, after a pause. 'The way that you've brought out the character of the hero is simply wonderful.'

'Do you think so?' he answered, with a pleased flush. 'I often tell myself that there's more in me than my mo— than people think.'

'There's an enormous amount in you.'

'Then, won't you let me send an essay on "The Ways of Bank-Clerks" to *Tit-Bits*, and get the guinea prize?'

'That wasn't exactly what I meant, old fellow: perhaps it would be better to wait a little and go ahead with the galley story.'

'Ah, but I sha'n't get the credit of that. *Tit-Bits* would publish my name and address if I win. What are you grinning at? They *would*.'

'I know it. Suppose you go for a walk. I want to look through my notes about our story.'

Now this reprehensible youth who left me, a little hurt and put back, might for aught he or I knew have been one of the crew of the *Argo* – had been certainly slave or comrade to Thorfin Karlsefne. Therefore he was deeply interested in guinea competitions. Remembering what Grish Chunder had said I laughed aloud. The Lords of Life and Death would never allow Charlie Mears to speak with full knowledge of his pasts, and I must even piece out what he had told me with my own poor inventions while Charlie wrote of the ways of bank-clerks.

I got together and placed on one file all my notes; and the net result was not cheering. I read them a second time. There was nothing that might not have been compiled at second-hand from other people's books – except, perhaps, the story of the fight in the harbour. The adventures of a Viking had been written many times before; the history of a Greek galley-slave was no new thing, and though I wrote both, who could challenge or confirm the accuracy of my details? I might as well tell a tale of two thousand years hence. The Lords of Life and Death were as cunning as Grish Chunder had hinted. They would allow nothing to escape that might trouble or make easy the minds of men. Though I was convinced of this, yet I could not leave the tale alone. Exaltation followed reaction, not once, but twenty times in the next few weeks. My moods varied with the March sunlight and flying clouds. By night or in the beauty of a spring morning I perceived that I could write that tale and shift continents thereby. In the wet windy afternoons, I saw that the tale might indeed be written, but would be nothing more than a faked, false-varnished, sham-rusted piece of Wardour Street work in the end. Then I blessed Charlie in many ways – though it was no fault of his. He seemed to be busy with prize competitions, and I saw less and less of him as the weeks went by and the earth cracked and grew ripe to spring, and the buds swelled in their sheaths. He did not care to read or talk of what he had read, and there was a new ring of self-assertion in his voice. I hardly cared to remind him of the galley when we met; but Charlie alluded to it on every occasion, always as a story from which money was to be made.

'I think I deserve twenty-five per cent, don't I, at least?' he said, with beautiful frankness. 'I supplied all the ideas, didn't I?'

This greediness for silver was a new side to his nature. I assumed that it had been developed in the City, where Charlie was picking up the curious nasal drawl of the underbred City man.

'When the thing's done we'll talk about it. I can't make anything of it at present. Red-haired or black-haired heroes are equally difficult.'

He was sitting by the fire staring at the red coals. '*I* can't understand what you find so difficult. It's all as clear as mud to me,' he replied. A jet of gas puffed out between the bars, took light, and whistled softly. 'Suppose we take the red-haired hero's adventures first, from the time that he came south to my galley and captured it and sailed to the Beaches.'

I knew better now than to interrupt Charlie. I was out of reach of pen and paper, and dared not move to get them lest I should break the current. The gas-jet puffed and whinnied, Charlie's voice dropped almost to a whisper, and he told a tale of the sailing of an open galley to Furdurstrandi, of sunsets on the open sea, seen under the curve of the one sail evening after evening when the galley's beak was notched into the centre of the sinking disc, and 'we sailed by that for we had no other guide,' quoth Charlie. He spoke of a landing on an island and explorations in its woods, where the crew killed three men whom they found asleep under the pines. Their ghosts, Charlie said, followed the galley, swimming and choking in the water, and the crew cast lots and threw one of their number overboard as a sacrifice to the strange gods whom they had offended. Then they ate sea-weed when their provisions failed, and their legs swelled, and their leader, the red-haired man, killed two rowers who mutinied, and after a year spent among the woods they set sail for their own country, and a wind that never failed carried them back so safely that they all slept at night. This, and much more, Charlie told. Sometimes the voice fell so low that I could not catch the words, though every nerve was on the strain. He spoke of their leader, the red-haired man, as a pagan speaks of his God; for it was he who cheered them and slew them impartially as he thought best for their needs; and it was he who steered them for three days among floating ice, each floe crowded with strange beasts that 'tried to sail with us,' said Charlie, 'and we beat them back with the handles of the oars.'

The gas-jet went out, a burnt coal gave way, and the fire settled with a tiny crash to the bottom of the grate. Charlie ceased speaking, and I said no word.

'By Jove!' he said at last, shaking his head. 'I've been staring at the fire till I'm dizzy. What was I going to say?'

'Something about the galley book.'

'I remember now. It's twenty-five per cent of the profits, isn't it?'

'It's anything you like when I've done the tale.'

'I wanted to be sure of that. I must go now. I've – I've an appointment.' And he left me.

Had not my eyes been held I might have known that that broken muttering over the fire was the swan-song of Charlie Mears. But I thought it the prelude to fuller revelation. At last and at last I should cheat the Lords of Life and Death!

When next Charlie came to me I received him with rapture. He was nervous and embarrassed, but his eyes were very full of light, and his lips a little parted.

'I've done a poem,' he said; and then, quickly: 'It's the best I've ever done. Read it.' He thrust it into my hand and retreated to the window.

I groaned inwardly. It would be the work of half an hour to criticise – that is to say, praise – the poem sufficiently to please Charlie. Then I had good reason to groan, for Charlie, discarding his favourite centipede metres, had launched into shorter and choppier verse, and verse with a motive at the back of it. This is what I read:

> The day is most fair, the cheery wind
> Halloos behind the hill,
> Where he bends the wood as seemeth good,
> And the sapling to his will!
> Riot, O wind; there is that in my blood
> That would not have thee still!
>
> She gave me herself, O Earth, O Sky;
> Grey sea, she is mine alone!
> Let the sullen boulders hear my cry,
> And rejoice tho' they be but stone!
>
> Mine! I have won her, O good brown earth,
> Make merry! 'Tis hard on Spring;
> Make merry; my love is doubly worth
> All worship your fields can bring!
> Let the hind that tills you feel my mirth
> At the early harrowing!

'Yes, it's the early harrowing, past a doubt,' I said, with a dread at my heart. Charlie smiled, but did not answer.

> Red cloud of the sunset, tell it abroad;
>   I am victor. Greet me, O Sun,
> Dominant master and absolute lord
>   Over the soul of one!

'Well?' said Charlie, looking over my shoulder.

I thought it far from well, and very evil indeed, when he silently laid a photograph on the paper – the photograph of a girl with a curly head and a foolish slack mouth.

'Isn't it – isn't it wonderful?' he whispered, pink to the tips of his ears, wrapped in the rosy mystery of first love. 'I didn't know; I didn't think – it came like a thunderclap.'

'Yes. It comes like a thunderclap. Are you very happy, Charlie?'

'My God – she – she loves me!' He sat down repeating the last words to himself. I looked at the hairless face, the narrow shoulders already bowed by desk-work, and wondered when, where, and how he had loved in his past lives.

'What will your mother say?' I asked cheerfully.

'I don't care a damn what she says!'

At twenty the things for which one does not care a damn should, properly, be many, but one must not include mothers in the list. I told him this gently; and he described Her, even as Adam must have described to the newly-named beasts the glory and tenderness and beauty of Eve. Incidentally I learned that She was a tobacconist's assistant with a weakness for pretty dress, and had told him four or five times already that She had never been kissed by a man before.

Charlie spoke on and on, and on; while I, separated from him by thousands of years, was considering the beginnings of things. Now I understood why the Lords of Life and Death shut the doors so carefully behind us. It is that we may not remember our first and most beautiful wooings. Were this not so, our world would be without inhabitants in a hundred years.

'Now, about that galley story,' I said still more cheerfully, in a pause in the rush of the speech.

Charlie looked up as though he had been hit. 'The galley – what galley? Good heavens, don't joke, man! This is serious! You don't know how serious it is!'

Grish Chunder was right. Charlie had tasted the love of woman that kills remembrance, and the finest story in the world would never be written.

The Record of Badalia Herodsfoot

The year's at the spring
And day's at the dawn;
Morning's at seven;
The hillside's dew-pearled;
The lark's on the wing;
The snail's on the thorn:
God's in His heaven –
All's right with the world!

Pippa Passes

THIS IS NOT THAT BADALIA whose spare names were Joanna, Pugnacious, and M'Canna, as the song says, but another and a much nicer lady.

In the beginning of things she had been unregenerate; had worn the heavy fluffy fringe which is the ornament of the costermonger's girl, and there is a legend in Gunnison Street that on her wedding-day she, a flare-lamp in either hand, danced dances on a discarded lover's winkle-barrow, till a policeman interfered, and then Badalia danced with the Law amid shoutings. Those were her days of fatness, and they did not last long, for her husband after two years took to himself another woman, and passed out of Badalia's life, over Badalia's senseless body; for he stifled protest with blows. While she was enjoying her widow-hood the baby that the husband had not taken away died of croup, and Badalia was altogether alone. With rare fidelity she listened to no proposals for a second marriage according to the customs of Gunnison Street, which do not differ from those of the Barralong. 'My man,' she explained to her suitors, ' 'e'll come back one o' these days, an' then, like as not, 'e'll take an' kill me if I was livin' 'long o' you. You don't know Tom; I do. Now you go. I can do for myself – not 'avin' a kid.' She did for herself with a mangle, some tending of babies, and an occasional sale of flowers. This latter trade is one that needs capital, and takes the vendor very far westward, insomuch that the return journey from, let us say, the Burlington Arcade to Gunnison Street, E., is an excuse for drink, and then, as Badalia pointed out, 'You come 'ome with your shawl 'arf off of your back, an' your bonnick under your arm, and the price of nothing-at-all in your pocket, let alone a slop takin' care o' you.' Badalia did not drink, but she knew her sisterhood, and gave them rude counsel. Otherwise she kept herself to herself, and meditated a great deal upon Tom Herodsfoot, her husband, who would come back someday, and the baby who would never return. In what manner these thoughts wrought upon her mind will not be known.

Her entry into society dates from the night when she rose literally under the feet of the Reverend Eustace Hanna, on the landing of No. 17 Gunnison Street, and told him that he was a fool without discernment in the dispensation of his district charities.

'You give Lascar Loo custids,' said she, without the formality of introduction; 'give her pork-wine. Garn! Give 'er blankits. Garn 'ome! 'Er mother, she eats 'em all, and drinks the blankits. Gits 'em back from the shop, she does, before you come visiting again, so as to 'ave 'em all handy an' proper; an' Lascar Loo she sez to you, "Oh, my mother's that good to me!" she do. Lascar Loo 'ad better talk so, bein' sick abed, 'r else 'er mother would kill 'er. Garn! you're a bloomin' gardener – you an' yer custids! Lascar Loo don't never smell of 'em even.'

Thereon the curate, instead of being offended, recognised in the heavy eyes under the fringe the soul of a fellow-worker, and so bade Badalia mount guard over Lascar Loo, when the next jelly or custard should arrive, to see that the invalid actually ate it. This Badalia did, to the disgust of Lascar Loo's mother, and the sharing of a black eye between the three; but Lascar Loo got her custard, and coughing heartily, rather enjoyed the fray.

Later on, partly through the Reverend Eustace Hanna's swift recognition of her uses, and partly through certain tales poured out with moist eyes and flushed cheeks by Sister Eva, youngest and most impressionable of the Little Sisters of the Red Diamond, it came to pass that Badalia, arrogant, fluffy-fringed, and perfectly unlicensed in speech, won a recognised place among such as labour in Gunnison Street.

These were a mixed corps, zealous or hysterical, faint-hearted or only very wearied of battle against misery, according to their lights. The most part were consumed with small rivalries and personal jealousies, to be retailed confidentially to their own tiny cliques in the pauses between wrestling with death for the body of a moribund laundress, or scheming for further mission-grants to resole a consumptive compositor's very consumptive boots. There was a rector that lived in dread of pauperising the poor, would fain have held bazaars for fresh altar-cloths, and prayed in secret for a large new brass bird, with eyes of red glass, fondly believed to be carbuncles. There was Brother Victor, of the Order of Little Ease, who knew a great deal about altar-cloths, but kept his knowledge in the background while he strove to propitiate Mrs Jessel, the Secretary of the Tea Cup Board, who had money to dispense, but hated Rome – even though Rome would, on its honour, do no more than fill the stomach, leaving the dazed soul to the mercies of Mrs Jessel. There were all the Little Sisters of the Red Diamond, daughters of the horseleech, crying 'Give' when their own charity was exhausted, and pitifully explaining to such as demanded an account of their disbursements in return for one half-sovereign, that relief-work in a bad district can hardly be systematised on the accounts' side without expensive duplication of staff. There was the Reverend Eustace Hanna, who worked impartially with Ladies' Committees, Androgynous Leagues and Guilds, Brother Victor, and anybody else who could give him money, boots, or blankets, or that more precious help that allows itself to be directed by those who know. And all these people learned, one by one, to consult Badalia on matters of personal character, right to relief, and hope of eventual reformation in Gunnison Street. Her answers were seldom cheering, but she possessed special knowledge and complete confidence in herself.

'I'm Gunnison Street,' she said to the austere Mrs Jessel. 'I know what's what, *I* do, an' they don't want your religion, mum, not a single – Excuse me. It's all right when they comes to die, mum, but till they die what they wants is things to eat. The men they'll shif' for themselves. That's why Nick Lapworth sez to you that 'e wants to be confirmed an' all that. 'E won't never lead no new life, nor 'is wife won't get no good out o' all the money you gives 'im. No more you can't pauperise them as 'asn't things to begin with. They're bloomin' well pauped. The women they can't shif' for themselves – 'specially bein' always confined. 'Ow should they? They wants things if they can get 'em anyways. If not they dies, and a good job too, for women is cruel put upon in Gunnison Street.'

'Do you believe that – that Mrs Herodsfoot is altogether a proper person to trust funds to?' said Mrs Jessel to the curate after this conversation. 'She seems to be utterly godless in her speech at least.'

The curate agreed. She was godless according to Mrs Jessel's views, but did not Mrs Jessel think that since Badalia knew Gunnison Street and its needs, as none other knew it, she might in a humble way be, as it were, the scullion of charity from purer sources, and that if, say, the Tea Cup Board could give a few shillings a week, and the Little Sisters of the Red Diamond a few more, and, yes, he himself could raise yet a few more, the total, not at all likely to be excessive, might be handed over to Badalia to dispense among her associates. Thus Mrs Jessel

herself would be set free to attend more directly to the spiritual wants
of certain large-limbed hulking men who sat picturesquely on the
lower benches of her gatherings and sought for truth – which is quite as
precious as silver, when you know the market for it.

'She'll favour her own friends,' said Mrs Jessel. The curate refrained
from mirth, and, after wise flattery, carried his point. To her un-
bounded pride Badalia was appointed the dispenser of a grant – a
weekly trust, to be held for the benefit of Gunnison Street.

'I don't know what we can get together each week,' said the curate to
her. 'But here are seventeen shillings to start with. You do what you
like with them among your people, only let me know how it goes so
that we shan't get muddled in the accounts. D'you see?'

'Ho yuss! 'Taint much though, is it?' said Badalia, regarding the white
coins in her palm. The sacred fever of the administrator, only known to
those who have tasted power, burned in her veins. 'Boots is boots,
unless they're give you, an' then they ain't fit to wear unless they're
mended top an' bottom; an' jellies is jellies; an' I don't think anything o'
that cheap pork-wine, but it all comes to something. It'll go quicker 'n a
quartern of gin – seventeen bob. An' I'll keep a book – same as I used to
do before Tom went an' took up 'long o' that pan-faced slut in
Hennessy's Rents. We was the only barrer that kep' regular books, me
an' – 'im.'

She bought a large copy-book – her unschooled handwriting
demanded room – and in it she wrote the story of her war; boldly, as
befits a general, and for no other eyes than her own and those of the
Reverend Eustace Hanna. Long ere the pages were full the mottled
cover had been soaked in kerosene – Lascar Loo's mother, defrauded
of her percentage on her daughter's custards, invaded Badalia's room
in 17 Gunnison Street, and fought with her to the damage of the lamp
and her own hair. It was hard, too, to carry the precious 'pork-wine' in
one hand and the book in the other through an eternally thirsty land;
so red stains were added to those of the oil. But the Reverend Eustace
Hanna, looking at the matter of the book, never objected. The
generous scrawls told their own tale, Badalia every Saturday night
supplying the chorus between the written statements thus –

*Mrs Hikkey, very ill brandy 3d. Cab for hospital, she had to go, 1s. Mrs
Poone confined. In money for tea (she took it, I know, sir) 6d. Met her husband
out looking for work.*

'I slapped 'is face for a bone-idle beggar! 'E won't get no work becos
'e's – excuse me, sir. Won't you go on?' The curate continued –

*Mrs Vincent. Confid. No linning for baby. Most untidy. In money 2s. 6d.
Some cloths from Miss Evva.*

'Did Sister Eva do that?' said the curate very softly. Now charity was Sister Eva's bounden duty, yet to one man's eyes each act of her daily toil was a manifestation of angelic grace and goodness – a thing to perpetually admire.

'Yes, sir. She went back to the Sisters' 'Ome an' took 'em off 'er own bed. Most beautiful marked too. Go on, sir. That makes up four and thruppence.'

Mrs Junnet to keep good fire coals is up. 7d.

Mrs Lockhart took a baby to nurse to earn a triffle but mother can't pay husband summons over and over. He won't help. Cash 2s. 2d. Worked in a ketchin but had to leave. Fire, tea, and shin of beef 1s. 7½d.

'There was a fight there, sir,' said Badalia. 'Not me, sir. 'Er 'usband, o' course 'e come in at the wrong time, was wishful to 'ave the beef, so I calls up the next floor an' down comes that mulatter man wot sells the sword-stick canes, top o' Ludgate-'ill. "Muley," sez I, "you big black beast, you, take an' kill this big white beast 'ere." I knew I couldn't stop Tom Lockart 'alf drunk, with the beef in 'is 'ands. "I'll beef 'm," sez Muley, an' 'e did it, with that pore woman a-cryin' in the next room, an' the top banisters on that landin' is broke out, but she got 'er beef-tea, an' Tom 'e's got 'is gruel. Will you go on, sir?'

'No, I think it will be all right. I'll sign for the week,' said the curate. One gets so used to these things profanely called human documents.

'Mrs Churner's baby's got diptheery,' said Badalia, turning to go.

'Where's that? The Churners of Painter's Alley, or the other Churners in Houghton Street?'

'Houghton Street. The Painter's Alley people, they're sold out an' left.'

'Sister Eva's sitting one night a week with old Mrs Probyn in Houghton Street – isn't she?' said the curate uneasily.

'Yes; but she won't sit no longer. *I've* took up Mrs Probyn. I can't talk 'er no religion, but she don't want it; an' Miss Eva she don't want no diptheery, tho' she sez she does. Don't *you* be afraid for Miss Eva.'

'But – but you'll get it, perhaps.'

'Like as not.' She looked the curate between the eyes, and her own eyes flamed under the fringe. 'Maybe I'd like to get it, for aught you know.'

The curate thought upon these words for a little time till he began to think of Sister Eva in the grey cloak with the white bonnet ribbons under the chin. Then he thought no more of Badalia.

What Badalia thought was never expressed in words, but it is known in Gunnison Street that Lascar Loo's mother, sitting blind drunk on her own doorstep, was that night captured and wrapped up in the war-cloud of Badalia's wrath, so that she did not know whether she stood on her head or her heels, and after being soundly bumped on every particular stair up to her room, was set down on Badalia's bed, there to whimper and quiver till the dawn, protesting that all the world was against her, and calling on the names of children long since slain by dirt and neglect. Badalia, snorting, went out to war, and since the hosts of the enemy were many, found enough work to keep her busy till the dawn.

As she had promised, she took Mrs Probyn into her own care, and began by nearly startling the old lady into a fit with the announcement that 'there ain't no God like as not, an' if there *is* it don't matter to you or me, an' any'ow you take this jelly.' Sister Eva objected to being shut off from her pious work in Houghton Street, but Badalia insisted, and by fair words and the promise of favours to come so prevailed on three or four of the more sober men of the neighbourhood, that they blockaded the door whenever Sister Eva attempted to force an entry, and pleaded the diphtheria as an excuse. 'I've got to keep 'er out o' 'arm's way,' said Badalia, 'an' out she keeps. The curick won't care a — for me, but – he wouldn't any'ow.'

The effect of that quarantine was to shift the sphere of Sister Eva's activity to other streets, and notably those most haunted by the Reverend Eustace Hanna and Brother Victor, of the Order of Little Ease. There exists, for all their human bickerings, a very close brotherhood in the ranks of those whose work lies in Gunnison Street. To begin with, they have seen pain – pain that no word or deed of theirs can alleviate – life born into Death, and Death crowded down by unhappy life. Also they understand the full significance of drink, which is a knowledge hidden from very many well-meaning people, and some of them have fought with the beasts at Ephesus. They meet at unseemly hours in unseemly places, exchange a word or two of hasty counsel, advice, or suggestion, and pass on to their appointed toil, since time is precious and lives hang in the balance of five minutes. For many, the gas-lamps are their sun, and the Covent Garden wains the chariots of the twilight. They have all in their station begged for money, so that the freemasonry of the mendicant binds them together.

To all these influences there was added in the case of two workers that thing which men have agreed to call Love. The chance that Sister Eva might catch diphtheria did not enter into the curate's head till Badalia had spoken. Then it seemed a thing intolerable and monstrous that she should be exposed not only to this risk, but any accident whatever of the streets. A wain coming round a corner might kill her; the rotten staircases on which she trod daily and nightly might collapse and maim her; there was danger in the tottering coping-stones of certain crazy houses that he knew well; danger more deadly within those houses. What if one of a thousand drunken men crushed out that precious life? A woman had once flung a chair at the curate's head. Sister Eva's arm would not be strong enough to ward off a chair. There were also knives that were quick to fly. These and other considerations cast the soul of the Reverend Eustace Hanna into torment that no leaning upon Providence could relieve. God was indubitably great and terrible – one had only to walk through Gunnison Street to see that much – but it would be better, vastly better, that Eva should have the protection of his own arm. And the world that was not too busy to watch might have seen a woman, not too young, light-haired and light-eyed, slightly assertive in her speech, and very limited in such ideas as lay beyond the immediate sphere of her duty, where the eyes of the Reverend Eustace Hanna turned to follow the footsteps of a Queen crowned in a little grey bonnet with white ribbons under the chin.

If that bonnet appeared for a moment at the bottom of a courtyard, or nodded at him on a dark staircase, then there was hope yet for Lascar Loo, living on one lung and the memory of past excesses, hope even for whining sodden Nick Lapworth, blaspheming, in the hope of money, over the pangs of a 'true conversion this time, s'elp me Gawd, sir'. If that bonnet did not appear for a day, the mind of the curate was filled with lively pictures of horror, visions of stretchers, a crowd at some villainous crossing, and a policeman – he could see that policeman – jerking out over his shoulder the details of the accident, and ordering the man who would have set his body against the wheels – heavy dray wheels, he could see them – to 'move on'. Then there was less hope for the salvation of Gunnison Street and all in it.

This agony Brother Victor beheld one day when he was coming from a death-bed. He saw the light in the eye, the relaxing muscles of the mouth, and heard a new ring in the voice that had told flat all the forenoon. Sister Eva had turned into Gunnison Street after a forty-eight hours' eternity of absence. She had not been run over. Brother Victor's heart must have suffered in some human fashion, or he would never have seen what he saw. But the Law of his Church made suffering easy. His duty was to go on with his work until he died, even as Badalia went on. She, magnifying her office, faced the drunken husband; coaxed the doubly shiftless, thriftless girl-wife into a little forethought, and begged clothes when and where she could for the scrofulous babes that multiplied like the green scum on the untopped water-cisterns.

The story of her deeds was written in the book that the curate signed weekly, but she never told him any more of fights and tumults in the street. 'Mis' Eva does 'er work 'er way. I does mine mine. But I do more than Mis' Eva ten times over, an' "Thank yer, Badalia," sez 'e, "that'll do for this week." I wonder what Tom's doin' now long o' that – other woman. Seems like as if I'd go an' look at 'im one o' these days. But I'd cut 'er liver out – couldn't 'elp myself. Better not go, p'raps.'

Hennessy's Rents lay more than two miles from Gunnison Street, and were inhabited by much the same class of people. Tom had established himself there with Jenny Wabstow, his new woman, and for weeks lived in great fear of Badalia's suddenly descending upon him. The prospect of actual fighting did not scare him; but he objected to the police-court that would follow, and the orders for maintenance and other devices of a law that cannot understand the simple rule that 'when a man's tired of a woman 'e ain't such a bloomin' fool as to live with 'er no more, an' that's the long an' short of it'. For some months his new wife wore very well, and kept Tom in a state of decent fear and consequent orderliness. Also work was plentiful. Then a baby was born, and, following the law of his kind, Tom, little interested in the children he helped to produce, sought distraction in drink. He had confined himself, as a rule, to beer, which is stupefying and compara-tively innocuous: at least, it clogs the legs, and though the heart may ardently desire to kill, sleep comes swiftly, and the crime often remains undone. Spirits, being more volatile, allow both the flesh and the soul to work together – generally to the inconvenience of others. Tom discovered that there was merit in whisky – if you only took enough of it – cold. He took as much as he could purchase or get given him, and by the time that his woman was fit to go abroad again, the two rooms of their household were stripped of many valuable articles. Then the woman spoke her mind, not once, but several times, with point, fluency, and metaphor; and Tom was indignant at being deprived of peace at the end of his day's work, which included much whisky. He therefore withdrew himself from the solace and companionship of Jenny Wabstow, and she therefore pursued him with more metaphors. At the last, Tom would turn round and hit her – sometimes across the head, and sometimes across the breast, and the bruises furnished material for discussion on doorsteps among such women as had been treated in like manner by their husbands. They were not few.

But no very public scandal had occurred till Tom one day saw fit to open negotiations with a young woman for matrimony according to the laws of free selection. He was getting very tired of Jenny, and the young woman was earning enough from flower-selling to keep him in

THE BEST SHORT STORIES

comfort, whereas Jenny was expecting another baby, and most unrea-
sonably expected consideration on this account. The shapelessness of
her figure revolted him, and he said as much in the language of his
breed. Jenny cried till Mrs Hart, lineal descendant, and Irish of the
'mother to Mike of the donkey-cart', stopped her on her own staircase
and whispered: 'God be good to you, Jenny, my woman, for I see how
'tis with you.' Jenny wept more than ever, and gave Mrs Hart a penny
and some kisses, while Tom was conducting his own wooing at the
corner of the street.

The young woman, prompted by pride, not by virtue, told Jenny of
his offers, and Jenny spoke to Tom that night. The altercation began in
their own rooms, but Tom tried to escape; and in the end all
Hennessy's Rents gathered themselves upon the pavement and formed
a court to which Jenny appealed from time to time, her hair loose on
her neck, her raiment in extreme disorder, and her steps astray from
drink. 'When your man drinks, you'd better drink too! It don't 'urt so
much when 'e 'its you then,' says the Wisdom of the Women. And
surely they ought to know.

'Look at 'im!' shrieked Jenny. 'Look at 'im, standin' there without
any word to say for himself, that 'ud smitch off and leave me an' never
so much as a shillin' lef' be'ind! You call yourself a man – you call
yourself the bleedin' shadow of a man? I've seen better men than you
made outer chewed paper and spat out arterwards. Look at 'im!' 'E's
been drunk since Thursday last, an' 'e'll be drunk s' long's 'e can get
drink. 'E's took all I've got, an' me – an' me – as you see – '

A murmur of sympathy from the women.

'Took it all, he did, an' atop of his blasted pickin' an' stealin' – yes,
you, you thief – 'e goes off an' tries to take up long o' that' – here
followed a complete and minute description of the young woman.
Luckily, she was not on the spot to hear. ' 'E'll serve 'er as 'e served me!
'E'll drink every bloomin' copper she makes an' then leave 'er alone,
same as 'e done me! O women, look you, I've bore 'im one an' there's
another on the way, an' 'e'd up an' leave me as I am now – the stinkin'
dorg. An' you *may* leave me. I don't want none o' your leavin's. Go
away. Get away!' The hoarseness of passion overpowered the voice.
The crowd attracted a policeman as Tom began to slink away.

'Look at 'im,' said Jenny, grateful for the new listener. 'Ain't there no
law for such as 'im? 'E's took all my money, 'e's beat me once, twice an'
over. 'E's swine drunk when 'e ain't mad drunk, an' now, an' now 'e's
trying to pick up along o' another woman. 'Im I give up a four times
better man for. Ain't there no law?'

'What's the matter now? You go into your 'ouse. I'll see to the man.

'As 'e been 'itting you?' said the policeman.

' 'Ittin' me? 'E's cut my 'eart in two, an' 'e stands there grinnin' as tho' 'twas all a play to 'im.'

'You go on into your 'ouse an' lie down a bit.'

'I'm a married woman, I tell you, an' I'll 'ave my 'usband!'

'I ain't done her no bloomin' 'arm,' said Tom from the edge of the crowd. He felt that public opinion was running against him.

'You ain't done me any bloomin' good, you dorg. I'm a married woman, I am, an' I won't 'ave my 'usband took from me.'

'Well, if you *are* a married woman, cover your breasts,' said the policeman soothingly. He was used to domestic brawls.

'Shan't – thank you for your impidence. Look 'ere!' She tore open her dishevelled bodice and showed such crescent-shaped bruises as are made by a well-applied chair-back. 'That's what 'e done to me acause my heart wouldn't break quick enough! 'E's tried to get in an' break it. Look at that, Tom, that you gave me last night; an' I made it up with you. But that was before I knew what you were tryin' to do long o' that woman – '

'D'you charge 'im?' said the policeman. ' 'E'll get a month for it, per'aps.'

'No,' said Jenny firmly. It was one thing to expose her man to the scorn of the street, and another to lead him to jail.

'Then you go in an' lie down, and you' – this to the crowd – 'pass along the pavement, there. Pass along. 'Taint nothing to laugh at.' To Tom, who was being sympathised with by his friends, 'It's good for you she didn't charge you, but mind this now, the next time,' etc.

Tom did not at all appreciate Jenny's forbearance, nor did his friends help to compose his mind. He had whacked the woman because she was a nuisance. For precisely the same reason he had cast about for a new mate. And all his kind acts had ended in a truly painful scene in the street, a most unjustifiable exposure by and of his woman, and a certain loss of caste – this he realised dimly – among his associates. Consequently, all women were nuisances, and consequently whisky was a good thing. His friends condoled with him. Perhaps he had been more hard on his woman than she deserved, but her disgraceful conduct under provocation excused all offence.

'I wouldn't 'ave no more to do with 'er – a woman like that there,' said one comforter.

'Let 'er go an' dig for her bloomin' self. A man wears 'isself out to 'is bones shovin' meat down their mouths, while they sit at 'ome easy all day; an' the very fust time, mark you, you 'as a bit of a difference, an very proper too for a man as *is* a man, she ups an' 'as you out into the street, callin' you Gawd knows what all. What's the good o' that, I arx you?' So spoke the second comforter.

The whisky was the third, and his suggestion struck Tom as the best of all. He would return to Badalia his wife. Probably she would have been doing something wrong while he had been away, and he could then vindicate his authority as a husband. Certainly she would have money. Single women always seemed to possess the pence that God and the Government denied to hard-working men. He refreshed himself with more whisky. It was beyond any doubt that Badalia would have done something wrong. She might even have married another man. He would wait till the new husband was out of the way, and, after kicking Badalia, would get money and a long absent sense of satisfaction. There is much virtue in a creed or a law, but when all is prayed and suffered, drink is the only thing that will make clean all a man's deeds in his own eyes. Pity it is that the effects are not permanent.

Tom parted with his friends, bidding them tell Jenny that he was going to Gunnison Street, and would return to her arms no more. Because this was the devil's message, they remembered and severally delivered it, with drunken distinctness, in Jenny's ears. Then Tom took more drink till his drunkenness rolled back and stood off from him as a wave rolls back and stands off the wreck it will swamp. He reached the traffic-polished black asphalt of a side-street and trod warily among the reflections of the shop-lamps that burned in gulfs of pitchy darkness, fathoms beneath his boot-heels. He was very sober indeed. Looking down his past, he beheld that he was justified of all his actions so entirely and perfectly that if Badalia had in his absence dared to lead a blameless life he would smash her for not having gone wrong.

Badalia at that moment was in her own room after the regular nightly skirmish with Lascar Loo's mother. To a reproof as stinging as a Gunnison Street tongue could make it, the old woman, detected for the hundredth time in the theft of the poor delicacies meant for the invalid, could only cackle and answer –

'D'you think Loo's never bilked a man in 'er life? She's dyin' now – on'y she's so cunning long about it. Me! I'll live for twenty years yet.'

Badalia shook her, more on principle than in any hope of curing her, and thrust her into the night, where she collapsed on the pavement and called upon the devil to slay Badalia.

He came upon the word in the shape of a man with a very pale face who asked for her by name. Lascar Loo's mother remembered. It was Badalia's husband – and the return of a husband to Gunnison Street was generally followed by beatings.

'Where's my wife?' said Tom. 'Where's my slut of a wife?'

'Upstairs an' be — to her,' said the old woman, falling over on her side. ' 'Ave you come back for 'er, Tom?'

'Yes. 'Oo's she took up while I bin gone?'

'All the bloomin' curicks in the parish. She's that set up you wouldn't know 'er.'

' 'Strewth she is!'

'Oh, yuss. Mor'n that, she's always round an' about with them sniffin' Sisters of Charity an' the curick. Mor'n that, 'e gives 'er money – pounds an' pounds a week. Been keepin' her that way for months, 'e 'as. No wonder you wouldn't 'ave nothin' to do with 'er when you left. An' she keeps me outer the food-stuff they gets for me lyin' dyin' out 'ere like a dorg. She's been a blazin' bad un has Badalia since you lef'.'

'Got the same room still, 'as she?' said Tom, striding over Lascar Loo's mother, who was picking at the chinks between the pave-stones.

'Yes, but so fine you wouldn't know it.'

Tom went up the stairs and the old lady chuckled. Tom was angry. Badalia would not be able to bump people for some time to come, or to interfere with the heaven-appointed distribution of custards.

Badalia, undressing to go to bed, heard feet on the stair that she knew well. Ere they stopped to kick at her door she had, in her own fashion, thought over very many things.

'Tom's back,' she said to herself. 'An' I'm glad . . . spite o' the curick an' everythink.'

She opened the door, crying his name.

The man pushed her aside.

'I don't want none o' your kissin's an' slaverin's. I'm sick of 'em,' said he.

'You ain't 'ad so many neither to make you sick these two years past.'

'I've 'ad better. Got any money?'

'On'y a little – orful little.'

'That's a — lie, an' you know it.'

' 'Taint – and, oh Tom, what's the use o' talkin' money the minute you come back? Didn't you like Jenny? I knowed you wouldn't.'

'Shut your 'ead. Ain't you got enough to make a man drunk fair?'

'You don't want bein' made more drunk any. You're drunk a'ready. You come to bed, Tom.'

'To you?'

'Ay, to me. Ain't I nothin' – spite o' Jenny?'

She put out her arms as she spoke. But the drink held Tom fast.

'Not for me,' said he, steadying himself against the wall. 'Don't I know 'ow you've been goin' on while I was away, yah!'

'Arsk about!' said Badalia indignantly, drawing herself together.

' 'Oo sez anythink agin me 'ere?'

' 'Oo sez? W'y, everybody. I ain't come back more'n a minute fore I finds you've been with the curick Gawd knows where. Wot curick was 'e?'

'The curick that's 'ere always,' said Badalia hastily. She was thinking of anything rather than the Revd Eustace Hanna at that moment. Tom sat down gravely in the only chair in the room. Badalia continued her arrangements for going to bed.

'Pretty thing that,' said Tom, 'to tell your own lawful married 'usband – an' I guv five bob for the weddin'-ring. Curick that's 'ere always! Cool as brass you are. Ain't you got no shame? Ain't 'e under the bed now?'

'Tom, you're bleedin' drunk. I ain't done nothin' to be 'shamed of.'

'You! You don't know wot shame is. But I ain't come 'ere to mess with you. Give me wot you've got, an' then I'll dress you down an' go to Jenny.'

'I ain't got nothin' 'cept some coppers an' a shillin' or so.'

'Wot's that about the curick keepin' you on five poun' a week?'

' 'Oo told you that?'

'Lascar Loo's mother, lyin' on the pavemint outside, an' more honest than you'll ever be. Give me wot you've got!'

Badalia passed over to a little shell pin-cushion on the mantelpiece, drew thence four shillings and threepence – the lawful earnings of her trade – and held them out to the man who was rocking in his chair and surveying the room with wide-opened, rolling eyes.

'That ain't five poun',' said he drowsily.

'I ain't got no more. Take it an' go – if you won't stay.'

Tom rose slowly, gripping the arms of the chair. 'Wot about the curick's money that 'e guv you?' said he. 'Lascar Loo's mother told me. You give it over to me now, or I'll make you.'

'Lascar Loo's mother don't know anything about it.'

'She do, an' more than you want her to know.'

'She don't. I've bumped the 'eart out of 'er, and I can't give you the money. Anythin' else but that, Tom, an' everythin' else but that, Tom, I'll give willin' and true. 'Taint my money. Won't the dollar be enough? That money's my trust. There's a book along of it too.'

'Your trust? Wot are you doin' with any trust that your 'usband don't know of? You an' your trust! Take you that!'

Tom stepped towards her and delivered a blow of the clenched fist across the mouth. 'Give me wot you've got,' said he, in the thick, abstracted voice of one talking in dreams.

'I won't,' said Badalia, staggering to the washstand. With any other man than her husband she would have fought savagely as a wild cat; but Tom had been absent two years, and, perhaps, a little timely submission would win him back to her. None the less, the weekly trust was sacred.

The wave that had so long held back descended on Tom's brain. He caught Badalia by the throat and forced her to her knees. It seemed just to him in that hour to punish an erring wife for two years of wilful desertion; and the more, in that she had confessed her guilt by refusing to give up the wage of sin.

Lascar Loo's mother waited on the pavement without for the sounds of lamentation, but none came. Even if Tom had released her gullet Badalia would not have screamed.

'Give it up, you slut!' said Tom. 'Is that 'ow you pay me back for all I've done?'

'I can't. 'Tain't my money. Gawd forgive you, Tom, for wot you're — ,' the voice ceased as the grip tightened, and Tom heaved Badalia against the bed. Her forehead struck the bedpost, and she sank, half kneeling, on the floor. It was impossible for a self-respecting man to refrain from kicking her: so Tom kicked with the deadly intelligence born of whisky. The head drooped to the floor, and Tom kicked at that till the crisp tingle of hair striking through his nailed boot with the chill of cold water, warned him that it might be as well to desist.

'Where's the curick's money, you kep' woman?' he whispered in the blood-stained ear. But there was no answer – only a rattling at the door, and the voice of Jenny Wabstow crying ferociously, 'Come out o' that, Tom, an' come 'ome with me! An' you, Badalia, I'll tear your face off its bones!'

Tom's friends had delivered their message, and Jenny, after the first flood of passionate tears, rose up to follow Tom, and, if possible, to win him back. She was prepared even to endure an exemplary whacking for her performances in Hennessy's Rents. Lascar Loo's mother guided her to the chamber of horrors, and chuckled as she retired down the staircase. If Tom had not banged the soul out of Badalia, there would at least be a royal fight between that Badalia and Jenny. And Lascar Loo's mother knew well that Hell has no fury like a woman fighting above the life that is quick in her.

Still there was no sound audible in the street. Jenny swung back the unbolted door, to discover her man stupidly regarding a heap by the bed. An eminent murderer has remarked that if people did not die so untidily, most men, and all women, would commit at least one murder in their lives. Tom was reflecting on the present untidiness, and the whisky was fighting with the clear current of his thoughts.

'Don't make that noise,' he said. 'Come in quick.'

'My Gawd!' said Jenny, checking like a startled wild beast. 'What's all this 'ere? You ain't – '

'Dunno. 'Spose I did it.'

'Did it! You done it a sight too well this time.'

'She was aggravatin',' said Tom thickly, dropping back into the chair. 'That aggravatin' you'd never believe. Livin' on the fat o' the land among these aristocratic parsons an' all. Look at them white curtings on the bed. *We* ain't got no white curtings. What I want to know is – ' The voice died as Badalia's had died, but from a different cause. The whisky was tightening its grip after the accomplished deed, and Tom's eyes were beginning to close. Badalia on the floor breathed heavily.

'No, nor like to 'ave,' said Jenny. 'You've done for 'er this time. You go!'

'Not me. She won't hurt. Do 'er good. I'm goin' to sleep. Look at those there clean sheets! Aint you comin' too?'

Jenny bent over Badalia, and there was intelligence in the battered woman's eyes – intelligence and much hate.

'I never told 'im to do such,' Jenny whispered. ' 'Twas Tom's own doin' – none o' mine. Shall I get 'im took, dear?'

The eyes told their own story. Tom, who was beginning to snore, must not be taken by the Law.

'Go,' said Jenny. 'Get out! Get out of 'ere.'

'You – told – me – that – this afternoon,' said the man very sleepily. 'Lemme go asleep.'

'That wasn't nothing. You'd only 'it me. This time it's murder – murder – murder! Tom, you've killed 'er now.' She shook the man from his rest, and understanding with cold terror filled his fuddled brain.

'I done it for your sake, Jenny,' he whimpered feebly, trying to take her hand.

'You killed 'er for the money, same as you would ha' killed me. Get out o' this. Lay 'er on the bed first, you brute!'

They lifted Badalia on to the bed, and crept forth silently.

'I can't be took along o' you – and if you was took you'd say I made you do it, an' try to get me 'anged. Go away – anywhere outer 'ere,' said Jenny, and she dragged him down the stairs.

'Goin' to look for the curick?' said a voice from the pavement. Lascar Loo's mother was still waiting patiently to hear Badalia squeal.

'Wot curick?' said Jenny swiftly. There was a chance of salving her conscience yet in regard to the bundle upstairs.

' 'Anna – 63 Roomer Terrace – close 'ere,' said the old woman. She had never been favourably regarded by the curate. Perhaps, since Badalia had not squealed, Tom preferred smashing the man to the woman. There was no accounting for tastes.

Jenny thrust her man before her till they reached the nearest main road. 'Go away, now,' she gasped. 'Go off anywheres, but don't come back to me. I'll never go with you again; an', Tom – Tom, d'you 'ear me? – clean your boots.'

Vain counsel. The desperate thrust of disgust which she bestowed upon him sent him staggering face-down into the kennel, where a policeman showed interest in his welfare.

'Took for a common drunk. Gawd send they don't look at 'is boots! 'Anna, 63 Roomer Terrace!' Jenny settled her hat and ran.

The excellent housekeeper of the Roomer Chambers still remembers how there arrived a young person, blue-lipped and gasping, who cried only: 'Badalia, 17 Gunnison Street. Tell the curick to come at once – at once – at once!' and vanished into the night. This message was borne to the Revd Eustace Hanna, then enjoying his beauty-sleep. He saw there was urgency in the demand, and unhesitatingly knocked up Brother Victor across the landing. As a matter of etiquette, Rome and England divided their cases in the district according to the creeds of the sufferers; but Badalia was an institution, and not a case, and there was no district-relief etiquette to be considered. 'Something has happened to Badalia,' the curate said, 'and it's your affair as well as mine. Dress and come along.'

'I am ready,' was the answer. 'Is there any hint of what's wrong?'

'Nothing beyond a runaway-knock and a call.'

'Then it's a confinement or a murderous assault. Badalia wouldn't wake us up for anything less. I'm qualified for both, thank God.'

The two men raced to Gunnison Street, for there were no cabs abroad, and under any circumstances a cab-fare means two days' good firing for such as are perishing with cold. Lascar Loo's mother had gone to bed, and the door was naturally on the latch. They found considerably more than they had expected in Badalia's room, and the Church of Rome acquitted itself nobly with bandages, while the Church of England could only pray to be delivered from the sin of envy. The Order of Little Ease, recognising that the soul is in most cases accessible through the body, take their measures and train their men accordingly.

'She'll do now,' said Brother Victor, in a whisper. 'It's internal bleeding, I fear, and a certain amount of injury to the brain. She has a husband, of course?'

'They all have, more's the pity.'

'Yes, there's a domesticity about these injuries that shows their origin.' He lowered his voice. 'It's a perfectly hopeless business, you understand. Twelve hours at the most.'

Badalia's right hand began to beat on the counterpane, palm down.

'I think you are wrong,' said the Church of England. 'She is going.'

'No, that's not the picking at the counterpane,' said the Church of Rome. 'She wants to say something; you know her better than I.'

The curate bent very low.

'Send for Miss Eva,' said Badalia, with a cough.

'In the morning. She will come in the morning,' said the curate, and Badalia was content. Only the Church of Rome, who knew something of the human heart, knitted his brows and said nothing. After all the law of his Order was plain. His duty was to watch till the dawn while the moon went down.

It was a little before her sinking that the Revd Eustace Hanna said, 'Hadn't we better send for Sister Eva? She seems to be going fast.'

Brother Victor made no answer, but as early as decency admitted there came one to the door of the house of the Little Sisters of the Red Diamond and demanded Sister Eva, that she might soothe the pain of Badalia Herodsfoot. That man, saying very little, led her to Gunnison Street, No. 17, and into the room where Badalia lay. Then he stood on the landing, and bit the flesh of his fingers in agony, because he was a priest trained to know, and knew how the hearts of men and women beat back at the rebound, so that Love is born out of horror, and passion declares itself when the soul is quivering with pain.

Badalia, wise to the last, husbanded her strength till the coming of Sister Eva. It is generally maintained by the Little Sisters of the Red Diamond that she died in delirium, but since one Sister at least took a half of her dying advice, this seems uncharitable.

She tried to turn feebly on the bed, and the poor broken human machinery protested according to its nature.

Sister Eva started forward, thinking that she heard the dread forerunner of the death-rattle. Badalia lay still conscious, and spoke with startling distinctness, the irrepressible irreverence of the street-hawker, the girl who had danced on the winkle-barrow twinkling; in her one available eye.

'Sounds jest like Mrs Jessel, don't it? Before she's 'ad 'er lunch an' 'as been talkin' all the mornin' to her classes.'

Neither Sister Eva nor the curate said anything. Brother Victor stood without the door, and the breath came harshly between his teeth, for he was in pain.

'Put a cloth over my 'ead,' said Badalia. 'I've got it good, an' I don't want Miss Eva to see. I ain't pretty this time.'

'Who was it?' said the curate.

'Man from outside. Never seed 'im no more'n Adam. Drunk, I s'pose. S'elp me Gawd, that's truth! Is Miss Eva 'ere? I can't see under the towel. I've got it good, Miss Eva. Excuse my not shakin' 'ands with you, but I'm not strong, an' it's fourpence for Mrs Imeny's beef-tea, an' wot you can give 'er for baby-linning. Allus 'avin' kids, these people. I 'adn't oughter talk, for *my* 'usband 'e never come a-nigh me these two years, or I'd a-bin as bad as the rest; but 'e never come a-nigh me . . . A man come and 'it me over the 'ead, an' 'e kicked me, Miss Eva; so it was just the same's if I had ha' had a 'usband, ain't it? The book's in the drawer, Mister 'Anna, an' it's all right, an' I never guv up a copper o' the trust money – not a copper. You look under the chist o' drawers – all wot isn't spent this week is there . . . An', Miss Eva, don't you wear that grey bonnick no more. I kep' you from the diptheery, an' – an' I didn't want to keep you so, but the curick said it 'ad to be done. I'd a sooner ha' took up with 'im than anyone, only Tom 'e come, an' then – you see, Miss Eva, Tom 'e never come a-nigh me for two years, nor I 'aven't seen 'im yet. S'elp me Gawd, I 'aven't. Do you 'ear? But you two go along, and make a match of it. I've wished otherways often, but o' course it was not for the likes o' me. If Tom 'ad come back, which 'e never did, I'd ha' been like the rest – sixpence for beef-tea for the baby, an' a shilling for layin' out the baby. You've seen it in the books, Mister 'Anna. That's what it is; an' o' course, you couldn't never 'ave nothing to do with me. But a woman she wishes as she looks, an' never you 'ave no doubt about 'im, Miss Eva. I've seen it in 'is face time an' agin – time an' agin . . . Make it a four pound ten funeral – with a pall.'

It was a seven pound fifteen shilling funeral, and all Gunnison Street turned out to do it honour. All but two; for Lascar Loo's mother saw that a Power had departed, and that her road lay clear to the custards. Therefore, when the carriages rattled off, the cat on the doorstep heard the wail of the dying prostitute who could not die –

'Oh, mother, mother, won't you even let me lick the spoon!'

The Ship that Found Herself

We now, held in captivity,
    Spring to our labour nor grieve!
See now, how it is blesseder,
    Brothers, to give than receive!
Keep trust, wherefore ye were made
    Paying the duty ye owe;
For a clean thrust and the sheer of the blade
    Shall carry us where we should go.

Song of the Engines

IT WAS HER FIRST VOYAGE, and though she was but a cargo-steamer of twelve hundred tons, she was the very best of her kind, the outcome of forty years of experiments and improvements in framework and machinery; and her designers and owner thought as much of her as though she had been the *Lucania*. Anyone can make a floating hotel that will pay expenses, if he puts enough money into the saloon, and charges for private baths, suites of rooms, and such like; but in these days of competition and low freights every square inch of a cargo-boat must be built for cheapness, great hold-capacity, and a certain steady speed. This boat was, perhaps, two hundred and forty feet long and thirty-two feet wide, with arrangements that enabled her to carry cattle on her main and sheep on her upper deck if she wanted to; but her great glory was the amount of cargo that she could store away in her holds. Her owners – they were a very well known Scotch firm – came round with her from the north, where she had been launched and christened and fitted, to Liverpool, where she was to take cargo for New York; and the owner's daughter, Miss Frazier, went to and fro on the clean decks, admiring the new paint and the brass work, and the patent winches, and particularly the strong, straight bow, over which she had cracked a bottle of champagne when she named the steamer the *Dimbula*. It was a beautiful September afternoon, and the boat in all her newness – she was painted lead-colour with a red funnel – looked very fine indeed. Her house-flag was flying, and her whistle from time to time acknowledged the salutes of friendly boats, who saw that she was new to the High and Narrow Seas and wished to make her welcome.

'And now,' said Miss Frazier delightedly, to the captain, 'she's a real ship, isn't she? It seems only the other day father gave the order for her, and now – and now – isn't she a beauty!' The girl was proud of the firm, and talked as though she were the controlling partner.

'Oh, she's no so bad,' the skipper replied cautiously. 'But I'm sayin' that it takes more than christenin' to mak' a ship. In the nature o' things, Miss Frazier, if ye follow me, she's just irons and rivets and plates put into the form of a ship. She has to find herself yet.'

'I thought father said she was exceptionally well found.'

'So she is,' said the skipper, with a laugh. 'But it's this way wi' ships, Miss Frazier. She's all here, but the parrts of her have not learned to work together yet. They've had no chance.'

'The engines are working beautifully. I can hear them.'

'Yes, indeed. But there's more than engines to a ship. Every inch of her, ye'll understand, has to be livened up and made to work wi' its neighbour – sweetenin' her, we call it, technically.'

'And how will you do it?' the girl asked.

'We can no more than drive and steer her, and so forth; but if we have rough weather this trip – it's likely – she'll learn the rest by heart! For a ship, ye'll obsairve, Miss Frazier, is in no sense a reegid body closed at both ends. She's a highly complex structure o' various an' conflictin' strains, wi' tissues that must give an' tak' accordin' to her personal modulus of elasteecity.' Mr Buchanan, the chief engineer, was coming towards them. 'I'm sayin' to Miss Frazier, here, that our little *Dimbula* has to be sweetened yet, and nothin' but a gale will do it. How's all wi' your engines, Buck?'

'Well enough – true by plumb an' rule, o' course; but there's no spontaneeity yet.' He turned to the girl. 'Take my word, Miss Frazier, and maybe ye'll comprehend later; even after a pretty girl's christened a ship it does not follow that there's such a thing as a ship under the men that work her.'

'I was sayin' the very same, Mr Buchanan,' the skipper interrupted.

'That's more metaphysical than I can follow,' said Miss Frazier, laughing.

'Why so? Ye're good Scotch, an' – I knew your mother's father, he was fra' Dumfries – ye've a vested right in metapheesics, Miss Frazier, just as ye have in the *Dimbula*,' the engineer said.

'Eh, well, we must go down to the deep watters, an' earn Miss Frazier her deevidends. Will you not come to my cabin for tea?' said the skipper. 'We'll be in dock the night, and when you're goin' back to Glasgie ye can think of us loadin' her down an' drivin' her forth – all for your sake.'

In the next few days they stowed some two thousand tons' dead weight into the *Dimbula*, and took her out from Liverpool. As soon as she met the lift of the open water, she naturally began to talk. If you lay your ear to the side of the cabin the next time you are in a steamer, you will hear hundreds of little voices in every direction, thrilling and buzzing, and whispering and popping, and gurgling and sobbing and squeaking exactly like a telephone in a thunderstorm. Wooden ships shriek and growl and grunt, but iron vessels throb and quiver through all their hundreds of ribs and thousands of rivets. The *Dimbula* was very strongly built, and every piece of her had a letter or number, or both, to describe it; and every piece had been hammered, or forged, or rolled, or punched by man, and had lived in the roar and rattle of the ship-yard for months. Therefore, every piece had its own separate voice in exact proportion to the amount of trouble spent upon it. Cast-iron, as a rule, says very little; but mild steel plates and wrought-iron, and ribs and beams that have been much bent and welded and riveted, talk continuously. Their conversation, of course, is not half as wise as our human talk, because they are all, though they do not know it, bound down one to the other in a black darkness, where they cannot tell what is happening near them, nor what will overtake them next.

As soon as she had cleared the Irish coast a sullen, grey-headed old wave of the Atlantic climbed leisurely over her straight bows, and sat down on her steam-capstan used for hauling up the anchor. Now the capstan and the engine that drove it had been newly painted red and green; besides which, nobody likes being ducked.

'Don't you do that again,' the capstan sputtered through the teeth of his cogs. 'Hi! Where's the fellow gone?'

The wave had slouched overside with a plop and a chuckle; but 'Plenty more where he came from,' said a brother-wave, and went through and over the capstan, who was bolted firmly to an iron plate on the iron deck-beams below.

'Can't you keep still up there?' said the deck-beams. 'What's the matter with you? One minute you weigh twice as much as you ought to, and the next you don't!'

'It isn't my fault,' said the capstan. 'There's a green brute outside that comes and hits me on the head.'

'Tell that to the shipwrights. You've been in position for months and you've never wriggled like this before. If you aren't careful you'll strain *us*.'

'Talking of strain,' said a low, rasping, unpleasant voice, 'are any of you fellows – you deck-beams, we mean – aware that those exceedingly ugly knees of yours happen to be riveted into our structure – *ours*?'

'Who might you be?' the deck-beams enquired.

'Oh, nobody in particular,' was the answer. 'We're only the port and starboard upper-deck stringers; and if you persist in heaving and hiking like this, we shall be reluctantly compelled to take steps.'

Now the stringers of the ship are long iron girders, so to speak, that run lengthways from stern to bow. They keep the iron frames (what are called ribs in a wooden ship) in place, and also help to hold the ends of the deck-beams, which go from side to side of the ship. Stringers always consider themselves most important, because they are so long.

'You will take steps – will you?' This was a long echoing rumble. It came from the frames – scores and scores of them, each one about eighteen inches distant from the next, and each riveted to the stringers in four places. 'We think you will have a certain amount of trouble in *that*'; and thousands and thousands of the little rivets that held everything together whispered: 'You will. You will! Stop quivering and be quiet. Hold on, brethren! Hold on! Hot Punches! What's that?'

Rivets have no teeth, so they cannot chatter with fright; but they did their best as a fluttering jar swept along the ship from stern to bow, and she shook like a rat in a terrier's mouth.

An unusually severe pitch, for the sea was rising, had lifted the big throbbing screw nearly to the surface, and it was spinning round in a kind of soda-water – half sea and half air – going much faster than was proper, because there was no deep water for it to work in. As it sank again, the engines – and they were triple expansion, three cylinders in a row – snorted through all their three pistons. 'Was that a joke, you fellow outside? It's an uncommonly poor one. How are we to do our work if you fly off the handle that way?'

'I didn't fly off the handle,' said the screw, twirling huskily at the end of the screw-shaft. 'If I had, you'd have been scrap-iron by this time. The sea dropped away from under me, and I had nothing to catch on to. That's all.'

'That's all, d'you call it?' said the thrust-block, whose business it is to take the push of the screw; for if a screw had nothing to hold it back it would crawl right into the engine-room. (It is the holding back of the screwing action that gives the drive to a ship.) 'I know I do my work deep down and out of sight, but I warn you I expect justice. All I ask for is bare justice. Why can't you push steadily and evenly, instead of whizzing like a whirligig, and making me hot under all my collars.' The thrust-block had six collars, each faced with brass, and he did not wish to get them heated.

All the bearings that supported the fifty feet of screw-shaft as it ran to the stern whispered: 'Justice – give us justice.'

'I can only give you what I can get,' the screw answered. 'Look out! It's coming again!'

He rose with a roar as the *Dimbula* plunged, and 'whack – flack – whack – whack' went the engines, furiously, for they had little to check them.

'I'm the noblest outcome of human ingenuity – Mr Buchanan says so,' squealed the high-pressure cylinder. 'This is simply ridiculous!' The piston went up savagely, and choked, for half the steam behind it was mixed with dirty water. 'Help! Oiler! Fitter! Stoker! Help! I'm choking,' it gasped. 'Never in the history of maritime invention has such a calamity overtaken one so young and strong. And if I go, who's to drive the ship?'

'Hush! oh, hush!' whispered the Steam, who, of course, had been to sea many times before. He used to spend his leisure ashore in a cloud, or a gutter, or a flower-pot, or a thunderstorm, or anywhere else where water was needed. 'That's only a little priming, a little carrying-over, as they call it. It'll happen all night, on and off. I don't say it's nice, but it's the best we can do under the circumstances.'

'What difference can circumstances make? I'm here to do my work – on clean, dry steam. Blow circumstances!' the cylinder roared.

'The circumstances will attend to the blowing. I've worked on the North Atlantic run a good many times – it's going to be rough before morning.'

'It isn't distressingly calm now,' said the extra-strong frames – they were called web-frames – in the engine-room. 'There's an upward thrust that we don't understand, and there's a twist that is very bad for our brackets and diamond-plates, and there's a sort of west-north-westerly pull that follows the twist, which seriously annoys us. We mention this because we happened to cost a good deal of money, and we feel sure that the owner would not approve of our being treated in this frivolous way.'

'I'm afraid the matter is out of the owner's hands for the present,' said the Steam, slipping into the condenser. 'You're left to your own devices till the weather betters.'

'I wouldn't mind the weather,' said a flat bass voice below; 'it's this confounded cargo that's breaking my heart. I'm the garboard-strake, and I'm twice as thick as most of the others, and I ought to know something.'

The garboard-strake is the lowest plate in the bottom of a ship, and the *Dimbula's* garboard-strake was nearly three-quarters of an inch mild steel.

'The sea pushes me up in a way I should never have expected,' the strake grunted, 'and the cargo pushes me down, and, between the two, I don't know what I'm supposed to do.'

'When in doubt, hold on,' rumbled the Steam, making head in the boilers.

'Yes; but there's only dark, and cold, and hurry, down here; and how do I know whether the other plates are doing their duty? Those bulwark-plates up above, I've heard, ain't more than five-sixteenths of an inch thick – scandalous, I call it.'

'I agree with you,' said a huge web-frame by the main cargo-hatch. He was deeper and thicker than all the others, and curved half-way across the ship in the shape of half an arch, to support the deck where deck-beams would have been in the way of cargo coming up and down. 'I work entirely unsupported, and I observe that I am the sole strength of this vessel, so far as my vision extends. The responsibility, I assure you, is enormous. I believe the money-value of the cargo is over one hundred and fifty thousand pounds. Think of that!'

'And every pound of it is dependent on my personal exertions.' Here spoke a sea-valve that communicated directly with the water outside, and was seated not very far from the garboard-strake. 'I rejoice to think that I am a Prince-Hyde Valve, with best Pará rubber facings. Five patents cover me – I mention this without pride – five separate and several patents, each one finer than the other. At present I am screwed fast. Should I open, you would immediately be swamped. This is incontrovertible!'

Patent things always use the longest words they can. It is a trick that they pick up from their inventors.

'That's news,' said a big centrifugal bilge-pump. 'I had an idea that you were employed to clean decks and things with. At least, I've used you for that more than once. I forget the precise number, in thousands, of gallons which I am guaranteed to throw per hour; but I assure you, my complaining friends, that there is not the least danger. I alone am capable of clearing any water that may find its way here. By my Biggest Deliveries, we pitched then!'

The sea was getting up in a workmanlike style. It was a dead westerly gale, blown from under a ragged opening of green sky, narrowed on all sides by fat, grey clouds; and the wind bit like pincers as it fretted the spray into lacework on the flanks of the waves.

'I tell you what it is,' the foremast telephoned down its wire-stays. 'I'm up here, and I can take a dispassionate view of things. There's an organised conspiracy against us. I'm sure of it, because every single one of these waves is heading directly for our bows. The whole sea is concerned in it – and so's the wind. It's awful!'

'What's awful?' said a wave, drowning the capstan for the hundredth time.

'This organised conspiracy on your part,' the capstan gurgled, taking his cue from the mast.

'Organised bubbles and spindrift! There has been a depression in the Gulf of Mexico. Excuse me!' He leaped overside; but his friends took up the tale one after another.

'Which has advanced – ' That wave hove green water over the funnel.

'As far as Cape Hatteras – ' He drenched the bridge.

'And is now going out to sea – to sea – to sea!' The third went free in three surges, making a clean sweep of a boat, which turned bottom up and sank in the darkening troughs alongside, while the broken falls whipped the davits.

'That's all there is to it,' seethed the white water roaring through the scuppers. 'There's no animus in our proceedings. We're only meteorological corollaries.'

'Is it going to get any worse?' said the bow-anchor chained down to the deck, where he could only breathe once in five minutes.

'Not knowing, can't say. Wind may blow a bit by midnight. Thanks awfully. Goodbye.'

The wave that spoke so politely had travelled some distance aft, and found itself all mixed up on the deck amidships, which was a well-deck sunk between high bulwarks. One of the bulwark plates, which was hung on hinges to open outward, had swung out, and passed the bulk of the water back to the sea again with a clean smack.

'Evidently that's what I'm made for,' said the plate, closing again with a sputter of pride. 'Oh no, you don't, my friend!'

The top of a wave was trying to get in from the outside, but as the plate did not open in that direction, the defeated water spurted back.

'Not bad for five-sixteenths of an inch,' said the bulwark-plate. 'My work, I see, is laid down for the night;' and it began opening and shutting with the motion of the ship as it was designed to do.

'We are not what you might call idle,' groaned all the frames together, as the *Dimbula* climbed a big wave, lay on her side at the top, and shot into the next hollow, twisting in the descent. A huge swell pushed up exactly under her middle, and her bow and stern hung free with nothing to support them. Then one joking wave caught her up at the bow, and another at the stern, while the rest of the water slunk away from under her just to see how she would like it; so she was held up at her two ends only, and the weight of the cargo and the machinery fell on the groaning iron keels and bilge-stringers.

'Ease off! Ease off, there!' roared the garboard-strake. 'I want one-eighth of an inch fair play. D'you hear me, you rivets!'

'Ease off! Ease off!' cried the bilge-stringers. 'Don't hold us so tight to the frames!'

'Ease off!' grunted the deck-beams, as the *Dimbula* rolled fearfully. 'You've cramped our knees into the stringers, and we can't move. Ease off, you flat-headed little nuisances.'

Then two converging seas hit the bows, one on each side, and fell away in torrents of streaming thunder.

'Ease off!' shouted the forward collision-bulkhead. 'I want to crumple up, but I'm stiffened in every direction. Ease off, you dirty little forge-filings. Let me breathe!'

All the hundreds of plates that are riveted to the frames, and make the outside skin of every steamer, echoed the call, for each plate wanted to shift and creep a little, and each plate, according to its position, complained against the rivets.

'We can't help it! *We* can't help it!' they murmured in reply. 'We're put here to hold you, and we're going to do it; you never pull us twice in the same direction. If you'd say what you were going to do next, we'd try to meet your views.'

'As far as I could feel,' said the upper-deck planking, and that was four inches thick, 'every single iron near me was pushing or pulling in opposite directions. Now, what's the sense of that? My friends, let us all pull together.'

'Pull any way you please,' roared the funnel, 'so long as you don't try your experiments on *me*. I need seven wire ropes, all pulling in different directions, to hold me steady. Isn't that so?'

'We believe you, my boy!' whistled the funnel-stays through their clinched teeth, as they twanged in the wind from the top of the funnel to the deck.

'Nonsense! We must all pull together,' the decks repeated. 'Pull lengthways.'

'Very good,' said the stringers; 'then stop pushing sideways when you get wet. Be content to run gracefully fore and aft, and curve in at the ends as we do.'

'No – no curves at the end! A very slight workmanlike curve from side to side, with a good grip at each knee, and little pieces welded on,' said the deck-beams.

'Fiddle!' cried the iron pillars of the deep, dark hold. 'Who ever heard of curves? Stand up straight; be a perfectly round column, and carry tons of good solid weight – like that! There!' A big sea smashed on the deck above, and the pillars stiffened themselves to the load.

'Straight up and down is not bad,' said the frames, who ran that way in the sides of the ship, 'but you must also expand yourselves sideways. Expansion is the law of life, children. Open out! open out!'

'Come back!' said the deck-beams savagely, as the upward heave of the sea made the frames try to open. 'Come back to your bearings, you slack-jawed irons!'

'Rigidity! Rigidity! Rigidity!' thumped the engines. 'Absolute, unvarying rigidity – rigidity!'

'You see!' whined the rivets in chorus. 'No two of you will ever pull alike, and – and you blame it all on us. We only know how to go through a plate and bite down on both sides so that it can't, and mustn't, and shan't move.'

'I've got one-fraction of an inch play, at any rate,' said the garboard-strake, triumphantly. So he had, and all the bottom of the ship felt the easier for it.

'Then we're no good,' sobbed the bottom rivets. 'We were ordered – we were ordered – never to give; and we've given, and the sea will come in, and we'll all go to the bottom together! First we're blamed for everything unpleasant, and now we haven't the consolation of having done our work.'

'Don't say I told you,' whispered the Steam consolingly; 'but, between you and me and the last cloud I came from, it was bound to happen sooner or later. You *had* to give a fraction, and you've given without knowing it. Now, hold on, as before.'

'What's the use?' a few hundred rivets chattered. 'We've given – we've given; and the sooner we confess that we can't keep the ship together, and go off our little heads, the easier it will be. No rivet forged can stand this strain.'

'No one rivet was ever meant to. Share it among you,' the Steam answered.

'The others can have my share. I'm going to pull out,' said a rivet in one of the forward plates.

'If you go, others will follow,' hissed the Steam. 'There's nothing so contagious in a boat as rivets going. Why, I knew a little chap like you – he was an eighth of an inch fatter, though – on a steamer – to be sure, she was only nine hundred tons, now I come to think of it – in exactly the same place as you are. He pulled out in a bit of a bobble of a sea, not half as bad as this, and he started all his friends on the same butt-strap, and the plates opened like a furnace door, and I had to climb into the nearest fog-bank, while the boat went down.'

'Now that's peculiarly disgraceful,' said the rivet. 'Fatter than me, was he, and in a steamer half our tonnage? Reedy little peg! I blush for the family, sir.' He settled himself more firmly than ever in his place, and the Steam chuckled.

'You see,' he went on, quite gravely, 'a rivet, and especially a rivet in your position, is really the one indispensable part of the ship.'

The Steam did not say that he had whispered the very same thing to every single piece of iron aboard. There is no sense in telling too much truth.

And all that while the little *Dimbula* pitched and chopped, and swung and slewed, and lay down as though she were going to die, and got up as though she had been stung, and threw her nose round and round in circles half a dozen times as she dipped; for the gale was at its worst. It was inky black, in spite of the tearing white froth on the waves, and, to top everything, the rain began to fall in sheets, so that you could not see your hand before your face. This did not make much difference to the ironwork below, but it troubled the foremast a good deal.

'Now it's all finished,' he said dismally. 'The conspiracy is too strong for us. There is nothing left but to – '

'*Hurraar! Brrrraaah! Brrrrrrp!*' roared the Steam through the fog-horn, till the decks quivered. 'Don't be frightened, below. It's only me, just throwing out a few words, in case anyone happens to be rolling round tonight.'

'You don't mean to say there's anyone except *us* on the sea in such weather?' said the funnel in a husky snuffle.

'Scores of 'em,' said the Steam, clearing its throat; '*Rrrrrraaa! Brraaaaa! Prrrp!* It's a trifle windy up here; and, Great Boilers! how it rains!'

'We're drowning,' said the scuppers. They had been doing nothing else all night, but this steady thrash of rain above them seemed to be the end of the world.

'That's all right. We'll be easier in an hour or two. First the wind and then the rain. Soon you may make sail again! *Grrraaaaaah! Drrrraaaa! Drrrp!* I have a notion that the sea is going down already. If it does you'll learn something about rolling. We've only pitched till now. By the way, aren't you chaps in the hold a little easier than you were?'

There was just as much groaning and straining as ever, but it was not so loud or squeaky in tone; and when the ship quivered she did not jar stiffly, like a poker hit on the floor, but gave with a supple little waggle, like a perfectly balanced golf-club.

'We have made a most amazing discovery,' said the stringers, one after another. 'A discovery that entirely changes the situation. We have found, for the first time in the history of shipbuilding, that the inward pull of the deck-beams and the outward thrust of the frames lock us, as it were, more closely in our places, and enables us to endure a strain which is entirely without parallel in the records of marine architecture.'

The Steam turned a laugh quickly into a roar up the fog-horn. 'What massive intellects you great stringers have,' he said softly, when he had finished.

'We also,' began the deck-beams, 'are discoverers and geniuses. We are of opinion that the support of the hold-pillars materially helps us. We find that we lock up on them when we are subjected to a heavy and singular weight of sea above.'

Here the *Dimbula* shot down a hollow, lying almost on her side – righting at the bottom with a wrench and a spasm.

'In these cases – are you aware of this, Steam? – the plating at the bows, and particularly at the stern – we would also mention the floors beneath us – help *us* to resist any tendency to spring.' The frames spoke, in the solemn, awed voice which people use when they have just come across something entirely new for the very first time.

'I'm only a poor puffy little flutterer,' said the Steam, 'but I have to stand a good deal of pressure in my business. It's all tremendously interesting. Tell us some more. You fellows are so strong.'

'Watch us and you'll see,' said the bow-plates, proudly. 'Ready, behind there! Here's the Father and Mother of Waves coming! Sit tight, rivets all!' A great sluicing comber thundered by, but through the scuffle and confusion the Steam could hear the low, quick cries of the ironwork as the various strains took them – cries like these: 'Easy, now – easy! *Now* push for all your strength! Hold out! Give a fraction! Hold up! Pull in! Shove crossways! Mind the strain at the ends! Grip, now! Bite tight! Let the water get away from under – and there she goes!'

The wave raced off into the darkness, shouting, 'Not bad, that, if it's your first run!' and the drenched and ducked ship throbbed to the beat of the engines inside her. All three cylinders were white with the salt spray that had come down through the engine-room hatch; there was white fur on the canvas-bound steam-pipes, and even the bright-work deep below was speckled and soiled; but the cylinders had learned to make the most of steam that was half water, and were pounding along cheerfully.

'How's the noblest outcome of human ingenuity hitting it?' said the Steam, as he whirled through the engine-room.

'Nothing for nothing in this world of woe,' the cylinders answered, as though they had been working for centuries, 'and precious little for seventy-five pounds' head. We've made two knots this last hour and a quarter! Rather humiliating for eight hundred horse-power, isn't it?'

'Well, it's better than drifting astern, at any rate. You seem rather less – how shall I put it? – stiff in the back than you were.'

'If you'd been hammered as we've been this night, you wouldn't be stiff – iff – iff, either. Theoreti – retti – retti – cally, of course, rigidity is the thing. Purrr – purr – practically, there has to be a little give and take. *We* found that out by working on our sides for five minutes at a stretch – cheh – chh. How's the weather?'

'Sea's going down fast,' said the Steam.

'Good business,' said the high-pressure cylinder. 'Whack her up, boys. They've given us five pounds more steam,' and he began humming the first bars of 'Said the young Obadiah to the old Obadiah', which, as you may have noticed, is a pet tune among engines not built for high speed. Racing-liners with twin-screws sing 'The Turkish Patrol' and the overture to the 'Bronze Horse', and 'Madame Angot', till something goes wrong, and then they render Gounod's 'Funeral March of a Marionette', with variations.

'You'll learn a song of your own some fine day,' said the Steam, as he flew up the fog-horn for one last bellow.

Next day the sky cleared and the sea dropped a little, and the *Dimbula* began to roll from side to side till every inch of iron in her was sick and giddy. But luckily they did not all feel ill at the same time: otherwise she would have opened out like a wet paper box.

The Steam whistled warnings as he went about his business: it is in this short, quick roll and tumble that follows a heavy sea that most of the accidents happen, for then everything thinks that the worst is over and goes off guard. So he orated and chattered till the beams and frames and floors and stringers and things had learned how to lock down and lock up on one another, and endure this new kind of strain.

They found ample time to practise, for they were sixteen days at sea, and it was foul weather till within a hundred miles of New York. The *Dimbula* picked up her pilot, and came in covered with salt and red rust. Her funnel was dirty grey from top to bottom; two boats had been carried away; three copper ventilators looked like hats after a fight with the police; the bridge had a dimple in the middle of it; the house that covered the steam steering-gear was split as with hatchets; there was a bill for small repairs in the engine-room almost as long as the screw-shaft; the forward cargo-hatch fell into bucket-staves when they raised the iron cross-bars; and the steam-capstan had been badly wrenched on its bed. Altogether, as the skipper said, it was 'a pretty general average'.

'But she's soupled,' he said to Mr Buchanan. 'For all her dead weight she rode like a yacht. Ye mind that last blow off the Banks? I am proud of her, Buck.'

'It's vera good,' said the chief engineer, looking along the dishevelled decks. 'Now, a man judgin' superfeecially would say we were a wreck, but we know otherwise – by experience.'

Naturally everything in the *Dimbula* fairly stiffened with pride, and the foremast and the forward collision-bulkhead, who are pushing creatures, begged the Steam to warn the Port of New York of their arrival. 'Tell those big boats all about us,' they said. 'They seem to take us quite as a matter of course.'

It was a glorious, clear, dead calm morning, and in single file, with less than half a mile between each, their bands playing and their tug-boats shouting and waving handkerchiefs, were the *Majestic*, the *Paris*, the *Touraine*, the *Servia*, the *Kaiser Wilhelm II*, and the *Werkendam*, all statelily going out to sea. As the *Dimbula* shifted her helm to give the great boats clear way, the Steam (who knows far too much to mind making an exhibition of himself now and then) shouted:

'Oyez! Oyez! Oyez! Princes, Dukes, and Barons of the High Seas! Know ye by these presents, we are the *Dimbula*, fifteen days nine hours from Liverpool, having crossed the Atlantic with three thousand ton of cargo for the first time in our career! We have not foundered. We are here. 'Eer! 'Eer! We are not disabled. But we have had a time wholly unparalleled in the annals of ship-building! Our decks were swept! We pitched; we rolled! We thought we were going to die! *Hi! Hi!* But we didn't. We wish to give notice that we have come to New York all the way across the Atlantic, through the worst weather in the world; and we are the *Dimbula!* We are – arr – ha – ha – ha-r-r-r!'

The beautiful line of boats swept by as steadily as the procession of the Seasons. The *Dimbula* heard the *Majestic* say, 'Hmph!' and the *Paris* grunted, 'How!' and the *Touraine* said, 'Oui!' with a little coquettish flicker of steam; and the *Servia* said, 'Haw!' and the *Kaiser* and the *Werkendam* said, 'Hoch!' Dutch-fashion – and that was absolutely all.

'I did my best,' said the Steam, gravely, 'but I don't think they were much impressed with us, somehow. Do you?'

'It's simply disgusting,' said the bow-plates. 'They might have seen what we've been through. There isn't a ship on the sea that has suffered as we have – is there, now?'

'Well, I wouldn't go so far as that,' said the Steam, 'because I've worked on some of those boats, and sent them through weather quite as bad as the fortnight that we've had, in six days; and some of them are a little over ten thousand tons, I believe. Now I've seen the *Majestic*, for instance, ducked from her bows to her funnel; and I've helped the *Arizona*, I think she was, to back off an iceberg she met with one dark night; and I had to run out of the *Paris*'s engine-room, one day, because there was thirty foot of water in it. Of course, I don't deny – ' The

Steam shut off suddenly, as a tug-boat, loaded with a political club and a brass band, that had been to see a New York senator off to Europe, crossed their bows, going to Hoboken. There was a long silence that reached, without a break, from the cut-water to the propeller-blades of the *Dimbula*.

Then a new, big voice said slowly and thickly, as though the owner had just waked up: 'It's my conviction that I have made a fool of myself.'

The Steam knew what had happened at once; for when a ship finds herself all the talking of the separate pieces ceases and melts into one voice, which is the soul of the ship.

'Who are you?' he said, with a laugh.

'I am the *Dimbula*, of course. I've never been anything else except that – and a fool!'

The tug-boat, which was doing its very best to be run down, got away just in time, its band playing clashily and brassily a popular but impolite air:

> In the days of old Rameses – are you on?
> In the days of old Rameses – are you on?
> In the days of old Rameses,
> That story had paresis,
> Are you on – are you on – are you on?

'Well, I'm glad you've found yourself,' said the Steam. 'To tell the truth I was a little tired of talking to all those ribs and stringers. Here's Quarantine. After that we'll go to our wharf and clean up a little, and – next month we'll do it all over again.'

The Maltese Cat

THEY HAD GOOD REASON to be proud, and better reason to be afraid, all twelve of them; for, though they had fought their way, game by game, up the teams entered for the polo tournament, they were meeting the Archangels that afternoon in the final match; and the Archangels' men were playing with half a dozen ponies apiece. As the game was divided into six quarters of eight minutes each, that meant a fresh pony after every halt. The Skidars' team, even supposing there were no accidents, could only supply one pony for every other change; and two to one is heavy odds. Again, as Shiraz, the grey Syrian, pointed out, they were meeting the pink and pick of the polo ponies of Upper India; ponies that had cost from a thousand rupees each, while they themselves were a cheap lot gathered, often from country carts, by their masters who belonged to a poor but honest native infantry regiment.

'Money means pace and weight,' said Shiraz, rubbing his black silk nose dolefully along his neat-fitting boot, 'and by the maxims of the game as I know it – '

'Ah, but we aren't playing the maxims,' said the Maltese Cat. 'We're playing the game, and we've the great advantage of knowing the game. Just think a stride, Shiraz. We've pulled up from bottom to second place in two weeks against all those fellows on the ground here; and that's because we play with our heads as well as with our feet.'

'It makes me feel undersized and unhappy all the same,' said Kittiwynk, a mouse-coloured mare with a red browband and the cleanest pair of legs that ever an aged pony owned. 'They've twice our size, these others.'

Kittiwynk looked at the gathering and sighed. The hard, dusty Umballa polo-ground was lined with thousands of soldiers, black and white, not counting hundreds and hundreds of carriages, and drags, and dog-carts, and ladies with brilliant-coloured parasols, and officers in uniform and out of it, and crowds of natives behind them; and orderlies on camels who had halted to watch the game, instead of carrying letters up and down the station, and native horse-dealers running about on thin-eared Biluchi mares, looking for a chance to sell a few first-class polo ponies. Then there were the ponies of thirty teams that had entered for the Upper India Free-for-All Cup – nearly every pony of worth and dignity from Mhow to Peshawar, from Allahabad to Multan; prize ponies, Arabs, Syrian, Barb, country bred, Deccanee, Waziri, and Kabul ponies of every colour and shape and temper that you could imagine. Some of them were in mat-roofed stables close to the polo-ground, but most were under saddle while their masters, who had been defeated in the earlier games, trotted in and out and told each other exactly how the game should be played.

It was a glorious sight, and the come-and-go of the little quick hoofs, and the incessant salutations of ponies that had met before on other polo-grounds or racecourses, were enough to drive a four-footed thing wild.

But the Skidars' team were careful not to know their neighbours, though half the ponies on the ground were anxious to scrape acquaintance with the little fellows that had come from the North, and, so far, had swept the board.

'Let's see,' said a soft, golden-coloured Arab, who had been playing very badly the day before, to the Maltese Cat, 'didn't we meet in Abdul Rahman's stable in Bombay four seasons ago? I won the Paikpattan Cup next season, you may remember.'

'Not me,' said the Maltese Cat politely. 'I was at Malta then, pulling a vegetable cart. I don't race. I play the game.'

'O–oh!' said the Arab, cocking his tail and swaggering off.

'Keep yourselves to yourselves,' said the Maltese Cat to his companions. 'We don't want to rub noses with all those goose-rumped half-breeds of Upper India. When we've won this cup they'll give their shoes to know us.'

'*We* shan't win the cup,' said Shiraz. 'How do you feel?'

'Stale as last night's feed when a muskrat has run over it,' said Polaris, a rather heavy-shouldered grey, and the rest of the team agreed with him.

'The sooner you forget that the better,' said the Maltese Cat cheerfully. 'They've finished tiffin in the big tent. We shall be wanted now. If your saddles are not comfy, kick. If your bits aren't easy, rear, and let the *saises* know whether your boots are tight.'

Each pony had his *sais*, his groom, who lived and ate and slept with the pony, and had betted a great deal more than he could afford on the result of the game. There was no chance of anything going wrong, and, to make sure, each *sais* was shampooing the legs of his pony to the last minute. Behind the *saises* sat as many of the Skidars' regiment as had leave to attend the match – about half the native officers, and a hundred or two dark, black-bearded men with the regimental pipers nervously

fingering the big beribboned bagpipes. The Skidars were what they call
a Pioneer regiment; and the bagpipes made the national music of half
the men. The native officers held bundles of polo-sticks, long cane-
handled mallets, and as the grandstand filled after lunch they arranged
themselves by ones and twos at different points round the ground, so
that if a stick were broken the player would not have far to ride for a
new one. An impatient British cavalry band struck up 'If you want to
know the time, ask a p'leeceman!' and the two umpires in light dust-
coats danced out on two little excited ponies. The four players of the
Archangels' team followed, and the sight of their beautiful mounts
made Shiraz groan again.

'Wait till we know,' said the Maltese Cat. 'Two of 'em are playing in
blinkers, and that means they can't see to get out of the way of their
own side, or they *may* shy at the umpires' ponies. They've *all* got white
web reins that are sure to stretch or slip!'

'And,' said Kittiwynk, dancing to take the stiffness out of her, 'they
carry their whips in their hands instead of on their wrists. Hah!'

'True enough. No man can manage his stick and his reins, and his
whip that way,' said the Maltese Cat. 'I've fallen over every square yard
of the Malta ground, and *I* ought to know.' He quivered his little flea-
bitten withers just to show how satisfied he felt; but his heart was not so
light. Ever since he had drifted into India on a troopship, taken, with an
old rifle, as part payment for a racing debt, the Maltese Cat had played
and preached polo to the Skidars' team on the Skidars' stony polo-
ground. Now a polo-pony is like a poet. If he is born with a love for the
game he can be made. The Maltese Cat knew that bamboos grew
solely in order that polo-balls might be turned from their roots, that
grain was given to ponies to keep them in hard condition, and that
ponies were shod to prevent them slipping on a turn. But, besides all
these things, he knew every trick and device of the finest game of the
world, and for two seasons he had been teaching the others all he knew
or guessed.

'Remember,' he said for the hundredth time as the riders came up,
'we *must* play together, and you *must* play with your heads. Whatever
happens, follow the ball. Who goes out first?'

Kittiwynk, Shiraz, Polaris, and a short high little bay fellow with
tremendous hocks and no withers worth speaking of (he was called
Corks) were being girthed up, and the soldiers in the background
stared with all their eyes.

'I want you men to keep quiet,' said Lutyens, the captain of the team,
'and especially *not* to blow your pipes.'

'Not if we win, Captain Sahib?' asked a piper.

'If we win, you can do what you please,' said Lutyens, with a smile, as he slipped the loop of his stick over his wrist, and wheeled to canter to his place. The Archangels' ponies were a little bit above themselves on account of the many-coloured crowd so close to the ground. Their riders were excellent players, but they were a team of crack players instead of a crack team; and that made all the difference in the world. They honestly meant to play together, but it is very hard for four men, each the best of the team he is picked from, to remember that in polo no brilliancy of hitting or riding makes up for playing alone. Their captain shouted his orders to them by name, and it is a curious thing that if you call his name aloud in public after an Englishman you make him hot and fretty. Lutyens said nothing to his men because it had all been said before. He pulled up Shiraz, for he was playing 'back', to guard the goal. Powell on Polaris was half-back, and Macnamara and Hughes on Corks and Kittiwynk were forwards. The tough bamboo-root ball was put into the middle of the ground one hundred and fifty yards from the ends, and Hughes crossed sticks, heads-up, with the captain of the Archangels, who saw fit to play forward, and that is a place from which you cannot easily control the team. The little click as the cane-shafts met was heard all over the ground, and then Hughes made some sort of quick wrist-stroke that just dribbled the ball a few yards. Kittiwynk knew that stroke of old, and followed as a cat follows a mouse. While the captain of the Archangels was wrenching his pony round Hughes struck with all his strength, and next instant Kittiwynk was away, Corks followed close behind her, their little feet pattering like raindrops on glass.

'Pull out to the left,' said Kittiwynk between her teeth, 'it's coming our way, Corks!'

The back and half-back of the Archangels were tearing down on her just as she was within reach of the ball. Hughes leaned forward with a loose rein, and cut it away to the left almost under Kittiwynk's feet, and it hopped and skipped off to Corks, who saw that, if he were not quick, it would run beyond the boundaries. That long bouncing drive gave the Archangels time to wheel and send three men across the ground to head off Corks. Kittiwynk stayed where she was, for she knew the game. Corks was on the ball half a fraction of a second before the others came up, and Macnamara, with a back-handed stroke, sent it back across the ground to Hughes, who saw the way clear to the Archangels' goal, and smacked the ball in before anyone quite knew what had happened.

'That's luck,' said Corks, as they changed ends. 'A goal in three minutes for three hits and no riding to speak of.'

'Don't know,' said Polaris. 'We've made 'em angry too soon.

Shouldn't wonder if they try to rush us off our feet next time.'

'Keep the ball hanging then,' said Shiraz. 'That wears out every pony that isn't used to it.'

Next time there was no easy galloping across the ground. All the Archangels closed up as one man, but there they stayed, for Corks, Kittiwynk, and Polaris were somewhere on the top of the ball, marking time among the rattling sticks, while Shiraz circled about outside, waiting for a chance.

'*We* can do this all day,' said Polaris, ramming his quarters into the side of another pony. 'Where do you think you're shoving to?'

'I'll – I'll be driven in an *ekka* if I know,' was the gasping reply, 'and I'd give a week's feed to get my blinkers off. I can't see anything.'

'The dust is rather bad. Whew! That was one for my off hock. Where's the ball, Corks?'

'Under my tail. At least a man's looking for it there. This is beautiful. They can't use their sticks, and it's driving 'em wild. Give old blinkers a push and he'll go over!'

'Here, don't touch me! I can't see. I'll – I'll back out, I think,' said the pony in blinkers, who knew that if you can't see all round your head you cannot prop yourself against a shock.

Corks was watching the ball where it lay in the dust close to his near fore with Macnamara's shortened stick tap-tapping it from time to time. Kittiwynk was edging her way out of the scrimmage, whisking her stump of a tail with nervous excitement.

'Ho! They've got it,' she snorted. 'Let me out!' and she galloped like a rifle-bullet just behind a tall lanky pony of the Archangels, whose rider was swinging up his stick for a stroke.

'Not today, thank you,' said Hughes, as the blow slid off his raised stick, and Kittiwynk laid her shoulder to the tall pony's quarters, and shoved him aside just as Lutyens on Shiraz sent the ball where it had come from, and the tall pony went skating and slipping away to the left. Kittiwynk, seeing that Polaris had joined Corks in the chase for the ball up the ground, dropped into Polaris's place, and then time was called.

The Skidars' ponies wasted no time in kicking or fuming. They knew each minute's rest meant so much gain, and trotted off to the rails and their *saises*, who began to scrape and blanket and rub them at once.

'Whew!' said Corks, stiffening up to get all the tickle out of the big vulcanite scraper. 'If we were playing pony for pony we'd bend those Archangels double in half an hour. But they'll bring out fresh ones, and fresh ones, and fresh ones after that – you see.'

'Who cares?' said Polaris. 'We've drawn first blood. Is my hock swelling?'

'Looks puffy,' said Corks. 'You must have had rather a swipe. Don't let it stiffen. You'll be wanted again in half an hour.'

'What's the game like?' said the Maltese Cat.

'Ground's like your shoe, except where they've put too much water on it,' said Kittiwynk. 'Then it's slippery. Don't play in the centre. There's a bog there. I don't know how their next four are going to behave, but we kept the ball hanging and made 'em lather for nothing. Who goes out? Two Arabs and a couple of countrybreds! That's bad. What a comfort it is to wash your mouth out!'

Kitty was talking with a neck of a leather-covered soda-water bottle between her teeth and trying to look over her withers at the same time. This gave her a very coquettish air.

'What's bad?' said Grey Dawn, giving to the girth and admiring his well-set shoulders.

'You Arabs can't gallop fast enough to keep yourselves warm – that's what Kitty means', said Polaris, limping to show that his hock needed attention. 'Are you playing "back", Grey Dawn?'

'Looks like it,' said Grey Dawn, as Lutyens swung himself up. Powell mounted the Rabbit, a plain bay countrybred much like Corks, but with mulish ears. Macnamara took Faiz Ullah, a handy short-backed little red Arab with a long tail, and Hughes mounted Benami, an old and sullen brown beast, who stood over in front more than a polo pony should.

'Benami looks like business,' said Shiraz. 'How's your temper, Ben?' The old campaigner hobbled off without answering, and the Maltese Cat looked at the new Archangel ponies prancing about on the ground. They were four beautiful blacks, and they saddled big enough and strong enough to eat the Skidars' team and gallop away with the meal inside them.

'Blinkers again,' said the Maltese Cat. 'Good enough!'

'They're chargers – cavalry chargers!' said Kittiwynk indignantly. '*They'll* never see thirteen three again.'

'They've all been fairly measured and they've all got their certificates,' said the Maltese Cat, 'or they wouldn't be here. We must take things as they come along, and keep our eyes on the ball.'

The game began, but this time the Skidars were penned to their own end of the ground, and the watching ponies did not approve of that.

'Faiz Ullah is shirking, as usual,' said Polaris, with a scornful grunt.

'Faiz Ullah is eating whip,' said Corks. They could hear the leather-thonged polo quirt lacing the little fellow's well-rounded barrel. Then the Rabbit's shrill neigh came across the ground. 'I can't do all the work,' he cried.

'Play the game, don't talk,' the Maltese Cat whickered; and all the ponies wriggled with excitement, and the soldiers and the grooms gripped the railings and shouted. A black pony with blinkers had singled out old Benami, and was interfering with him in every possible way. They could see Benami shaking his head up and down and flapping his underlip.

'There'll be a fall in a minute,' said Polaris. 'Benami is getting stuffy.'

The game flickered up and down between goal-post and goal-post, and the black ponies were getting more confident as they felt they had the legs of the others. The ball was hit out of a little scrimmage, and Benami and the Rabbit followed it; Faiz Ullah only too glad to be quiet for an instant.

The blinkered black pony came up like a hawk, with two of his own side behind him, and Benami's eye glittered as he raced. The question was which pony should make way for the other; each rider was perfectly willing to risk a fall in a good cause. The black who had been driven nearly crazy by his blinkers trusted to his weight and his temper; but Benami knew how to apply his weight and how to keep his temper. They met, and there was a cloud of dust. The black was lying on his side with all the breath knocked out of his body. The Rabbit was a hundred yards up the ground with the ball, and Benami was sitting down. He had slid nearly ten yards, but he had had his revenge, and sat cracking his nostrils till the black pony rose.

'That's what you get for interfering. Do you want any more?' said Benami, and he plunged into the game. Nothing was done because Faiz Ullah would not gallop, though Macnamara beat him whenever he could spare a second. The fall of the black pony had impressed his companions tremendously, and so the Archangels could not profit by Faiz Ullah's bad behaviour.

But as the Maltese Cat said, when time was called and the four came back blowing and dripping, Faiz Ullah ought to have been kicked all round Umballa. If he did not behave better next time, the Maltese Cat promised to pull out his Arab tail by the root and eat it.

There was no time to talk, for the third four were ordered out.

The third quarter of a game is generally the hottest, for each side thinks that the others must be pumped; and most of the winning play in a game is made about that time.

Lutyens took over the Maltese Cat with a pat and a hug, for Lutyens valued him more than anything else in the world. Powell had Shikast, a little grey rat with no pedigree and no manners outside polo; Macnamara mounted Bamboo, the largest of the team, and Hughes took Who's Who, *alias* The Animal. He was supposed to have Australian blood in his veins, but he looked like a clothes horse, and you could whack him on the legs with an iron crow-bar without hurting him.

They went out to meet the very flower of the Archangels' team, and when Who's Who saw their elegantly booted legs and their beautiful satiny skins he grinned a grin through his light, well-worn bridle.

'My word!' said Who's Who. 'We must give 'em a little football. Those gentlemen need a rubbing down.'

'No biting,' said the Maltese Cat warningly, for once or twice in his career Who's Who had been known to forget himself in that way.

'Who said anything about biting? I'm not playing tiddlywinks. I'm playing the game.'

The Archangels came down like a wolf on the fold, for they were tired of football and they wanted polo. They got it more and more. Just after the game began, Lutyens hit a ball that was coming towards him rapidly, and it rose in the air, as a ball sometimes will, with the whirr of a frightened partridge. Shikast heard, but could not see it for the minute, though he looked everywhere and up into the air as the Maltese Cat had taught him. When he saw it ahead and overhead, he went forward with Powell as fast as he could put foot to ground. It was then that Powell, a quiet and level-headed man as a rule, became inspired and played a stroke that sometimes comes off successfully on a quiet afternoon of long practice. He took his stick in both hands, and standing up in his stirrups, swiped at the ball in the air, Munipore fashion. There was one second of paralysed astonishment, and then all four sides of the ground went up in a yell of applause and delight as the ball flew true (you could see the amazed Archangels ducking in their saddles to get out of the line of flight, and looking at it with open mouths), and the regimental pipes of the Skidars squealed from the railings as long as the piper had breath.

Shikast heard the stroke; but he heard the head of the stick fly off at the same time. Nine hundred and ninety-nine ponies out of a thousand would have gone tearing on after the ball with a useless player pulling at their heads, but Powell knew him, and he knew Powell; and the instant he felt Powell's right leg shift a trifle on the saddle-flap he headed to the boundary, where a native officer was frantically waving a new stick. Before the shouts had ended Powell was armed again.

Once before in his life the Maltese Cat had heard that very same stroke played off his own back, and had profited by the confusion it made. This time he acted on experience, and leaving Bamboo to guard the goal in case of accidents, came through the others like a flash, head and tail low, Lutyens standing up to ease him – swept on and on before the other side knew what was the matter, and nearly pitched on his head between the Archangels' goalpost as Lutyens tipped the ball in after a straight scurry of a hundred and fifty yards. If there was one thing more than another upon which the Maltese Cat prided himself it was on this quick, streaking kind of run half across the ground. He did not believe in taking balls round the field unless you were clearly over-matched. After this they gave the Archangels five minutes' football, and an expensive fast pony hates football because it rumples his temper.

Who's Who showed himself even better than Polaris in this game. He did not permit any wriggling away, but bored joyfully into the scrimmage as if he had his nose in a feed-box, and were looking for something nice. Little Shikast jumped on the ball the minute it got clear, and every time an Archangel pony followed it he found Shikast standing over it asking what was the matter.

'If we can live through this quarter,' said the Maltese Cat, 'I shan't care. Don't take it out of yourselves. Let them do the lathering.'

So the ponies, as their riders explained afterwards, 'shut up'. The Archangels kept them tied fast in front of their goal, but it cost the Archangels' ponies all that was left of their tempers; and ponies began to kick, and men began to repeat compliments, and they chopped at the legs of Who's Who, and he set his teeth and stayed where he was, and the dust stood up like a tree over the scrimmage till that hot quarter ended.

They found the ponies very excited and confident when they went to their *saises*; and the Maltese Cat had to warn them that the worst of the game was coming.

'Now *we* are all going in for the second time,' said he, 'and *they* are trotting out fresh ponies. You'll think you can gallop, but you'll find you can't; and then you'll be sorry.'

'But two goals to nothing is a halter-long lead,' said Kittiwynk prancing.

'How long does it take to get a goal?' the Maltese Cat answered. 'For pity's sake, don't run away with the notion that the game is half-won just because we happen to be in luck now. They'll ride you into the grandstand if they can; you must *not* give 'em a chance. Follow the ball.'

'Football, as usual?' said Polaris. 'My hock's half as big as a nose-bag.'

'Don't let them have a look at the ball if you can help it. Now leave me alone. I must get all the rest I can before the last quarter.'

He hung down his head and let all his muscles go slack; Shikast, Bamboo, and Who's Who copying his example.

'Better not watch the game,' he said. 'We aren't playing, and we shall only take it out of ourselves if we grow anxious. Look at the ground and pretend it's fly-time.'

They did their best, but it was hard advice to follow. The hoofs were drumming and the sticks were rattling all up and down the ground, and yells of applause from the English troops told that the Archangels were pressing the Skidars hard. The native soldiers behind the ponies groaned and grunted, and said things in undertones, and presently they heard a long-drawn shout and a clatter of hurrahs!

'One to the Archangels,' said Shikast, without raising his head. 'Time's nearly up. Oh, my sire and dam!'

'Faiz Ullah,' said the Maltese Cat, 'if you don't play to the last nail in your shoes this time, I'll kick you on the ground before all the other ponies.'

'I'll do my best when my time comes,' said the little Arab sturdily.

The *saises* looked at each other gravely as they rubbed their ponies' legs. This was the first time when long purses began to tell, and everybody knew it. Kittiwynk and the others came back with the sweat dripping over their hoofs and their tails telling sad stories.

'They're better than we are,' said Shiraz. 'I knew how it would be.'

'Shut your big head,' said the Maltese Cat; 'we've one goal to the good yet.'

'Yes, but it's two Arabs and two countrybreds to play now,' said Corks. 'Faiz Ullah, remember!' He spoke in a biting voice.

As Lutyens mounted Grey Dawn he looked at his men, and they did not look pretty. They were covered with dust and sweat in streaks. Their yellow boots were almost black, their wrists were red and lumpy, and their eyes seemed two inches deep in their heads, but the expression in the eyes was satisfactory.

'Did you take anything at tiffin?' said Lutyens, and the team shook their heads. They were too dry to talk.

'All right. The Archangels did. They are worse pumped than we are.'

'They've got the better ponies,' said Powell. 'I shan't be sorry when this business is over.'

That fifth quarter was a sad one in every way. Faiz Ullah played like a little red demon; and the Rabbit seemed to be everywhere at once, and Benami rode straight at anything and everything that came in his way, while the umpires on their ponies wheeled like gulls outside the shifting game. But the Archangels had the better mounts – they had kept their racers till late in the game – and never allowed the Skidars to play football. They hit the ball up and down the width of the ground till Benami and the rest were outpaced. Then they went forward, and time and again Lutyens and Grey Dawn were just, and only just, able to send the ball away with a long splitting backhander. Grey Dawn forgot that he was an Arab; and turned from grey to blue as he galloped. Indeed, he forgot too well, for he did not keep his eyes on the ground as an Arab should, but stuck out his nose and scuttled for the dear honour of the game. They had watered the ground once or twice between the quarters, and a careless waterman had emptied the last of his skinful all in one place near the Skidars' goal. It was close to the end of play, and for the tenth time Grey Dawn was bolting after a ball when his near hind foot slipped on the greasy mud and he rolled over and over, pitching Lutyens just clear of the goalpost; and the triumphant Archangels made their goal. Then time was called – two goals all; but Lutyens had to be helped up, and Grey Dawn rose with his near hind leg strained somewhere.

'What's the damage?' said Powell, his arm round Lutyens.

'Collar-bone, of course,' said Lutyens between his teeth. It was the third time he had broken it in two years, and it hurt him.

Powell and the others whistled. 'Game's up,' said Hughes.

'Hold on. We've five good minutes yet, and it isn't my right hand,' said Lutyens. 'We'll stick it out.'

'I say,' said the captain of the Archangels, trotting up. 'Are you hurt, Lutyens? We'll wait if you care to put in a substitute. I wish – I mean – the fact is, you fellows deserve this game if any team does. Wish we could give you a man or some of our ponies – or something.'

'You're awfully good, but we'll play it to a finish, I think.'

The captain of the Archangels stared for a little. 'That's not half bad,' he said, and went back to his own side, while Lutyens borrowed a scarf from one of his native officers and made a sling of it. Then an Archangel galloped up with a big bath-sponge and advised Lutyens to put it under his arm-pit to ease his shoulder, and between them they tied up his left arm scientifically, and one of the native officers leaped forward with four long glasses that fizzed and bubbled.

The team looked at Lutyens piteously, and he nodded. It was the last quarter, and nothing would matter after that. They drank out the dark golden drink, and wiped their moustaches, and things looked more hopeful.

The Maltese Cat had put his nose into the front of Lutyens' shirt, and was trying to say how sorry he was.

'He knows,' said Lutyens, proudly. 'The beggar knows. I've played him without a bridle before now – for fun.'

'It's no fun now,' said Powell. 'But we haven't a decent substitute.'

'No,' said Lutyens. 'It's the last quarter, and we've got to make our goal and win. I'll trust the Cat.'

'If you fall this time you'll suffer a little,' said Macnamara.

'I'll trust the Cat,' said Lutyens.

'You hear that?' said the Maltese Cat proudly to the others. 'It's worth while playing polo for ten years to have that said of you. Now then, my sons, come along. We'll kick up a little bit, just to show the Archangels *this* team haven't suffered.'

And, sure enough, as they went on to the ground the Maltese Cat, after satisfying himself that Lutyens was home in the saddle, kicked out three or four times, and Lutyens laughed. The reins were caught up anyhow in the tips of his strapped hand, and he never pretended to rely on them. He knew the Cat would answer to the least pressure of the leg, and by way of showing off – for his shoulder hurt him very much – he bent the little fellow in a close figure-of-eight in and out between the goalposts. There was a roar from the native officers and men, who dearly loved a piece of *dugabashi* (horse-trick work), as they called it, and the pipes very quietly and scornfully droned out the first bars of a common bazaar-tune called 'Freshly Fresh and Newly New', just as a warning to the other regiments that the Skidars were fit. All the natives laughed.

'And now,' said the Cat, as they took their place, 'remember that this is the last quarter, and follow the ball!'

'Don't need to be told,' said Who's Who.

'Let me go on. All those people on all four sides will begin to crowd in – just as they did at Malta. You'll hear people calling out, and moving forward and being pushed back, and that is going to make the Archangel ponies very unhappy. But if a ball is struck to the boundary, you go after it, and let the people get out of your way. I went over the pole of a four-in-hand once, and picked a game out of the dust by it. Back me up when I run, and follow the ball.'

There was a sort of an all-round sound of sympathy and wonder as the last quarter opened, and then there began exactly what the Maltese Cat had foreseen. People crowded in close to the boundaries, and the Archangels' ponies kept looking sideways at the narrowing space. If you know how a man feels to be cramped at tennis – not because he wants to run out of the court, but because he likes to know that he can at a pinch – you will guess how ponies must feel when they are playing in a box of human beings.

'I'll bend some of those men if I can get away,' said Who's Who, as he rocketed behind the ball; and Bamboo nodded without speaking. They were playing the last ounce in them, and the Maltese Cat had left the goal undefended to join them. Lutyens gave him every order that he could to bring him back, but this was the first time in his career that the little wise grey had ever played polo on his own responsibility, and he was going to make the most of it.

'What are you doing here?' said Hughes, as the Cat crossed in front of him and rode off an Archangel.

'The Cat's in charge – mind the goal!' shouted Lutyens, and bowing forward hit the ball full, and followed on, forcing the Archangels towards their own goal.

'No football,' said the Cat. 'Keep the ball by the boundaries and cramp 'em. Play open order and drive 'em to the boundaries.'

Across and across the ground in big diagonals flew the ball, and whenever it came to a flying rush and a stroke close to the boundaries the Archangel ponies moved stiffly. They did not care to go headlong at a wall of men and carriages, though if the ground had been open they could have turned on a sixpence.

'Wriggle her up the sides,' said the Cat. 'Keep her close to the crowd. They hate the carriages. Shikast, keep her up this side.'

Shikast with Powell lay left and right behind the uneasy scuffle of an open scrimmage, and every time the ball was hit away Shikast galloped on it at such an angle that Powell was forced to hit it towards the boundary; and when the crowd had been driven away from that side, Lutyens would send the ball over to the other, and Shikast would slide desperately after it till his friends came down to help. It was billiards, and no football, this time – billiards in a corner pocket; and the cues were not well chalked.

'If they get us out in the middle of the ground they'll walk away from us. Dribble her along the sides,' cried the Cat.

So they dribbled all along the boundary, where a pony could not come on their right-hand side; and the Archangels were furious, and the umpires had to neglect the game to shout at the people to get back, and several blundering mounted policemen tried to restore order, all close to the scrimmage, and the nerves of the Archangels' ponies stretched and broke like cobwebs.

Five or six times an Archangel hit the ball up into the middle of the ground, and each time the watchful Shikast gave Powell his chance to send it back, and after each return, when the dust had settled, men could see that the Skidars had gained a few yards.

Every now and again there were shouts of ' 'Side! Off side!' from the spectators; but the teams were too busy to care, and the umpires had all they could do to keep their maddened ponies clear of the scuffle.

At last Lutyens missed a short easy stroke, and the Skidars had to fly back helter-skelter to protect their own goal, Shikast leading. Powell stopped the ball with a backhander when it was not fifty yards from the goalposts, and Shikast spun round with a wrench that nearly hoisted Powell out of his saddle.

'Now's our last chance,' said the Cat, wheeling like a cockchafer on a pin. 'We've got to ride it out. Come along.'

Lutyens felt the little chap take a deep breath, and, as it were, crouch under his rider. The ball was hopping towards the right-hand boundary, an Archangel riding for it with both spurs and a whip; but neither spur nor whip would make his pony stretch himself as he neared the crowd. The Maltese Cat glided under his very nose, picking up his hind legs sharp, for there was not a foot to spare between his quarters and the other pony's bit. It was as neat an exhibition as fancy figure-skating. Lutyens hit with all the strength he had left, but the stick slipped a little in his hand, and the ball flew off to the left instead of keeping close to the boundary. Who's Who was far across the ground, thinking hard as he galloped. He repeated, stride for stride, the Cat's manoeuvres with another Archangel pony, nipping the ball away from under his bridle, and clearing his opponent by half a fraction of an inch, for Who's Who was clumsy behind. Then he drove away towards the right as the Maltese Cat came up from the left; and Bamboo held a middle course exactly between them. The three were making a sort of Government-broad-arrow-shaped attack; and there was only the Arch-angels' back to guard the goal; but immediately behind them were three Archangels racing all they knew, and mixed up with them was Powell, sending Shikast along on what he felt was their last hope. It takes a very good man to stand up to the rush of seven crazy ponies in the last quarters of a cup game, when men are riding with their necks for sale, and the ponies are delirious. The Archangels' back missed his stroke, and pulled aside just in time to let the rush go by. Bamboo and Who's Who shortened stride to give the Maltese Cat room, and Lutyens got the goal with a clean, smooth, smacking stroke that was heard all over the field. But there was no stopping the ponies. They poured through the goalposts in one mixed mob, winners and losers together, for the pace had been terrific. The Maltese Cat knew by experience what would happen, and, to save Lutyens, turned to the right with one last effort that strained a back-sinew beyond hope of repair. As he did so he heard the right-hand goal-post crack as a pony cannoned into it – crack, splinter, and fall like a mast. It had been sawed three parts through in case of accidents, but it upset the pony nevertheless, and he blundered into another, who blundered into the left-hand post, and then there was confusion and dust and wood. Bamboo was lying on the ground, seeing stars; an Archangel pony rolled beside him, breathless and angry; Shikast had sat down dog-fashion to avoid falling over the others, and was sliding along on his little bobtail in a cloud of dust; and Powell was sitting on the ground, hammering with his stick and trying to cheer. All the others were shouting at the top of what was left of their voices, and the men who had been split were shouting too. As soon as the people saw no one was hurt, ten thousand native and English shouted and clapped and yelled, and before anyone could stop them the pipers of the Skidars broke on to the ground, with all the native officers and men behind them, and marched up and down, playing a wild northern tune called 'Zakhme Bagãn', and through the insolent blaring of the pipes and the high-pitched native yells you could hear the Archangels' band hammering, 'For they are all jolly good fellows', and then reproachfully to the losing team, 'Ooh, Kafoozalum! Kafoozalum! Kafoozalum!'

Besides all these things and many more, there was a Commander-in-Chief, and an Inspector-General of Cavalry, and the principal veterinary officer in all India, standing on the top of a regimental coach, yelling like schoolboys; and brigadiers and colonels and com-missioners, and hundreds of pretty ladies joined the chorus. But the Maltese Cat stood with his head down, wondering how many legs were left to him; and Lutyens watched the men and ponies pick themselves out of the wreck of the two goalposts, and he patted the Cat very tenderly.

'I say,' said the captain of the Archangels, spitting a pebble out of his mouth, 'will you take three thousand for that pony – as he stands?'

'No, thank you. I've an idea he's saved my life,' said Lutyens, getting off and lying down at full length. Both teams were on the ground too, waving their boots in the air, and coughing and drawing deep breaths, as the *saises* ran up to take away the ponies, and an officious water-carrier sprinkled the players with dirty water till they sat up.

'My Aunt!' said Powell, rubbing his back and looking at the stumps of the goalposts, 'that was a game!'

They played it over again, every stroke of it, that night at the big dinner, when the Free-for-All Cup was filled and passed down the table, and emptied and filled again, and everybody made most eloquent speeches. About two in the morning, when there might have been some singing, a wise little, plain little, grey little head looked in through the open door.

'Hurrah! Bring him in,' said the Archangels; and his *sais*, who was very happy indeed, patted the Maltese Cat on the flank, and he limped in to the blaze of light and the glittering uniforms, looking for Lutyens. He was used to messes, and men's bedrooms, and places where ponies are not usually encouraged, and in his youth had jumped on and off a mess-table for a bet. So he behaved himself very politely, and ate bread dipped in salt, and was petted all round the table, moving gingerly; and they drank his health, because he had done more to win the Cup than any man or horse on the ground.

That was glory and honour enough for the rest of his days, and the Maltese Cat did not complain much when his veterinary surgeon said that he would be no good for polo any more. When Lutyens married, his wife did not allow him to play, so he was forced to be an umpire; and his pony on these occasions was a flea-bitten grey with a neat polo-tail, lame all round, but desperately quick on his feet, and, as everybody knew, Past Pluperfect Prestissimo Player of the Game.

KASPAR'S SONG IN 'VARDA'
(from the Swedish of Stagnelius)

Eyes aloft, over dangerous places,
   The children follow where Psyche flies,
And, in the sweat of their upturned faces,
   Slash with a net at the empty skies.

So it goes they fall amid brambles,
   And sting their toes on the nettle-tops,
Till after a thousand scratches and scrambles
   They wipe their brows, and the hunting stops.

Then to quiet them comes their father
   And stills the riot of pain and grief,
Saying, 'Little ones, go and gather
   Out of my garden a cabbage leaf.

'You will find on it whorls and clots of
   Dull grey eggs that, properly fed,
Turn, by way of the worm, to lots of
   Radiant Psyches raised from the dead.'

'Heaven is beautiful, Earth is ugly,'
   The three-dimensioned preacher saith,
So we must not look where the snail and the slug lie
   For Psyche's birth . . . And that is our death!

'Wireless'

'IT'S A FUNNY THING, this Marconi business, isn't it?' said Mr Shaynor, coughing heavily. 'Nothing seems to make any difference, by what they tell me – storms, hills, or anything; but if that's true we shall know before morning.'

'Of course it's true,' I answered, stepping behind the counter. 'Where's old Mr Cashell?'

'He's had to go to bed on account of his influenza. He said you'd very likely drop in.'

'Where's his nephew?'

'Inside, getting the things ready. He told me that the last time they experimented they put the pole on the roof of one of the big hotels here, and the batteries electrified all the water-supply, and' – he giggled – 'the ladies got shocks when they took their baths.'

'I never heard of that.'

'The hotel wouldn't exactly advertise it, would it? Just now, by what Mr Cashell tells me, they're trying to signal from here to Poole, and they're using stronger batteries than ever. But, you see, he being the guvnor's nephew and all that (and it will be in the papers too), it doesn't matter how they electrify things in this house. Are you going to watch?'

'Very much. I've never seen this game. Aren't you going to bed?'

'We don't close till ten on Saturdays. There's a good deal of influenza in town, too, and there'll be a dozen prescriptions coming in before morning. I generally sleep in the chair here. It's warmer than jumping out of bed every time. Bitter cold, isn't it?'

'Freezing hard. I'm sorry your cough's worse.'

'Thank you. I don't mind cold so much. It's this wind that fair cuts me to pieces.' He coughed again hard and hackingly, as an old lady came in for ammoniated quinine. 'We've just run out of it in bottles, madam,' said Mr Shaynor, returning to the professional tone, 'but if you will wait two minutes, I'll make it up for you, madam.'

I had used the shop for some time, and my acquaintance with the proprietor had ripened into friendship. It was Mr Cashell who revealed to me the purpose and power of Apothecaries' Hall what time a fellow-chemist had made an error in a prescription of mine, had lied to cover his sloth, and when error and lie were brought home to him had written vain letters.

'A disgrace to our profession,' said the thin, mild-eyed man, hotly, after studying the evidence. 'You couldn't do a better service to the profession than report him to Apothecaries' Hall.'

I did so, not knowing what djinns I should evoke; and the result was such an apology as one might make who had spent a night on the rack. I conceived great respect for Apothecaries' Hall, and esteem for Mr Cashell, a zealous craftsman who magnified his calling. Until Mr Shaynor came down from the North his assistants had by no means agreed with Mr Cashell. 'They forget,' said he, 'that, first and foremost, the compounder is a medicine-man. On him depends the physician's reputation. He holds it literally in the hollow of his hand, sir.'

Mr Shaynor's manners had not, perhaps, the polish of the grocery and Italian warehouse next door, but he knew and loved his dispensary work in every detail. For relaxation he seemed to go no farther afield than the romance of drugs – their discovery, preparation, packing, and export – but it led him to the ends of the earth, and on this subject, and the Pharmaceutical Formulary, and Nicholas Culpepper, most confident of physicians, we met.

Little by little I grew to know something of his beginnings and his hopes – of his mother, who had been a schoolteacher in one of the northern counties, and of his red-headed father, a small job-master at Kirby Moors, who died when he was a child; of the examinations he had passed and of their exceeding and increasing difficulty; of his dreams of a shop in London; of his hate for the price-cutting Co-operative stores; and, most interesting, of his mental attitude towards customers.

'There's a way you get into,' he told me, 'of serving them carefully, and I hope, politely, without stopping your own thinking. I've been reading Christie's *New Commercial Plants* all this autumn, and that needs keeping your mind on it, I can tell you. So long as it isn't a prescription, of course, I can carry as much as half a page of Christie in my head, and at the same time I could sell out all that window twice over, and not a penny wrong at the end. As to prescriptions, I think I could make up the general run of 'em in my sleep, almost.'

For reasons of my own, I was deeply interested in Marconi experiments at their outset in England; and it was of a piece with Mr Cashell's unvarying thoughtfulness that, when his nephew the electrician appropriated the house for a long-range installation, he should, as I have said, invite me to see the result.

The old lady went away with her medicine, and Mr Shaynor and I stamped on the tiled floor behind the counter to keep ourselves warm. The shop, by the light of the many electrics, looked like a Paris-diamond mine, for Mr Cashell believed in all the ritual of his craft. Three superb glass jars – red, green, and blue – of the sort that led Rosamund to parting with her shoes – blazed in the broad plate-glass windows, and there was a confused smell of orris, Kodak films, vulcanite, tooth-powder, sachets, and almond-cream in the air. Mr Shaynor fed the dispensary stove, and we sucked cayenne-pepper jujubes and menthol lozenges. The brutal east wind had cleared the streets, and the few passers-by were muffled to their puckered eyes. In the Italian warehouse next door some gay feathered birds and game, hung upon hooks, sagged to the wind across the left edge of our window-frame.

'They ought to take these poultry in – all knocked about like that,' said Mr Shaynor. 'Doesn't it make you feel fair perishing? See that old hare! The wind's nearly blowing the fur off him.'

I saw the belly-fur of the dead beast blown apart in ridges and streaks as the wind caught it, showing bluish skin underneath. 'Bitter cold,' said Mr Shaynor, shuddering. 'Fancy going out on a night like this! Oh, here's young Mr Cashell.'

The door of the inner office behind the dispensary opened, and an energetic, spade-bearded man stepped forth, rubbing his hands.

'I want a bit of tin-foil, Shaynor,' he said. 'Good-evening. My uncle told me you might be coming.' This to me, as I began the first of a hundred questions.

'I've everything in order,' he replied. 'We're only waiting until Poole calls us up. Excuse me a minute. You can come in whenever you like – but I'd better be with the instruments. Give me that tin-foil. Thanks.'

While we were talking, a girl – evidently no customer – had come into the shop, and the face and bearing of Mr Shaynor changed. She leaned confidently across the counter.

'But I can't,' I heard him whisper uneasily – the flush on his cheek was dull red, and his eyes shone like a drugged moth's. 'I can't. I tell you I'm alone in the place.'

'No, you aren't. Who's *that*? Let him look after it for half an hour. A brisk walk will do you good. Ah, come now, John.'

'But he isn't – '

'I don't care. I want you to; we'll only go round by St Agnes. If you don't – '

He crossed to where I stood in the shadow of the dispensary counter, and began some sort of broken apology about a lady-friend.

'Yes,' she interrupted. 'You take the shop for half an hour – to oblige *me*, won't you?'

She had a singularly rich and promising voice that well matched her outline.

'All right,' I said. 'I'll do it – but you'd better wrap yourself up, Mr Shaynor.'

'Oh, a brisk walk ought to help me. We're only going round by the church.' I heard him cough grievously as they went out together.

I refilled the stove, and, after reckless expenditure of Mr Cashell's coal, drove some warmth into the shop. I explored many of the glass-knobbed drawers that lined the walls, tasted some disconcerting drugs, and, by the aid of a few cardamoms, ground ginger, chloric-ether, and dilute alcohol, manufactured a new and wildish drink, of which I bore a glassful to young Mr Cashell, busy in the back office. He laughed shortly when I told him that Mr Shaynor had stepped out – but a frail coil of wire held all his attention, and he had no word for me bewildered among the batteries and rods. The noise of the sea on the beach began to make itself heard as the traffic in the street ceased. Then briefly, but very lucidly, he gave me the names and uses of the mechanism that crowded the tables and the floor.

'When do you expect to get the message from Poole?' I demanded, sipping my liquor out of a graduated glass.

'About midnight, if everything is in order. We've got our installation-pole fixed to the roof of the house. I shouldn't advise you to turn on a tap or anything tonight. We've connected up with the plumbing, and all the water will be electrified.' He repeated to me the history of the agitated ladies at the hotel at the time of the first installation.

'But what *is* it?' I asked. 'Electricity is out of my beat altogether.'

'Ah, if you knew *that* you'd know something nobody knows. It's just It – what we call Electricity, but the magic – the manifestations – the Hertzian waves – are all revealed by *this*. The coherer, we call it.'

He picked up a glass tube not much thicker than a thermometer, in which, almost touching, were two tiny silver plugs, and between them an infinitesimal pinch of metallic dust. 'That's all,' he said, proudly, as though himself responsible for the wonder. 'That is the thing that will reveal to us the Powers whatever the Powers may be – at work – through space – a long distance away.'

Just then Mr Shaynor returned alone and stood coughing his heart out on the mat.

'Serves you right for being such a fool,' said young Mr Cashell, as annoyed as myself at the interruption. 'Never mind – we've all the night before us to see wonders.'

Shaynor clutched the counter, his handkerchief to his lips. When he brought it away I saw two bright red stains.

'I – I've got a bit of a rasped throat from smoking cigarettes,' he panted. 'I think I'll try a cubeb.'

'Better take some of this. I've been compounding while you've been away.' I handed him the brew.

' 'Twon't make me drunk, will it? I'm almost a teetotaller. My word! That's grateful and comforting.'

He set down the empty glass to cough afresh.

'Brr! But it was cold out there! I shouldn't care to be lying in my grave a night like this. Don't *you* ever have a sore throat from smoking?' He pocketed the handkerchief after a furtive peep.

'Oh, yes, sometimes,' I replied, wondering, while I spoke, into what agonies of terror I should fall if ever I saw those bright-red danger-signals under my nose. Young Mr Cashell among the batteries coughed slightly to show that he was quite ready to continue his scientific explanations, but I was thinking still of the girl with the rich voice and the significantly cut mouth, at whose command I had taken charge of the shop. It flashed across me that she distantly resembled the seductive shape on a gold-framed toilet-water advertisement whose charms were unholily heightened by the glare from the red bottle in the window. Turning to make sure, I saw Mr Shaynor's eyes bent in the same direction, and by instinct recognised that the flamboyant thing was to him a shrine. 'What do you take for your – cough?' I asked.

'Well, I'm the wrong side of the counter to believe much in patent medicines. But there are asthma cigarettes and there are pastilles. To tell you the truth, if you don't object to the smell, which is very like incense, I believe, though I'm not a Roman Catholic, Blaudett's Cathedral Pastilles relieve me as much as anything.'

'Let's try.' I had never raided a chemist's shop before, so I was thorough. We unearthed the pastilles – brown, gummy cones of benzoin – and set them alight under the toilet-water advertisement, where they fumed in thin blue spirals.

'Of course,' said Mr Shaynor, to my question, 'what one uses in the shop for one's self comes out of one's pocket. Why, stocktaking in our business is nearly the same as with jewellers – and I can't say more than that. But one gets them' – he pointed to the pastille-box – 'at trade-prices.' Evidently the censing of the gay, seven-tinted wench with the teeth was an established ritual which cost something.

'And when do we shut up shop?'

'We stay like this all night. The guv – old Mr Cashell – doesn't believe in locks and shutters as compared with electric light. Besides, it brings trade. I'll just sit here in the chair by the stove and write a letter, if you don't mind. Electricity isn't my prescription.'

The energetic young Mr Cashell snorted within, and Shaynor settled himself up in his chair over which he had thrown a staring red, black, and yellow Austrian jute blanket, rather like a table-cover. I cast about, amid patent-medicine pamphlets, for something to read, but finding little, returned to the manufacture of the new drink. The Italian warehouse took down its game and went to bed. Across the street blank shutters flung back the gaslight in cold smears; the dried pavement seemed to rough up in goose-flesh under the scouring of the savage wind, and we could hear, long ere he passed, the policeman flapping his arms to keep himself warm. Within, the flavours of cardamoms and chloric-ether disputed those of the pastilles and a score of drugs and perfume and soap scents. Our electric lights, set low down in the windows before the tun-bellied Rosamund jars, flung inward three monstrous daubs of red, blue, and green, that broke into kaleidoscopic lights on the facetted knobs of the drug-drawers, the cut-glass scent flagons, and the bulbs of the sparklet bottles. They flushed the white-tiled floor in gorgeous patches; splashed along the nickel-silver counter-rails, and turned the polished mahogany counter-panels to the likeness of intricate grained marbles – slabs of porphyry and malachite. Mr Shaynor unlocked a drawer, and ere he began to write, took out a meagre bundle of letters. From my place by the stove, I could see the scalloped edges of the paper with a flaring monogram in the corner and could even smell the reek of chypre. At each page he turned toward the toilet-water lady of the advertisement and devoured her with over-luminous eyes. He had drawn the Austrian blanket over his shoulders, and among those warring lights he looked more than ever the incarnation of a drugged moth – a tiger-moth as I thought.

He put his letter into an envelope, stamped it with stiff mechanical movements, and dropped it in the drawer. Then I became aware of the silence of a great city asleep – the silence that underlaid the even voice of the breakers along the sea-front – a thick, tingling quiet of warm life stilled down for its appointed time, and unconsciously I moved about the glittering shop as one moves in a sick-room. Young Mr Cashell was adjusting some wire that crackled from time to time with the tense, knuckle-stretching sound of the electric spark. Upstairs, where a door shut and opened swiftly, I could hear his uncle coughing abed.

'Here,' I said, when the drink was properly warmed, 'take some of this, Mr Shaynor.'

He jerked in his chair with a start and a wrench, and held out his hand for the glass. The mixture, of a rich port-wine colour, frothed at the top.

'It looks,' he said, suddenly, 'it looks – those bubbles – like a string of pearls winking at you – rather like the pearls round that young lady's neck.' He turned again to the advertisement where the female in the dove-coloured corset had seen fit to put on all her pearls before she cleaned her teeth.

'Not bad, is it?' I said.

'Eh?'

He rolled his eyes heavily full on me, and, as I stared, I beheld all meaning and consciousness die out of the swiftly dilating pupils. His figure lost its stark rigidity, softened into the chair, and, chin on chest, hands dropped before him, he rested open-eyed, absolutely still.

'I'm afraid I've rather cooked Shaynor's goose,' I said, bearing the fresh drink to young Mr Cashell. 'Perhaps it was the chloric-ether.'

'Oh, he's all right.' The spade-bearded man glanced at him pityingly. 'Consumptives go off in those sort of doses very often. It's exhaustion . . . I don't wonder. I dare say the liquor will do him good. It's grand stuff,' he finished his share appreciatively. 'Well, as I was saying – before he interrupted – about this little coherer. The pinch of dust, you see, is nickel-filings. The Hertzian waves, you see, come out of space from the station that despatches 'em, and all these little particles are attracted together – cohere, we call it – for just so long as the current passes through them. Now, it's important to remember that the current is an induced current. There are a good many kinds of induction – '

'Yes, but what *is* induction?'

'That's rather hard to explain untechnically. But the long and the short of it is that when a current of electricity passes through a wire there's a lot of magnetism present round that wire; and if you put another wire parallel to, and within what we call its magnetic field – why then, the second wire will also become charged with electricity.'

'On its own account?'

'On its own account.'

'Then let's see if I've got it correctly. Miles off, at Poole, or wherever it is – '

'It will be anywhere in ten years.'

'You've got a charged wire – '

'Charged with Hertzian waves which vibrate, say, two hundred and thirty million times a second.' Mr Cashell snaked his forefinger rapidly through the air.

'All right – a charged wire at Poole, giving out these waves into space. Then this wire of yours sticking out into space – on the roof of the house – in some mysterious way gets charged with those waves from Poole – '

'Or anywhere – it only happens to be Poole tonight.'

'And those waves set the coherer at work, just like an ordinary telegraph-office ticker?'

'No! That's where so many people make the mistake. The Hertzian waves wouldn't be strong enough to work a great heavy Morse instrument like ours. They can only just make that dust cohere, and while it coheres (a little while for a dot and a longer while for a dash) the current from this battery – the home battery' – he laid his hand on the thing – 'can get through to the Morse printing-machine to record the dot or dash. Let me make it clearer. Do you know anything about steam?'

'Very little. But go on.'

'Well, the coherer is like a steam-valve. Any child can open a valve and start a steamer's engines, because a turn of the hand lets in the main steam, doesn't it? Now, this home battery here ready to print is the main steam. The coherer is the valve, always ready to be turned on. The Hertzian wave is the child's hand that turns it.'

'I see. That's marvellous.'

'Marvellous, isn't it? And, remember, we're only at the beginning. There's nothing we shan't be able to do in ten years. I want to live – my God, how I want to live, and see it develop!' He looked through the door at Shaynor breathing lightly in his chair. 'Poor beast! And he wants to keep company with Fanny Brand.'

'Fanny *who?*' I said, for the name struck an obscurely familiar chord in my brain – something connected with a stained handkerchief, and the word 'arterial'.

'Fanny Brand – the girl you kept shop for.' He laughed. 'That's all I know about her, and for the life of me I can't see what Shaynor sees in her, or she in him.'

'*Can't* you see what he sees in her?' I insisted.

'Oh, yes, if *that's* what you mean. She's a great, big, fat lump of a girl, and so on. I suppose that's why he's so crazy after her. She isn't his sort. Well, it doesn't matter. My uncle says he's bound to die before the year's out. Your drink's given him a good sleep, at any rate.' Young Mr Cashell could not catch Mr Shaynor's face, which was half turned to the advertisement.

I stoked the stove anew, for the room was growing cold, and lighted another pastille. Mr Shaynor in his chair, never moving, looked through and over me with eyes as wide and lustreless as those of a dead hare.

'Poole's late,' said young Mr Cashell, when I stepped back. 'I'll just send them a call.'

He pressed a key in the semi-darkness, and with a rending crackle there leaped between two brass knobs a spark, streams of sparks, and sparks again.

'Grand, isn't it? *That's* the Power – our unknown Power – kicking and fighting to be let loose,' said young Mr Cashell. 'There she goes – kick – kick – kick into space. I never get over the strangeness of it when I work a sending-machine – waves going into space, you know. T. R. is our call. Poole ought to answer with L. L. L.'

We waited two, three, five minutes. In that silence, of which the boom of the tide was an orderly part, I caught the clear '*kiss – kiss – kiss*' of the halliards on the roof, as they were blown against the installation-pole.

'Poole is not ready. I'll stay here and call you when he is.'

I returned to the shop, and set down my glass on a marble slab with a careless clink. As I did so, Shaynor rose to his feet, his eyes fixed once more on the advertisement, where the young woman bathed in the light from the red jar simpered pinkly over her pearls. His lips moved without cessation. I stepped nearer to listen. 'And threw – and threw – and threw,' he repeated, his face all sharp with some inexplicable agony.

I moved forward astonished. But it was then he found words – delivered roundly and clearly. These –

> And threw warm gules on Madeleine's young breast.

The trouble passed off his countenance, and he returned lightly to his place, rubbing his hands.

It had never occurred to me, though we had many times discussed reading and prize-competitions as a diversion, that Mr Shaynor ever read Keats, or could quote him at all appositely. There was, after all, a certain stained-glass effect of light on the high bosom of the highly-polished picture which might, by stretch of fancy, suggest, as a vile chromo recalls some incomparable canvas, the line he had spoken. Night, my drink, and solitude were evidently turning Mr Shaynor into a poet. He sat down again and wrote swiftly on his villainous note-paper, his lips quivering.

I shut the door into the inner office and moved up behind him. He made no sign that he saw or heard. I looked over his shoulder, and read, amid half-formed words, sentences, and wild scratches –

> – Very cold it was. Very cold
> The hare – the hare – the hare –
> The birds –

He raised his head sharply, and frowned toward the blank shutters of the poulterer's shop where they jutted out against our window. Then one clear line came –

> The hare, in spite of fur, was very cold.

The head, moving machine-like, turned right to the advertisement where the Blaudett's Cathedral Pastille reeked abominably. He grunted, and went on –

> Incense in a censer –
> Before her darling picture framed in gold –
> Maiden's picture – angel's portrait –

'Hsh!' said Mr Cashell guardedly from the inner office, as though in the presence of spirits. 'There's something coming through from somewhere; but it isn't Poole.' I heard the crackle of sparks as he depressed the keys of the transmitter. In my own brain, too, something crackled, or it might have been the hair on my head. Then I heard my own voice, in a harsh whisper: 'Mr Cashell, there is something coming through here, too. Leave me alone till I tell you.'

'But I thought you'd come to see this wonderful thing – sir,' indignantly at the end.

'Leave me alone till I tell you. Be quiet.'

I watched – I waited. Under the blue-veined hand – the dry hand of the consumptive – came away clear, without erasure –

> And my weak spirit fails
> To think how the dead must freeze –

he shivered as he wrote –

> Beneath the churchyard mould.

Then he stopped, laid the pen down, and leaned back.

For an instant, that was half an eternity, the shop spun before me in a rainbow-tinted whirl, in and through which my own soul most dispassionately considered my own soul as that fought with an over-mastering fear. Then I smelt the strong smell of cigarettes from Mr Shaynor's clothing, and heard, as though it had been the rending of trumpets, the rattle of his breathing. I was still in my place of observation, much as one would watch a rifle-shot at the butts, half-bent, hands on my knees, and head within a few inches of the black, red, and yellow blanket of his shoulder. I was whispering encouragement, evidently to my other self, sounding sentences, such as men pronounce in dreams.

'If he has read Keats, it proves nothing. If he hasn't – like causes *must* beget like effects. There is no escape from this law. *You* ought to be grateful that you know 'St Agnes' Eve' without the book; because, given the circumstances, such as Fanny Brand, who is the key of the enigma, and approximately represents the latitude and longitude of Fanny Brawne; allowing also for the bright red colour of the arterial blood upon the handkerchief, which was just what you were puzzling over in the shop just now; and counting the effect of the professional environment, here almost perfectly duplicated – the result is logical and inevitable. As inevitable as induction.'

Still, the other half of my soul refused to be comforted. It was cowering in some minute and inadequate corner – at an immense distance.

Hereafter, I found myself one person again, my hands still gripping my knees, and my eyes glued on the page before Mr Shaynor. As dreamers accept and explain the upheaval of landscapes and the resurrection of the dead, with excerpts from the evening hymn or the multiplication-table, so I had accepted the facts, whatever they might be, that I should witness, and had devised a theory, sane and plausible to my mind, that explained them all. Nay, I was even in advance of my facts, walking hurriedly before them, assured that they would fit my theory. And all that I now recall of that epoch-making theory are the lofty words: 'If he has read Keats it's the chloric-ether. If he hasn't, it's the identical bacillus, or Hertzian wave of tuberculosis, *plus* Fanny Brand and the professional status which, in conjunction with the main-stream of subconscious thought common to all mankind, has thrown up temporarily an induced Keats.'

Mr Shaynor returned to his work, erasing and rewriting as before with swiftness. Two or three blank pages he tossed aside. Then he wrote, muttering –

The little smoke of a candle that goes out.

'No,' he muttered. 'Little smoke – little smoke – little smoke. What else?' He thrust his chin forward toward the advertisement, where-under the last of the Blaudett's Cathedral Pastilles fumed in its holder. 'Ah!' Then with relief –

The little smoke that dies in moonlight cold.

Evidently he was snared by the rhymes of his first verse, for he wrote and rewrote 'gold – cold – mould' many times. Again he sought inspiration from the advertisement, and set down, without erasure, the line I had overheard –

>		And threw warm gules on Madeleine's young breast.

As I remembered the original it is 'fair' – a trite word – instead of 'young', and I found myself nodding approval, though I admitted that the attempt to reproduce 'its little smoke in pallid moonlight died' was a failure.

Followed without a break ten or fifteen lines of bald prose – the naked soul's confession of its physical yearning for its beloved – unclean as we count uncleanliness; unwholesome, but human exceedingly; the raw material, so it seemed to me in that hour and in that place, whence Keats wove the twenty-sixth, seventh, and eighth stanzas of his poem. Shame I had none in overseeing this revelation; and my fear had gone with the smoke of the pastille.

'That's it,' I murmured. 'That's how it's blocked out. Go on! Ink it in, man. Ink it in!'

Mr Shaynor returned to broken verse wherein 'loveliness' was made to rhyme with a desire to look upon 'her empty dress'. He picked up a fold of the gay, soft blanket, spread it over one hand, caressed it with infinite tenderness, thought, muttered, traced some snatches which I could not decipher, shut his eyes drowsily, shook his head, and dropped the stuff. Here I found myself at fault, for I could not then see (as I do now) in what manner a red, black, and yellow Austrian blanket coloured his dreams.

In a few minutes he laid aside his pen, and, chin on hand, considered the shop with thoughtful and intelligent eyes. He threw down the blanket, rose, passed along a line of drug-drawers, and read the names on the labels aloud. Returning, he took from his desk Christie's *New Commercial Plants* and the old Culpepper that I had given him, opened and laid them side by side with a clerky air, all trace of passion gone from his face, read first in one and then in the other, and paused with pen behind his ear.

'What wonder of Heaven's coming now?' I thought.

'Manna – manna – manna,' he said at last, under wrinkled brows. 'That's what I wanted. Good! Now then! Now then! Good! Good! Oh, by God, that's good!' His voice rose and he spoke rightly and fully without a falter –

>		Candied apple, quince and plum and gourd,
>		And jellies smoother than the creamy curd,
>		And lucent syrups tinct with cinnamon,
>		Manna and dates in Argosy transferred
>		From Fez; and spiced dainties, every one
>		From silken Samarkand to cedared Lebanon.

He repeated it once more, using 'blander' for 'smoother' in the second line; then wrote it down without erasure, but this time (my set eyes missed no stroke of any word) he substituted 'soother' for his atrocious second thought, so that it came away under his hand as it is written in the book – as it is written in the book.

A wind went shouting down the street, and on the heels of the wind followed a spurt and rattle of rain.

After a smiling pause – and good right had he to smile – he began anew, always tossing the last sheet over his shoulder –

> The sharp rain falling on the window-pane,
> Rattling sleet – the wind-blown sleet.

Then prose: 'It is very cold of mornings when the wind brings rain and sleet with it. I heard the sleet on the window-pane outside, and thought of you, my darling. I am always thinking of you. I wish we could both run away like two lovers into the storm and get that little cottage by the sea which we are always thinking about, my own dear darling. We could sit and watch the sea beneath our windows. It would be a fairyland all of our own – a fairy sea – a fairy sea . . . '

He stopped, raised his head, and listened. The steady drone of the Channel along the seafront that had borne us company so long leaped up a note to the sudden fuller surge that signals the change from ebb to flood. It beat in like the change of step throughout an army – this renewed pulse of the sea – and filled our ears till they, accepting it, marked it no longer.

> A fairyland for you and me
> Across the foam – beyond . . .
> A magic foam, a perilous sea.

He grunted again with effort and bit his underlip. My throat dried, but I dared not gulp to moisten it lest I should break the spell that was drawing him nearer and nearer to the high-water mark but two of the sons of Adam have reached. Remember that in all the millions permitted there are no more than five – five little lines – of which one can say: 'These are the pure Magic. These are the clear Vision. The rest is only poetry.' And Mr Shaynor was playing hot and cold with two of them!

I vowed no unconscious thought of mine should influence the blindfold soul, and pinned myself desperately to the other three, repeating and re-repeating –

> A savage spot as holy and enchanted
> As e'er beneath a waning moon was haunted
> By woman wailing for her demon lover.

But though I believed my brain thus occupied, my every sense hung upon the writing under the dry, bony hand, all brown-fingered with chemicals and cigarette-smoke.

> Our windows fronting on the dangerous foam,

(he wrote, after long, irresolute snatches), and then –

> Our open casements facing desolate seas
> Forlorn – forlorn –

Here again his face grew peaked and anxious with that sense of loss I had first seen when the Power snatched him. But this time the agony was tenfold keener. As I watched it mounted like mercury in the tube. It lighted his face from within till I thought the visibly scourged soul must leap forth naked between his jaws, unable to endure. A drop of sweat trickled from my forehead down my nose and splashed on the back of my hand.

> Our windows facing on the desolate seas
> And pearly foam of magic fairyland –

'Not yet – not yet,' he muttered, 'wait a minute. *Please* wait a minute. I shall get it then –

> Our magic windows fronting on the sea,
> The dangerous foam of desolate seas . . .
> For aye.

Ouh, my God!'

From head to heel he shook – shook from the marrow of his bones outwards – then leaped to his feet with raised arms, and slid the chair screeching across the tiled floor where it struck the drawers behind and fell with a jar. Mechanically, I stooped to recover it.

As I rose, Mr Shaynor was stretching and yawning at leisure.

'I've had a bit of a doze,' he said. 'How did I come to knock the chair over? You look rather – '

'The chair startled me,' I answered. 'It was so sudden in this quiet.'

Young Mr Cashell behind his shut door was offendedly silent.

'I suppose I must have been dreaming,' said Mr Shaynor.

'I suppose you must,' I said. 'Talking of dreams – I – I noticed you writing – before – '

He flushed consciously.

'I meant to ask you if you've ever read anything written by a man called Keats.'

'Oh! I haven't much time to read poetry, and I can't say that I remember the name exactly. Is he a popular writer?'

'Middling. I thought you might know him because he's the only poet who was ever a druggist. And he's rather what's called the lover's poet.'

'Indeed. I must dip into him. What did he write about?'

'A lot of things. Here's a sample that may interest you.'

Then and there, carefully, I repeated the verse he had twice spoken and once written not ten minutes ago.

'Ah! Anybody could see he was a druggist from that line about the tinctures and syrups. It's a fine tribute to our profession.'

'I don't know,' said young Mr Cashell, with icy politeness, opening the door one half-inch, 'if you still happen to be interested in our trifling experiments. But, should such be the case – '

I drew him aside, whispering, 'Shaynor seemed going off into some sort of fit when I spoke to you just now. I thought, even at the risk of being rude, it wouldn't do to take you off your instruments just as the call was coming through. Don't you see?'

'Granted – granted as soon as asked,' he said, unbending. 'I *did* think it a shade odd at the time. So that was why he knocked the chair down?'

'I hope I haven't missed anything,' I said.

'I'm afraid I can't say that, but you're just in time for the end of a rather curious performance. You can come in too, Mr Shaynor. Listen, while I read it off.'

The Morse instrument was ticking furiously. Mr Cashell interpreted: ' "K.K.V. Can make nothing of your signals." ' A pause. ' "M.M.V. M.M.V. Signals unintelligible. Purpose anchor Sandown Bay. Examine instruments tomorrow." Do you know what that means? It's a couple of men-o'-war working Marconi signals off the Isle of Wight. They are trying to talk to each other. Neither can read the other's messages, but all their messages are being taken in by our receiver here. They've been going on for ever so long. I wish you could have heard it.'

'How wonderful!' I said. 'Do you mean we're overhearing Portsmouth ships trying to talk to each other – that we're eavesdropping across half South England?'

'Just that. Their transmitters are all right, but their receivers are out of order, so they only get a dot here and a dash there. Nothing clear.'

'Why is that?'

'God knows – and Science will know tomorrow. Perhaps the induction is faulty; perhaps the receivers aren't tuned to receive just the number of vibrations per second that the transmitter sends. Only a word here and there. Just enough to tantalise.'

Again the Morse sprang to life.

'That's one of 'em complaining now. Listen: "*Disheartening – most disheartening.*" It's quite pathetic. Have you ever seen a spiritualistic seance? It reminds me of that sometimes – odds and ends of messages coming out of nowhere – a word here and there – no good at all.'

'But mediums are all impostors,' said Mr Shaynor, in the doorway, lighting an asthma-cigarette. 'They only do it for the money they can make. I've seen 'em.'

'Here's Poole, at last – clear as a bell. L.L.L. Now we shan't be long.' Mr Cashell rattled the keys merrily. 'Anything you'd like to tell 'em?'

'No, I don't think so,' I said. 'I'll go home and get to bed. I'm feeling a little tired.'

THE RETURN OF THE CHILDREN

Neither the harps nor the crowns amused, nor the cherubs' dove-
    winged races –
Holding hands forlornly the Children wandered beneath the Dome;
Plucking the radiant robes of the passers-by, and with pitiful faces
Begging what Princes and Powers refused: 'Ah, please will you let us
    go home?'

Over the jewelled floor, nigh weeping, ran to them Mary the Mother,
Kneeled and caressed and made promise with kisses, and drew them
    along to the gateway –
Yea, the all-iron unbribeable Door which Peter must guard and none
    other,
Straightway She took the Keys from his keeping, and opened and freed
    them straightway.

Then to Her Son, Who had seen and smiled, She said: 'On the night
    that I bore Thee,
What didst Thou care for a love beyond mine or a heaven that was not
    my arm?
Didst Thou push from the nipple, O Child, to hear the angels adore
    Thee?
When we two lay in the breath of the kine?' And He said: 'Thou hast
    done no harm.'

So through the Void the Children ran homeward merrily hand in
    hand,
Looking neither to left nor right where the breathless Heavens stood
    still;
And the Guards of the Void resheathed their swords, for they heard the
    Command:
'Shall I that have suffered the Children to come to me hold them
    against their will?'

'They'

ONE VIEW CALLED ME to another; one hilltop to its fellow, half across the county, and since I could answer at no more trouble than the snapping forward of a lever, I let the county flow under my wheels. The orchid-studded flats of the East gave way to the thyme, ilex, and grey grass of the Downs; these again to the rich cornland and fig trees of the lower coast, where you carry the beat of the tide on your left hand for fifteen level miles; and when at last I turned inland through a huddle of rounded hills and woods I had run myself clean out of my known marks. Beyond that precise hamlet which stands godmother to the capital of the United States, I found hidden villages where bees, the only things awake, boomed in eighty-foot lindens that overhung grey Norman churches; miraculous brooks diving under stone bridges built for heavier traffic than would ever vex them again; tithe-barns larger than their churches, and an old smithy that cried out aloud how it had once been a hall of the Knights of the Temple. Gypsies I found on a common where the gorse, bracken, and heath fought it out together up a mile of Roman road; and a little farther on I disturbed a red fox rolling dog-fashion in the naked sunlight.

As the wooded hills closed about me I stood up in the car to take the bearings of that great Down whose ringed head is a landmark for fifty miles across the low countries. I judged that the lie of the country would bring me across some westward-running road that went to his feet, but I did not allow for the confusing veils of the woods. A quick turn plunged me first into a green cutting brim-full of liquid sunshine, next into a gloomy tunnel where last year's dead leaves whispered and scuffled about my tyres. The strong hazel stuff meeting overhead had not been cut for a couple of generations at least, nor had any axe helped the moss-cankered oak and beech to spring above them. Here the road changed frankly into a carpeted ride on whose brown velvet spent primrose-clumps showed like jade, and a few sickly, white-stalked blue-bells nodded together. As the slope favoured I shut off the power and slid over the whirled leaves, expecting every moment to meet a keeper; but I only heard a jay, far off, arguing against the silence under the twilight of the trees.

Still the track descended. I was on the point of reversing and working my way back on the second speed ere I ended in some swamp, when I saw sunshine through the tangle ahead and lifted the brake.

It was down again at once. As the light beat across my face my fore-wheels took the turf of a great still lawn from which sprang horsemen ten feet high with levelled lances, monstrous peacocks, and sleek round-headed maids of honour – blue, black, and glistening – all of clipped yew. Across the lawn – the marshalled woods besieged it on three sides – stood an ancient house of lichened and weather-worn stone, with mullioned windows and roofs of rose-red tile. It was flanked by semi-circular walls, also rose-red, that closed the lawn on the fourth side, and at their feet a box hedge grew man-high. There were doves on the roof about the slim brick chimneys, and I caught a glimpse of an octagonal dove-house behind the screening wall.

Here, then, I stayed; a horseman's green spear laid at my breast; held by the exceeding beauty of that jewel in that setting.

'If I am not packed off for a trespasser, or if this knight does not ride a wallop at me,' thought I, 'Shakespeare and Queen Elizabeth at least must come out of that half-open garden door and ask me to tea.'

A child appeared at an upper window, and I thought the little thing waved a friendly hand. But it was to call a companion, for presently another bright head showed. Then I heard a laugh among the yew-peacocks, and turning to make sure (till then I had been watching the house only) I saw the silver of a fountain behind a hedge thrown up against the sun. The doves on the roof cooed to the cooing water; but between the two notes I caught the utterly happy chuckle of a child absorbed in some light mischief.

The garden door – heavy oak sunk deep in the thickness of the wall – opened further: a woman in a big garden hat set her foot slowly on the time-hollowed stone step and as slowly walked across the turf. I was forming some apology when she lifted up her head and I saw that she was blind.

'I heard you,' she said. 'Isn't that a motor car?'

'I'm afraid I've made a mistake in my road. I should have turned off up above – I never dreamed . . . ' I began.

'But I'm very glad. Fancy a motor car coming into the garden! It will be such a treat –'

She turned and made as though looking about her. 'You – you haven't seen anyone, have you – perhaps?'

'No one to speak to, but the children seemed interested at a distance.'

'Which?'

'I saw a couple up at the window just now, and I think I heard a little chap in the grounds.'

'Oh, lucky you!' she cried, and her face brightened. 'I hear them, of course, but that's all. You've seen them and heard them?'

'Yes,' I answered. 'And if I know anything of children, one of them's having a beautiful time by the fountain yonder. Escaped, I should imagine.'

'You're fond of children?'

I gave her one or two reasons why I did not altogether hate them.

'Of course, of course,' she said. 'Then you understand. Then you won't think it foolish if I ask you to take your car through the gardens, once or twice – quite slowly. I'm sure they'd like to see it. They see so little, poor things. One tries to make their life pleasant, but – ' she threw out her hands towards the woods. 'We're so out of the world here.'

'That will be splendid,' I said. 'But I can't cut up your grass.'

She faced to the right. 'Wait a minute,' she said. 'We're at the South gate, aren't we? Behind those peacocks there's a flagged path. We call it the Peacocks' Walk. You can't see it from here, they tell me, but if you squeeze along by the edge of the wood you can turn at the first peacock and get on to the flags.'

It was sacrilege to wake that dreaming house-front with the clatter of machinery, but I swung the car to clear the turf, brushed along the edge of the wood and turned in on the broad stone path where the fountain-basin lay like one star-sapphire.

'May I come too?' she cried. 'No, please don't help me. They'll like it better if they see me.'

She felt her way lightly to the front of the car, and with one foot on the step she called: 'Children, oh, children! Look and see what's going to happen!'

The voice would have drawn lost souls from the Pit, for the yearning that underlay its sweetness, and I was not surprised to hear an answering shout behind the yews. It must have been the child by the fountain, but he fled at our approach, leaving a little toy boat in the water. I saw the glint of his blue blouse among the still horsemen.

Very disposedly we paraded the length of the walk and at her request backed again. This time the child had got the better of his panic, but stood far off and doubting.

'The little fellow's watching us,' I said. 'I wonder if he'd like a ride.'

'They're very shy still. Very shy. But, oh, lucky you to be able to see them! Let's listen.'

I stopped the machine at once, and the humid stillness, heavy with the scent of box, cloaked us deep. Shears I could hear where some gardener was clipping; a mumble of bees and broken voices that might have been the doves.

'Oh, unkind!' she said weariedly.

'Perhaps they're only shy of the motor. The little maid at the window looks tremendously interested.'

'Yes?' She raised her head. 'It was wrong of me to say that. They are really fond of me. It's the only thing that makes life worth living – when they're fond of you, isn't it? I daren't think what the place would be without them. By the way, is it beautiful?'

'I think it is the most beautiful place I have ever seen.'

'So they all tell me. I can feel it, of course, but that isn't quite the same thing.'

'Then have you never – ?' I began, but stopped abashed.

'Not since I can remember. It happened when I was only a few months old, they tell me. And yet I must remember something, else how could I dream about colours. I see light in my dreams, and colours, but I never see *them*. I only hear them just as I do when I'm awake.'

'It's difficult to see faces in dreams. Some people can, but most of us haven't the gift,' I went on, looking up at the window where the child stood all but hidden.

'I've heard that too,' she said. 'And they tell me that one never sees a dead person's face in a dream. Is that true?'

'I believe it is – now I come to think of it.'

'But how is it with yourself – yourself?' The blind eyes turned towards me.

'I have never seen the faces of my dead in any dream,' I answered.

'Then it must be as bad as being blind.'

The sun had dipped behind the woods and the long shades were possessing the insolent horsemen one by one. I saw the light die from off the top of a glossy-leaved lance and all the brave hard green turn to soft black. The house, accepting another day at end, as it had accepted an hundred thousand gone, seemed to settle deeper into its rest among the shadows.

'Have you ever wanted to?' she said after the silence

'Very much sometimes,' I replied. The child had left the window as the shadows closed upon it.

'Ah! So've I, but I don't suppose it's allowed . . . Where d'you live?'

'Quite the other side of the county – sixty miles and more, and I must be going back. I've come without my big lamp.'

'But it's not dark yet. I can feel it.'

'I'm afraid it will be by the time I get home. Could you lend me someone to set me on my road at first? I've utterly lost myself.'

'I'll send Madden with you to the crossroads. We are so out of the world, I don't wonder you were lost! I'll guide you round to the front of the house; but you will go slowly, won't you, till you're out of the grounds? It isn't foolish, do you think?'

'I promise you I'll go like this,' I said, and let the car start herself down the flagged path.

We skirted the left wing of the house, whose elaborately cast lead guttering alone was worth a day's journey; passed under a great rose-grown gate in the red wall, and so round to the high front of the house which in beauty and stateliness as much excelled the back as that all others I had seen.

'Is it so very beautiful?' she said wistfully when she heard my raptures. 'And you like the lead-figures too? There's the old azalea garden behind. They say that this place must have been made for children. Will you help me out, please? I should like to come with you as far as the crossroads, but I mustn't leave them. Is that you, Madden? I want you to show this gentleman the way to the crossroads. He has lost his way but – he has seen them.'

A butler appeared noiselessly at the miracle of old oak that must be called the front door, and slipped aside to put on his hat. She stood looking at me with open blue eyes in which no sight lay, and I saw for the first time that she was beautiful.

'Remember,' she said quietly, 'if you are fond of them you will come again,' and disappeared within the house.

The butler in the car said nothing till we were nearly at the lodge gates, where catching a glimpse of a blue blouse in a shrubbery I swerved amply lest the devil that leads little boys to play should drag me into child-murder.

'Excuse me,' he asked of a sudden, 'but why did you do that, sir?'

'The child yonder.'

'Our young gentleman in blue?'

'Of course.'

'He runs about a good deal. Did you see him by the fountain, sir?'

'Oh, yes, several times. Do we turn here?'

'Yes, sir. And did you 'appen to see them upstairs too?'

'At the upper window? Yes.'

'Was that before the mistress come out to speak to you, sir?'

'A little before that. Why d'you want to know?'

He paused a little. 'Only to make sure that – that they had seen the car, sir, because with children running about, though I'm sure you're driving particularly careful, there might be an accident. That was all, sir. Here are the crossroads. You can't miss your way from now on.

Thank you, sir, but that isn't *our* custom, not with – '

'I beg your pardon,' I said, and thrust away the British silver.

'Oh, it's quite right with the rest of 'em as a rule. Goodbye, sir.'

He retired into the armour-plated conning tower of his caste and walked away. Evidently a butler solicitous for the honour of his house, and interested, probably through a maid, in the nursery.

Once beyond the signposts at the crossroads I looked back, but the crumpled hills interlaced so jealously that I could not see where the house had lain. When I asked its name at a cottage along the road, the fat woman who sold sweetmeats there gave me to understand that people with motor cars had small right to live – much less to 'go about talking like carriage folk'. They were not a pleasant-mannered community.

When I retraced my route on the map that evening I was little wiser. Hawkin's Old Farm appeared to be the Survey title of the place, and the old County Gazetteer, generally so ample, did not allude to it. The big house of those parts was Hodnington Hall, Georgian with early Victorian embellishments, as an atrocious steel engraving attested. I carried my difficulty to a neighbour – a deep-rooted tree of that soil – and he gave me a name of a family which conveyed no meaning.

A month or so later – I went again, or it may have been that my car took the road of her own volition. She over-ran the fruitless Downs, threaded every turn of the maze of lanes below the hills, drew through the high-walled woods, impenetrable in their full leaf, came out at the crossroads where the butler had left me, and a little farther on developed an internal trouble which forced me to turn her in on a grass way-waste that cut into a summer-silent hazel wood. So far as I could make sure by the sun and a six-inch Ordnance map, this should be the road flank of that wood which I had first explored from the heights above. I made a mighty serious business of my repairs and a glittering shop of my repair kit, spanners, pump, and the like, which I spread out orderly upon a rug. It was a trap to catch all childhood, for on such a day, I argued, the children would not be far off. When I paused in my work I listened, but the wood was so full of the noises of summer (though the birds had mated) that I could not at first distinguish these from the tread of small cautious feet stealing across the dead leaves. I rang my bell in an alluring manner, but the feet fled, and I repented, for to a child a sudden noise is very real terror. I must have been at work half an hour when I heard in the wood the voice of the blind woman crying: 'Children, oh, children! Where are you?' and the stillness made slow to close on the perfection of that cry. She came towards me, half feeling her way between the tree boles, and though a child it seemed clung to her skirt, it swerved into the leafage like a rabbit as she drew nearer.

'Is that you?' she said, 'from the other side of the county?'

'Yes, it's me from the other side of the county.'

'Then why didn't you come through the upper woods? They were there just now.'

'They were here a few minutes ago. I expect they knew my car had broken down, and came to see the fun.'

'Nothing serious, I hope? How do cars break down?'

'In fifty different ways. Only mine has chosen the fifty-first.'

She laughed merrily at the tiny joke, cooed with delicious laughter, and pushed her hat back.

'Let me hear,' she said.

'Wait a moment,' I cried, 'and I'll get you a cushion.'

She set her foot on the rug all covered with spare parts, and stooped above it eagerly. 'What delightful things!' The hands through which she saw glanced in the chequered sunlight. 'A box here – another box! Why, you've arranged them like playing shop!'

'I confess now that I put it out to attract them. I don't need half those things really.'

'How nice of you! I heard your bell in the upper wood. You say they were here before that?'

'I'm sure of it. Why are they so shy? That little fellow in blue who was with you just now ought to have got over his fright. He's been watching me like a Red Indian.'

'It must have been your bell,' she said. 'I heard one of them go past me in trouble when I was coming down. They're shy – so shy even with me.' She turned her face over her shoulder and cried again: 'Children, oh, children! Look and see!'

'They must have gone off together on their own affairs,' I suggested, for there was a murmur behind us of lowered voices broken by the sudden squeaking giggles of childhood. I returned to my tinkerings and she leaned forward, her chin on her hand, listening interestedly.

'How many are they?' I said at last. The work was finished, but I saw no reason to go.

Her forehead puckered a little in thought. 'I don't quite know,' she said simply. 'Sometimes more – sometimes less. They come and stay with me because I love them, you see.'

'That must be very jolly,' I said, replacing a drawer, and as I spoke I heard the inanity of my answer.

'You – you aren't laughing at me,' she cried. 'I – I haven't any of my own. I never married. People laugh at me sometimes about them because – because – '

'Because they're savages,' I returned. 'It's nothing to fret for. That sort laugh at everything that isn't in their own fat lives.'

'I don't know. How should I? I only don't like being laughed at about *them*. It hurts; and when one can't see . . . I don't want to seem silly,' her chin quivered like a child's as she spoke, 'but we blindies have only one skin, I think. Everything outside hits straight at our souls. It's different with you. You've such good defences in your eyes – looking out – before anyone can really pain you in your soul. People forget that with us.'

I was silent reviewing that inexhaustible matter – the more than inherited (since it is also carefully taught) brutality of the Christian peoples, beside which the mere heathendom of the West Coast nigger is clean and restrained. It led me a long distance into myself.

'Don't do that!' she said of a sudden, putting her hands before her eyes.

'What?'

She made a gesture with her hand.

'That! It's – it's all purple and black. Don't! That colour hurts.'

'But, how in the world do you know about colours?' I exclaimed, for here was a revelation indeed.

'Colours as colours?' she asked.

'No. *Those* Colours which you saw just now.'

'You know as well as I do,' she laughed, 'else you wouldn't have asked that question. They aren't in the world at all. They're in *you* – when you went so angry.'

'D'you mean a dull purplish patch, like port wine mixed with ink?' I said.

'I've never seen ink or port wine, but the colours aren't mixed. They are separate – all separate.'

'Do you mean black streaks and jags across the purple?'

She nodded. 'Yes – if they are like this,' and zigzagged her finger again, 'but it's more red than purple – that bad colour.'

'And what are the colours at the top of the – whatever you see?'

Slowly she leaned forward and traced on the rug the figure of the Egg itself.

'I see them so,' she said, pointing with a grass stem, 'white, green, yellow, red, purple, and when people are angry or bad, black across the red – as you were just now.'

'Who told you anything about it – in the beginning?' I demanded.

'About the Colours? No one. I used to ask what colours were when I was little – in table-covers and curtains and carpets, you see – because

THE BEST SHORT STORIES

some colours hurt me and some made me happy. People told me; and when I got older that was how I saw people.' Again she traced the outline of the Egg which it is given to very few of us to see.

'All by yourself?' I repeated.

'All by myself. There wasn't anyone else. I only found out afterwards that other people did not see the Colours.'

She leaned against the tree-bole plaiting and unplaiting chance-plucked grass stems. The children in the wood had drawn nearer. I could see them with the tail of my eye frolicking like squirrels.

'Now I am sure you will never laugh at me,' she went on after a long silence. 'Nor at *them.*'

'Goodness! No!' I cried, jolted out of my train of thought. 'A man who laughs at a child – unless the child is laughing too – is a heathen!'

'I didn't mean that, of course. You'd never laugh *at* children, but I thought – I used to think – that perhaps you might laugh about *them.* So now I beg your pardon . . . What are you going to laugh at?'

I had made no sound, but she knew.

'At the notion of your begging my pardon. If you had done your duty as a pillar of the State and a landed proprietress you ought to have summoned me for trespass when I barged through your woods the other day. It was disgraceful of me – inexcusable.'

She looked at me, her head against the tree trunk – long and steadfastly – this woman who could see the naked soul.

'How curious,' she half whispered. 'How very curious.'

'Why, what have I done?'

'You don't understand . . . and yet you understood about the Colours. Don't you understand?'

She spoke with a passion that nothing had justified, and I faced her bewilderedly as she rose. The children had gathered themselves in a roundel behind a bramble bush. One sleek head bent over something smaller, and the set of the little shoulders told me that fingers were on lips. They, too, had some child's tremendous secret. I alone was hopelessly astray there in the broad sunlight.

'No,' I said, and shook my head as though the dead eyes could note. 'Whatever it is, I don't understand yet. Perhaps I shall later – if you'll let me come again.'

'You will come again,' she answered. 'You will surely come again and walk in the wood.'

'Perhaps the children will know me well enough by that time to let me play with them – as a favour. You know what children are like.'

'It isn't a matter of favour but of right,' she replied, and while I wondered what she meant, a dishevelled woman plunged round the bend of the road, loose-haired, purple, almost lowing with agony as she ran. It was my rude, fat friend of the sweetmeat shop. The blind woman heard and stepped forward. 'What is it, Mrs Madehurst?' she asked.

The woman flung her apron over her head and literally grovelled in the dust, crying that her grandchild was sick to death, that the local doctor was away fishing, that Jenny the mother was at her wits' end, and so forth, with repetitions and bellowings.

'Where's the next nearest doctor?' I asked between paroxysms.

'Madden will tell you. Go round to the house and take him with you. I'll attend to this. Be quick!' She half supported the fat woman into the shade. In two minutes I was blowing all the horns of Jericho under the front of the House Beautiful, and Madden, in the pantry, rose to the crisis like a butler and a man.

A quarter of an hour at illegal speeds caught us a doctor five miles away. Within the half-hour we had decanted him, much interested in motors, at the door of the sweetmeat shop, and drew up the road to await the verdict.

'Useful things cars,' said Madden, all man and no butler. 'If I'd had one when mine took sick she wouldn't have died.'

'How was it?' I asked.

'Croup. Mrs Madden was away. No one knew what to do. I drove eight miles in a tax cart for the doctor. She was choked when we came back. This car 'd ha' saved her. She'd have been close on ten now.'

'I'm sorry,' I said. 'I thought you were rather fond of children from what you told me going to the crossroads the other day.'

'Have you seen 'em again, sir – this mornin'?'

'Yes, but they're well broke to cars. I couldn't get any of them within twenty yards of it.'

He looked at me carefully as a scout considers a stranger – not as a menial should lift his eyes to his divinely appointed superior.

'I wonder why,' he said just above the breath that he drew.

We waited on. A light wind from the sea wandered up and down the long lines of the woods, and the wayside grasses, whitened already with summer dust, rose and bowed in sallow waves.

A woman, wiping the suds off her arms, came out of the cottage next the sweetmeat shop.

'I've be'n listenin' in de backyard,' she said cheerily. 'He says Arthur's unaccountable bad. Did ye hear him shruck just now? Unaccountable bad. I reckon 'twill come Jenny's turn to walk in de wood nex' week along, Mr Madden.'

'Excuse me, sir, but your lap-robe is slipping,' said Madden deferentially. The woman started, dropped a curtsey, and hurried away.

'What does she mean by "walking in the wood"?' I asked.

'It must be some saying they use hereabouts. I'm from Norfolk myself,' said Madden. 'They're an independent lot in this county. She took you for a chauffeur, sir.'

I saw the doctor come out of the cottage followed by a draggle-tailed wench who clung to his arm as though he could make treaty for her with Death. 'Dat sort,' she wailed – 'dey're just as much to us dat has 'em as if dey was lawful born. Just as much – just as much! An' God he'd be just as pleased if you saved 'un, doctor. Don't take it from me. Miss Florence will tell ye de very same. Don't leave 'im, doctor!'

'I know, I know,' said the man; 'but he'll be quiet for a while now. We'll get the nurse and the medicine as fast as we can.' He signalled me to come forward with the car, and I strove not to be privy to what followed; but I saw the girl's face, blotched and frozen with grief, and I felt the hand without a ring clutching at my knees when we moved away.

The doctor was a man of some humour, for I remember he claimed my car under the Oath of Aesculapius, and used it and me without mercy. First we convoyed Mrs Madehurst and the blind woman to wait by the sick bed till the nurse should come. Next we invaded a neat county town for prescriptions (the doctor said the trouble was cerebro-spinal meningitis), and when the County Institute, banked and flanked with scared market cattle, reported itself out of nurses for the moment we literally flung ourselves loose upon the county. We conferred with the owners of great houses – magnates at the ends of overarching avenues whose big-boned womenfolk strode away from their tea-tables to listen to the imperious doctor. At last a white-haired lady sitting under a cedar of Lebanon and surrounded by a court of magnificent Borzois – all hostile to motors – gave the doctor, who received them as from a princess, written orders which we bore many miles at top speed, through a park, to a French nunnery, where we took over in exchange a pallid-faced and trembling Sister. She knelt at the bottom of the tonneau telling her beads without pause till, by short cuts of the doctor's invention, we had her to the sweetmeat shop once more. It was a long afternoon crowded with mad episodes that rose and dissolved like the dust of our wheels; cross-sections of remote and incomprehensible lives through which we raced at right angles; and I went home in the dusk, wearied out, to dream of the clashing horns of cattle; round-eyed nuns walking in a garden of graves; pleasant tea-parties beneath shaded trees; the carbolic-scented, grey-painted corridors of the County Institute; the steps of shy children in the wood, and the hands that clung to my knees as the motor began to move.

I had intended to return in a day or two, but it pleased Fate to hold me from that side of the county, on many pretexts, till the elder and the wild rose had fruited. There came at last a brilliant day, swept clear from the south-west, that brought the hills within hand's reach – a day of unstable airs and high filmy clouds. Through no merit of my own I was free, and set the car for the third time on that known road. As I reached the crest of the Downs I felt the soft air change, saw it glaze under the sun; and, looking down at the sea, in that instant beheld the blue of the Channel turn through polished silver and dulled steel to dingy pewter. A laden collier hugging the coast steered outward for deeper water, and, across copper-coloured haze, I saw sails rise one by one on the anchored fishing-fleet. In a deep dene behind me an eddy of sudden wind drummed through sheltered oaks, and spun aloft the first dry sample of autumn leaves. When I reached the beach road the sea-fog fumed over the brickfields, and the tide was telling all the groins of the gale beyond Ushant. In less than an hour summer England vanished in chill grey. We were again the shut island of the North, all the ships of the world bellowing at our perilous gates; and between their outcries ran the piping of bewildered gulls. My cap dripped moisture, the folds of the rug held it in pools or sluiced it away in runnels, and the salt-rime stuck to my lips.

Inland the smell of autumn loaded the thickened fog among the trees, and the drip became a continuous shower. Yet the late flowers – mallow of the wayside, scabious of the field, and dahlia of the garden – showed gay in the mist, and beyond the sea's breath there was little sign of decay in the leaf. Yet in the villages the house doors were all open, and bare-legged, bare-headed children sat at ease on the damp doorsteps to shout 'pip-pip' at the stranger.

I made bold to call at the sweetmeat shop, where Mrs Madehurst met me with a fat woman's hospitable tears. Jenny's child, she said, had died two days after the nun had come. It was, she felt, best out of the way, even though insurance offices, for reasons which she did not pretend to follow, would not willingly insure such stray lives. 'Not but what Jenny didn't tend to Arthur as though he'd come all proper at de end of de first year – like Jenny herself.' Thanks to Miss Florence, the child had been buried with a pomp which, in Mrs Madehurst's opinion, more than covered the small irregularity of its birth. She described the coffin, within and without, the glass hearse, and the evergreen lining of the grave.

'But how's the mother?' I asked.

'Jenny? Oh, she'll get over it. I've felt dat way with one or two o' my own. She'll get over. She's walkin' in de wood now.'

'In this weather?'

Mrs Madehurst looked at me with narrowed eyes across the counter. 'I dunno but it opens de 'eart like. Yes it opens de 'eart. Dat's where losin' and bearin' comes so alike in de long run, we do say.'

Now the wisdom of the old wives is greater than that of all the Fathers, and this last oracle sent me thinking so extendedly as I went up the road, that I nearly ran over a woman and a child at the wooded corner by the lodge gates of the House Beautiful.

'Awful weather!' I cried, as I slowed dead for the turn.

'Not so bad,' she answered placidly out of the fog. 'Mine's used to 'un. You'll find yours indoors, I reckon.'

Indoors, Madden received me with professional courtesy, and kind enquiries for the health of the motor, which he would put under cover.

I waited in a still, nut-brown hall, pleasant with late flowers and warmed with a delicious wood fire – a place of good influence and great peace. (Men and women may sometimes, after great effort, achieve a creditable lie; but the house, which is their temple, cannot say anything save the truth of those who have lived in it.) A child's cart and a doll lay on the black-and-white floor, where a rug had been kicked back. I felt that the children had only just hurried away – to hide themselves, most like – in the many turns of the great adzed staircase that climbed statelily out of the hall, or to crouch at gaze behind the lions and roses of the carven gallery above. Then I heard her voice above me, singing as the blind sing – from the soul:

> 'In the pleasant orchard-closes . . .'

And all my early summer came back at the call.

> 'In the pleasant orchard-closes,
>   God bless all our gains say we –
> But may God bless all our losses,
>   Better suits with our degree.'

She dropped the marring fifth line, and repeated –

> 'Better suits with our degree!'

I saw her lean over the gallery, her linked hands white as pearl against the oak.

'Is that you – from the other side of the county?' she called.

'Yes, me – from the other side of the county,' I answered, laughing.

'What a long time before you had to come here again.' She ran down the stairs, one hand lightly touching the broad rail. 'It's two months and four days. Summer's gone!'

'I meant to come before, but Fate prevented.'

'I knew it. Please do something to that fire. They won't let me play with it, but I can feel it's behaving badly. Hit it!'

I looked on either side of the deep fireplace, and found but a half-charred hedge-stake with which I punched a black log into flame.

'It never goes out, day or night,' she said, as though explaining. 'In case anyone comes in with cold toes, you see.'

'It's even lovelier inside than it was out,' I murmured. The red light poured itself along the age-polished dusky panels till the Tudor roses and lions of the gallery took colour and motion. An old eagle-topped convex mirror gathered the picture into its mysterious heart, distorting afresh the distorted shadows, and curving the gallery lines into the curves of a ship. The day was shutting down in half a gale as the fog turned to stringy scud. Through the uncurtained mullions of the broad window I could see valiant horsemen of the lawn rear and recover against the wind that taunted them with legions of dead leaves.

'Yes, it must be beautiful,' she said. 'Would you like to go over it? There's still light enough upstairs.'

I followed her up the unflinching, wagon-wide staircase to the gallery whence opened the thin fluted Elizabethan doors.

'Feel how they put the latch low down for the sake of the children.' She swung a light door inward.

'By the way, where are they?' I asked. 'I haven't even heard them today.'

She did not answer at once. Then, 'I can only hear them,' she replied softly. 'This is one of their rooms – everything ready, you see.'

She pointed into a heavily-timbered room. There were little low gate tables and children's chairs. A doll's house, its hooked front half open, faced a great dappled rocking-horse, from whose padded saddle it was but a child's scramble to the broad window-seat overlooking the lawn. A toy gun lay in a corner beside a gilt wooden cannon.

'Surely they've only just gone,' I whispered. In the failing light a door creaked cautiously. I heard the rustle of a frock and the patter of feet – quick feet through a room beyond.

'I heard that,' she cried triumphantly. 'Did you? Children, oh, children! Where are you?'

The voice filled the walls that held it lovingly to the last perfect note, but there came no answering shout such as I had heard in the garden. We hurried on from room to oak-floored room; up a step here, down three steps there; among a maze of passages; always mocked by our quarry. One might as well have tried to work an unstopped warren with a single ferret. There were bolt-holes innumerable – recesses in walls, embrasures of deep-slit windows now darkened, whence they could start up behind us; and abandoned fireplaces, six feet deep in the masonry, as well as the tangle of communicating doors. Above all, they had the twilight for their helper in our game. I had caught one or two joyous chuckles of evasion, and once or twice had seen the silhouette of a child's frock against some darkening window at the end of a passage; but we returned empty-handed to the gallery, just as a middle-aged woman was setting a lamp in its niche.

'No, I haven't seen her either this evening, Miss Florence,' I heard her say, 'but that Turpin he says he wants to see you about his shed.'

'Oh, Mr Turpin must want to see me very badly. Tell him to come to the hall, Mrs Madden.'

I looked down into the hall whose only light was the dulled fire, and deep in the shadow I saw them at last. They must have slipped down while we were in the passages, and now thought themselves perfectly hidden behind an old gilt leather screen. By child's law, my fruitless chase was as good as an introduction, but since I had taken so much trouble I resolved to force them to come forward later by the simple trick, which children detest, of pretending not to notice them. They lay close, in a little huddle, no more than shadows except when a quick flame betrayed an outline.

'And now we'll have some tea,' she said. 'I believe I ought to have offered it you at first, but one doesn't arrive at manners somehow when one lives alone and is considered – h'm – peculiar.' Then with very pretty scorn, 'Would you like a lamp to see to eat by?'

'The firelight's much pleasanter, I think.' We descended into that delicious gloom and Madden brought tea.

I took my chair in the direction of the screen ready to surprise or be surprised as the game should go, and at her permission, since a hearth is always sacred, bent forward to play with the fire.

'Where do you get these beautiful short faggots from?' I asked idly. 'Why, they are tallies!'

'Of course,' she said. 'As I can't read or write I'm driven back on the early English tally for my accounts. Give me one and I'll tell you what it meant.'

I passed her an unburned hazel-tally, about a foot long, and she ran her thumb down the nicks.

'This is the milk record for the home farm for the month of April last year, in gallons,' said she. 'I don't know what I should have done without tallies. An old forester of mine taught me the system. It's out of date now for every one else; but my tenants respect it. One of them's coming now to see me. Oh, it doesn't matter. He has no business here out of office hours. He's a greedy, ignorant man – very greedy or – he wouldn't come here after dark.'

'Have you much land then?'

'Only a couple of hundred acres in hand, thank goodness. The other six hundred are nearly all let to folk who knew my folk before me, but this Turpin is quite a new man – and a highway robber.'

'But are you sure I shan't be – ?'

'Certainly not. You have the right. He hasn't any children.'

'Ah, the children!' I said, and slid my low chair back till it nearly touched the screen that hid them. 'I wonder whether they'll come out for me.'

There was a murmur of voices – Madden's and a deeper note – at the low, dark side door, and a ginger-headed, canvas-gaitered giant of the unmistakable tenant-farmer type stumbled or was pushed in.

'Come to the fire, Mr Turpin,' she said.

'If – if you please, miss, I'll – I'll be quite as well by the door.' He clung to the latch as he spoke like a frightened child. Of a sudden I realised that he was in the grip of some almost overpowering fear.

'Well?'

'About that new shed for the young stock – that was all. These first autumn storms settin' in . . . but I'll come again, miss.' His teeth did not chatter much more than the door latch.

'I think not,' she answered levelly. 'The new shed – m'm. What did my agent write you on the 15th?'

'I – fancied p'raps that if I came to see you – ma – man to man like, miss. But – '

His eyes rolled into every corner of the room wide with horror. He half opened the door through which he had entered, but I noticed it shut again – from without and firmly.

'He wrote what I told him,' she went on. 'You are overstocked already. Dunnett's Farm never carried more than fifty bullocks – even in Mr Wright's time. And *he* used cake. You've sixty-seven and you don't cake. You've broken the lease in that respect. You're dragging the heart out of the farm.'

'I'm – I'm getting some minerals – superphosphates – next week. I've as good as ordered a truck-load already. I'll go down to the station tomorrow about 'em. Then I can come and see you man to man like, miss, in the daylight . . . That gentleman's not going away, is he?' He almost shrieked.

I had only slid the chair a little farther back, reaching behind me to tap on the leather of the screen, but he jumped like a rat.

'No. Please attend to me, Mr Turpin.' She turned in her chair and faced him with his back to the door. It was an old and sordid little piece of scheming that she forced from him – his plea for the new cowshed at his landlady's expense, that he might with the covered manure pay his next year's rent out of the valuation after, as she made clear, he had bled the enriched pastures to the bone. I could not but admire the intensity of his greed, when I saw him out-facing for its sake whatever terror it was that ran wet on his forehead.

I ceased to tap the leather – was, indeed, calculating the cost of the shed – when I felt my relaxed hand taken and turned softly between the soft hands of a child. So at last I had triumphed. In a moment I would turn and acquaint myself with those quick-footed wanderers . . .

The little brushing kiss fell in the centre of my palm – as a gift on which the fingers were, once, expected to close: as the all-faithful half-reproachful signal of a waiting child not used to neglect even when grown-ups were busiest – a fragment of the mute code devised very long ago.

Then I knew. And it was as though I had known from the first day when I looked across the lawn at the high window.

I heard the door shut. The woman turned to me in silence, and I felt that she knew.

What time passed after this I cannot say. I was roused by the fall of a log, and mechanically rose to put it back. Then I returned to my place in the chair very close to the screen.

'Now you understand,' she whispered, across the packed shadows.

'Yes, I understand – now. Thank you.'

'I – I only hear them.' She bowed her head in her hands. 'I have no right, you know – no other right. I have neither borne nor lost – neither borne nor lost!'

'Be very glad then,' said I, for my soul was torn open within me.

'Forgive me!'

She was still, and I went back to my sorrow and my joy.

'It was because I loved them so,' she said at last, brokenly. '*That* was why it was, even from the first – even before I knew that they – they were all I should ever have. And I loved them so!'

She stretched out her arms to the shadows and the shadows within the shadow.

'They came because I loved them – because I needed them. I – I must have made them come. Was that wrong, think you?'

'No – no.'

'I – I grant you that the toys and – and all that sort of thing were nonsense, but – but I used to so hate empty rooms myself when I was little.' She pointed to the gallery. 'And the passages all empty . . . And how could I ever bear the garden door shut? Suppose – '

'Don't! For pity's sake, don't!' I cried. The twilight had brought a cold rain with gusty squalls that plucked at the leaded windows.

'And the same thing with keeping the fire in all night. *I* don't think it so foolish – do you?'

I looked at the broad brick hearth, saw, through tears I believe, that there was no unpassable iron on or near it, and bowed my head.

'I did all that and lots of other things – just to make believe. Then they came. I heard them, but I didn't know that they were not mine by right till Mrs Madden told me – '

'The butler's wife? What?'

'One of them – I heard – she saw. And knew. Hers! *Not* for me. I didn't know at first. Perhaps I was jealous. Afterwards, I began to understand that it was only because I loved them not because . . . Oh, you *must* bear or lose,' she said piteously. 'There is no other way – and yet they love me. They must! Don't they?'

There was no sound in the room except the lapping voices of the fire, but we two listened intently, and she at least took comfort from what she heard. She recovered herself and half rose. I sat still in my chair by the screen.

'Don't think me a wretch to whine about myself like this, but – but I'm all in the dark, you know, and *you* can see.'

In truth I could see, and my vision confirmed me in my resolve, though that was like the very parting of spirit and flesh. Yet a little longer I would stay since it was the last time.

'You think it is wrong, then?' she cried sharply, though I had said nothing.

'Not for you. A thousand times no. For you it is right . . . I am grateful to you beyond words. For me it would be wrong. For me only . . . '

'Why?' she said, but passed her hand before her face as she had done at our second meeting in the wood. 'Oh, I see,' she went on simply as a child. 'For you it would be wrong.' Then with a little indrawn laugh, 'And, d'you remember, I called you lucky – once – at first. You who must never come here again!'

She left me to sit a little longer by the screen, and I heard the sound of her feet die out along the gallery above.

FROM LYDEN'S *Irenius*
ACT III, SC. II

Gow. – Had it been your Prince instead of a groom caught in this noose there's not an astrologer of the city –

Prince – Sacked! Sacked! We were a city yesterday.

Gow. – So be it, but I was not governor. Not an astrologer, but would ha' sworn he'd foreseen it at the last versary of Venus, when Vulcan caught her with Mars in the house of stinking Capricorn. But since 'tis Jack of the Straw that hangs, the forgetful stars had it not on their tablets.

Prince – Another life! Were there any left to die? How did the poor fool come by it?

Gow. – *Simpliciter* thus. She that damned him to death knew not that she did it, or would have died ere she had done it. For she loved him. He that hangs him does so in obedience to the Duke, and asks no more than 'Where is the rope?' The Duke, very exactly he hath told us, works God's will, in which holy employ he's not to be questioned. We have then left upon his finger, only Jack whose soul now plucks the left sleeve of Destiny in Hell to overtake why she clapped him up like a fly on a sunny wall. Whuff! Soh!

Prince – Your cloak, Ferdinand. I'll sleep now.

Ferdinand – Sleep, then . . . He too, loved his life?

Gow. – He was born of woman . . . but at the end threw life from him, like your Prince, for a little sleep . . . 'Have I any look of a King?' said he, clanking his chain – 'to be so baited on all sides by Fortune, that I must e'en die now to live with myself one day longer.' I left him railing at Fortune and woman's love.

Ferdinand – Ah, woman's love!

(*Aside*)   Who knows not Fortune, glutted on easy thrones,
                Stealing from feasts as rare to coneycatch,
                Privily in the hedgerows for a clown
                With that same cruel-lustful hand and eye,
                Those nails and wedges, that one hammer and lead,
                And the very gerb of long-stored lightnings loosed
                Yesterday 'gainst some King.

Mrs Bathurst

THE DAY THAT I CHOSE to visit HMS *Peridot* in Simon's Bay was the day that the Admiral had chosen to send her up the coast. She was just steaming out to sea as my train came in, and since the rest of the Fleet were either coaling or busy at the rifle-ranges a thousand feet up the hill, I found myself stranded, lunchless, on the sea-front with no hope of return to Cape Town before 5 p.m. At this crisis I had the luck to come across my friend Inspector Hooper, Cape Government Railways, in command of an engine and a brake-van chalked for repair.

'If you get something to eat,' he said, 'I'll run you down to Glengariff siding till the goods comes along. It's cooler there than here, you see.'

I got food and drink from the Greeks who sell all things at a price, and the engine trotted us a couple of miles up the line to a bay of drifted sand and a plank-platform half buried in sand not a hundred yards from the edge of the surf. Moulded dunes, whiter than any snow, rolled far inland up a brown and purple valley of splintered rocks and dry scrub. A crowd of Malays hauled at a net beside two blue and green boats on the beach; a picnic party danced and shouted barefoot where a tiny river trickled across the flat, and a circle of dry hills, whose feet were set in sands of silver, locked us in against a seven-coloured sea. At either horn of the bay the railway line cut just above high-water mark, ran round a shoulder of piled rocks, and disappeared.

'You see there's always a breeze here,' said Hooper, opening the door as the engine left us in the siding on the sand, and the strong south-easter buffeting under Elsie's Peak dusted sand into our tickey* beer. Presently he sat down to a file full of spiked documents. He had returned from a long trip up-country, where he had been reporting on damaged rolling-stock, as far away as Rhodesia. The weight of the bland wind on my eyelids; the song of it under the car roof, and high up among the rocks; the drift of fine grains chasing each other musically ashore; the tramp of the surf; the voices of the picnickers; the rustle of Hooper's file, and the presence of the assured sun, joined with the beer to cast me into magical slumber. The hills of False Bay were just dissolving into those of fairyland when I heard footsteps on the sand

* old South African threepenny bit

outside, and the clink of our couplings.

'Stop that!' snapped Hooper, without raising his head from his work. 'It's those dirty little Malay boys, you see: they're always playing with the trucks . . .'

'Don't be hard on 'em. The railway's a general refuge in Africa,' I replied.

' 'Tis – up-country at any rate. That reminds me,' he felt in his waistcoat-pocket, 'I've got a curiosity for you from Wankies – beyond Buluwayo. It's more of a souvenir perhaps than – '

'The old hotel's inhabited,' cried a voice. 'White men, from the language. Marines to the front! Come on, Pritch. Here's your Belmont. Wha–i–i!'

The last word dragged like a rope as Mr Pyecroft ran round to the open door, and stood looking up into my face. Behind him an enormous Sergeant of Marines trailed a stalk of dried seaweed, and dusted the sand nervously from his fingers.

'What are you doing here?' I asked. 'I thought the *Hierophant* was down the coast?'

'We came in last Tuesday – from Tristan de Cunha – for overhaul, and we shall be in dockyard 'ands for two months, with boiler-seatings.'

'Come and sit down.' Hooper put away the file.

'This is Mr Hooper of the Railway,' I exclaimed, as Pyecroft turned to haul up the black-moustached sergeant.

'This is Sergeant Pritchard, of the *Agaric*, an old shipmate,' said he. 'We were strollin' on the beach.' The monster blushed and nodded. He filled up one side of the van when he sat down.

'And this is my friend, Mr Pyecroft,' I added to Hooper, already busy with the extra beer which my prophetic soul had bought from the Greeks.

'*Moi aussi*,' quoth Pyecroft, and drew out beneath his coat a labelled quart bottle.

'Why, it's Bass!' cried Hooper.

'It was Pritchard,' said Pyecroft. 'They can't resist him.'

'That's not so,' said Pritchard mildly.

'Not *verbatim* per'aps, but the look in the eye came to the same thing.'

'Where was it?' I demanded.

'Just on beyond here – at Kalk Bay. She was slappin' a rug in a back verandah. Pritch 'adn't more than brought his batteries to bear, before she stepped indoors an' sent it flyin' over the wall.'

Pyecroft patted the warm bottle.

'It was all a mistake,' said Pritchard. 'I shouldn't wonder if she mistook me for Maclean. We're about of a size.'

I had heard householders of Muizenburg, St James's, and Kalk Bay complain of the difficulty of keeping beer or good servants at the seaside, and I began to see the reason. None the less, it was excellent Bass, and I too drank to the health of that large-minded maid.

'It's the uniform that fetches 'em, an' they fetch it,' said Pyecroft. 'My simple navy blue is respectable, but not fascinatin'. Now Pritch in 'is Number One rig is always "purr Mary, on the terrace" – *ex officio* as you might say.'

'She took me for Maclean, I tell you,' Pritchard insisted. 'Why – why – to listen to him you wouldn't think that only yesterday – '

'Pritch,' said Pyecroft, 'be warned in time. If we begin tellin' what we know about each other we'll be turned out of the pub. Not to mention aggravated desertion on several occasions – '

'Never anything more than absence without leaf – I defy you to prove it,' said the Sergeant hotly. 'An' if it comes to that, how about Vancouver in '87?'

'How about it? Who pulled bow in the gig going ashore? Who told Boy Niven . . . ?'

'Surely you were court-martialled for that?' I said. The story of Boy Niven who lured seven or eight able-bodied seamen and marines into the woods of British Columbia used to be a legend of the Fleet.

'Yes, we were court-martialled to rights,' said Pritchard, 'but we should have been tried for murder if Boy Niven 'adn't been unusually tough. He told us he had an uncle 'oo'd give us land to farm. 'E said he was born at the back o' Vancouver Island, and *all* the time the beggar was a balmy Barnardo Orphan!'

'*But* we believed him,' said Pyecroft. 'I did – you did – Paterson did – an' 'oo was the Marine that married the cocoanut-woman afterwards – him with the mouth?'

'Oh, Jones, Spit-Kid Jones. I 'aven't thought of 'im in years,' said Pritchard. 'Yes, Spit-Kid believed it, an' George Anstey and Moon. We were very young an' very curious.'

'*But* lovin' an' trustful to a degree,' said Pyecroft.

'Remember when 'e told us to walk in single file for fear o' bears? Remember, Pye, when 'e 'opped about in that bog full o' ferns an' sniffed an' said 'e could smell the smoke of 'is uncle's farm? An' *all* the time it was a dirty little outlyin' uninhabited island. We walked round it in a day, an' come back to our boat lyin' on the beach. A whole day Boy Niven kept us walkin' in circles lookin' for 'is uncle's farm! He said his uncle was compelled by the law of the land to give us a farm!'

'Don't get hot, Pritch. We believed,' said Pyecroft.

'He'd been readin' books. He only did it to get a run ashore an' have himself talked of. A day an' a night – eight of us – followin' Boy Niven round an uninhabited island in the Vancouver archipelago! Then the picket came for us an' a nice pack o' idiots we looked!'

'What did you get for it?' Hooper asked.

'Heavy thunder with continuous lightning for two hours. Thereafter sleet-squalls, a confused sea, and cold, unfriendly weather till conclusion o' cruise,' said Pyecroft. 'It was only what we expected, but what we felt – an' I assure you, Mr Hooper, even a sailor-man has a heart to break – was bein' told that we able seamen an' promisin' marines 'ad misled Boy Niven. Yes, we poor back-to-the-landers was supposed to 'ave misled him! He rounded on us, o' course, an' got off easy.'

'Excep' for what we gave him in the steerin'-flat when we came out o' cells. 'Eard anything of 'im lately, Pye?'

'Signal Boatswain in the Channel Fleet, I believe – Mr L. L. Niven is.'

'An' Anstey died o' fever in Benin,' Pritchard mused. 'What come to Moon? Spit-Kid we know about.'

'Moon – Moon! Now where did I last . . . ? Oh yes, when I was in the *Palladium*. I met Quigley at Buncrana Station. He told me Moon 'ad run when the *Astrild* sloop was cruising among the South Seas three years back. He always showed signs o' bein' a Mormonastic beggar. Yes, he slipped off quietly an' they 'adn't time to chase 'im round the islands even if the navigatin' officer 'ad been equal to the job.'

'Wasn't he?' said Hooper.

'Not so. Accordin' to Quigley the *Astrild* spent half her commission rompin' up the beach like a she-turtle, an' the other half hatching turtles' eggs on the top o' numerous reefs. When she was docked at Sydney her copper looked like Aunt Maria's washing on the line – an' her 'mid-ship frames was sprung. The commander swore the dockyard 'ad done it haulin' the pore thing on to the slips. They *do* do strange things at sea, Mr Hooper.'

'Ah! I'm not a taxpayer,' said Hooper, and opened a fresh bottle. The Sergeant seemed to be one who had a difficulty in dropping subjects.

'How it all comes back, don't it?' he said. 'Why, Moon must 'ave 'ad sixteen years' service before he ran.'

'It takes 'em at all ages. Look at – you know,' said Pyecroft.

'Who?' I asked.

'A service man within eighteen months of his pension is the party you're thinkin' of,' said Pritchard. 'A warrant 'oo's name begins with a V, isn't it?'

'But, in a way o' puttin' it, we can't say that he actually did desert,' Pyecroft suggested.

'Oh no,' said Pritchard. 'It was only permanent absence up-country without leave. That was all.'

'Up-country?' said Hooper. 'Did they circulate his description?'

'What for?' said Pritchard, most impolitely.

'Because deserters are like columns in the war. They don't move away from the line, you see. I've known a chap caught at Salisbury that way tryin' to get to Nyassa. They tell me, but o' course I don't know, that they don't ask questions on the Nyassa Lake Flotilla up there. I've heard of a P. & O. quartermaster in full command of an armed launch there.'

'Do you think Click 'ud ha' gone up that way?' Pritchard asked.

'There's no saying. He was sent up to Bloemfontein to take over some Navy ammunition left in the fort. We know he took it over and saw it into the trucks. Then there was no more Click – then or thereafter. Four months ago it transpired, and thus the *casus belli* stands at present,' said Pyecroft.

'What were his marks?' said Hooper again.

'Does the Railway get a reward for returnin' 'em, then?' said Pritchard.

'If I did d'you suppose I'd talk about it?' Hooper retorted angrily.

'You seemed so very interested,' said Pritchard with equal crispness.

'Why was he called Click?' I asked, to tide over an uneasy little break in the conversation. The two men were staring at each other very fixedly.

'Because of an ammunition hoist carryin' away,' said Pyecroft. 'And it carried away four of 'is teeth – on the lower port side, wasn't it, Pritch? The substitutes which he bought weren't screwed home, in a manner o' sayin'. When he talked fast they used to lift a little on the bed-plate. 'Ence, "Click". They called 'im a superior man, which is what we'd call a long, black-'aired, genteelly speakin', 'alf-bred beggar on the lower deck.'

'Four false teeth in the lower left jaw,' said Hooper, his hand in his waistcoat-pocket. 'What tattoo marks?'

'Look here,' began Pritchard, half rising. 'I'm sure we're very grateful to you as a gentleman for your 'orspitality, but per'aps we may 'ave made an error in – '

I looked at Pyecroft for aid – Hooper was crimsoning rapidly.

'If the fat marine now occupying the fo'c's'le will kindly bring 'is *status quo* to an anchor yet once more, we may be able to talk like gentlemen – not to say friends,' said Pyecroft. 'He regards you, Mr Hooper, as a emissary of the Law.'

'I only wish to observe that when a gentleman exhibits such a peculiar, or I should rather say, such a *bloomin'* curiosity in identification marks as our friend here – '

'Mr Pritchard,' I interposed, 'I'll take all the responsibility for Mr Hooper.'

'An' *you*'ll apologise all round,' said Pyecroft. 'You're a rude little man, Pritch.'

'But how was I – ' he began, wavering.

'I don't know an' I don't care. Apologise!'

The giant looked round bewildered and took our little hands into his vast grip, one by one.

'I was wrong,' he said meekly as a sheep. 'My suspicions was unfounded. Mr Hooper, I apologise.'

'You did quite right to look out for your own end o' the line,' said Hooper. 'I'd ha' done the same with a gentleman I didn't know, you see. If you don't mind I'd like to hear a little more o' your Mr Vickery. It's safe with me, you see.'

'Why did Vickery run?' I began, but Pyecroft's smile made me turn my question to 'Who was she?'

'She kep' a little hotel at Hauraki – near Auckland,' said Pyecroft.

'By Gawd!' roared Pritchard, slapping his hand on his leg. 'Not Mrs Bathurst!'

Pyecroft nodded slowly, and the Sergeant called all the powers of darkness to witness his bewilderment.

'So far as I could get at it, Mrs B. was the lady in question.'

'But Click was married,' cried Pritchard.

'An' 'ad a fifteen-year-old daughter. 'E's shown me her photograph. Settin' that aside, so to say, 'ave you ever found these little things make much difference? Because I haven't.'

'Good Lord Alive an' Watchin'! . . . Mrs Bathurst . . .' Then with another roar: 'You can say what you please, Pye, but you don't make me believe it was any of 'er fault. She wasn't *that!*'

'If I was going to say what I please, I'd begin by callin' you a silly ox an' work up to the higher pressures at leisure. I'm trying to say solely what transpired. M'rover, for once you're right. It wasn't her fault.'

'You couldn't 'aven't made me believe it if it 'ad been,' was the answer.

Such faith in a Sergeant of Marines interested me greatly. 'Never mind about that,' I cried. 'Tell me what she was like.'

'She was a widow,' said Pyecroft. 'Left so very young and never re-spliced. She kep' a little hotel for warrants and non-coms close to Auckland, an' she always wore black silk, and 'er neck – '

'You ask what she was like,' Pritchard broke in. 'Let me give you an instance. I was at Auckland first in '97, at the end o' the *Marroquin's* commission, an' as I'd been promoted I went up with the others. She used to look after us all, an' she never lost by it – not a penny! "Pay me now," she'd say, "or settle later. I know you won't let me suffer. Send the money from home if you like." Why, gentlemen all, I tell you I've seen that lady take her own gold watch an' chain off her neck in the bar an' pass it to a bosun 'oo'd come ashore without 'is ticker an' 'ad to catch the last boat. "I don't know your name," she said, "but when you've done with it, you'll find plenty that know me on the front. Send it back by one o' them." And it was worth thirty pounds if it was worth 'arf a crown. The little gold watch, Pye, with the blue monogram at the back. But, as I was sayin', in those days she kep' a beer that agreed with me – Slits it was called. One way an' another I must 'ave punished a good few bottles of it while we was in the bay – comin' ashore every night or so. Chaffin' across the bar like, once when we were alone, "Mrs B.," I said, "when next I call I want you to remember that this is my particular – just as you're my particular." (She'd let you go *that* far!) "Just as you're my particular," I said. "Oh, thank you, Sergeant Pritchard," she says, an' put 'er hand up to the curl be'ind 'er ear. Remember that way she had, Pye?'

'I think so,' said the sailor.

'Yes, "Thank you, Sergeant Pritchard," she says. "The least I can do is to mark it for you in case you change your mind. There's no great demand for it in the Fleet," she says, "but to make sure I'll put it at the back o' the shelf," an' she snipped off a piece of her hair ribbon with that old dolphin cigar-cutter on the bar – remember it, Pye? – an' she tied a bow round what was left – just four bottles. That was '97 – no, '96. In '98 I was in the *Resiliant* – China station – full commission. In Nineteen One, mark you, I was in the *Carthusian*, back in Auckland Bay again. Of course I went up to Mrs B.'s with the rest of us to see how things were goin'. They were the same as ever. (Remember the big tree on the pavement by the side-bar, Pye?) I never said anythin' in special (there was too many of us talkin' to her), but she saw me at once.'

'That wasn't difficult?' I ventured.

'Ah, but wait. I was comin' up to the bar, when, "Ada," she says to her niece, "get me Sergeant Pritchard's particular," and, gentlemen all, I tell you before I could shake 'ands with the lady, there were those four bottles o' Slits, with 'er 'air ribbon in a bow round each o' their necks, set down in front o' me, an' as she drew the cork she looked at me under her eyebrows in that blindish way she had o' lookin', an', "Sergeant Pritchard," she says, "I do 'ope you 'aven't changed your mind about your particulars." That's the kind o' woman she was – after five years!'

'I don't *see* her yet somehow,' said Hooper, but with sympathy.

'She – she never scrupled to feed a lame duck or set 'er foot on a scorpion at any time of 'er life,' Pritchard added valiantly.

'That don't help me either. My mother's like that for one.'

The giant heaved inside his uniform and rolled his eyes at the car-roof. Said Pyecroft suddenly –

'How many women have you been intimate with all over the world, Pritch?'

Pritchard blushed plum colour to the short hairs of his seventeen-inch neck.

' 'Undreds,' said Pyecroft. 'So've I. How many of 'em can you remember in your own mind, settin' aside the first – an' per'aps the last – *and one more*?'

'Few, wonderful few, now I tax myself,' said Sergeant Pritchard relievedly.

'An' how many times might you 'ave been at Auckland?'

'One – two,' he began – 'why, I can't make it more than three times in ten years. But I can remember every time that I ever saw Mrs B.'

'So can I – an' I've only been to Auckland twice – how she stood an' what she was sayin' an' what she looked like. That's the secret. 'Tisn't beauty, so to speak, nor good talk necessarily. It's just It. Some women'll stay in a man's memory if they once walk down a street, but most of 'em you can live with a month on end, an' next commission you'd be put to it to certify whether they talked in their sleep or not, as one might say.'

'Ah!' said Hooper. 'That's more the idea. I've known just two women of that nature.'

'An' it was no fault o' theirs?' asked Pritchard.

'None whatever. I know *that*!'

'An' if a man gets struck with that kind o' woman, Mr Hooper?' Pritchard went on.

'He goes crazy – or just saves himself,' was the slow answer.

'You've hit it,' said the Sergeant. 'You've seen an' known somethin' in the course o' your life, Mr Hooper. I'm lookin' at you!' He set down his bottle.

'And how often had Vickery seen her?' I asked.

'That's the dark an' bloody mystery,' Pyecroft answered. 'I'd never come across him till I come out in the *Hierophant* just now, an' there wasn't anyone in the ship who knew much about him. You see, he was what you call a superior man. 'E spoke to me once or twice about Auckland and Mrs B. on the voyage out. I called that to mind subsequently. There must 'ave been a good deal between 'em, to my way o' thinkin'. Mind you, I'm only giving you my *résumé* of it all, because all I know is second-'and so to speak, or rather I should say more than second-'and.'

'How?' said Hooper peremptorily. 'You must have seen it or heard it.'

'Ye–es,' said Pyecroft. 'I used to think seein' and hearin' was the only regulation aids to ascertainin' facts, but as we get older we get more accommodatin'. The cylinders work easier, I suppose . . . Were you in Cape Town last December when Phyllis's Circus came?'

'No – up-country,' said Hooper, a little nettled at the change of venue.

'I ask because they had a new turn of a scientific nature called "Home and Friends for a Tickey".'

'Oh, you mean the cinematograph – the pictures of prize-fights and steamers. I've seen 'em up-country.'

'Biograph or cinematograph was what I was alludin' to. London Bridge with the omnibuses – a troopship goin' to the war – marines on parade at Portsmouth, an' the Plymouth Express arrivin' at Paddin'ton.'

'Seen 'em all. Seen 'em all,' said Hooper impatiently.

'We *Hierophants* came in just before Christmas week an' leaf was easy.'

'I think a man gets fed up with Cape Town quicker than anywhere else on the station. Why, even Durban's more like Nature. We was there for Christmas,' Pritchard put in.

'Not bein' a devotee of Indian *peeris*, as our doctor said to the Pusser, I can't exactly say. Phyllis's was good enough after musketry practice at Mozambique. I couldn't get off the first two or three nights on account of what you might call an imbroglio with our Torpedo Lieutenant in the submerged flat, where some pride of the West country had sugared up a gyroscope; but I remember Vickery went ashore with our Carpenter Rigdon – old Crocus we called him. As a general rule Crocus never left 'is ship unless an' until he was 'oisted out with a winch, but *when* 'e went 'e would return noddin' like a lily gemmed with dew. We smothered him down below that night, but the things 'e said about Vickery as a fittin' playmate for a Warrant Officer of 'is cubic capacity, before we got him quiet, was what I should call pointed.'

'I've been with Crocus – in the *Redoubtable*,' said the Sergeant. 'He's a character if there is one.'

'Next night I went into Cape Town with Dawson and Pratt; but just at the door of the Circus I came across Vickery. "Oh!" he says, "you're the man I'm looking for. Come and sit next me. This way to the shillin'

places!" I went astern at once, protestin' because tickey seats better
suited my so-called finances. "Come on," says Vickery, "I'm payin'."
Naturally I abandoned Pratt and Dawson in anticipation o' drinks to
match the seats. "No," he says, when this was 'inted – "not now. Not
now. As many as you please afterwards, but I want you sober for the
occasion." I caught 'is face under a lamp just then, an' the appearance
of it quite cured me of my thirsts. Don't mistake. It didn't frighten me.
It made me anxious. I can't tell you what it was like, but that was the
effect which it 'ad on me. If you want to know, it reminded me of those
things in bottles in those herbalistic shops at Plymouth – preserved in
spirits of wine. White an' crumply things – previous to birth as you
might say.'

'You 'ave a beastial mind, Pye,' said the Sergeant, relighting his pipe.

'Perhaps. We were in the front row, an' "Home an' Friends" came
on early. Vickery touched me on the knee when the number went up.
"If you see anything that strikes you," he says, "drop me a hint;" then
he went on clicking. We saw London Bridge an' so forth an' so on, an'
it was most interestin'. I'd never seen it before. You 'eard a little
dynamo like buzzin', but the pictures were the real thing – alive an'
movin'.'

'I've seen 'em,' said Hooper. 'Of course they are taken from the very
thing itself – you see.'

'Then the Western Mail came in to Paddin'ton on the big magic
lantern sheet. First we saw the platform empty an' the porters standin'
by. Then the engine come in, head on, an' the women in the front row
jumped: she headed so straight. Then the doors opened and the
passengers came out and the porters got the luggage – just like life.
Only – only when anyone came down too far towards us that was
watchin', they walked right out o' the picture, so to speak. I was 'ighly
interested, I can tell you. So were all of us. I watched an old man with a
rug 'oo'd dropped a book an' was tryin' to pick it up, when quite slowly,
from be'ind two porters – carryin' a little reticule an' lookin' from side
to side – comes out Mrs Bathurst. There was no mistakin' the walk in a
hundred thousand. She come forward – right forward – she looked out
straight at us with that blindish look which Pritch alluded to. She
walked on and on till she melted out of the picture – like – like a
shadow jumpin' over a candle, an' as she went I 'eard Dawson in the
tickey seats be'ind sing out: "Christ! there's Mrs B.!" '

Hooper swallowed his spittle and leaned forward intently.

'Vickery touched me on the knee again. He was clickin' his four false
teeth with his jaw down like an enteric at the last kick. "Are you sure?"
says he. "Sure," I says, "didn't you 'ear Dawson give tongue? Why, it's

the woman herself." "I was sure before," he says, "but I brought you to make sure. Will you come again with me tomorrow?"

' "Willingly," I says, "it's like meetin' old friends."

' "Yes," he says, openin' his watch, "very like. It will be four-and-twenty hours less four minutes before I see her again Come and have a drink," he says. "It may amuse you, but it's no sort of earthly use to me." He went out shaking his head an' stumblin' over people's feet as if he was drunk already. I anticipated a swift drink an' a speedy return, because I wanted to see the performin' elephants. Instead o' which Vickery began to navigate the town at the rate o' knots, lookin' in at a bar every three minutes approximate Greenwich time. I'm not a drinkin' man, though there are those present' – he cocked his unforget-table eye at me – 'who may have seen me more or less imbued with the fragrant spirit. None the less when I drink I like to do it at anchor an' not at an average speed of eighteen knots on the measured mile. There's a tank as you might say at the back o' that big hotel up the hill – what do they call it?'

'The Molteno Reservoir,' I suggested, and Hooper nodded.

'That was his limit o' drift. We walked there an' we come down through the Gardens – there was a South-Easter blowin' – an' we finished up by the Docks. Then we bore up the road to Salt River, and wherever there was a pub Vickery put in sweatin'. He didn't look at what he drunk – he didn't look at the change. He walked an' he drunk an' he perspired in rivers. I understood why old Crocus 'ad come back in the condition 'e did, because Vickery an' I 'ad two an' a half hours o' this gypsy manoeuvre, an' when we got back to the station there wasn't a dry atom on or in me.'

'Did he say anything?' Pritchard asked.

'The sum total of 'is conversation from 7.45 p.m. till 11.15 p.m. was "Let's have another." Thus the mornin' an' the evenin' were the first day, as Scripture says . . . To abbreviate a lengthy narrative, I went into Cape Town for five consecutive nights with Master Vickery, and in that time I must 'ave logged about fifty knots over the ground an' taken in two gallon o' all the worst spirits south the Equator. The evolution never varied. Two shilling seats for us two; five minutes o' the pictures, an' perhaps forty-five seconds o' Mrs B. walking down towards us with that blindish look in her eyes an' the reticule in her hand. Then out walk – and drink till train time.'

'What did you think?' said Hooper, his hand fingering his waistcoat-pocket.

'Several things,' said Pyecroft. 'To tell you the truth, I aren't quite done thinkin' about it yet. Mad? The man was a dumb lunatic – must

'ave been for months – years p'raps. I know somethin' o' maniacs, as
every man in the Service must. I've been shipmates with a mad skipper –
an' a lunatic Number One, but never both together I thank 'Eaven. I
could give you the names o' three captains now 'oo ought to be in an
asylum, but you don't find me interferin' with the mentally afflicted till
they begin to lay about 'em with rammers an' winch-handles. Only once
I crept up a little into the wind towards Master Vickery. "I wonder what
she's doin' in England," I says. "Don't it seem to you she's lookin' for
somebody?" That was in the Gardens again, with the South-Easter
blowin' as we were makin' our desperate round. "She's lookin' for me,"
he says, stoppin' dead under a lamp an' clickin'. When he wasn't
drinkin', in which case all 'is teeth clicked on the glass, 'e was clickin' 'is
four false teeth like a Marconi ticker. "Yes! lookin' for me," he said, an'
he went on very softly an' as you might say affectionately. "*But*," he
went on, "in future, Mr Pyecroft, I should take it kindly of you if you'd
confine your remarks to the drinks set before you. Otherwise," he says,
"with the best will in the world towards you, I may find myself guilty of
murder! Do you understand?" he says. "Perfectly," I says, "but would it
at all soothe you to know that in such a case the chances o' your being
killed are precisely equivalent to the chances o' me being outed." "Why,
no," he says, "I'm almost afraid that 'ud be a temptation." Then I said –
we was right under the lamp by that arch at the end o' the Gardens
where the trams come round – "Assumin' murder was done – or
attempted murder – I put it to you that you would still be left so badly
crippled, as one might say, that your subsequent capture by the police –
to 'oom you would 'ave to explain – would be largely inevitable."
"That's better," 'e says, passin' 'is hands over his forehead. "That's
much better, because," he says, "do you know, as I am now, Pye, I'm not
so sure if I could explain anything much." Those were the only
particular words I had with 'im in our walks as I remember.'

    'What walks!' said Hooper. 'Oh my soul, what walks!'

    'They were chronic,' said Pyecroft gravely, 'but I didn't anticipate
any danger till the Circus left. Then I anticipated that, bein' deprived
of 'is stimulant, he might react on me, so to say, with a hatchet.
Consequently, after the final performance an' the ensuin' wet walk, I
kep' myself aloof from my superior officer on board in the execution of
'is duty, as you might put it. Consequently, I was interested when the
sentry informs me while I was passin' on my lawful occasions that Click
had asked to see the captain. As a general rule warrant officers don't
dissipate much of the owner's time, but Click put in an hour and more
be'ind that door. My duties kep' me within eyeshot of it. Vickery came
out first, an' 'e actually nodded at me an' smiled. This knocked me out

o' the boat, because, havin' seen 'is face for five consecutive nights, I didn't anticipate any change there more than a condenser in hell, so to speak. The owner emerged later. His face didn't read off at all, so I fell back on his cox, 'oo'd been eight years with him and knew him better than boat signals. Lamson – that was the cox's name – crossed 'is bows once or twice at low speeds an' dropped down to me visibly concerned. "He's shipped 'is court-martial face," says Lamson. "Someone's goin' to be 'ung. I've never seen that look but once before when they chucked the gun-sights overboard in the *Fantastic*." Throwin' gun-sights overboard, Mr Hooper, is the equivalent for mutiny in these degenerate days. It's done to attract the notice of the authorities an' the *Western Mornin' News* – generally by a stoker. Naturally, word went round the lower deck an' we had a private over'aul of our little consciences. But, barrin' a shirt which a second-class stoker said 'ad walked into 'is bag from the marines' flat by itself, nothin' vital transpired. The owner went about flyin' the signal for "attend public execution," so to say, but there was no corpse at the yard-arm. 'E lunched on the beach an' 'e returned with 'is regulation harbour-routine face about 3 p.m. Thus Lamson lost prestige for raising false alarms. The only person 'oo might 'ave connected the epicycloidal gears correctly was one Pyecroft, when he was told that Mr Vickery would go up-country that same evening to take over certain naval ammunition left after the war in Bloemfontein Fort. No details was ordered to accompany Master Vickery. He was told off first person singular – as a unit – by himself.'

The marine whistled penetratingly.

'That's what I thought,' said Pyecroft. 'I went ashore with him in the cutter an' 'e asked me to walk through the station. He was clickin' audibly, but otherwise seemed happy-ish.

' "You might like to know," he says, stoppin' just opposite the Admiral's front gate, "that Phyllis's Circus will be performin' at Worcester tomorrow night. So I shall see 'er yet once again. You've been very patient with me," he says.

' "Look here, Vickery," I said, "this thing's come to be just as much as I can stand. Consume your own smoke. I don't want to know any more."

' "You!" he said. "What have you got to complain of? – you've only 'ad to watch. I'm *it*," he says, "but that's neither here nor there," he says. "I've one thing to say before shakin' 'ands. Remember," 'e says – we were just by the Admiral's garden-gate then – "remember, that I am *not* a murderer, because my lawful wife died in childbed six weeks after I came out. That much at least I am clear of," 'e says.

' "Then what have you done that signifies?" I said. "What's the rest of it?"

' "The rest," 'e says, "is silence," an' he shook 'ands and went clickin' into Simonstown station.'

'Did he stop to see Mrs Bathurst at Worcester?' I asked.

'It's not known. He reported at Bloemfontein, saw the ammunition into the trucks, and then 'e disappeared. Went out – deserted, if you care to put it so – within eighteen months of his pension, an' if what 'e said about 'is wife was true he was a free man as 'e then stood. How do you read it off?'

'Poor devil!' said Hooper. 'To see her that way every night! I wonder what it was.'

'I've made my 'ead ache in that direction many a long night.'

'But I'll swear Mrs B. 'ad no 'and in it,' said the Sergeant, unshaken.

'No. Whatever the wrong or deceit was, he did it, I'm sure o' that. I 'ad to look at 'is face for five consecutive nights. I'm not so fond o' navigatin' about Cape Town with a South-Easter blowin' these days. I can hear those teeth click, so to say.'

'Ah, those teeth,' said Hooper, and his hand went to his waistcoat-pocket once more. 'Permanent things false teeth are. You read about 'em in all the murder trials.'

'What d'you suppose the captain knew – or did?' I asked.

'I've never turned my searchlight that way,' Pyecroft answered unblushingly.

We all reflected together, and drummed on empty beer bottles as the picnic-party, sunburned, wet, and sandy, passed our door singing 'The Honeysuckle and the Bee'.

'Pretty girl under that kapje,' said Pyecroft.

'They never circulated his description?' said Pritchard.

'I was askin' you before these gentlemen came,' said Hooper to me, 'whether you knew Wankies – on the way to the Zambesi – beyond Buluwayo?'

'Would he pass there – tryin' to get to that Lake what's 'is name?' said Pritchard.

Hooper shook his head and went on: 'There's a curious bit o' line there, you see. It runs through solid teak forest – a sort o' mahogany really – seventy-two miles without a curve. I've had a train derailed there twenty-three times in forty miles. I was up there a month ago relievin' a sick inspector, you see. He told me to look out for a couple of tramps in the teak.'

'Two?' Pyecroft said. 'I don't envy that other man if – '

'We get heaps of tramps up there since the war. The inspector told me I'd find 'em at M'Bindwe siding waiting to go North. He'd given 'em some grub and quinine, you see. I went up on a construction train. I looked out for 'em. I saw them miles ahead along the straight, waiting in the teak. One of 'em was standin' up by the dead-end of the siding an' the other was squattin' down lookin' up at 'im, you see.'

'What did you do for 'em?' said Pritchard.

'There wasn't much I could do, except bury 'em. There'd been a bit of a thunderstorm in the teak, you see, and they were both stone dead and as black as charcoal. That's what they really were, you see – charcoal. They fell to bits when we tried to shift 'em. The man who was standin' up had the false teeth. I saw 'em shinin' against the black. Fell to bits he did too, like his mate squatting down an' watchin' him, both of 'em all wet in the rain. Both burned to charcoal, you see. And – that's what made me ask about marks just now – the false-toother was tattooed on the arms and chest – a crown and foul anchor with M. V. above.'

'I've seen that,' said Pyecroft quickly. 'It was so.'

'But if he was all charcoal-like?' said Pritchard, shuddering.

'You know how writing shows up white on a burned letter? Well, it was like that, you see. We buried 'em in the teak and I kept . . . But he was a friend of you two gentlemen, you see.'

Mr Hooper brought his hand away from his waistcoat-pocket – empty.

Pritchard covered his face with his hands for a moment, like a child shutting out an ugliness.

'And to think of her at Hauraki!' he murmured – 'with 'er 'air-ribbon on my beer. "Ada," she said to her niece . . . Oh, my Gawd! . . . '

'On a summer afternoon, when the honeysuckle blooms,
    And all Nature seems at rest,
Underneath the bower, 'mid the perfume of the flower,
    Sat a maiden with the one she loves the best – '

sang the picnic-party waiting for their train at Glengariff.

'Well, I don't know how you feel about it,' said Pyecroft, 'but 'avin' seen 'is face for five consecutive nights on end, I'm inclined to finish what's left of the beer an' thank Gawd he's dead!'

'OUR FATHERS ALSO'

By – they are by with mirth and tears,
   Wit or the works of Desire –
Cushioned about on the kindly years
   Between the wall and the fire.

The grapes are pressed, the corn is shocked –
   Standeth no more to glean;
For the Gates of Love and Learning locked
   When they went out between.

All lore our Lady Venus bares
   Signalled it was or told
By the dear lips long given to theirs
   And longer to the mould.

All Profit, all Device, all Truth
   Written it was or said
By the mighty men of their mighty youth,
   Which is mighty being dead.

The film that floats before their eyes
   The Temple's Veil they call;
And the dust that on the Shewbread lies
   Is holy over all.

Warn them of seas that slip our yoke
   Of slow conspiring stars –
The ancient Front of Things unbroke
   But heavy with new wars?

By – they are by with mirth and tears,
   Wit or the waste of Desire –
Cushioned about on the kindly years
   Between the wall and the fire.

Below the Mill Dam

'Book – Book – Domesday Book!' They were letting in the water for the evening stint at Robert's Mill, and the wooden Wheel where lived the Spirit of the Mill settled to its nine-hundred-year-old song: 'Here Azor, a freeman, held one rod, but it never paid geld. *Nun-nun-nunquam geldavit.* Here Reinbert has one villein and four cottars with one plough – and wood for six hogs and two fisheries of sixpence and a mill of ten shillings – *unum molinum* – one mill. Reinbert's mill – Robert's Mill. Then and afterwards and now – *tunc et post et modo* – Robert's Mill. Book – Book – Domesday Book!'

'I confess,' said the Black Rat on the crossbeam, luxuriously trimming his whiskers – 'I confess I am not above appreciating my position and all it means.' He was a genuine old English black rat, a breed which, report says, is rapidly diminishing before the incursions of the brown variety.

'Appreciation is the surest sign of inadequacy,' said the Grey Cat, coiled up on a piece of sacking.

'But I know what you mean,' she added. 'To sit by right at the heart of things – eh?'

'Yes,' said the Black Rat, as the old mill shook and the heavy stones thuttered on the grist. 'To possess – er – all this environment as an integral part of one's daily life must insensibly of course . . . You see?'

'I feel,' said the Grey Cat. 'Indeed, if *we* are not saturated with the spirit of the Mill, who should be?'

'Book – Book – Domesday Book!' The Wheel, set to his work, was running off the tenure of the whole rape, for he knew Domesday Book backwards and forwards: '*In Ferle tenuit Abbatia de Wiltuna unam hidam et unam virgam et dimidiam. Nunquam geldavit.* And Agemond, a freeman, has half a hide and one rod. I remember Agemond well. Charmin' fellow – friend of mine. He married a Norman girl in the days when we rather looked down on the Normans as upstarts. An' Agemond's dead? So he is. Eh, dearie me! dearie me! I remember the wolves howling outside his door in the big frost of Ten Fifty-Nine . . . *Essewelde hundredum nunquam geldum reddidit.* Book! Book! Domesday Book!'

'After all,' the Grey Cat continued, 'atmosphere is life. It is the influences under which we live that count in the long run. Now, outside' – she cocked one ear towards the half-opened door – 'there is an absurd convention that rats and cats are, I won't go so far as to say natural enemies, but opposed forces. Some such ruling may be crudely effective – I don't for a minute presume to set up my standards as final – among the ditches; but from the larger point of view that one gains by living at the heart of things, it seems for a rule of life a little overstrained. Why, because some of your associates have, shall I say, liberal views on the ultimate destination of a sack of – er – middlings don't they call them – '

'Something of that sort,' said the Black Rat, a most sharp and sweet-toothed judge of everything ground in the mill for the last three years.

'Thanks – middlings be it. *Why*, as I was saying, must I disarrange my fur and my digestion to chase you round the dusty arena whenever we happen to meet?'

'As little reason,' said the Black Rat, 'as there is for me, who, I trust, am a person of ordinarily decent instincts, to wait till you have gone on a round of calls, and then to assassinate your very charming children.'

'Exactly! It has its humorous side though.' The Grey Cat yawned. 'The miller seems afflicted by it. He shouted large and vague threats to my address, last night at tea, that he wasn't going to keep cats who "caught no mice". Those were his words. I remember the grammar sticking in my throat like a herring-bone.'

'And what did you do?'

'What does one do when a barbarian utters? One ceases to utter and removes. I removed – towards his pantry. It was a *riposte* he might appreciate.'

'Really those people grow absolutely insufferable,' said the Black Rat. 'There is a local ruffian who answers to the name of Mangles – a builder – who has taken possession of the outhouses on the far side of the Wheel for the last fortnight. He has constructed cubical horrors in red brick where those deliciously picturesque pigsties used to stand. Have you noticed?'

'There has been much misdirected activity of late among the humans. They jabber inordinately. I haven't yet been able to arrive at their reason for existence.' The Cat yawned.

'A couple of them came in here last week with wires, and fixed them all about the walls. Wires protected by some abominable composition, ending in iron brackets with glass bulbs. Utterly useless for any purpose and artistically absolutely hideous. What do they mean?'

'Aaah! I have known *four*-and-twenty leaders of revolt in Faenza,' said the Cat, who kept good company with the boarders spending a summer at the Mill Farm. 'It means nothing except that humans occasionally bring their dogs with them. I object to dogs in all forms.'

'Shouldn't object to dogs,' said the Wheel sleepily . . . 'The Abbot of Wilton kept the best pack in the county. He enclosed all the Harryngton Woods to Sturt Common. Aluric, a freeman, was dispossessed of his holding. They tried the case at Lewes, but he got no change out of William de Warrenne on the bench. William de Warrenne fined Aluric eight and fourpence for treason, and the Abbot of Wilton excommunicated him for blasphemy. Aluric was no sportsman. Then the Abbot's brother married . . . I've forgotten her name, but she was a charmin' little woman. The Lady Philippa was her daughter. That was after the barony was conferred. She rode devilish straight to hounds. They were a bit throatier than we breed now, but a good pack: one of the best. The Abbot kept 'em in splendid shape. Now, who was the woman the Abbot kept? Book – Book! I shall have to go right back to Domesday and work up the centuries: *Modo per omnia reddit burgum tunc – tunc – tunc!* Was it *burgum* or *hundredum?* I shall remember in a minute. There's no hurry.' He paused as he turned over silvered with showering drops.

'This won't do,' said the Waters in the sluice. 'Keep moving.'

The Wheel swung forward; the Waters roared on the buckets and dropped down to the darkness below.

'Noisier than usual,' said the Black Rat. 'It must have been raining up the valley.'

'Floods maybe,' said the Wheel dreamily. 'It isn't the proper season, but they can come without warning. I shall never forget the big one – when the Miller went to sleep and forgot to open the hatches. More than two hundred years ago it was, but I recall it distinctly. Most unsettling.'

'We lifted that wheel off his bearings,' cried the Waters. 'We said, "Take away that bauble!" And in the morning he was five miles down the valley – hung up in a tree.'

'Vulgar!' said the Cat. 'But I am sure he never lost his dignity.'

'We don't know. He looked like the Ace of Diamonds when we had finished with him . . . Move on there! Keep on moving. Over! Get over!'

'And why on this day more than any other,' said the Wheel statelily. 'I am not aware that my department requires the stimulus of external pressure to keep it up to its duties. I trust I have the elementary instincts of a gentleman.'

'Maybe,' the Waters answered together, leaping down on the buckets. 'We only know that you are very stiff on your bearings. Over, get over!'

The Wheel creaked and groaned. There was certainly greater pressure upon him than he had ever felt, and his revolutions had increased from six and three-quarters to eight and a third per minute. But the uproar between the narrow, weed-hung walls annoyed the Grey Cat.

'Isn't it almost time,' she said plaintively, 'that the person who is paid to understand these things shuts off those vehement drippings with that screw-thing on the top of that box-thing.'

'They'll be shut off at eight o'clock as usual,' said the Rat; 'then we can go to dinner.'

'But we shan't be shut off till ever so late,' said the Waters gaily. 'We shall keep it up all night.'

'The ineradicable offensiveness of youth is partially compensated for by its eternal hopefulness,' said the Cat. 'Our dam is not, I am glad to say, designed to furnish water for more than four hours at a time. Reserve is Life.'

'Thank goodness!' said the Black Rat. 'Then they can return to their native ditches.'

'Ditches!' cried the Waters; 'Raven's Gill Brook is no ditch. It is almost navigable, and *we* come from there away.' They slid over solid and compact till the Wheel thudded under their weight.

'Raven's Gill Brook,' said the Rat. 'I never heard of Raven's Gill.'

'We are the waters of Harpenden Brook – down from under Callton Rise. Phew! how the race stinks compared with the heather country.' Another five foot of water flung itself against the Wheel, broke, roared, gurgled, and was gone.

'Indeed,' said the Grey Cat, 'I am sorry to tell you that Raven's Gill Brook is cut off from this valley by an absolutely impassable range of mountains, and Callton Rise is more than nine miles away. It belongs to another system entirely.'

'Ah yes,' said the Rat, grinning, 'but we forget that, for the young, water always runs uphill.'

'Oh, hopeless! hopeless! hopeless!' cried the Waters, descending open-palmed upon the Wheel. 'There is nothing between here and Raven's Gill Brook that a hundred yards of channelling and a few square feet of concrete could not remove; and hasn't removed!'

'And Harpenden Brook is north of Raven's Gill and runs into Raven's Gill at the foot of Callton Rise, where the big ilex trees are, and *we* come from there!' These were the glassy, clear waters of the high chalk.

'And Batten's Ponds, that are fed by springs, have been led through Trott's Wood, taking the spare water from the old Witches' Spring

under Churt Haw, and we – we – we are their combined waters!'
Those were the Waters from the upland bogs and moors – a porter-
coloured, dusky, and foam-flecked flood.

'It's all very interesting,' purred the Cat to the sliding waters, 'and I
have no doubt that Trott's Woods and Bott's Woods are tremendously
important places; but if you could manage to do your work – whose
value I don't in the least dispute – a little more soberly, I, for one,
should be grateful.'

'Book – book – book – book – book – Domesday Book!' The urged
Wheel was fairly clattering now: 'In Burgelstaltone a monk holds of
Earl Godwin one hide and a half with eight villeins. There is a church –
and a monk . . . I remember that monk. Blessed if he could rattle his
rosary off any quicker than I am doing now . . . and wood for seven
hogs. I must be running twelve to the minute . . . almost as fast as
Steam. Damnable invention, Steam! . . . Surely it's time we went to
dinner or prayers – or something. Can't keep up this pressure, day in
and day out, and not feel it. I don't mind for myself, of course. *Noblesse
oblige*, you know. I'm only thinking of the Upper and the Nether
Millstones. They came out of the common rock. They can't be
expected to – '

'Don't worry on our account, please,' said the Millstones huskily. 'So
long as you supply the power we'll supply the weight and the bite.'

'Isn't it a trifle blasphemous, though, to work you in this way?'
grunted the Wheel. 'I seem to remember something about the Mills of
God grinding "slowly". *Slowly* was the word!'

'But we are not the Mills of God. We're only the Upper and the
Nether Millstones. We have received no instructions to be anything
else. We are actuated by power transmitted through you.'

'Ah, but let us be merciful as we are strong. Think of all the beautiful
little plants that grow on my woodwork. There are five varieties of rare
moss within less than one square yard – and all these delicate jewels of
nature are being grievously knocked about by this excessive rush of the
water.'

'Umph!' growled the Millstones. 'What with your religious scruples
and your taste for botany we'd hardly know you for the Wheel that put
the carter's son under last autumn. You never worried about *him*!'

'He ought to have known better.'

'So ought your jewels of nature. Tell 'em to grow where it's safe.'

'How a purely mercantile life debases and brutalises!' said the Cat to
the Rat.

'They were such beautiful little plants too,' said the Rat tenderly.
'Maiden's-tongue and hart's-hair fern trellising all over the wall just as

they do on the sides of churches in the Downs. Think what a joy the sight of them must be to our sturdy peasants pulling hay!'

'Golly!' said the Millstones. 'There's nothing like coming to the heart of things for information,' and they returned to the song that all English water-mills have sung from time beyond telling:

> 'There was a jovial miller once
> Lived on the River Dee,
> And this the burden of his song
> For ever used to be . . . '

Then, as fresh grist poured in and dulled the note:

> 'I care for nobody – no, not I,
> And nobody cares for me.'

'Even these stones have absorbed something of our atmosphere,' said the Grey Cat. 'Nine-tenths of the trouble in this world comes from lack of detachment.'

'One of your people died from forgetting that, didn't she?' said the Rat.

'One only. The example has sufficed us for generations.'

'Ah! but what happened to Don't Care?' the Waters demanded.

'Brutal riding to death of the casual analogy is another mark of provincialism!' The Grey Cat raised her tufted chin. 'I am going to sleep. With my social obligations I must snatch rest when I can; but, as our old friend here says, *Noblesse oblige* . . . Pity me! Three functions tonight in the village, and a barn-dance across the valley!'

'There's no chance, I suppose, of your looking in on the loft about two. Some of our young people are going to amuse themselves with a new sacque-dance – best white flour only,' said the Black Rat.

'I believe I am officially supposed not to countenance that sort of thing, but youth is youth . . . By the way, the humans set my milk-bowl in the loft these days; I hope your youngsters respect it.'

'My dear lady,' said the Black Rat, bowing, 'you grieve me. You hurt me inexpressibly. After all these years, too!'

'A general crush is so mixed – highways and hedges – all that sort of thing – and no one can answer for one's best friends. *I* never try. So long as mine are amusin' and in full voice, and can hold their own at a tile-party, I'm as catholic as these mixed waters in the dam here!'

'We aren't mixed. We *have* mixed. We are one now,' said the Waters sulkily.

'Still uttering?' said the Cat. 'Never mind, here's the Miller coming to shut you off. Ye–es, I have known – *four* – or five is it? – and twenty leaders of revolt in Faenza . . . A little more babble in the dam, a little more noise in the sluice, a little extra splashing on the wheel, and then – '

'They will find that nothing has occurred,' said the Black Rat. 'The old things persist and survive and are recognised – our old friend here first of all. By the way,' he turned toward the Wheel, 'I believe we have to congratulate you on your latest honour.'

'Profoundly well deserved – even if he had never – as he has – laboured strenuously through a long life for the amelioration of millkind,' said the Cat, who belonged to many tile and outhouse committees. 'Doubly deserved, I may say, for the silent and dignified rebuke his existence offers to the clattering, fidgety-footed demands of – er – some people. What form did the honour take?'

'It was,' said the Wheel bashfully, 'a machine-moulded pinion.'

'Pinions! Oh, how heavenly!' the Black Rat sighed. 'I never see a bat without wishing for wings.'

'Not exactly that sort of pinion,' said the Wheel, 'but a really ornate circle of toothed iron wheels. Absurd, of course, but gratifying. Mr Mangles and an associate herald invested me with it personally – on my left rim – the side that you can't see from the mill. I hadn't meant to say anything about it – or the new steel straps round my axles – bright red, you know – to be worn on all occasions – but, without false modesty, I assure you that the recognition cheered me not a little.'

'How intensely gratifying!' said the Black Rat. 'I must really steal an hour between lights someday and see what they are doing on your left side.'

'By the way, have you any light on this recent activity of Mr Mangles?' the Grey Cat asked. 'He seems to be building small houses on the far side of the tail-race. Believe me, I don't ask from any vulgar curiosity.'

'It affects our Order,' said the Black Rat simply but firmly.

'Thank you,' said the Wheel. 'Let me see if I can tabulate it properly. Nothing like system in accounts of all kinds. Book! Book! Book! On the side of the Wheel towards the hundred of Burgelstaltone, where till now was a stye of three hogs, Mangles, a freeman, with four villeins and two carts of two thousand bricks, has a new small house of five yards and a half, and one roof of iron and a floor of cement. Then, now, and afterwards beer in large tankards. And Felden, a stranger, with three villeins and one very great cart, deposits on it one engine of iron and brass and a small iron mill of four feet, and a broad strap of leather. And Mangles, the builder, with two villeins, constructs the floor for the same, and a floor of new brick with wires for the small mill. There are there also chalices filled with iron and water, in number fifty-seven. The whole is valued at one hundred and seventy-four pounds . . . I'm sorry I can't make myself clearer, but you can see for yourself.'

'Amazingly lucid,' said the Cat. She was the more to be admired because the language of Domesday Book is not, perhaps, the clearest medium wherein to describe a small but complete electric-light installation, deriving its power from a water-wheel by means of cogs and gearing.

'See for yourself – by all means, see for yourself,' said the Waters, spluttering and choking with mirth.

'Upon my word,' said the Black Rat furiously, 'I may be at fault, but I wholly fail to perceive where these offensive eavesdroppers – er – come in. We were discussing a matter that solely affected our Order.'

Suddenly they heard, as they had heard many times before, the Miller shutting off the water. To the rattle and rumble of the labouring stones succeeded thick silence, punctuated with little drops from the stayed wheel. Then some water-bird in the dam fluttered her wings as she slid to her nest, and the plop of a water-rat sounded like the fall of a log in the water.

'It is all over – it always is all over at just this time. Listen, the Miller is going to bed – as usual. Nothing has occurred,' said the Cat.

Something creaked in the house where the pigstyes had stood, as metal engaged on metal with a clink and a burr.

'Shall I turn her on?' cried the Miller.

'Ay,' said the voice from the dynamo-house.

'A human in Mangles' new house!' the Rat squeaked.

'What of it?' said the Grey Cat. 'Even supposing Mr Mangles' cat's-meat-coloured hovel ululated with humans, can't you see for yourself – that – ?'

There was a solid crash of released waters leaping upon the wheel more furiously than ever, a grinding of cogs, a hum like the hum of a hornet, and then the unvisited darkness of the old mill was scattered by intolerable white light. It threw up every cobweb, every burl and knot in the beams and the floor; till the shadows behind the flakes of rough plaster on the wall lay clear-cut as shadows of mountains on the photographed moon.

'See! See! See!' hissed the Waters in full flood. 'Yes, see for yourselves. Nothing has occurred. Can't you see?'

The Rat, amazed, had fallen from his foothold and lay half-stunned on the floor. The Cat, following her instinct, leaped nigh to the ceiling, and with flattened ears and bared teeth backed in a corner ready to fight whatever terror might be loosed on her. But nothing happened.

Through the long aching minutes nothing whatever happened, and her wire-brush tail returned slowly to its proper shape.

'Whatever it is,' she said at last, 'it's overdone. They can never keep it up, you know.'

'Much you know,' said the Waters. 'Over you go, old man. You can take the full head of us now. Those new steel axle-straps of yours can stand anything. Come along, Raven's Gill, Harpenden, Callton Rise, Batten's Ponds, Witches' Spring, all together! Let's show these gentlemen how to work!'

'But – but – I thought it was a decoration. Why – why – why – it only means more work for *me*!'

'Exactly. You're to supply about sixty eight-candle lights when required. But they won't be all in use at once – '

'Ah! I thought as much,' said the Cat. 'The reaction is bound to come.'

'*And*,' said the Waters, 'you will do the ordinary work of the mill as well.'

'Impossible!' the old Wheel quivered as it drove. 'Aluric never did it – nor Azor, nor Reinbert. Not even William de Warrenne or the Papal Legate. There's no precedent for it. I tell you there's no precedent for working a wheel like this.'

'Wait a while! We're making one as fast as we can. Aluric and Co. are dead. So's the Papal Legate. You've no notion how dead they are, but we're here – the Waters of Five Separate Systems. We're just as interesting as Domesday Book. Would you like to hear about the land-tenure in Trott's Wood? It's squat-right, chiefly.' The mocking Waters leaped one over the other, chuckling and chattering profanely.

'In that hundred Jenkins, a tinker, with one dog – *unus canis* – holds, by the Grace of God and a habit he has of working hard, *unam hidam* – a large potato patch. Charmin' fellow, Jenkins. Friend of ours. Now, who the dooce did Jenkins keep? . . . In the hundred of Callton is one charcoal-burner *irreligiosissimus homo* – a bit of a rip – but a thorough sportsman. *Ibi est ecclesia. Non multum.* Not much of a church, *quia* because, *episcopus* the Vicar irritated the Nonconformists *tunc et post et modo* – then and afterwards and now – until they built a cut-stone Congregational chapel with red brick facings that did not return itself – *defendebat se* – at four thousand pounds.'

'Charcoal-burners, vicars, schismatics, and red brick facings,' groaned the Wheel. 'But this is sheer blasphemy. What waters have they let in upon me?'

'Floods from the gutters. Faugh, this light is positively sickening!' said the Cat, rearranging her fur.

'We come down from the clouds or up from the springs, exactly like all other waters everywhere. Is that what's surprising you?' sang the Waters.

'Of course not. I know my work if you don't. What I complain of is your lack of reverence and repose. You've no instinct of deference towards your betters – your heartless parody of the Sacred volume (the Wheel meant Domesday Book) proves it.'

'Our betters?' said the Waters most solemnly. 'What is there in all this dammed race that hasn't come down from the clouds, or – '

'Spare me that talk please,' the Wheel persisted. 'You'd *never* understand. It's the tone – your tone that we object to.'

'Yes. It's your tone,' said the Black Rat, picking himself up limb by limb.

'If you thought a trifle more about the work you're supposed to do, and a trifle less about your precious feelings, you'd render a little more duty in return for the power vested in you – we mean wasted on you,' the Waters replied.

'I have been some hundreds of years laboriously acquiring the knowledge which you see fit to challenge so light-heartedly,' the Wheel jarred.

'Challenge him! Challenge him!' clamoured the little waves riddling down through the tail-race. 'As well now as later. Take him up!'

The main mass of the Waters plunging on the Wheel shocked that well-bolted structure almost into the box-lids by saying: 'Very good. Tell us what you suppose yourself to be doing at the present moment.'

'Waiving the offensive form of your question, I answer, purely as a matter of courtesy, that I am engaged in the trituration of farinaceous substances whose ultimate destination it would be a breach of the trust reposed in me to reveal.'

'Fiddle!' said the Waters. 'We knew it all along! The first direct question shows his ignorance of his own Job. Listen, old thing. Thanks to us, you are now actuating a machine of whose construction you know nothing, that that machine may, over wires of whose ramifications you are, by your very position, profoundly ignorant, deliver a power which you can never realise, to localities beyond the extreme limits of your mental horizon, with the object of producing phenomena which in your wildest dreams (if you ever dream) you could never comprehend. Is that clear, or would you like it all in words of four syllables?'

'Your assumptions are deliciously sweeping, but may I point out that a decent and – the dear old Abbot of Wilton would have put it in his resonant monkish Latin much better than I can – a scholarly reserve does not necessarily connote blank vacuity of mind on all subjects.'

'Ah, the dear old Abbot of Wilton,' said the Rat sympathetically, as one nursed in that bosom. 'Charmin' fellow – thorough scholar and gentleman. Such a pity!'

'Oh, Sacred Fountains!' – the Waters were fairly boiling. 'He goes out of his way to expose his ignorance by triple bucketfuls. He creaks to high Heaven that he is hopelessly behind the common order of things! He invites the streams of Five Watersheds to witness his su-su-supernal incompetence, and then he talks as though there were untold reserves of knowledge behind him that he is too modest to bring forward. For a bland, circular, absolutely sincere impostor, you're a miracle, O Wheel!'

'I do not pretend to be anything more than an integral portion of an accepted and not altogether mushroom institution.'

'Quite so,' said the Waters. 'Then go round – hard – '

'To what end?' asked the Wheel.

'Till a big box of tanks in your house begins to fizz and fume – gassing is the proper word.'

'It would be,' said the Cat, sniffing.

'That will show that your accumulators are full. When the accumulators are exhausted, and the lights burn badly, you will find us whacking you round and round again.'

'The end of life as decreed by Mangles and his creatures is to go whacking round and round for ever,' said the Cat.

'In order,' the Rat said, 'that you may throw raw and unnecessary illumination upon all the unloveliness in the world. Unloveliness which we shall – er – have always with us. At the same time you will riotously neglect the so-called little but vital graces that make up Life.'

'Yes, Life,' said the Cat, 'with its dim delicious half-tones and veiled indeterminate distances. Its surprisals, escapes, encounters, and dizzying leaps – its full-throated choruses in honour of the morning star, and its melting reveries beneath the sun-warmed wall.'

'Oh, you can go on the tiles, Pussalina, just the same as usual,' said the laughing Waters. 'We shan't interfere with you.'

'On the tiles, forsooth!' hissed the Cat.

'Well, that's what it amounts to,' persisted the Waters. 'We see a good deal of the minor graces of life on our way down to our job.'

'And – but I fear I speak to deaf ears – do they never impress you?' said the Wheel.

'Enormously,' said the Waters. 'We have already learned six refined synonyms for loafing.'

'But (here again I feel as though preaching in the wilderness) it never occurs to you that there may exist some small difference between the wholly animal – ah – rumination of bovine minds and the discerning, well-apportioned leisure of the finer type of intellect?'

'Oh, yes. The bovine mind goes to sleep under a hedge and makes no bones about it when it's shouted at. We've seen *that* – in haying-time – all along the meadows. The finer type is wide awake enough to fudge up excuses for shirking, and mean enough to get stuffy when its excuses aren't accepted. Turn over!'

'But, my good people, no gentleman gets stuffy as you call it. A certain proper pride, to put it no higher, forbids – '

'Nothing that he wants to do if he really wants to do it. Get along! What are you giving us? D'you suppose we've scoured half heaven in the clouds, and half earth in the mists, to be taken in at this time of the day by a bone-idle, old hand-quern of your type?'

'It is not for me to bandy personalities with you. I can only say that I simply decline to accept the situation.'

'Decline away. It doesn't make any odds. They'll probably put in a turbine if you decline too much.'

'What's a turbine?' said the Wheel quickly.

'A little thing you don't see, that performs surprising revolutions. But you won't decline. You'll hang on to your two nice red-strapped axles and your new machine-moulded pinions like – a – like a leech on a lily stem! There's centuries of work in your old bones if you'd only apply yourself to it; and, mechanically, an overshot wheel with this head of water is about as efficient as a turbine.'

'So in future I am to be considered mechanically? I have been painted by at least five Royal Academicians.'

'Oh, you can be painted by five hundred when you aren't at work, of course. But while you are at work you'll work. You won't half-stop and think and talk about rare plants and dicky-birds and farinaceous fiduciary interests. You'll continue to revolve, and this new head of water will see that you do so continue.'

'It is a matter on which it would be exceedingly ill-advised to form a hasty or a premature conclusion. I will give it my most careful consideration,' said the Wheel.

'Please do,' said the Waters gravely. 'Hullo! Here's the Miller again.'

The Cat coiled herself in a picturesque attitude on the softest corner of a sack, and the Rat without haste, yet certainly without rest, slipped behind the sacking as though an appointment had just occurred to him.

In the doorway, with the young Engineer, stood the Miller grinning amazedly.

'Well – well – well! 'tis true-ly won'erful. An' what a power o' dirt! It come over me now looking at these lights, that I've never rightly seen my own mill before. She needs a lot bein' done to her.'

'Ah! I suppose one must make oneself moderately agreeable to the baser sort. They have their uses. This thing controls the dairy.' The Cat, pincing on her toes, came forward and rubbed her head against the Miller's knee.'

'Ay, you pretty puss,' he said, stooping. 'You're as big a cheat as the rest of 'em that catch no mice about me. A won'erful smooth-skinned, rough-tongued cheat you be. I've more than half a mind – '

'She does her work well,' said the Engineer, pointing to where the Rat's beady eyes showed behind the sacking. 'Cats and Rats livin' together – see?'

'Too much they do – too long they've done. I'm sick and tired of it. Go and take a swim and larn to find your own vittles honest when you come out, Pussy.'

'My word!' said the Waters, as a sprawling Cat landed all unannounced in the centre of the tail-race. 'Is that you, Mewsalina? You seem to have been quarrelling with your best friend. Get over to the left. It's shallowest there. Up on that alder-root with all four paws. Good-night!'

'You'll never get any they rats,' said the Miller, as the young Engineer struck wrathfully with his stick at the sacking. 'They're not the common sort. They're the old black English sort.'

'Are they, by Jove? I must catch one to stuff, someday.'

Six months later, in the chill of a January afternoon, they were letting in the Waters as usual.

'Come along! It's both gears this evening,' said the Wheel, kicking joyously in the first rush of the icy stream. 'There's a heavy load of grist just in from Lamber's Wood. Eleven miles it came in an hour and a half in our new motor-lorry, and the Miller's rigged five new five-candle lights in his cow-stables. I'm feeding 'em tonight. There's a cow due to calve. Oh, while I think of it, what's the news from Callton Rise?'

'The waters are finding their level as usual – but why do you ask?' said the deep outpouring Waters.

'Because Mangles and Felden and the Miller are talking of increasing the plant here and running a sawmill by electricity. I was wondering whether we – '

'I beg your pardon,' said the Waters, chuckling. '*What* did you say?'

'Whether *we*, of course, had power enough for the job. It will be a biggish contract. There's all Harpenden Brook to be considered and

Batten's Ponds as well, and Witches' Fountain, and the Churt's Hawd system.'

'We've power enough for anything in the world,' said the Waters. 'The only question is whether you could stand the strain if we came down on you full head.'

'Of course I can,' said the Wheel. 'Mangles is going to turn me into a set of turbines – beauties.'

'Oh – er – I suppose it's the frost that has made us a little thick-headed, but to whom are we talking?' asked the amazed Waters.

'To me – the Spirit of the Mill, of course.'

'Not to the old Wheel, then?'

'I happen to be living in the old Wheel just at present. When the turbines are installed I shall go and live in them. What earthly difference does it make?'

'Absolutely none,' said the Waters, 'in the earth or in the waters under the earth. But we thought turbines didn't appeal to you.'

'Not like turbines? Me? My dear fellows, turbines are good for fifteen hundred revolutions a minute – and with our power we can drive 'em at full speed. Why there's nothing we couldn't grind or saw or illuminate or heat with a set of turbines! That's to say if all the Five Watersheds are agreeable.'

'Oh, we've been agreeable for ever so long.'

'Then why didn't you tell me?'

'Don't know. Suppose it slipped our memory.' The Waters were holding themselves in for fear of bursting with mirth.

'How careless of you! You should keep abreast of the age, my dear fellows. We might have settled it long ago, if you'd only spoken. Yes, four good turbines and a neat brick penstock – eh? This old Wheel's absurdly out of date.'

'Well,' said the Cat, who after a little proud seclusion had returned to her place impenitent as ever. 'Praised be Pasht and the Old Gods, that whatever may have happened I, at least, have preserved the Spirit of the Mill!'

She looked round as if expecting her faithful ally, the Black Rat; but that very week the Engineer had caught and stuffed him, and had put him in a glass case; he being a genuine old English black rat. That breed, the report says, is rapidly diminishing before the incursions of the brown variety.

WORDSWORTH CLASSICS

REQUESTS FOR INSPECTION COPIES Lecturers wishing to obtain copies of Wordsworth Classics, Wordsworth Poetry Library or Wordsworth Classics of World Literature titles on inspection are invited to contact: Dennis Hart, Wordsworth Editions Ltd, Crib Street, Ware, Herts SG12 9ET; E-mail: dennis.hart@wordsworth-editions.com. Please quote the author, title and ISBN of the titles in which you are interested; together with your name, academic address, E-mail address, the course on which the books will be used and the expected enrolment.

Teachers wishing to inspect specific core titles for GCSE or A level courses are also invited to contact Wordsworth Editions at the above address.

Inspection copies are sent solely at the discretion of Wordsworth Editions Ltd.

JANE AUSTEN
Emma
Mansfield Park
Northanger Abbey
Persuasion
Pride and Prejudice
Sense and Sensibility

ARNOLD BENNETT
Anna of the Five Towns
The Old Wives' Tale

R. D. BLACKMORE
Lorna Doone

M. E. BRADDON
Lady Audley's Secret

ANNE BRONTË
Agnes Grey
*The Tenant of
Wildfell Hall*

CHARLOTTE BRONTË
Jane Eyre
The Professor
Shirley
Villette

EMILY BRONTË
Wuthering Heights

JOHN BUCHAN
Greenmantle
The Island of Sheep
John Macnab
Mr Standfast
The Thirty-Nine Steps
The Three Hostages

SAMUEL BUTLER
Erewhon
The Way of All Flesh

LEWIS CARROLL
Alice in Wonderland

M. CERVANTES
Don Quixote

ANTON CHEKHOV
Selected Stories

G. K. CHESTERTON
*The Club of Queer
Trades*
*Father Brown:
Selected Stories*
*The Man Who Was
Thursday*
*The Napoleon of
Notting Hill*

ERSKINE CHILDERS
The Riddle of the Sands

JOHN CLELAND
*Fanny Hill – Memoirs of
a Woman of Pleasure*

WILKIE COLLINS
The Moonstone
The Woman in White

JOSEPH CONRAD
Almayer's Folly
Heart of Darkness
Lord Jim
Nostromo
Sea Stories
The Secret Agent
Selected Short Stories
Victory

J. FENIMORE COOPER
The Last of the Mohicans

STEPHEN CRANE
The Red Badge of Courage

THOMAS DE QUINCEY
*Confessions of an English
Opium Eater*

DANIEL DEFOE
Moll Flanders
Robinson Crusoe

CHARLES DICKENS
Barnaby Rudge
Bleak House
Christmas Books
David Copperfield
Dombey and Son
Ghost Stories
Great Expectations
Hard Times
Little Dorrit
Martin Chuzzlewit
The Mystery of Edwin Drood
Nicholas Nickleby
The Old Curiosity Shop
Oliver Twist
Our Mutual Friend
Pickwick Papers
Sketches by Boz
A Tale of Two Cities

BENJAMIN DISRAELI
Sybil

FYODOR DOSTOEVSKY
Crime and Punishment
The Idiot

ARTHUR CONAN DOYLE
*The Adventures of
Sherlock Holmes*
*The Case-Book of
Sherlock Holmes*
*The Return of
Sherlock Holmes*
*The Best of
Sherlock Holmes*
*The Hound of the
Baskervilles*
*The Lost World &
Other Stories*
Sir Nigel
*A Study in Scarlet & The
Sign of Four*
The Valley of Fear
The White Company

DISTRIBUTION

AUSTRALIA & PAPUA NEW GUINEA
Peribo Pty Ltd
58 Beaumont Road, Mount Kuring-Gai
NSW 2080, Australia
Tel: (02) 457 0011 Fax: (02) 457 0022

CZECH REPUBLIC
Bohemian Ventures s r. o.,
Delnicka 13, 170 00 Prague 7
Tel: 042 2 877837 Fax: 042 2 801498

FRANCE
Copernicus Diffusion
81 Rue des Entrepreneurs, Paris 75015
Tel: 01 53 95 38 00 Fax: 01 53 95 38 01

GERMANY & AUSTRIA
Taschenbuch-Vertrieb
Ingeborg Blank GmbH
Lager und Buro Rohrmooser Str 1
85256 Vierkirchen/Pasenbach
Tel: 08139-8130/8184 Fax: 08139-8140

Tradis Verlag und Vertrieb GmbH (Bookshops)
Postfach 90 03 69, D-51113 Köln
Tel: 022 03 31059 Fax: 022 03 39340

GREAT BRITAIN
Wordsworth Editions Ltd
Cumberland House, Crib Street
Ware, Hertfordshire SG12 9ET
Tel: 01920 465167 Fax: 01920 462267

INDIA
Om Books International
4379/4B, Prakash House, Ansari Road
Darya Ganj, New Delhi – 110002
Tel: 3263363/3265303 Fax: 3278091
E-mail: sales@ombooks.com

IRELAND
Easons & Son Limited
Furry Park Industrial Estate
Santry 9, Eire
Tel: 003531 8733811 Fax: 003531 8733945

ISRAEL
Sole Agent – **Timmy Marketing Limited**
Israel Ben Zeev 12, Ramont Gimmel, Jerusalem
Tel: 972-2-5865266 Fax: 972-2-5860035
Sole Distributor – Sefer ve Sefel Ltd
Tel & Fax: 972-2-6248237

ITALY
Logos – Edizioni e distribuzione libri
Via Curtatona 5/J
41100 Modena, Italy
Tel: 059-418820/418821 Fax: 059-418786

NEW ZEALAND & FIJI
Allphy Book Distributors Ltd
4-6 Charles Street,
Eden Terrace,
Auckland,
Tel: (09) 3773096 Fax: (09) 3022770

MALAYSIA & BRUNEI
Vintrade SDN BHD
5 & 7 Lorong Datuk Sulaiman 7
Taman Tun Dr Ismail
60000 Kuala Lumpur,
Malaysia
Tel: (603) 717 3333 Fax: (603) 719 2942

MALTA & GOZO
Agius & Agius Ltd
42A South Street, Valletta VLT 11
Tel: 234038 - 220347 Fax: 241175

PHILIPPINES
I J Sagun Enterprises
P O Box 4322 CPO Manila
2 Topaz Road, Greenheights Village,
Taytay, Rizal
Tel: 631 80 61 TO 66

SOUTH AFRICA
Chapter Book Agencies
Postnet Private bag X10016
Edenvale, 1610 Gauteng
South Africa
Tel: (++27) 11 425 5990
Fax: (++27) 11 425 5997

SLOVAK REPUBLIC
Slovak Ventures s r. o.,
Stefanikova 128, 949 01 Nitra
Tel/Fax: 042 87 525105/6/7

SPAIN
Ribera Libros, S.L.
Poligono Martiartu, Calle 1 - no 6
48480 Arrigorriaga, Vizcaya
Tel: 34 4 6713607 (Almacen)
        34 4 4418787 (Libreria)
Fax: 34 4 6713608 (Almacen)
        34 4 4418029 (Libreria)

UNITED STATES OF AMERICA
NTC/Contemporary Publishing Company
4225 West Touhy Avenue
Lincolnwood (Chicago)
Illinois 60646-4622
USA
Tel: (847) 679 5500 Fax: (847) 679 2494

DIRECT MAIL
Bibliophile Books
5 Thomas Road, London E14 7BN,
Tel: 0171-515 9222 Fax: 0171-538 4115
Order hotline 24 hours Tel: 0171-515 9555
Cash with order + £2.50 p&p (UK)